Prais
#1 *New York*
De

"Popular romance writer Debbie Macomber has a gift for evoking the emotions that are at the heart of the genre's popularity."
—*Publishers Weekly*

"It's clear that Debbie Macomber cares deeply about her fully realized characters and their families, friends and loves, along with their hopes and dreams. She also makes her readers care about them."
—*Bookreporter.com*

"Debbie Macomber is one of the most reliable, versatile romance writers around."
—*Milwaukee Journal Sentinel*

"Readers won't be able to get enough of Macomber's gentle storytelling."
—*RT Book Reviews*

"Bestselling Macomber...sure has a way of pleasing readers."
—*Booklist*

"It's impossible not to cheer for Macomber's characters.... When it comes to creating a special place and memorable, honorable characters, nobody does it better than Macomber."
—*BookPage*

"Macomber is a master storyteller."
—*Times Record News*

DEBBIE MACOMBER

Country Proposals

Country Bride and *The Courtship of Carol Sommars*

MIRA

MIRA™

ISBN-13: 978-0-7783-6832-8

Country Proposals

For questions and comments about the quality of this book, please contact us at CustomerService@Harlequin.com.

TM is a trademark of Harlequin Enterprises ULC.

Mira
22 Adelaide St. West, 41st Floor
Toronto, Ontario M5H 4E3, Canada
MIRABooks.com

Printed in U.S.A.

Also available from Debbie Macomber and MIRA

Blossom Street

The Shop on Blossom Street
A Good Yarn
Susannah's Garden
Back on Blossom Street
Twenty Wishes
Summer on Blossom Street
Hannah's List
"The Twenty-First Wish"
(in *The Knitting Diaries*)
A Turn in the Road

Cedar Cove

16 Lighthouse Road
204 Rosewood Lane
311 Pelican Court
44 Cranberry Point
50 Harbor Street
6 Rainier Drive
74 Seaside Avenue
8 Sandpiper Way
92 Pacific Boulevard
1022 Evergreen Place
Christmas in Cedar Cove
(*5-B Poppy Lane* and
A Cedar Cove Christmas)
1105 Yakima Street
1225 Christmas Tree Lane

The Dakota Series

Dakota Born
Dakota Home
Always Dakota
Buffalo Valley

The Manning Family

The Manning Sisters
(*The Cowboy's Lady* and
The Sheriff Takes a Wife)
The Manning Brides
(*Marriage of Inconvenience* and
Stand-In Wife)
The Manning Grooms
(*Bride on the Loose* and
Same Time, Next Year)

Christmas Books

Home for the Holidays
Glad Tidings
(*There's Something About Christmas* and *Here Comes Trouble*)
Christmas in Alaska
(*Mail-Order Bride* and
The Snow Bride)
Trading Christmas
Christmas Letters
The Perfect Christmas (includes
Can This Be Christmas?)
Choir of Angels
(*Shirley, Goodness and Mercy*,
Those Christmas Angels and
Where Angels Go)
Call Me Mrs. Miracle
The Gift of Christmas
A Country Christmas
(*Kisses in the Snow* and
The Christmas Basket)

Heart of Texas

Texas Skies
(*Lonesome Cowboy* and
Texas Two-Step)
Texas Nights
(*Caroline's Child* and *Dr. Texas*)
Texas Home
(*Nell's Cowboy* and *Lone Star Baby*)
Promise, Texas
Return to Promise

Midnight Sons

Alaska Skies
(*Brides for Brothers* and
The Marriage Risk)
Alaska Nights
(*Daddy's Little Helper* and
Because of the Baby)
Alaska Home
(*Falling for Him*, *Ending in Marriage* and *Midnight Sons and Daughters*)

This Matter of Marriage
Montana
Thursdays at Eight
Between Friends
Changing Habits
The Sooner the Better
Three Brides, No Groom
Summer Breezes
(*Fallen Angel* and
The Way to a Man's Heart)
Seaside Springtime
(*For All My Tomorrows* and
Yours and Mine)
Fairy-Tale Forever
(*Cindy and the Prince* and
Some Kind of Wonderful)
Perfect Partners
(*Rainy Day Kisses* and
Love 'n' Marriage)
Finally You
(*All Things Considered* and
No Competition)
Winning Hearts
(*Laughter in the Rain* and
Love by Degree)
Finding You Again
(*White Lace and Promises* and
Jury of His Peers)
A Second Glance
(*Shadow Chasing* and
Yesterday Once More)
Longing for Yesterday
(*Reflections of Yesterday* and
Yesterday's Hero)
The Night We Met
(*Starlight*)
Time for Love
(*A Friend or Two* and
The Trouble with Caasi)
Their Perfect Match
(*Promise Me Forever* and
Adam's Image)
Married in Seattle
(*First Comes Marriage* and
Wanted: Perfect Partner)
Right Next Door
(*Father's Day* and
The Courtship of Carol Sommars)
Wyoming Brides
(*Denim and Diamonds* and
The Wyoming Kid)
A Wish Upon a Dress
(*The First Man You Meet* and
The Man You'll Marry)
Weddings in Orchard Valley
(*Valerie* and *Stephanie*)
Married in Texas (*Norah* and
Lone Star Lovin')
An Engagement in Seattle
(*Groom Wanted* and
Bride Wanted)
North to Alaska
(*That Wintry Feeling* and
Borrowed Dreams)

Debbie Macomber's Cedar Cove Cookbook
Debbie Macomber's Christmas Cookbook

CONTENTS

Country Bride

One

"I now pronounce you husband and wife."

A burst of organ music crescendoed through the largest church in Nightingale, Oregon, as a murmur of shared happiness rose from the congregation.

Standing at the altar, Clay Franklin claimed his right to kiss Rorie Campbell Franklin, his bride.

Kate Logan did her best to look delighted for her friends, even though she felt as if a giant fist had been slammed into her stomach. Tears gathered in her eyes and she lowered her gaze, unable to watch as the man she'd loved for most of her life wrapped his arm around his new bride's waist.

Clay should be marrying me, Kate cried silently. *I should be the one he's looking at so tenderly. Me!* During the past few weeks, Kate had repeatedly reassured herself that she'd done the right thing in stepping aside to bring Clay and Rorie together. But that fact didn't lessen her pain now. Kate loved Clay, and that wasn't going to change. He was her best friend and confidant, her compass, her North Star. And now Clay was married to another woman—someone he loved far more than he could ever care for Kate.

A clean white handkerchief was thrust into her hand by Luke Rivers, her father's foreman. Kate knew he'd been waiting for this moment, convinced she'd dissolve into a puddle of tears.

She declined the use of his handkerchief by gently shaking her head.

"I'm here," he whispered in her ear.

"So is half of Nightingale," she returned wryly. Luke seemed determined to rescue her from this pain—as if that was possible. All she wanted was to survive this day with her dignity intact, and his open sympathy threatened the composure she'd painfully mustered.

"You're doing fine."

"Luke," she muttered, "stop making a fuss over me. Please." She'd managed to get through the ceremony without breaking down. The last thing she needed now was to have Luke calling attention to her.

It was ironic that Kate had been the one responsible for bringing Clay and Rorie together. She should be feeling noble and jubilant and honorable. But the only emotion she felt was a deep, abiding sense of loss.

Rorie and Clay walked down the center aisle, and from somewhere deep inside her, Kate found the strength to raise her head and smile blindly in their direction. Luke's hands gripped her shoulders as though to lend her strength. His concern should have been a comfort, but it wasn't.

"I'll walk you to the reception hall," Luke said, slipping his arm through hers.

"I'm perfectly capable of making it there on my own," she snapped, not wanting his pity. She would've argued more, but since they were sitting near the front of the church, they were among the first to be ushered out. Holding her head high, Kate walked past her friends and neighbors, doing her best to appear cheerful and serene.

At least she *looked* her best; Kate had made certain of that. She'd curled her thick blond hair until it lightly brushed her shoulders. The style emphasized her blue eyes and sculpted cheekbones. She'd shopped long and hard for the perfect dress and had found one that enhanced her slender waist and outlined her trim figure. The minute she'd tried on the soft blue silk and viewed herself in the mirror, Kate had known this was the dress. Although the lines were simple, the look was both classic and sophisticated, a look she'd never bothered to cultivate before. Too often in the past, she'd been mistaken for a teenager, mostly, she supposed, because she dressed the part. But she was a woman now and she had the broken heart to prove it.

Kate paused in the church vestibule, waiting for her father. Devin was sitting with Dorothea Murphy, his widow friend. Her father's interest in the older woman was something of a mystery to Kate. Tall and plump and outspoken, she was completely unlike Kate's late mother, who'd been delicate and reserved. Kate sometimes wondered what it was about Dorothea that attracted her father. They'd been seeing a lot of each other in recent weeks, but the possibility of their contemplating marriage filled Kate with a sudden, overwhelming sense of alarm. Kate pushed the thought from her mind. Losing Clay was all she could deal with right now.

"Are you all right, Princess?" Devin asked when he joined her.

"I wish everyone would stop worrying about me. I'm fine." It wasn't the truth, but Kate was well aware that she had to put on a breezy, unconcerned front. At least for the next few hours.

Her father patted her hand. "I know how hard this is for you. Do you want to go to the reception or would you prefer to head home?" His eyes were warm and sympathetic, and Kate felt a rush of love for him. A part of her longed to slip away unnoticed, but she couldn't and she knew it.

"Kate's already agreed to accompany me," Luke inserted, daring her to contradict him.

Indignation rose inside her. Instead of helping, Luke was making everything worse. The pain of watching Clay pledge his life to another woman was difficult enough, without Luke's unsought demands.

"I'm glad to hear that," Devin Logan said, clearly relieved. He smiled as he slipped his arm around Dorothea's waist. "Mrs. Murphy invited me to sit with her and, frankly, I was looking forward to doing that." He released Kate's hand, kissed her on the cheek, then strolled nonchalantly away.

"Shall we?" Grinning, Luke reached for Kate's limp hand and tucked it into the crook of his arm. As if they'd been a couple for years, he casually led her out of the church.

The early evening air was crisp and clear. Autumn had crested on an October tide of bronze and gold leaves, huge pumpkins and early twilights. Normally, this time of year invigorated Kate. If she hadn't been fortifying herself against Clay's wedding, she could have appreciated the season more.

The walk across the parking lot to the reception hall

was a short one. Kate didn't say another word to Luke, mentally preparing herself for the coming encounter with Clay and his bride. With each step her heart grew heavier. Rorie had asked her to be a bridesmaid, and although Kate was honored by the request, she'd declined. Rorie understood and hadn't pressured her. Despite the fact that they both loved the same man, Rorie and Kate had become close. Their friendship made everything more difficult for Kate, yet somehow easier, too.

By the time they arrived at the old brick building, Kate's pulse was so loud it echoed like a drum in her ear. Just outside the double doors leading into the hall, she stopped abruptly.

"I can't go in there," she told Luke. Panic had worked its way into her voice, which was low and trembling. "I can't face them and pretend… I just can't do it."

"Yes, you can."

"How could you possibly know what I can and can't do?" she demanded, wanting to bury her face in her hands and weep. These past few hours had taken their toll and she couldn't keep up the charade much longer.

Luke gazed down on her and for the briefest of moments his eyes registered sympathy and regret.

"You can go in there and you will," he repeated.

Kate saw determination in his serious dark eyes and swallowed an angry retort, knowing he was right.

At six feet, Luke towered over her, and the hard set of his mouth did more than hint at determination and a will of iron. "If you don't attend the reception, everyone in Nightingale will talk. Is that what you want?"

"Yes," she cried, then lowered her head, battling down wave after wave of depression and self-pity. "No," she said reluctantly, loath to agree with him.

"I'm here for you, Kate. Lean on me for once in your life, and let me help you through the next few hours."

"I'm doing fine. I—"

He wouldn't allow her to finish. "Quit fighting me. I'm your friend, remember?"

His words, hushed and tender, brought a burning to her eyes. Her fingers tightened around his arm and she nodded, calling upon a reserve of strength she didn't know she possessed. "Just don't be so bossy with me. Please. I can bear almost anything but that." She'd made it through the wedding ceremony on her own. Now she needed someone at her side to help her appear strong and steady, in control of her emotions, when she felt as though the entire universe was pitching and heaving.

"Anything you say, Princess."

Although she'd objected earlier, she felt comforted by his strong arm against her. She heard his voice, as if from a distance, too preoccupied with her own pain to respond to his concern. But his presence restored her determination to acquit herself well during the long evening ahead.

"Only Daddy calls me Princess," she said distractedly.

"You mind?"

"I don't know… I suppose it's all right."

"Good." His fingers intertwined with hers as he guided her into the brightly decorated reception hall.

The next half hour was a blur. Drawing upon Luke's silent strength, Kate managed to make it through the reception line without a problem. Still, her knees felt shaky by the time she reached Clay, who kissed her cheek and thanked her for being so wonderful. Kate certainly didn't *feel* wonderful—even particularly admirable—

but she smiled. And she was sincere when she offered Clay and Rorie her very best wishes.

Somehow Luke must have known how frail she felt because he took her hand and led her to one of the round lace-covered tables. His fingers were cool and callused, while Kate's were damp with her stubborn resolve to hide her pain.

Wordlessly, she sat beside Luke until the cake had been cut and the first piece ceremonially fed to the bride and groom. The scene before her flickered like an old silent movie. Kate held herself still, trying not to feel anything, but not succeeding.

"Would you like me to get you something to eat?" Luke asked, when a line formed to gather refreshments.

She stared at him, hardly able to comprehend his words. Then she blinked and her eyes traveled across the hall to the three-tiered heart-shaped wedding cake. "No," she said automatically.

"When was the last time you ate?"

Kate didn't remember. She shrugged. "Breakfast, I guess." As she spoke she realized that wasn't true. Dinner the night before was the last time she'd eaten. No wonder she felt so shaky and light-headed.

"I'm getting you some wedding cake," Luke announced grimly.

"Don't. I'm—I'm not hungry."

He was doing it again! Taking over, making decisions on her behalf because he felt sorry for her. She would have argued with him, but he was already walking away, blithely unaware of her frustration.

Kate watched him, suddenly seeing him with fresh eyes. Luke Rivers had lived and worked on the Circle L for a decade, but Kate knew next to nothing about his past. His official title was foreman, but he was much more than that. He'd initiated several successful cattle-breeding programs and been involved in a profit-sharing venture with her father almost from the first. Devin had often remarked that Luke was certainly capable of maintaining his own spread. But year after year, he stayed on at the Circle L. This realization—that she knew so little of his past and even less about his thoughts and plans—shocked Kate. He'd always been just plain Luke. And he'd always been around—or so it seemed.

She had to admit that Luke puzzled her. He was handsome enough, but he rarely dated any woman for long, although plenty of Nightingale's finest had made their interest obvious. He was a "catch" who refused to play ball. He could be as tough as leather and mean as a saddle sore when the mood struck him, but it seldom did. Tall, lean and rugged adequately described him on the surface. It was what lay below that piqued her interest now.

Kate's musings about Luke were interrupted by the man himself as he pulled out the chair beside her and sat down. He pushed a delicate china plate filled with cheese and mixed nuts in her direction.

"I thought you were bringing me cake." His own plate was loaded with a huge piece, in addition to a few nuts and pastel mints.

"I brought you some protein instead. Sugar's not a good idea on an empty stomach."

"I don't believe you," she muttered, her sarcasm fuelled by his arrogance. "First you insist on bringing me cake, and then just when I'm looking forward to it, you decide I shouldn't be eating sweets."

Luke ignored her, slicing into his cake. "Just a minute

ago, you said it would be a waste of time for me to bring you anything. Fact is, you downright refused to eat."

"That...was before."

He smiled, and that knowing cocky smile of his infuriated her.

"You'll feel sick if you eat sugar," he announced in an authoritative voice.

So much for helping her through the evening! All he seemed to want to do was quarrel. "Apparently you know how my stomach's going to react to various food groups. You amaze me, Luke Rivers. I had no idea you knew so much about my body's metabolism."

"You'd be shocked if I told you all the things I know about you and your body, Princess."

Kate stood abruptly. "I don't think it's a good idea for you to call me that. I'm not your 'Princess.' I'm a woman, not a little girl."

"Honey, you don't need to tell me that. I already know. Now, sit down." His tone was brusque, and his smile humorless.

"I'll stand if I choose."

"Fine then. Look like a fool, if that's what you want."

No sooner had the words left his lips than she lowered herself back into the chair. The fight had gone out of her as quickly as it had come. Absently she scooped up a handful of nuts and chewed them vigorously, taking her frustration out on them.

Luke pushed his plate aside and took her hand, squeezing it gently. "I'm your friend. I've always been your friend and I'll continue to be your friend as long as I live. Don't ever doubt that."

Kate's eyes filled and her throat tightened painfully.

"I know. It's just that this is so much more…exhausting than I thought it would be."

Voices drew Kate's eyes to the front of the room, where Clay and Rorie were toasting each other with glasses of sparkling champagne. Soon flutes were being delivered around the room. Kate took one, holding the stem with both hands as if the champagne would lend her strength.

When the newlyweds were toasted, she took a sip. It bubbled and fizzed inside her mouth, then slid easily down her throat.

The soft strains of a violin drifted around the hall, and, mesmerized, Kate watched as Clay claimed his bride and led her onto the dance floor. Just watching the couple, so much in love, with eyes only for each other, heaped an extra burden of pain on Kate's shoulders. She looked away and, when she did, her gaze met Luke's. She tried to smile, to convince him she wasn't feeling a thing, but her effort failed dismally. Ready tears brimmed at the corners of her eyes and she bent her head, not wanting anyone to notice them, least of all Luke. He'd been wonderful; he'd been terrible. Kate couldn't decide which.

Soon others joined Clay and Rorie. First the matron of honor and then the bridesmaids and groomsmen, each couple swirling around the polished floor with practiced ease.

Luke got to his feet, walked to Kate's side and offered her his hand. His eyes held hers, silently demanding that she dance with him. Kate longed to tell him no, but she didn't have the energy to argue. It was simpler to give in than try to explain why she couldn't.

Together they approached the outskirts of the dance floor and Luke skillfully turned her into his arms.

"Everything's going to be all right," he whispered as his hand slid around her waist.

Kate managed a nod, grateful for his concern. She needed Luke this evening more than she'd realized. One thing was clear; she'd never make it through the remainder of the night without him.

During the past few years, Luke had danced with Kate any number of times. She'd never given it a second thought. Now they danced to one song and then another, but when she slipped into his embrace a third time, and his fingers spread across the small of her back, a shiver of unexpected awareness skidded up her spine. Kate paused, confused. Her steps faltered and in what seemed like an attempt to help her, Luke pulled her closer. Soon their bodies were so close together Kate could hear the steady beat of Luke's heart against her own. The quickening rate of his pulse told her he was experiencing the same rush of excitement she was.

Kate felt so light-headed she was almost giddy. Luke's arms were warm and secure, a solid foundation to hold on to when her world had been abruptly kicked off its axis. It might have been selfish, but Kate needed that warmth, that security. Smiling up at him, she closed her eyes and surrendered to the warm sensations carried on the soft, lilting music.

"Kate, there's something I need to tell you about the Circle L—"

She pressed her fingers against his lips, afraid that words would ruin this feeling. Arms twined around his neck, she grazed his jaw with the side of her face, reveling in the feel of him. Male and strong. Lean and hard.

"All right," he whispered, "we'll talk about it later."

They continued dancing and Luke rubbed his face against her hair, mussing it slightly, but Kate didn't mind.

Like a contented cat, she purred softly, the low sound coming from deep in her throat. The music ended all too quickly and with heavy reluctance, she dropped her arms and backed up one small step. Silently they stood an inch or so apart until the music resumed, when they reached for each other once again.

But this time Kate decided to figure out what was happening between them. Knowing how much she loved Clay, Luke was trying to help her through the evening. Yes, that was it. And doing a fine job, too. She felt…marvelous. It didn't make sense to her that she should experience this strong, unexpectedly sensual attraction to Luke, but at the moment she didn't care. He was concerned and gentle and she needed him.

They remained as they were, not speaking, savoring these warm sensations, until Kate lost count of the number of times they'd danced.

When the band took a ten-minute break, Luke released her with an unwillingness that made her heart soar. As though he couldn't bear to be separated from her, he took her hand, lacing her fingers with his.

He was leading her back to their table when they were interrupted by Beth Hammond, a pert blonde, who'd hurried toward them. "Hello, Luke," she said, ignoring Kate.

"Beth." He bowed his head politely, but it was evident that he didn't appreciate the intrusion.

The other woman placed a proprietary hand on his arm. "You promised me a dance, remember?"

Kate's eyes swivelled from Beth, who was pouting prettily, to Luke, who looked testy and impatient.

"If you'll excuse me a minute, I'm going to get a drink," Kate said. Her throat was parched and she didn't want to be left standing alone when the music started and Beth walked off with Luke.

The fruit punch was cold and refreshing, but she still felt warm. Kate decided to walk outside and let the cool night air clear her mind. Try though she might, she didn't really understand what was happening between her and Luke. It probably had to do with the confused state of her emotions, she decided. She'd think about it later.

The stars glittered like frost diamonds against a velvety black sky. Kate stood in the crisp evening air with her arms around her waist, gazing up at the heavens. She didn't hear Luke until he stepped behind her and lightly rested his hands on her shoulders. "I couldn't find you," he said in a voice that was softly accusing.

Kate didn't want to discuss Beth Hammond. For as long as she could remember, the other woman had been going out of her way to attract him.

"It's beautiful out, isn't it?" she asked instead. Instinctively she nestled closer to Luke, reclining against the lean strength of his body, seeking his warmth.

"Beautiful," he repeated, running his hands down her arms.

How content she felt with Luke, how comfortable—the way she imagined people felt when they'd been married for twenty years. But along with this familiar sense of ease, she experienced a prickle of anticipation. Her feelings were contradicting themselves. Secure and steady, and at the same time this growing sense of giddy excitement. It must be that glass of champagne.

The band started playing again and the music wafted outside. Gently Luke turned her to face him, slipping his hands around her as if to dance. Her arms reached for his neck, resuming their earlier position.

"We should talk," he whispered close to her ear.

"No," she murmured with a sigh. It seemed the most natural thing in the world to stand on the tips of her toes and brush her moist lips over his. Then she realized what she'd done. Her eyes widened and she abruptly stepped back, her heart hammering inside her chest.

Neither spoke. In the light that spilled from the hall, they stared at each other. Kate didn't know what her eyes told Luke, but his own were clouded with uncertainty. Kate half expected him to chastise her, or to tease her for behaving like such a flirt. Instead he reached for her once more, his eyes challenging her to stop him.

She couldn't.

The warmth of his mouth on hers produced a small sigh of welcome as her eyes slid languidly shut; she felt transported into a dreamworld, one she'd never visited before. This couldn't actually be happening, she told herself, and yet it felt so real. So right.

Luke's kiss was surprisingly tender, unlike anything she'd expected. "My darling Kate," he breathed against her hair, "I've dreamed of this so often."

"You have?" To her own ears, her voice sounded far, far away. Her head was swimming. If this was a dream, then she didn't want it to end. Sighing, she smiled beguilingly up at him.

"You little tease," he said, and laughed softly. He rained light kisses on her forehead, the corners of her eyes and her cheek, until she interrupted his meandering lips, seeking his mouth with her own.

He seemed to want the kiss as much as she did, but apparently saw no need to rush the experience, as if he feared hurrying would spoil it. Kate's mouth parted, inviting a deeper union. His willing compliance was so effective it buckled her knees.

"Kate?" Still holding her, he drew back, tilting his head to study her. Boldly she met his look, her eyes dancing with mischief. If he'd been kissing her out of pity, she was past caring.

A long moment passed before a slow, thoughtful smile played across his lips. "I think I'd better get you inside."

"No," she said, surprised at how vehement she felt about returning to the reception hall and the newlyweds. "I don't want to go back there."

"But—"

"Stay with me here. Dance with me. Hold me." He'd said he wanted to take care of her. Well, she was giving him the opportunity. She leaned into him and sighed, savoring his strength and support. This was Luke. Luke Rivers. Her trusted friend. Surely he understood; surely he'd help her through this most difficult night of her life. "I want you with me." She couldn't explain what was happening any more than she could deny it.

"You don't know what you're asking me." He stared down at her, searching her features for a long, breathless moment. Then the cool tips of his fingers brushed her face, moving along her cheekbones, stroking her skin as if he expected her to vanish.

Kate caught his hand with her own and gazed into

his dark eyes. They glittered like freshly polished onyx, full of light and a deep inner fire.

"I want you to kiss me. You taste so good." She moistened her lips and leaned closer to him, so close that she could feel the imprint of his buttons against her body. So close that the beat of his heart merged with her own. Excitement shivered through her in tremors so intense they frightened her. But not enough to make her pull away.

Her words spurred Luke into action, and when he kissed her their lips met with hungry insistence. Sensation erupted between them until Kate was weak and dizzy, clinging to him for support, her fingers bunching the material of his jacket. When he lifted his head, ending the kiss, Kate felt nearly faint from the rush of blood to her pounding temples.

There was a look of shock on Luke's face. His eyes questioned her, but Kate's thoughts were as scattered as autumn leaves tossed by the wind.

"How much champagne have you had?" he asked softly.

"One glass," she answered with a sigh, resting her forehead against his heaving chest. Luke hadn't said taking care of her would be this wonderful. Had she known, she wouldn't have resented it quite so much earlier.

Luke expelled a harsh breath. "You've had more than one glass. I doubt you even know who I am."

"Of course I do!" she flared. "You're Luke. Now, don't be ridiculous. Only..."

"Only what?"

"Only you never kissed me before. At least not like

that. Why didn't you tell me you were so good at this?" Finding herself exceptionally witty, she began to laugh.

"I'm taking you home," Luke said firmly, grabbing her elbow with such force that she was half lifted from the walkway.

"Luke," she cried. "I don't want to go back yet."

His grip relaxed immediately. "Kate Logan, you're drunk! Except you don't have the sense to know it."

"I most certainly am not!" She waved her index finger at him like a schoolmarm. "I'll have you know that it takes a lot more than one glass of champagne to do me in."

Luke obviously wasn't willing to argue the point. His hand cradling her elbow, he led her toward the parking lot.

"I want to stay," she protested.

He didn't answer. Then it dawned on her that perhaps she'd misread Luke. Maybe he was trying to get rid of her so he could return to Beth.

"Luke?"

"Kate, please, don't argue with me."

"Are you in love with Beth?"

"No." His answer was clipped and impatient.

"Thank heaven." Her hand fluttered over her heart. "I don't think I could bear it if you were."

Luke stopped abruptly and Kate realized they were standing in front of his truck. He opened the passenger door for her, but she had no intention of climbing in. At least not yet. She wanted to spend more time with Luke, their arms wrapped around each other the way they'd been before. The pain that had battered her heart for weeks had vanished the instant she stepped into his arms.

"Kiss me again, okay?"

"Kate, no."

"Please?"

"Kate, you're drunk."

"And I tell you I'm not." The one glass of champagne had been just enough to make her a little…reckless. It felt so good to surrender to these new emotions—to lean on Luke. From the moment they'd arrived at the wedding, he'd been telling her how much she needed him. Maybe he was right. There'd been so much upheaval in her life, and Luke was here, warm and kind and solid.

"I'm going to drive you home," he insisted. From the sound of his voice, Kate could tell he was growing frustrated.

The house would be dark and cold. How Kate feared being alone, and with Clay out of her life, there was only her father. And Luke. If Devin did decide to marry Mrs. Murphy, he might sell the ranch and then Luke would be gone, too. Alarmed at the thought, she placed her hands on his shoulders, her gaze holding his.

"Kate?" Luke coaxed.

"All right, I'll go back to the house, but on one condition."

"Kate, come on, be reasonable."

"I want you to do something for me. You keep telling me you're my friend and how much you want to help…."

"Just get inside the truck, would you, before someone comes along and finds us arguing?"

"I need your promise first."

Luke ignored her. "You've got a reputation to uphold. You can't let people in Nightingale see you tipsy. The school board will hear about this and that'll be the end of your career."

Kate smiled, shaking her head, then impulsively leaned forward and kissed him again. Being with Luke took the hurt away, and she refused to suffer that kind of pain ever again. "Will you please do what I want?"

"All right," he muttered, clearly exasperated. "What is it?"

"Oh, thank you," she murmured, and sighed expressively. This was going to shock him, but no more than it had already shocked her. She didn't know where the idea had come from, but it seemed suddenly, inarguably right.

Kate smiled at him, her heart shining through her eyes. "It's simple really. All I want you to do is marry me."

Two

Early the following day, Devin Logan walked hesitantly into the kitchen where Kate sat drinking her first cup of coffee. She smiled a greeting. "Morning, Dad."

"Morning, Princess." He circled the table twice before he sat down.

Kate watched him curiously, then rose to pour him a cup of coffee and bring it to the table. It was a habit she'd begun after her mother's death several years earlier.

"Did you and Mrs. Murphy have a good time last night?" Kate asked, before her father could comment on the rumors that were sure to be circulating about her and Luke Rivers. She hadn't seen Luke yet, but she would soon enough, and she was mentally bracing herself for the confrontation. What a fool she'd made of herself. She cringed at the thought of her marriage proposal and didn't doubt for a second that Luke was going to take a great deal of delight in tormenting her about it. She suspected it would be a long while before he let her live this one down.

"Looks like rain," Devin mumbled.

Kate grinned good-naturedly, wondering at her father's strange mood. "I asked you about last night, not about the weather."

Devin's eyes flared briefly with some unnamed emotion, which he quickly disguised. His gaze fell to the steaming mug cupped in his hands.

"Dad? Did you and Mrs. Murphy enjoy yourselves?"

"Why, sure, we had a grand time," he said with forced enthusiasm.

Kate waited for him to elaborate. Instead he reached for the sugar bowl and resolutely added three heaping teaspoons to his mug. He stirred it so briskly the coffee threatened to slosh over the edge. All the while, he stared blankly into space.

Kate didn't know what to make of Devin's unusual behavior. "Dad," she said, trying again, "is there something on your mind?"

His eyes darted about the room, reluctantly settling on Kate. "What makes you ask that?"

"You just added sugar to your coffee. You've been drinking it sugarless for forty years."

He glared down at the mug, surprise written on his tanned face. "I did?"

"I saw you myself."

"I did," he repeated firmly, as if that was what he'd intended all along. "I, ah, seem to have developed a sweet tooth lately."

It was becoming apparent to Kate that her father's experience at Clay and Rorie's wedding reception must have rivaled her own. "Instead of beating around the bush all morning, why don't you just tell me what's on your mind?"

Once more, her father lowered his eyes, then nodded

and swallowed tightly. "Dorothea and I had…a long talk last night," he began haltingly. "It all started innocently enough. Then again, I'm sure the wedding and all the good feelings floating around Clay and Rorie probably had a lot to do with it." He paused to take a sip of his coffee, grimacing at its sweetness. "The best I can figure, we started talking seriously after Nellie Jackson came by and told Dorothea and me that we made a handsome couple. At least that's what I remember."

"It's true," Kate said kindly. Personally she would have preferred her father to see someone who resembled her mother a bit more, but Mrs. Murphy was a pleasant, gentle woman and Kate was fond of her.

Her father smiled fleetingly. "Then the champagne was passed around and Dorothea and I helped ourselves." He paused, glancing at Kate as if that explained everything.

"Yes," Kate said, hiding a smile, "go on."

Slowly Devin straightened, and his eyes, forthright and unwavering, held hers. "You know I loved your mother. When Nora died, there was a time I wondered if I could go on living without her, but I have, and so have you."

"Of course you have, Dad." Suddenly it dawned on Kate exactly where this conversation was leading. It shouldn't have surprised her, and yet… Kate's heart was beginning to hammer uncomfortably. Her father didn't need to say another word; she knew what was coming as surely as if he'd already spoken the words aloud. He was going to marry Dorothea Murphy.

"Your mother's been gone nearly five years now and, well, a man gets lonely," her father continued. "I've been thinking about doing some traveling and, frankly, I don't want to do it alone."

"You should've said something earlier, Dad," Kate interjected. "I'd have loved traveling with you. Still would. That's one of the nice things about being a teacher," she rambled on. "My summers are free. And with Luke watching the ranch, you wouldn't have any worries about what's happening at home and—"

"Princess." His spoon made an irritating clicking sound against the sides of the ceramic mug, but he didn't seem to notice. "I asked Dorothea to marry me last night and she's graciously consented."

After only a moment's hesitation, Kate found the strength to smile and murmur, "Why, Dad, that's fantastic."

"I realize it's going to be hard on you, Princess—so soon after Clay's wedding and all. I want you to know I have no intention of abandoning you—you'll always be my little girl."

"Of course you aren't abandoning me." Tears edged their way into the corners of Kate's eyes and a cold numbness moved out from her heart and spread through her body. "I'm happy for you. Really happy." She meant it, too, but she couldn't help feeling a sense of impending loss. All the emotional certainties seemed to be disappearing from her life.

Her father gently squeezed her hand. "There are going to be some other changes, as well, I'm afraid. I'm selling the ranch."

Kate gasped before she could stop herself. He'd just confirmed all her fears. She'd lost Clay to another woman; now she was about to lose her father, and her home, too. Then another thought crystallized in her mind, a thought that had been half formed the night before. If the ranch was sold, Luke would be gone, too.

Clay. Her father. The Circle L. Luke. Everyone and everything she loved, gone in a matter of hours. It was almost more than she could absorb. Pressing her hand over her mouth, she blinked back the tears.

"Now, I don't want you to concern yourself," her father hurried to add. "You'll always have a home with me. Dorothea and I talked it over and we both want you to feel free to live with us in town as long as you like. You'll always be my Princess, and Dorothea understands that."

"Dad," Kate muttered, laughing and crying at the same time. "That's ridiculous. I'm twenty-four years old and perfectly capable of living on my own."

"Of course you are, but—"

She stopped him by raising her hand. "There's no need to discuss it further. You and Dorothea Murphy are going to be married, and… I couldn't be happier for you. Don't you worry about me. I'll find a place of my own in town and make arrangements to move as soon as I can."

Her father sighed, clearly relieved by her easy acceptance of his plans. "Well, Princess," he said with a grin, "I can't tell you how pleased I am. Frankly, I was worried you'd be upset."

"Oh, Dad…"

Still grinning broadly, Devin stroked the side of his jaw. "Dorothea isn't a bit like your mother—I don't know if you're aware of that or not. Fact is, the only reason I asked her out that first time was so she'd invite me over for some of her peach cobbler. Then before I knew it, I was making excuses to get into town and it wasn't because of her cobbler, either."

Kate made an appropriate reply, although a minute later she wasn't sure what she'd said. Soon afterward, her father kissed her cheek and then left the house, telling her he'd be back later that afternoon.

She poured herself a second cup of coffee and leaned against the kitchen counter, trying to digest everything that was happening to her well-organized life. She felt as though her whole world had been uprooted and flung about—as though a hurricane had landed in Nightingale.

Wandering aimlessly from room to room, she paused in front of the bookcase, where a photograph of her mother stood. Tears blurred her eyes as she picked it up and clutched it to her chest. Wave upon wave of emotion swept through her, followed by a flood of hot tears.

She relived the overwhelming grief she'd felt at her mother's death, and she was furious with her father for letting another woman take Nora's place in his life. At the same time, she couldn't begrudge him his new happiness.

Mrs. Murphy wasn't the type of woman Kate would have chosen for her father, but then she wasn't doing the choosing. Suddenly resolute, Kate dragged in a deep breath, exhaling the fear and uncertainty and inhaling acceptance of this sudden change in both their lives.

The back door opened and instinctively Kate closed her eyes, mentally composing herself. It could only be Luke, and he was the last person she wanted to see right now.

"Kate?"

With trembling hands, she replaced the faded photograph and wiped the tears from her face. "Good morning, Luke," she said as she entered the kitchen.

Luke had walked over to the cupboard and taken down a mug. "Your father just told me the news about him and Mrs. Murphy," he said carefully. "Are you going to be all right?"

"Of course. It's wonderful for Dad, isn't it?"

"For your father yes, but it must be a shock to you so soon..."

"After Clay and Rorie," she finished for him. Reaching for the coffeepot, she poured his cup and refilled her own. "I'm going to be just fine," she repeated, but Kate didn't know whether she was telling him this for his benefit or her own. "Naturally, the fact that Dad's marrying Dorothea means a few changes in all our lives, but I'll adjust."

"I haven't seen your father this happy in years."

Kate did her best to smile through the pain. "Yes, I know." To her horror tears formed again, and she lowered her eyes and blinked wildly in an effort to hide them.

"Kate?"

She whirled around and set her coffee aside, then started wiping invisible crumbs from the perfectly clean kitchen counter.

Luke's hands settled on her shoulders, and before she knew what was happening, Kate had turned and buried her face against his clean-smelling denim shirt. A single sob shook her shoulders and she gave a quivering sigh, embarrassed to be breaking down in front of him like this.

"Go on, baby," he whispered gently, his hands rubbing her back, "let it out."

She felt like such a weakling to be needing Luke so much, but he was so strong and steady, and Kate felt as helpless as a rowboat tossed in an angry sea. "Did…did you know Dad might sell the ranch?" she asked Luke.

"Yes." His voice was tight. "When did he tell you?"

"This morning, after he said he was marrying Mrs. Murphy."

"You don't have to worry about it."

"But I do," she said, sobbing brokenly. She felt Luke's chin caress the crown of her head and she snuggled into his warm, safe embrace. Luke was her most trusted friend. He'd seen her through the most difficult day of her life.

The thought of Clay and Rorie's wedding flashed into her mind, and with it came the burning memory of her marriage proposal to Luke. She stiffened in his arms, mortified at the blatant way she'd used him, the way she'd practically begged him to take care of her—to marry her. Breaking free of his arms, she straightened and offered him a watery smile.

"What would I do without you, Luke Rivers?"

"You won't ever need to find out." He slid his arms around her waist and gently kissed the tip of her nose. His smile was tender. "There must've been something in the air last night. First us, and now your father and Mrs. Murphy."

"About us," she began carefully. She drew in a steadying breath, but her eyes avoided Luke's. "I hope you realize that when I asked you to marry me I…didn't actually mean it."

He went very still and for a long moment he said nothing. "I took you seriously, Kate."

Kate freed herself from his arms and reached for

her coffee, gripping the mug tightly. "I'd had too much champagne."

"According to you, it was only one glass."

"Yes, but I drank it on an empty stomach, and with all the difficult emotions the wedding brought out, I… I simply wasn't myself."

Luke frowned. "Oh?"

"No, I wasn't," she said, feigning a light laugh. "The way we were dancing and the way I clung to you, and… and kissed you. That's nothing like me. I'm not going to hold you to that promise, Luke."

As if he found it difficult to remain standing, Luke turned a chair around and straddled it with familiar ease. Kate claimed the chair opposite him, grateful to sit down. Her nerves were stretched to the breaking point. Luke draped his forearms over the back of his chair, cupping the hot mug with both hands, and studied Kate with an intensity that made her blush.

"Listen," Kate said hesitantly, "you were the perfect gentleman and I want you to know how much I appreciate everything you did. But… I didn't mean half of what I said."

The sun-marked crow's feet at the corners of his eyes fanned out as Luke smiled slowly, confidently. "Now, that raises some interesting questions."

"I don't understand." Surely Luke knew what she was talking about, yet he seemed to enjoy watching her make an even bigger fool of herself by forcing her to explain.

"Well," he said in an easy drawl, "if you only meant half of what you said, then it leads me to wonder what you did mean and what you didn't."

"I can't remember *everything* I said," she murmured,

her cheeks hot enough to pop a batch of corn. "But I do know I'd greatly appreciate it if you'd forget the part about marrying me."

"I don't want to forget it."

"Luke, please," she cried, squeezing her eyes shut. "This is embarrassing me. Could you please drop it?"

Luke rubbed his jaw thoughtfully. "I don't think I can."

So Luke was going to demand his pound of flesh. Kate supposed she shouldn't be surprised. She had, after all, brought this on herself. "You were so kind to me at the reception… After the wedding ceremony you kept saying you wanted to help me and, Luke, you did, you honestly did. I don't think I could've made it through Clay's wedding without you, but…"

"You want to forget the kissing, too?"

"Yes, please." She nodded emphatically.

He frowned. "That's not what you said last night. In fact, you seemed a little stunned at how pleasant it was. As I recall you told me—and I quote—'why didn't you tell me you were so good at this?'"

"I said that?" Kate muttered, already knowing it was true.

"I'm afraid so."

She covered her face with both hands as the hot color mounted in her cheeks.

"And you made me promise to marry you."

She bit down hard on her lower lip. "Anyone else in the world would have mercifully forgotten I said that."

With a certain degree of ceremony, Luke set his hat farther back on his head and folded his arms. His face was a study in concentration. "I have no intention of forgetting it. I'm a man of my word and I never break my promises."

Kate groaned. In light of her father's news this morning, she'd hoped Luke might be a bit more understanding. "It's obvious you're deriving pleasure from this," she muttered angrily, then pressed her lips together to keep from saying more.

"No, not exactly. When would you like to have the wedding? And while we're at it, you might as well learn now that—"

"You can't be serious!" she interrupted, incredulous that he'd suggest they set a date. If this was a joke, he was carrying it too far.

"I'm dead serious. You asked me to marry you, I agreed, and anything less would be a breach of good faith."

"Then I… I absolve you from your promise." She waved her hands as if she was granting some kind of formal dispensation.

He stroked the side of his face, his forehead creased in a contemplative frown. "My word is my word and I stand firm on it."

"I didn't understand what I was saying—well, I did. Sort of. But you know as well as I do that the…heat of the moment was doing most of the talking."

Luke's frown deepened. "I suppose everybody in town will assume you're marrying me on the rebound. Either that, or I'll be the one they gossip about. That doesn't trouble me much, but I don't like the thought of folks saying anything about you."

"Will you stop?" she cried. "I have no intention of marrying anyone! Ever!" She was finished with love, finished with romance. Thirty years from now she'd be living alone with a few cats and her knitting needles.

"That wasn't what you said last night."

"Would you quit saying that? I wasn't myself, for heaven's sake!"

"Well, our getting married sounded like a hell of a good idea to me. Now, I know you've gone through a hard time, but our marriage will end all that."

Kate brushed a shaking hand across her eyes, hoping this was just part of a nightmare and she'd soon wake up. Unfortunately when she lowered her hand, Luke was still sitting there, as arrogant as could be. "I can't believe we're having this discussion. It's totally unreasonable, and if you're trying to improve my mood, you've failed."

"I'm serious, Kate. I told you that."

Keeping her head down, she spoke quickly, urgently. "It's really wonderful of you to even consider going through with the marriage, but it isn't necessary, Luke. More than anyone, you should know that I can't marry you. Not when I love Clay Franklin."

"Hogwash."

Kate's head jerked up. "I beg your pardon?"

"You're in love with me. You just don't know it yet."

It took Kate only half a second to respond. "Of all the egotistical, vain, high-handed..." She paused to suck in a breath. If Luke's intent was to shock her, he'd succeeded. She bolted to her feet and flailed the air with both hands. Unable to stand still, she started pacing the kitchen. "I don't understand you. I've tried, honestly I've tried. One moment you're the Rock of Gibraltar, steady and secure and everything I need, my best friend, and the next moment you're saying the most ridiculous things to me. It never used to be like this! Why have you changed?"

"Is it really that bad?" he cajoled softly, ignoring her question.

"I don't know what happened to you—to us—at the wedding reception, but like you said, something must've been in the air. Let's blame it on the champagne and drop it before one of us gets hurt."

"If you gave the idea of our getting married some serious thought, it might grow on you," he suggested next.

Then he got to his feet and moved purposefully toward her, his mouth twisted in a cocky grin. "Maybe this will help you decide what's best."

"I—"

He laid a finger across her mouth. "It seems to me you've forgotten it's not ladylike to be quite so stubborn." With that, he slipped his arm around her waist and pulled her gently against him.

Knowing what he intended, Kate opened her mouth to protest, but he fastened his lips over hers, sealing off the words, and to her chagrin, soon erasing them altogether. Her fingers gripped the collar of his blue button-snap shirt and against every dictate of her will her mouth parted, welcoming his touch.

When he released her, it was a minor miracle that she didn't collapse on the floor. He paused and a wide grin split his face.

"Yup," he said, looking pleased, "you love me all right."

Three

Kate had never felt more grateful for a Monday morning than she did the following day. At least when she was at school, she had the perfect excuse to avoid another confrontation with Luke. He seemed to believe he was somehow responsible for her and to take that responsibility quite seriously. She had absolutely no intention of holding him to his promise and couldn't understand why he was being so stubborn. To suggest she was in love with him simply because she'd proposed marriage and responded ardently to his kisses revealed how truly irrational Luke Rivers had become.

Kate paused and let that thought run through her mind a second time, then laughed aloud. No wonder Luke insisted on marrying her. Kate had to admit she could see why he might have the wrong impression. Still, she wished she could think of some way to set him straight.

Luke was right about a few things, though. She *did* love him—but not in the way he implied. She felt for him as a sister did toward a special older brother. As a woman did toward a confidant and companion of many years' standing. The feelings she'd experienced when he kissed her were something of a mystery, but could easily be attributed to the heightened emotions following Clay's wedding. There'd been so many changes in Kate's life during the past few months that she barely understood herself anymore.

She could never love Luke the way she'd loved Clay. For as long as Kate could remember, she'd pictured herself as Clay's wife. Joining her life with any other man's seemed not only wrong but completely foreign.

"Good morning, Miss Logan," seven-year-old Taylor Morgenroth said as he walked casually into the classroom. "I saw you at Mr. Franklin's wedding on Saturday."

"You did?" It shouldn't surprise her, since nearly every family in town had been represented at the wedding. Probably more of her students had seen her there.

"You were with Mr. Rivers, weren't you? My mom kept asking my dad who you were dancing with. That was Mr. Rivers, wasn't it?"

"Yes." Kate had to bite her tongue to keep from explaining that she hadn't actually been "with" Luke. He wasn't her official date, although they'd attended the wedding together. But explaining something like that to a second-grader would only confuse the child.

"My dad made me dance with my older sister. It was yucky."

Kate managed some remark about how much of a gentleman Taylor had been, but she doubted that he wanted to hear it.

Before long, the students of Nightingale Elementary were filing into the classroom and rushing toward their desks. From that point on, Kate didn't have time to think about Luke or Saturday night or anything else except her lesson plans for the day.

At noon she took her packed lunch to the staff room. Several of the other teachers were already seated at the circular tables.

“Kate!” Sally Daley, the sixth-grade teacher, waved her hand to gain Kate’s attention. She smiled, patting the empty chair beside her.

Reluctantly Kate joined the older woman, sending an apologetic look to her friend Linda Hutton, the third-grade teacher, with whom she usually had lunch. Sally had the reputation of being a busybody, but Kate couldn’t think of a way to elude her without being rude.

“We were just talking about you,” Sally said warmly, “and we thought it would be nice if you’d sit with us today.”

“I’ll be happy to,” Kate said, feeling a twinge of guilt at the lie. She opened her brown bag, taking out a container of peach-flavored yogurt and two rye crisps.

“Clay’s wedding was really lovely, wasn’t it?” Sally asked without preamble. “And now I understand your father and Dorothea Murphy are going to be tying the knot?” Her questioning tone indicated she wasn’t certain of her facts.

“That’s right,” Kate said cheerfully.

“Kind of a surprise, wasn’t it?”

“Kind of,” was all Kate would admit, although she realized she should’ve known her father was falling in love with Mrs. Murphy. They’d been spending more and more time together since early summer. If Kate hadn’t been so blinded by what was happening between her and Clay, she would’ve noticed how serious her father had become about Dorothea long before now.

"It's going to be difficult for you, isn't it, dear?" Sally asked sympathetically. "Everyone knows how close you and your father have been since Nora died."

"I'm very pleased my father's planning to remarry." And Kate was. The initial shock had worn off; she felt genuinely and completely happy that her father had found someone to love. He'd never complained, but Kate knew he'd been lonely during the past few years.

"Still, it must be a blow," Sally pressed, "especially coming on the heels of Clay and Rorie getting married. It seems your whole life's been turned upside down, doesn't it?"

Kate nodded, keeping her eyes focused on her sparse meal.

"Speaking of Clay and Rorie, their wedding *was* lovely," Susan Weaver, the kindergarten teacher, put in.

"I thought so, too," Kate said, smiling through the pain. "Rorie will be a perfect wife for him." The words nearly stuck in her throat, although she was fully aware of their truth. Rorie was an ideal complement to Clay. From the moment she'd stepped into their lives, she'd obviously belonged with him.

"The new Mrs. Franklin is certainly an ambitious soul. Why, the library hasn't been the same since she took over. There are education programs going on every other week. Displays. Lectures. I tell you, nothing but good has happened since she moved to Nightingale."

"I couldn't agree with you more."

Sally nodded. "You've taken this…disappointment over Clay rather well," she murmured with cloying sympathy. "And now your father remarrying so soon afterward…" She gently patted Kate's hand. "If there's anything I can do for you, Kate, anything at all, during this difficult time, I want you to call me. I know I speak for each and every staff member when I say that. Your father must see what a wonderful daughter you've been, and I'm sorry all of this is being added to your burden just now. But if it's ever more than you can bear, your friends at Nightingale Elementary will be honored to stand by your side. All you have to do is call." The other women nodded.

If Sally was expecting a lengthy response, Kate couldn't manage it. "Thank you. That's…really good to know," she said in a faltering voice. To hear Sally tell it, Kate was close to a nervous breakdown.

"We're prepared to help as you pick up the shattered pieces of your life. And furthermore, I think Luke Rivers is a fine man."

"Luke Rivers?" Kate repeated, nearly choking on her bite of rye crisp. A huge lump formed in her throat at Sally's implication.

"Why, yes." Sally smiled serenely. "Everyone in Nightingale saw how the two of you were gazing into each other's eyes at the dance. It was the most romantic thing I've seen in years."

"Dance?"

"At the wedding-reception dance," Sally elaborated. "From what I understand, Beth Hammond's been so depressed she hasn't left her house since that night."

"Whatever for?"

Sally laughed lightly. "Surely there's no reason to be so reticent—you're among friends. Everyone knows how she's had her eye on Luke for years."

Susan nodded vigorously. "Apparently they dated a few times a year ago, but Luke's kept her dangling ever since."

"I don't have a clue what you mean," Kate said faintly, her heart beating hard enough to pound its way out of her chest. She'd hoped that with her father's engagement, the rumors about her and Luke would naturally fade away. So much for wishful thinking.

Sally exchanged a meaningful look with the other teachers. "Well, I thought that, you know…that you and Luke Rivers were involved."

"Luke and me?" Kate gave a short, almost hysterical laugh. "Nothing could be further from the truth. Luke's a dear friend, and we've known each other for years, but we're not romantically involved. There's nothing going on between us. Absolutely nothing." She spoke more vehemently than necessary, feeling pleased that for once Sally couldn't get a single word in.

After a moment, she made a show of looking at her watch. "Excuse me, ladies, but I've got to get back to my classroom."

As she left the faculty lounge, she heard the whispers start. Groaning inwardly, Kate marched down the hall and into her own room. Sitting at her desk, she snapped the cracker in half and examined it closely before tossing it in the garbage.

"Don't you know it's wrong to waste food?" Linda Hutton said, leaning against the doorjamb, arms folded.

"I wished I'd never talked to that woman," Kate muttered, feeling foolish for allowing herself to be manipulated into conversation with a known busybody.

"Well, then," Linda said, with a grin, "why did you?"

"If I knew the answer to that, I'd be enjoying my lunch instead of worrying about the tales Sally's going to spread about me…and Luke Rivers."

Linda walked into the room.

"The least you could've done was rescue me," Kate complained.

"Hey, I leave that kind of work to the fire department." Linda planted her hands on the edge of Kate's desk. "Besides, I was curious myself."

"Curious about what? Luke and me? All we did was dance a couple of times. I...was feeling warm and went outside for a little bit. Luke met me there and after a few minutes, he...drove me home. What's the big deal, anyway?"

"A couple of dances... I see," Linda said, her words slow and thoughtful.

"I'd be interested in knowing exactly *what* you see. Everyone keeps making an issue of the dancing. Taylor came into class this morning and the first thing he said was that he'd seen me at the wedding. He didn't talk about running into me at the grocery store earlier that day."

"Did you have your arms wrapped around a man there, too?"

"Don't be silly!"

"I wasn't. Honestly, Kate, nearly everyone in Nightingale saw the way you and Luke were dancing. You acted as though there wasn't anyone else at the reception. Needless to say, rumors were floating in every direction. Everyone was watching the two of you, and neither you or Luke even noticed. Or cared. I heard the pastor mumble something about maybe performing another wedding soon, and he wasn't referring to your father and Dorothea Murphy—which is another matter entirely." Linda paused to suck in a deep breath. "Are you sure you're going to be able to handle this on top of—"

"Clay and Rorie? Yes," Kate answered her own question emphatically. "Oh, I had a few bad moments when Dad first told me, but I got over it." The comfort she'd found in Luke's arms had helped her more than she cared to admit. He seemed to be making a habit of helping her through difficult moments.

Linda eyed her sceptically. "There's been so much upheaval in your life these past few weeks. You know, sometimes people go into shock for weeks after a major change in their lives."

"Linda," Kate cried, "everyone keeps looking at me as though they expect me to have a nervous breakdown. What is it with you people?"

"It isn't us, Katie girl, it's you."

Kate pushed her hair off her forehead and kept her hand there. "What do I have to do to convince you that I'm fine? I'm happy for Clay and Rorie. I consider myself resilient and emotionally strong, but this makes me wonder why you and Sally and the others don't."

"I don't think anyone's waiting for you to fall apart," Linda countered. "We all have your best interests at heart. In fact, with one obvious exception, everyone's really pleased you have Luke."

"But I don't *have* him. Luke isn't a possession, he's a man. We're friends. You know that." Kate expected Linda, of all her friends and colleagues, to recognize the truth when she heard it. Instead she'd made it sound as though Kate's dancing with Luke and then letting him take her home meant instant wedding bells.

Linda shook her head. "To be honest, Kate, you're doing a whole lot of denying and I don't understand why. It seems to me that the person you're really trying to convince is yourself."

By the time Kate arrived home that evening, she was in a fine temper. Her father had already left for a meeting at the Eagles Lodge. He'd taped a note to the refrigerator door telling her not to worry about fixing him any dinner because he planned to stop at Dorothea's later for a bite to eat.

Kate read his scrawled note, pulled it off the fridge and crumpled it with both hands. She was angry and impatient for no reason she could identify.

Heating a bowl of soup, Kate stood by the stove stirring it briskly when Luke let himself in the back door. After her encounter with Sally and Linda, Luke was the last person she wanted to see. Nevertheless, her eyes flew anxiously to his.

"Evening, Kate."

"Hi."

He hung his hat on the peg next to the door, then walked to the kitchen counter and examined the empty soup can. "I hope you're going to eat more than this."

"Luke," she said, slowly expelling her breath, "I had a terrible day and I'm rotten company."

"What happened?"

Kate didn't want to talk about it. Dredging up her lunch-hour conversation with Sally Daley would only refuel her unhappiness.

"Kate?" Luke coaxed.

She shrugged. "The other teachers heard about Dad and Dorothea and seemed to think the shock would do me in, if you know what I mean."

"I think I do." As he was speaking, he took two bowls out of the cupboard and set them on the table.

Kate stirred the soup energetically, not looking at

him, almost afraid of his reaction. "In addition, people are talking about us."

When she glanced in his direction, Luke nodded, his eyes twinkling. "I thought they might be."

"I don't like it!" she burst out. The least Luke could do was show the proper amount of concern. "Sally Daley told me how pleased she was with the way I'd rebounded from a broken heart." She paused, waiting for his response. When he didn't give one, she added, "Sally seems to think you and I are perfect together."

Luke grinned. "And that upset you?"

"Yes!" she cried.

"Sally didn't mean anything. She's got a big heart."

"And an even bigger mouth," Kate retorted. "We're in trouble here, Luke Rivers, and I need to know how we're going to get out of it."

"The answer to that is simple. We should get married and put an end to all the speculation."

Kate's shoulders sagged in defeat. "Luke, please, I'm not in the mood for your teasing tonight. We have to get serious about..."

Her voice dwindled away as Luke, standing behind her, placed his hands on her shoulders and nuzzled her neck. "I'm willing."

His touch had a curious effect on Kate's senses, which sprang to sudden life. It took every ounce of fortitude she possessed to resist melting into his arms and accepting his comfort. But that was how they'd got into this mess in the first place.

"The gossips are having a field day and I hate it."

Luke drew her away from the stove and turned her toward him. He searched her face, but his own revealed not a hint of annoyance or distress. "I don't mind if folks talk. It's only natural, don't you think?"

"How can you *say* that?"

"Kate, you're making this out to be some kind of disaster."

"But don't you see? It is! There are people out there who actually believe we're falling in love."

"You do love me. I told you that earlier. Remember?"

"Oh, Luke," she cried, so disheartened she wanted to weep. "I know what you're trying to do and I appreciate it with all my heart, but it isn't necessary. It really isn't."

Luke looked baffled. "I don't understand."

"You've been so sweet." She laid her hand against his clean-shaven cheek. "Any other man would've laughed in my face when I made him promise to marry me, but you agreed and now, out of consideration for *my* pride, *my* feelings, you claim you're going through with it."

"Kate," he said, guiding her to the table and gently pressing her into a chair. "Sit down. I have something important to tell you—something I've been trying to tell you since the night of the wedding."

"What is it?" she asked, once she was seated.

Luke paced the floor directly in front of her chair. "I should've told you much sooner, but with everything else that's going on in your life, finding the right time has been difficult." He paused and frowned at her as though he was having trouble choosing his words.

"Yes?" she coaxed.

"I'm buying the Circle L."

The kitchen started to sway. Kate reached out and gripped the edge of the table. She'd hoped it would be months, at least, before a buyer was found. And it had never occurred to her that Luke might be that buyer.

"I see," she said, smiling through her shock. "I… I'd have thought Dad would've said something himself."

"I asked him not to."

Her troubled gaze clashed with Luke's. Despite her shock she felt curious. How could Luke afford to buy a ranch, especially one as large as this? She knew he'd been raised by an uncle, who had died years before. Had there been an inheritance? "Luke," she ventured shyly, "I know it's none of my business, but…"

"How did I come by the money?" he finished for her. "You have every right to ask. I inherited it from my uncle Dan—I've told you about him. He owned a couple of businesses in Wyoming, where I grew up. There was also a small sum left to me by my grandfather. I invested everything, together with most of what Devin's paid me over the years, and I've got enough now to buy the ranch outright—which'll leave your dad and Dorothea in good financial shape for their retirement. I'll be able to expand the operation, too."

Kate nodded absently. She hadn't known much about Luke's background, apart from the fact that he had very little family, that he'd lost his parents at an early age. She supposed those losses were the reason he'd been so sympathetic, such a comfort to her and Devin, at the time of Nora's death.

It still seemed too much to take in. Her home—it was going to belong to Luke. He'd move his things from the small foreman's house, though she knew he hadn't accumulated many possessions. But it meant that soon she'd be sorting through and packing up the memories of a lifetime…. She bit her lip.

He knelt in front of her, grasping her fingers with

his warm, hard hands. "I realize you've been through a lot of emotional upheaval lately, but this should help."

"Help!" she wailed. "How could it possibly—?"

"There's no reason for you to be uprooted now."

For a stunned second she didn't react. "I don't have the slightest idea what you're talking about."

"Once we're married, we'll live right here."

"Married!" she almost shouted. "I'm beginning to hate the sound of that word."

"You'd better get used to it, because the way I figure, we're going to be husband and wife before Christmas. We'll let Devin and Dorothea take their vows first—I don't want to steal their thunder—and then we'll wait a couple of weeks and have the Reverend Wilkins marry us."

"Luke, this is all very sweet of you, but *it isn't necessary.*" Kate was convinced that this sudden desire to make her his wife was founded in sympathy. He felt sorry for her because of all the unexpected jolts that had hit her recently. Including this latest one.

"I can't understand why you're arguing with me."

Her hand caressed his jaw. How square and strong it was, and the eyes that gazed at her had never seemed darker or more magnetic. She smiled sadly. "Don't you think it's a little…odd to be discussing marriage when you've never once said you love me?"

"I love you."

It should have been a solemn moment, but Kate couldn't help laughing. "Oh, Luke, that was terrible."

"I'm serious. I love you and you love me."

"Of course we love each other, but what we feel is what *friends* feel. The kind of love brothers and sisters share."

Fire leaped into his eyes, unlike anything she'd seen in him before. With any other man, she would have been frightened—but this was Luke….

"Instead of looking at me as if you're tempted to turn me over your knee, you should be grateful I'm not holding you to your word."

"Kate," he said loudly, "we're getting married." He spoke as though he was daring her to disagree with him.

She lowered her head and brushed his lips with her own. "No, we're not. I'll always be grateful to have a friend as good as you, Luke Rivers. Every woman deserves someone just as kind and thoughtful, but we'd be making the biggest mistake of our lives if we went through with this marriage."

"I don't think that's true."

"I'm sane and rational, and I'm not going to disintegrate under the emotional stress of Clay's wedding or my father's remarriage, or the sale of the ranch. Life goes on—I learned that after my mother died. It sounds so clichéd, but it's the truth. I learned to deal with losing her and I'll do the same with everything else."

"Kate, you don't get it. I *want* to marry you."

"Oh, Luke, it's so nice of you. But you don't love me. Not the way you should. Someday, you'll make some lucky woman a fantastic husband." Kate had grown accustomed to his comfortable presence. But while she felt at ease with him, she experienced none of the thrill, the urgent excitement, that being in love entailed. Well, of course, there was her reaction to Luke's kisses—but that was an aberration, she told herself.

With Clay, the intensity of emotion had wrapped itself around her so securely that she'd been sure it would last a lifetime. Kate hadn't fooled herself into believing

Clay felt as strongly for her. He'd been fond of her, and Kate had been willing to settle for that. But it hadn't been enough for him. And she wasn't allowing Luke to settle for second-best, either.

"People are going to talk, so we both have to do our best to put an end to the rumors."

"I don't intend to do any such thing," Luke said, his jaw rigid. His eyes narrowed. "Kate, darling, a marriage between us is inevitable. The sooner you accept that, the better it'll be for everyone involved."

Four

"The way I figure it," Kate said, munching on a carrot stick, "I'm only going to convince Luke I don't intend to marry him by dating someone else."

Linda looked as if she were about to swallow her apple whole. The two were seated in the school lunchroom on Friday afternoon, reviewing plans for the Thanksgiving play their two classes would present the following month.

"Dating someone else?" Linda echoed, still wearing a stunned expression. "A few days ago you said you were finished with love and completely opposed to the idea of men and marriage."

"I'm not expecting to fall in love again," Kate explained impatiently. "That would be ridiculous."

"You talk about being ridiculous?" Linda asked, setting down her half-eaten apple. "We were discussing Pilgrim costumes and suddenly you decide you want to start dating. I take it you're not referring to Miles Standish?"

"Of course not."

"That's what I thought."

Kate supposed she wasn't making a lot of sense to her friend. Luke and the issue of marriage had been on her mind all week, but she'd carefully avoided any mention of the subject. Until now. The rumors regarding her and Luke continued to burn like a forest fire through Nightingale, aided, Kate was sure, by the silly grin Luke wore around town, and the fact that he was buying her father's ranch. True, he hadn't pressured her into setting a wedding date again, but the thought was there, waiting to ambush her every time they were in the same room. She used to be able to laugh and joke with Luke, but lately, the minute they were together, Kate found herself raising protective barriers.

"All right, you've piqued my curiosity," Linda said, her eyes flashing with humor. "Tell me about this sudden interest in the opposite sex."

"I want to stop the rumors, naturally." And convince Luke that her marriage proposal had been rooted in self-pity. He'd been so strong and she'd felt so fragile....

Linda pushed aside the pages of the Thanksgiving project notes. "Have you picked anyone in particular?"

"No," Kate murmured, frowning. "I've been out of circulation for so long, I'm not sure who's available."

"No one," Linda told her in a despondent voice. "And I should know. If you want the truth, I think Nightingale would make an excellent locale for a convent. Have you ever considered the religious life?"

Kate ignored that. "Didn't I hear Sally Daley mention something about a new guy who recently moved to town? She seemed to think he was single."

"Eric Wilson. Attorney, mid-thirties, divorced, with a small mole on his left shoulder."

Kate was astonished. "Good heavens, how did Sally know all that?"

Linda shook her head. "I don't even want to guess."

"Eric Wilson." Kate repeated it slowly, letting each syllable roll off her tongue. She decided the name had a friendly feel, though it didn't really tell her anything about the man himself.

"Have you met him?" Kate asked her friend.

"No, but you're welcome to him, if you want. My track record with divorced men isn't exactly great. The only reason Sally said anything to me was that she assumed you and Luke would be married before the holidays were over." Linda grimaced. "She thought I'd need her help in finding a date for the wedding."

A sense of panic momentarily overtook Kate. This wedding nonsense was completely out of hand, which meant she had to come up with another man *now.*

"There's always Andy Barrett," she murmured. Andy worked at the pharmacy and was single. True, he wasn't exactly a heartthrob, but he was a decent-enough sort.

Linda immediately rejected that possibility. "No one in town would believe you'd choose Andy over Luke." A smile played across her mouth, as if she found the idea of Kate and Andy together somehow comical. "Andy's sweet, don't get me wrong," Linda amended, "but Luke's a real man."

"I'll think of someone," Kate murmured, her determination fierce.

Linda started to gather her Thanksgiving notes. "If you're serious about this, then you may have no choice but to import a man from Portland."

"You're kidding, I hope," Kate groaned.

"Nope. I'm dead serious," Linda said, shoving everything into her briefcase.

Her friend's words echoed depressingly through Kate's mind as she pushed her cart to the frozen-food section of the grocery store later that afternoon. She peered at the TV dinners, trying to choose something for dinner. Her father had dined with Dorothea every night since they'd become engaged, and the wedding was planned for early December.

"The beef burgundy is good," a resonant male voice said from behind her.

Kate turned to face a tall, friendly-looking man with flashing blue eyes and a lazy smile.

"Eric Wilson," he introduced himself, holding out his hand.

"Kate Logan," she said, her heart racing as they exchanged handshakes. It was all Kate could do not to tell him she'd been talking about him only minutes before and that she'd learned he was possibly the only single prospect in town—other than Luke, of course. How bizarre that they should run into each other almost immediately afterward. Perhaps not! Perhaps it was fate.

"The Salisbury steak isn't half-bad, either." As if to prove his point, he deposited both the beef burgundy and the Salisbury steak frozen dinners in his cart.

"You sound as though you know."

"I've discovered frozen entrées are less trouble than a wife."

He frowned as he spoke, so she guessed that his divorce had been unpleasant. Sally would be able to provide the details, and Kate made a mental note to ask her. She'd do it blatantly, of course, since Sally would spread Kate's interest in the transplanted lawyer all over the county.

"You're new in town, aren't you? An attorney?"

Eric nodded. "At your service."

Kate was thinking fast. It'd been a long time since she'd flirted with a man—if you didn't count the way she'd behaved at the wedding. "Does that mean I can sue you if the beef burgundy isn't to my liking?"

He grinned at that, and although her comment hadn't been especially witty, she felt encouraged by his smile.

"You might have trouble getting the judge to listen to your suit, though," he told her.

"Judge Webster is my uncle," she said, laughing.

"And I suppose you're his favorite niece."

"Naturally."

"In that case, might I suggest we avoid the possibility of a lawsuit and I buy you dinner?"

That was so easy Kate couldn't believe it. She'd been out of the dating game years, and she'd been sure it would take a while to get the hang of it again. "I'd be delighted."

It wasn't until Kate was home, high on her success, that she realized Eric, as a new man in town, was probably starved for companionship. That made her pride sag just a little, but she wasn't about to complain. Within hours of declaring that she wanted to start dating, she'd met a man. An attractive, pleasant man, too. It didn't matter that he'd asked her out because he was lonely or that he was obviously still embittered by his divorce. A date was a date.

Kate showered and changed into a mid-calf burgundy wool skirt and a rose-colored silk blouse. She was putting the last coat of polish on her nails when her father strolled into the kitchen. Even from her position at the far side of the room, Kate caught a strong whiff of his spicy aftershave. She smiled.

"You look nice, Dad."

"Thanks," he said, tugging on the lapels of his tweed jacket, then brushing the sleeves.

"Do you want me to wait up for you?"

A flush worked its way up Devin's neck. "Of course not."

Kate loved teasing him, and as their eyes met, they both started to laugh.

"You're looking awfully pretty yourself," Devin commented. "Are you and Luke going out?"

"Eric Wilson is taking me to dinner."

Devin regarded her quizzically. "Who? You're kidding, aren't you?"

"No." She gave him a warning frown. "Eric's new here. We met in the frozen-food section at the grocery store this afternoon and he asked me to dinner."

"And you accepted?" His eyes were wide with astonishment.

"Of course. It beats sitting around here and watching reruns on television."

"But...but what about Luke?"

"What about him?"

"I thought... I'd hoped after Clay's wedding that the two of you might—"

"Dad, Luke's a dear friend, but we're not in love with each other."

For a moment Devin looked as if he wanted to argue, but apparently decided against it. "He's a good man, Princess."

"Trust me, I know that. If it wasn't for Luke, I wouldn't have survived the last couple of months."

"Folks in town have the impression that you two might be falling in love, and I can't say I blame them after watching you at the wedding."

Kate focused her attention on polishing her nails, knowing that an identical shade of red had crept into her cheeks.

"Luke and I are friends, Dad, nothing more," she repeated.

"I don't mind letting you know, Kate, that I think very highly of Luke. If I were to handpick a husband for you, it would be him."

"I…think Luke's wonderful, too," she said, her words faltering.

"Now that he's buying the ranch, well, it seems natural that the two of you—"

"Dad, please," she whispered. "I'm not in love with Luke, and he doesn't love me."

"That's a real pity," came Devin's softly drawled response. He reached for his hat, then paused by the door. "I don't suppose Luke knows you're going out tonight, does he?"

"There isn't any reason to tell him." She tried to act nonchalant. But she desperately wanted to avoid another showdown with Luke. Pleadingly, she raised her eyes to her father. "You aren't going to tell him, are you?"

"I won't lie to him."

"Oh, I wouldn't expect you to do that," Kate murmured. She blew at the dark-red polish on her nails, trying to dry them quickly. With luck, Eric would arrive soon and she could make her escape before she encountered Luke.

Kate should have known that was asking too much. She was standing at the kitchen window beside the oak table, waiting for Eric's headlights to come down the long drive, when Luke walked into the house.

Kate groaned inwardly, but said nothing. Her fingers tightened on the curtain as she changed her silent entreaty. Now she prayed that Eric would be late.

"You've got your coat on," Luke observed as he poured a mug of coffee.

"I'll be leaving in a couple of minutes," she said, hoping she didn't sound as tense as she felt. Then, a little guiltily, she added, "I baked some oatmeal cookies yesterday. The cookie jar's full, so help yourself."

He did exactly that, then sat down at the table. "If I didn't know better, I'd think you were waiting for someone."

"I am."

"Who?"

"A...friend." Her back was to him, but Kate could feel the tension between them.

"Are you upset about something?"

"No. Should I be?" she asked in an offhand manner.

"You've been avoiding me all week," he said.

He was sitting almost directly behind her and Kate felt his presence acutely. Her knees were shaking, her breath coming in short, uneven gulps. She felt lightheaded. It had to be nerves. If Luke discovered she was going to dinner with Eric, there could be trouble. Yes, she told herself, that explained the strange physical reaction she was experiencing.

"Kate, love—"

"Please," she implored, "don't call me that." She released the curtain and turned to face him. "I made a mistake, and considering the circumstances, it was understandable. Please, Luke, can't you drop this whole marriage business? Please?"

His look of shocked surprise didn't do anything to settle her nerves. A strained moment passed before Luke relaxed, chuckling. "I've broken stallions who've given me less trouble than you."

"I'm no stallion."

Luke chuckled again, and before she could move, his arms reached out and circled her waist to pull her onto his lap.

Kate was so astonished that for a crazy moment she didn't react at all. "Let me go," she said stiffly, holding her chin at a regal angle.

He ignored her demand and lightly ran the tips of his fingers along the side of her jaw, stroking downward to cup her chin. "I've missed you this week, Princess."

A trail of warmth followed his cool fingers, and a foreign sensation nibbled at her stomach. Kate didn't know what was wrong with her—and she didn't *want* to know.

"I've decided to give you a chance to think everything through before we contact Pastor Wilkins—"

"Before we what?" she flared.

"Before we're married," he explained patiently, his voice much too low and seductive to suit her. "But every time we're together, you run away like a frightened kitten."

"Did you stop to think there might be a perfectly logical reason for that?" She'd told him repeatedly that she wasn't going to marry him, but it didn't seem to make any differences. "I'm sorry, I truly am, but I just don't see you that way."

"Oh?"

He raised his hand and threaded his fingers through her hair. She tried to pull away, to thwart him, with no effect.

"That's not the feeling I get when I kiss you."

She braced her hands against his shoulders. "I apologize if I've given you the wrong impression," she said, her voice feeble.

He cocked his eyebrows at her statement, and his lips quivered with the effort to suppress a smile. That infuriated Kate, but she held on to her temper, knowing an argument would be pointless.

"It seems to me," he continued, "that we need some time alone to explore what's happening between us."

Alarm rose in Kate's throat as she struggled to hide her response to him. The last thing she wanted was "time alone" with Luke.

"I'm afraid that's impossible tonight," she said hastily.

"Why's that?"

He was so close that his breath fanned her flushed face. It was all Kate could do to keep from closing her eyes and surrendering to the sensations that encircled her, like lazy curls of smoke from a campfire.

His mouth found her neck and he placed a series of kisses there, each one a small dart of pleasure that robbed her of clear thought. For a wild moment, she couldn't catch her breath. His hands were in her hair, and his mouth was working its magic....

"No," she breathed, her voice low and trembling. Any resistance she'd managed to rally had vanished.

"Yes, my darlin', Kate?"

He sought her mouth then, and excitement erupted

inside her. She clung to him, arms around his neck as his lips returned again and again to taste and tantalize her.

When he buried his face in the hollow of her throat, Kate moaned softly. She felt nearly faint from the rush of pleasure.

"Call Linda and cancel whatever plans you've made," he whispered.

Kate froze. "I can't."

"Yes, you can. I'll talk to her, if you want."

"I'm not going out with Linda."

"Then call whoever it is and cancel."

"No…"

A flash of headlights through the kitchen window announced Eric's arrival. With a burst of frantic energy, Kate leaped off Luke's lap, feeling disoriented and bewildered. She rubbed her hands over her face, realizing she'd probably smudged her makeup, but that didn't concern her as much as the unreserved way she'd submitted to Luke's touch. He'd kissed her before and it had been wonderful—more than wonderful. But in those brief moments when he'd held her, at the wedding and then again the next day, she hadn't experienced this burning *need.* It terrified her.

"Kate?"

She looked at Luke without really seeing him. "I've got to go," she insisted.

"There's a man here."

Kate opened the door for Eric. "Hi," she greeted him, doing her best to appear cheerful and animated, but suspecting that she looked and sounded as though she was coming down with a bad case of flu. "I see you found the place without a problem."

"Actually, I had one hell of a time," he said, glancing at his watch. "Didn't you notice I'm fifteen minutes late?"

Well, no, she hadn't. Not really.

"Kate, who is this man?" Luke demanded in a steely voice.

"Eric Wilson, this is Luke Rivers. Luke is buying the Circle L," she said breathlessly.

The two men exchanged the briefest of handshakes.

Kate didn't dare look in Luke's direction. She didn't need to; she could feel the resentment and annoyance that emanated from him like waves of heat. "Well, I suppose we should be on our way," Kate said to Eric, throwing him a tight, nervous smile.

"Yes, I suppose we should." Eric's gaze traveled from Kate to Luke, then back again. He seemed equally eager to escape.

"I'll say good-night, Luke," she said pointedly, her hand on the back door.

He didn't respond, which was just as well.

Once they were outside, Eric opened his car door for her. "You said Luke is buying the ranch?"

"Yes," she answered brightly.

"And nothing else?" he pressed, frowning. "The look he was giving me seemed to say you came with the property."

"That's not true." Even if Luke chose to believe otherwise. After tonight, she couldn't deny that they shared a strong physical attraction, but that was nothing on which to base a life together. She didn't *love* Luke; how could she, when she was still in love with Clay? She'd been crazy about Clay Franklin most of her life, and feelings that intense didn't change overnight simply because he'd married another woman.

When Clay and Rorie had announced their engagement, Kate had known with desolate certainty that she'd never love again. If she couldn't have Clay, then she would live the remainder of her life alone, treasuring the time they'd had together.

"You're absolutely certain Rivers has no claim on you?"

"None," Kate assured him.

"That's funny," Eric said with a humorless chuckle. "From the way he glared at me, I feel lucky to have walked away with my head still attached."

Kate forced a laugh. "I'm sure you're mistaken."

Eric didn't comment further, but she could tell he didn't believe her.

After their shaky beginning, dinner turned out to be a pleasant affair. Eric took Kate to the Red Bull, the one fancy restaurant in Nightingale, a steak house that specialized in thick T-bones and fat baked potatoes. A country-and-western band played local favorites in the lounge, which was a popular Friday-night attraction. The music drifted into the dining-room, creating a festive atmosphere.

Eric studied the menu, then requested a bottle of wine with their meal.

When the waitress had taken their order, he placed his elbows on the table and smiled at Kate. "Your eyes are lovely," he said, his voice a little too enthusiastic.

Despite herself, Kate blushed. "Thank you."

"They're the same color as my ex-wife's." He said this in bitter tones, as if he wished Kate's were any color other than blue. "I'm sorry," he added, looking chagrined. "I've got to stop thinking about Lonni. It's over. Finished. Kaput."

"I take it you didn't want the divorce."

"Do you mind if we don't talk about it?"

Kate felt foolish for bringing up the subject, especially since it was obviously so painful for him. "I'm sorry, that was thoughtless. You're trying to let go of the past."

The bottle of wine arrived and when Eric had sampled and approved it the waitress filled their glasses.

"Actually you remind me of Lonni," he said, after taking a sip of the chardonnay. "We met when we were both in college."

Kate looked down at her wineglass, twirling the delicate stem between her fingers. Eric was so clearly in love with his ex-wife that she wondered what had torn them apart.

"You were asking about the divorce?" He replenished his wine with a lavish hand.

"If it's too difficult, you don't need to talk about it."

"I don't think either Lonni or I ever intended to let it go this far," he said, and Kate was sure he hadn't even heard her. "I certainly didn't, but before I knew what was happening, the whole thing blew up in my face. There wasn't another man—I would've staked my life on that."

Their dinner salads were served and, picking up her fork, Kate asked, "What brought you to Nightingale?"

Eric drank his wine as if he were gulping cool water on a summer afternoon. "Lonni, of course."

"I beg your pardon?"

"Lonni. I decided I needed to make a clean break. Get a fresh start and all that."

"I see."

"You have to understand that when Lonni first suggested we should separate, I thought it was the right thing to do. We hadn't been getting along and, frankly, if she wanted out of the relationship, I wasn't going to stand in her way. It's best to discover these things before you have children, don't you agree?"

"Oh, yes." Kate nibbled at her salad, wondering what she could say that would help or comfort Eric.

An hour and another bottle of wine later, Kate realized he'd drunk the better part of both bottles and was in no condition to drive home. Now she had to tactfully make *him* realize that.

"Do you dance?" she asked, as he paid the dinner bill.

He frowned slightly. "This country-and-western stuff doesn't usually appeal to me, but I'm willing to give it a whirl, if you are."

Kate assumed all the wine he'd been drinking had quelled his reservations. When the band began a lively melody, Eric led Kate onto the crowded dance floor.

Kate was breathless by the time the song ended. To her relief, the next number was a much slower one. She recognized her mistake the minute Eric locked her in his embrace. His hands fastened at the small of her back, forcing her close. She tried to put some space between them, but Eric didn't seem to notice her efforts. His eyes were shut as he swayed to the leisurely beat. Kate wasn't fooled; her newfound friend was pretending he had Lonni in his arms. It was a good thing her ego wasn't riding on this date.

"I need a little more room," she whispered.

He loosened his grip for a moment, but as the song

continued, his hold gradually tightened again. Kate edged her forearms up and braced them on his chest, easing herself back an inch or two.

"Excuse me, please." A harsh male voice that was all too familiar came from behind Eric. Kate wished she could crawl into a hole and die the instant she heard it.

"I'm cutting in," Luke informed the other man, who turned his head and looked at the intruder incredulously.

Without a word of protest Eric dropped his arms and took a step in retreat. Neither man bothered to ask Kate what *she* wanted. She was about to complain when Luke reached for her hand and with a natural flair swept her into his arms. The immediate sense of welcome she experienced made her want to weep with frustration.

"Why did you cut in like that?" she demanded. She felt disheartened and irritable. Everything she'd worked for this evening was about to be undone.

"Did you mean for that city slicker to hold you so close?"

"How Eric holds me isn't any of your business."

"I'm making it my business."

His face was contorted with anger. His arms were so tight that Kate couldn't have escaped him if she'd tried. Judging by the looks they were receiving from the couples around them, they were quickly becoming the main attraction.

The instant the music ended, Kate abruptly left Luke's arms and returned to Eric. Her date stood in the corner of the room, nursing a shot glass filled with amber liquid. Kate groaned and hid her displeasure. Eric had already had enough wine without adding hard liquor.

"I thought you said there was nothing between you and Luke Rivers," he muttered, when she joined him.

"There isn't. We're just good friends."

"That's not the impression I'm getting."

Kate didn't know how to respond. "I apologize for the interruption. Do you want to dance?"

"Not if it's going to cost me my neck."

"It isn't," she promised.

Another lively song erupted from the band. Eric took her hand and she smiled encouragingly up at him. As they headed for the dance floor, Kate tried to ignore Luke's chilly glare.

Midway through the song, Eric stopped dancing. "I'm not very good at this fancy footwork," he declared. With that, he pulled her into his arms, tucking her securely against him.

"This is much better," he whispered, his mouth close to her ear. Once more his hold tightened.

"Eric, please. I'm having trouble breathing," Kate told him in a strangled voice.

"Oh, sorry." He relaxed his grip. "Lonni and I used to dance like this all the time."

Kate had guessed as much. It was on the tip of her tongue to remind him that she wasn't his ex-wife, but she doubted it would make any difference. Eric had spent much of the evening pretending she was.

At the moment, however, her date and his ex-wife were the least of Kate's problems. Tiny pinpricks moved up and down her spine, telling her that Luke was still glaring at her from the other side of the room. She did her best to act as though he wasn't there.

She smiled up at Eric, she laughed, she talked, but

with each breath she drew she could feel Luke's eyes on her, scrutinizing every move she made.

When the music stopped, Eric returned to their table and his drink, swallowing the remainder of it in one gulp. The music started again and he pulled Kate toward him.

"I think I'll sit this one out." She hoped that would appease Luke, who looked as if he were about to rip Eric in two.

Her gaze fell to her lap and she folded her hands, concentrating on not letting him know how much a single glance from him affected her.

"How much have you had to drink, Wilson?"

While her eyes were lowered, Luke had come over to their table. His voice was controlled but unmistakably furious.

"I can't say that's any of your concern, Rivers." For his part, Eric seemed nervous. He leaned back in his chair, balancing on two legs, and raised his empty shot glass.

"I don't agree," Luke countered, moving closer. "From what I can see, you've had plenty. I'm taking Kate home with me."

"Luke," she protested, "please don't do this."

"Your date's in no condition to drive."

It was all Kate could do not to stand up and defend Eric. Unfortunately Luke was right. She'd known it even before they'd finished dinner, but she wanted to handle things her own way.

"I can hold my liquor as well as the next man," Eric said, daring to wave his glass under Luke's nose. It was apparent to everyone that his courage had been fortified by whiskey. Few men would have taunted Luke in his present mood.

Luke turned to Kate. "You've got better sense than this, Kate."

Kate did. But she had no intention of telling him so. "I think Eric knows his own limit," she returned.

"Then you plan to ride home with him?"

"I'm not sure yet." She wouldn't, but she wasn't about to give Luke an armful of ammunition to use against her.

Luke scowled at her with such fury it was difficult for Kate to swallow normally.

Slowly he turned to Eric. "If you value your teeth, I suggest you stay exactly where you are. Bob," Luke called to the sheriff's deputy across the room, "would you see that this newcomer gets home without a problem?"

"Sure thing, Luke."

"Kate," he said, addressing her next, "you're coming with me."

"I most certainly am not."

Luke didn't leave her any option. He leaned forward and pulled her upright, as if she weighed no more than a bag of popcorn.

She struggled briefly but knew it was useless. "Luke, don't do this. Please, don't do this," she pleaded through clenched teeth, humiliated to the very roots of her hair.

"Either you come with me willingly or I carry you out of here." Luke's composure didn't falter. When she resisted, he swept his arms behind her legs and lifted her from the floor.

"Luke," Kate cried, "put me down this instant. I *demand* that you put me down."

He completely ignored her threat as he strode toward the door, his gaze focused impassively ahead of them. The waitress who'd served her dinner came running up to hand Kate her coat and bag. Her eyes were flashing with humor.

"Stick by your man, honey," she advised. "That city slicker can't hold a candle to Luke Rivers."

"Luke's the man for you," someone else shouted.

"When you gonna tie the knot?"

Two men were holding open the lounge door for them. The last thing Kate heard as Luke carried her into the cold night air was a robust round of applause from inside the lounge.

Five

"I have never been so embarrassed in my life," Kate stormed as Luke parked his pickup outside the house. "How could you *do* that to me? How could you?"

During the entire ride home, Luke hadn't spoken a word, nor had he even glanced at her. He'd held himself stiff, staring straight ahead. For all his concern about her riding with Eric, he drove as if the very devil were on their tail. Only when they entered the long, winding drive that led to the house had he reduced his speed.

"I'll never forgive you for this," she told him, grabbing the door handle and vaulting out of the truck. She couldn't get away from him fast enough. By morning every tongue in Nightingale would be wagging, telling how Luke Rivers had hauled Kate Logan out of the Red Bull.

To her dismay Luke followed her into the house.

"I couldn't care less if you forgive me or not," he said darkly.

"The women were laughing and the men snickering.… I won't be able to show my face in this town again."

"As far as I'm concerned, the problem is one of your own making."

"That's not true!" She'd had no way of knowing that Eric was going to start downing wine like soda pop. And she did *not* need a lecture from Luke Rivers. All she wanted him to do was leave, so she could lick her wounds in private and figure out how long it would be before she dared go out in public again.

Luke started pacing the kitchen floor. Each step was measured and precise. Clipped, like his voice.

"Please go," she beseeched wearily.

"I'm not leaving until I get some answers from you."

Gathering what remained of her dignity, which at this point wasn't much, Kate sank onto a chair. She wouldn't argue with Luke. Every time she tried, she came out the loser. Better to get this over with now rather than wait for morning. She sighed deeply.

"Who the hell is Eric Wilson and why were you having dinner with him?" Luke's heavy boots clicked against the kitchen floor as he paced.

Instead of answering, Kate asked, "What's happened to us?" She gazed sorrowfully up at Luke. "Do you remember how much fun we used to have together? Tonight wasn't fun, Luke. Just a few weeks ago I could laugh with you and cry with you. You were my friend and I was yours. Suddenly nothing's the same, and I don't understand why." Her voice quavered slightly. She fought an overwhelming desire to hide her face in her hands and weep.

She didn't win. Tears of pride and anguish spilled on to her cheeks. She brought her hands up, trying to hide her distress.

Luke knelt in front of her and pried her hands away.

His fingers tenderly caressed her face. "Everything has changed, hasn't it, Princess?"

She sucked in a shaky breath and nodded.

"You're confused, aren't you?" His hands cradled her face and he eased forward to press his warm mouth over hers. Even as she kissed him back, her confusion grew. He'd been so angry with her, more furious than she'd ever seen him. Yet, when he kissed her, he was achingly gentle.

Luke seemed to believe that her ready response to his kiss would answer the questions that haunted her. Instead it raised *more* questions, more qualms.

"Do you understand now?" he asked, his voice a husky murmur, his eyes closed.

How Kate wished she did. She shook her head, bewildered and still uncertain.

Luke stroked her lips with his index finger. His most innocent touches brought her nerves to life with a prickling, wary excitement. Refusing to think about her own impulse, she held his hand to her mouth and brushed her lips across his callused fingertips.

"Oh, love," he moaned, and bent forward, caressing her mouth with his once more. "We've got to put an end to this madness before I go insane."

"How?" she gasped, as she braced her hands against his broad chest. He felt so good, hard muscle and warm flesh, and so strong, as if nothing could stand in his way once he determined a course. Not heaven. Not hell. And not anything in between.

"How?" He repeated her question, then chuckled, the sound rumbling from deep within his chest. "We'll have to do what you suggested."

"What I suggested?"

His mouth continued to tease hers with a series of small, nibbling kisses that seemed to pluck at her soul. "There's only one way to cure what's between us, Kate."

"One way," she echoed weakly.

"You'll have to marry me. There's no help for it and, considering how I feel right now, the sooner the better."

Kate felt as if he'd dumped a bucket of ice water over her head. "Marry you," she shrieked, pushing him away so quickly that he nearly toppled backward. "Your answer to all this confusion is for us to get married?"

"Kate, don't be unreasonable. We're perfect for each other. You need me now more than at any time in your life and I'm here for you."

"Luke, please—"

"No." He stopped her with a look. "You're about to lose everything in life that you thought was secure—your father and your home. I don't have any intention of taking over Devin's role, but the way I figure it, I'd make you a decent husband."

"What about *love?*" Kate cried.

Luke sighed in frustration. "We've gone over that ten times. You already love me—"

"Like a brother."

"Princess, sisters don't kiss their brothers the way you just kissed me."

He apparently believed that was argument enough. Not knowing how else to respond, she shook her head. "I love Clay! You keep ignoring that or insisting I don't—but I do. I have for as long as I can remember. I can't marry you. I won't!"

"For heaven's sake, forget Clay."

"It's not so easy!" she shouted.

"It would be if you'd try a little harder," Luke muttered, obviously losing patience. "I'm asking you to marry me, Kate Logan, and a smart woman like you should know a good offer when she hears one."

So much for love. So much for romance. Luke wasn't even listening to her, and Kate doubted he'd understood a single thing she'd said. "This conversation isn't getting us anywhere."

"Kate—"

"I think you should leave."

"Kate," he said, firmly gripping her shoulders, "how long is it going to take you to realize that I love you and you love me?"

"Love you? How can you say that? Until a few weeks ago I was engaged to marry Clay Franklin!" Angrily she pushed away his hands and sprang to her feet.

"Yes. And all that time you were going to marry the wrong man."

Luke didn't seem to find that statement the least bit odd, as if women regularly chose to marry one man when they were really in love with another. Kate shook her head, releasing a harsh breath.

"It's the truth," he said calmly.

She glared at him. Reasoning with Luke was a waste of time. He repeated the same nonsensical statements over and over, as if his few words were explanation enough.

"I'm going to bed," she said, turning abruptly away from him. "You can do as you like."

A moment of stunned silence followed her words before he chuckled softly, seductively. "I'm sure you don't mean that the way it sounds."

* * *

As Kate expected, the small community buzzed with the news of her fiasco with Eric Wilson. Neighbor delighted in telling neighbor how Luke Rivers had swooped her into his arms and how the entire Friday-night crowd at the Red Bull had cheered as he'd carried her off the dance floor.

Kate needed every ounce of courage she possessed just to walk down Main Street. Her smile felt stiff and false and she was convinced she had the beginnings of an ulcer.

To worsen matters, all the townsfolk seemed to believe it was their place to offer her free advice.

"You stick with Luke Rivers. He's a far better man than that city slicker," the butcher told her Saturday afternoon.

Blushing heatedly, she ordered a pork roast and left as soon as she'd paid.

"I understand you and Luke Rivers caused quite a ruckus the other night at the steak house," the church secretary said Sunday morning after the service. "I heard about the romantic way Luke carried you outside."

Kate hadn't found being carried off the least bit romantic but she smiled kindly, made no comment and returned home without a word.

"What's this I hear about you and Luke Rivers?" The moment Kate entered her classroom Monday morning, Sally Daley appeared.

"Whatever you heard, I'm sure it was vastly exaggerated," Kate said hurriedly.

"That could be," Sally admitted with a delicate laugh. "You certainly know how to keep this town talking.

First Clay's wedding reception, and now this. By the way, Clay and Rorie are back from Hawaii, and I heard they both have marvelous tans."

"That often happens in Hawaii," Kate said, sarcastically, barely holding on to her composure.

No sooner had Sally left than Linda showed up. "Is it true?" she demanded, her eyes as round as quarters.

Kate shrugged. "Probably."

"Oh, good grief, the whole thing about squelching rumors backfired, didn't it?"

Miserably Kate nodded. She was afraid she'd dissolve in a puddle of tears the next time someone mentioned Luke's name. "After what happened to me Friday night, well… I just don't think it's possible to feel any more humiliated."

"I thought you said you hadn't met Eric," Linda said, clearly puzzled.

"I hadn't when you and I talked. Eric and I ran into each other at the grocery not ten minutes after you mentioned his name."

Linda slumped against the side of Kate's desk. "I try for months to meet a new man and nothing happens. It doesn't make sense. A few minutes after you decide to look, one pops up in front of you like a bird in a turkey shoot!"

"Beginner's luck." Except that Friday night could in no way be classified as lucky.

"Oh, Kate, you've really done it now."

"I know," she whispered in a tone of defeat.

Kate's day ended much as it had begun, which meant that by four o'clock she had a headache to rival all headaches. After school, she stopped at the pharmacy and bought a bottle of double-strength aspirin and some antacid tablets.

When she left the pharmacy, she headed for the library, wondering if Rorie would be back at work so soon after her honeymoon. Her friend's smiling face greeted Kate the instant she walked through the doors.

"Kate, it's so good to see you."

"Hi, Rorie." Kate still felt a little awkward with Clay's bride. She suffered no regrets about bringing them together, though it had been the most painful decision of her life.

"Sally Daley's right," Kate said with a light laugh as she kissed Rorie's cheek. "You're so tanned. You look wonderful."

Rorie accepted the praise with a smile that shone from her dark brown eyes. "To be honest, I never thought I'd get Clay to laze away seven whole days on the beach, but he did. Oh, Kate, we had the most wonderful time."

"I'm glad." And she was. Rorie radiated happiness, and the glow of it warmed Kate's numb heart.

"I was just about to go on my coffee break. Have you got time to join me?" Rorie invited, glancing at her watch.

"I'd love to." Kate crossed her fingers. She hoped Rorie hadn't heard any of the gossip—no doubt colorfully embroidered by now—about what had happened Friday night. At the moment, Kate needed a friend, a good friend, someone she could trust to be objective.

While Rorie arranged to leave the library in the hands of a volunteer assistant, Kate walked over to Nellie's Café, across the street from the pharmacy. She'd already ordered their coffee when Rorie slipped into the red upholstered booth across from her.

"What's this I've been hearing all day about you and Luke? Honestly, Kate, you know how to live dangerously, don't you? And now Luke's buying the Circle L and your father's marrying Mrs. Murphy. We were only gone seven days, but I swear it felt like a year with everything Mary had to tell us once we got home."

Kate tried to maintain a stoic expression, although the acid in her stomach seemed to be burning a hole straight through her. There were no secrets in this town.

"To tell you the truth, Luke and I haven't been getting along very well lately," she admitted, keeping her eyes lowered so as not to meet her friend's questioning gaze.

Rorie took a tentative sip of coffee. "Do you want to talk about it?"

Kate nodded. She felt embarrassingly close to tears and paid careful attention to the silverware, repositioning the fork and the spoon several times.

"Luke was so good to me after you and Clay became engaged. He couldn't have been a better friend. Then… after the wedding I was feeling lost and alone. Luke had been dancing with me and I felt so…secure in his arms, and I'm afraid I suggested something foolish…. And now Luke keeps reminding me of it."

"That doesn't sound like Luke." Rorie frowned in puzzlement. "Nor does suggesting 'something foolish' sound like you."

"I had a glass of champagne on an empty stomach," Kate offered as an excuse.

"What about Luke?"

"I don't know, but I swear, he's become so unreasonable about everything, and he keeps saying the most ridiculous things."

"Give me an example," Rorie said.

Kate shrugged. "He claims I love him."

Her remark was followed by a short silence. "What *do* you feel for Luke?" Rorie asked.

"I care about him, but not in the way he assumes." Her finger idly circled the rim of the coffee cup while she composed her thoughts. "What irritates me most is that Luke discounts everything I felt for Clay, as if my love for him was nothing more than wasted emotion." Kate felt awkward explaining this to her ex-fiancé's wife, but Rorie was the one person who'd understand.

"And now that Clay's married to me," Rorie said, "Luke seems to think some lightbulb has snapped on inside your brain."

"Exactly."

"He thinks you should have no hesitation about throwing yourself into *his* loving arms?"

"Yes!" Rorie explained it far better than Kate had. "He keeps insisting I need him and that if I thought about it I'd realize I do love him. If it was only Luke I could probably deal with it, but everyone in town, including my own father, thinks I should marry him, too."

"That's when you agreed to have dinner with that new attorney. What's his name again?"

"Eric Wilson. Yes, that was exactly the reason I went out with him. Rorie, I tell you I was desperate. Every time I turned around, Luke was there wearing this smug, knowing look and casually announcing that we'd be married before Christmas. He makes the whole thing sound like it's a foregone conclusion and if I resist him I'd be…going against nature or something." She paused and waved her hand dramatically.

Rorie laughed. "Is he really doing that?"

Kate nodded grimly. "Actually there's more." She felt she had to tell Rorie everything. "To be fair, you should know I have no one to blame but myself. Luke may be doing all this talking about us getting married. But I was the one who…suggested it."

"How? When? Oh. The 'something foolish' you mentioned."

Shredding the paper napkin into tiny strips, Kate nodded again, flinching at the memory. "Honestly, Rorie, I didn't mean it. We were standing in the moonlight at your wedding dance and everything was so serene and beautiful. The words just slipped out of my mouth before I stopped to think what I was saying."

"The incident with the attorney didn't help."

Kate sighed. "And now that Dad's marrying Mrs. Murphy and Luke's bought the ranch, everything's getting worse."

"Luke can be a bit overpowering at times, can't he?"

Kate rolled her eyes in agreement. "But you know, what bothers me even more than Luke's cavalier attitude is the way everyone else seems to be siding with him."

"You mean about marrying Luke?"

"Yes." Kate gave another forlorn sigh. "Look at my dad—he's the perfect example. And everyone in town seems to think that if I'm foolish enough to let another good man slip through my fingers, I'll end up thirty and a spinster for sure."

"That's crazy!"

Coming from San Francisco, Rorie couldn't understand how differently people in this small Oregon community viewed life, Kate mused. A woman already thirty years old and unmarried was likely to stay that way—at least in Nightingale. "You haven't lived here long enough to know how folks in this town think."

"Kate, you're over twenty-one. No one can force you to marry Luke. Remember that."

Kate rested her elbows on the table and cradled her coffee cup in both hands. "I feel like I'm caught in a current that's flowing too fast for me. I'm afraid to stand up for fear I'll lose my footing but I can't just allow it to carry me where it will, either."

"No, you can't," Rorie said and her mouth tightened.

"Luke—and practically everyone else—apparently sees me as a poor, spineless soul who can't possibly decide what's best for her own life."

"That's not true at all," Rorie declared. "And don't let anyone tell you you're weak! If that was the case, you would have married Clay yourself, instead of working so hard to make sure we found each other."

Kate dismissed that with a shake of her head. "I did the only thing I could."

"But not everyone would've been so unselfish. Clay and I owe our happiness to you." She clasped Kate's hands with her own. "I wish I knew how to help you. All I can tell you is to listen to your own heart."

"Oh, Rorie, I feel so much better talking to you." She knew her friend was right. She'd faltered for a step or two, but considering everything that had happened in the past little while, that was understandable. Luke might believe she needed him, but she didn't, not really. In the weeks to come, she'd have the opportunity to prove it.

"Before I forget," Rorie said, her voice eager, "Clay

and I want to invite you over for dinner one night soon. As I said, we feel deeply indebted to you and want to thank you for what you did."

"Dinner," Kate repeated, suddenly dismayed. She'd need time to prepare herself before facing Clay again. Here she was reassuring herself in one breath and then doubting herself in the next.

"Would next Tuesday be all right?" Rorie pressed.

"But you've hardly had time to settle in with Clay," Kate said, turning her attention back to her friend. "How about giving it another week or two?"

"Are you worried that I'm going to serve my special seafood fettuccine?" Rorie asked with a laugh. When she'd first been stranded in Nightingale, Rorie had cooked it for Clay and his younger brother, Skip, one night. But, unfortunately, because both men did strenuous physical jobs, they were far more interested in a hearty meat-and-potatoes meal at the end of the day. Neither of them had considered seafood in a cream sauce with fancy noodles a very satisfactory repast, though Clay had politely tried to hide his disappointment. Skip hadn't.

Kate smiled at the memory of that night and slowly shook her head. "You serve whatever you want. I'm much easier to please than Skip."

"Actually Mary will probably do the cooking. She's been the Franklins' housekeeper for so many years that I don't dare invade her kitchen just yet. After the fettuccine disaster, she doesn't trust me around her stove any more than Skip does."

They both laughed, and to Kate, it felt good to forget her troubles, even for a few minutes.

"I should get back to the library," Rorie said reluctantly.

"I need to head home myself." Kate left some change on the table and slid out of the booth. Impulsively she hugged Rorie, grateful for the time they'd spent together and for the other woman's support. "I'm glad you're my friend," she whispered, feeling a little self-conscious.

"I am, too," Rorie said, and hugged her back.

By the time Kate pulled into the Circle L driveway, she was filled with bold resolution. She hurried inside just long enough to set a roast in the oven and change her clothes. Then she went into the yard, intent on confronting Luke. She wanted to get this over with—as soon as possible.

As luck would have it, Luke wasn't in any of the places she normally found him. Bill Schmidt, a longtime ranch hand, was working in the barn by himself.

"Bill, have you seen Luke?" she asked.

Bill straightened and set his hat farther back on his head. "Can't say I have. At least, not in the past couple of hours. Said he was going out to look for strays. I imagine he'll be back pretty soon now."

"I see." Kate gnawed her lower lip, wondering what she should do. Without pausing to question the wisdom of her decision, she reached for a bridle.

"Bill, would you get Nonstop for me?" Nonstop was the fastest horse in their stable. Kate was in the mood for some exercise; if she didn't find Luke, that was fine, too. She could use a good hard ride to vent some of the frustration that had been binding her all week.

"Sure, Miz Logan." Bill left his task and headed for the corral, returning a few minutes later with Nonstop.

"Luke seemed to be in the mood to do some riding himself this afternoon," he commented as he helped her cinch the saddle. "Must be the weather."

"Must be," Kate agreed.

Minutes later Nonstop was cantering out of the yard. Kate hadn't ridden in weeks and she was surprised to realize just how long it had been. When she was engaged to Clay, she'd spent many a summer afternoon in the saddle, many a Saturday or Sunday riding by his side. That had ended about the same time as their wedding plans. She felt a stinging sense of loss but managed to dispel it with the memory of her talk with Rorie.

Bill pointed out the general direction Luke had taken, and Kate followed that course at a gallop. She found it wonderfully invigorating to be in the saddle again.

The afternoon remained mild, but the breeze carried the distinctive scent of autumn. These past few days had been Indian summer, with rare clement temperatures. Within the hour, the sun would set, bathing the rolling green hills in a golden haze.

"Kate." Her name floated on a whisper of wind.

Pulling back on the reins, Kate halted the mare and turned in the saddle to discover Luke trotting toward her. She raised her hand and waved. Much of her irritation had dissipated, replaced by a newly awakened sense of well-being. No longer did Kate feel her life was roaring out of control; she was in charge, and it exhilarated her.

Luke dismounted as soon as he reached her. "Is everything all right?"

"Of course," she said with a slight laugh. "I hope I didn't frighten you."

"No. I rode into the yard not more than fifteen minutes after you left, according to Bill. I was afraid I wasn't going to catch you. You were riding like a demon."

"I…had some thinking to do."

"Bill said you were looking for me."

"Yes," she agreed. "I wanted to talk to you." There was no better time than the present. And no better place. They were at the top of a grassy hill that looked out over a lush green valley. Several head of cattle dotted the pasture spread out below them, grazing in the last of the afternoon sun.

Luke lifted his hands to her waist, helping her out of the saddle. His eyes held hers as he lowered her to the ground. Once again, she was aware that his touch had a curious effect on her, but she stringently ignored it.

Still, Kate's knees felt a little shaky and she was more breathless than she should've been after her ride. She watched Luke loop the reins over the horses' heads to dangle on the ground. Both Nonstop and Silver Shadow, Luke's gelding, were content to graze leisurely.

"It's nice out this afternoon, isn't it?" she said, then sank down on the grass and drew up her legs.

Luke sat down beside her, gazing out over the valley. "It's a rare day. I don't expect many more like it."

"Rorie and Clay are back from Hawaii."

Luke had removed his leather work gloves to brush a stray curl from her temple, then stopped abruptly and withdrew his hand. "I take it you saw Rorie?"

She nodded, adding, "We had coffee at Nellie's."

"You're not upset?"

"Not at all."

"I thought you looked more at peace with yourself." He leaned back and rested his weight on the palms of his hands. His long legs were stretched in front of him, crossed at the ankles. "Did you finally recognize that you never did love Clay? That you're in love with me?"

"No," she said vehemently, amazed he could anger her so quickly.

Luke turned away. "I thought… I'd hoped you were willing to discuss a wedding date," he said stiffly.

"Oh, Luke," she whispered and closed her eyes. He was so worried for her, so concerned, and she didn't know how to reassure him.

"Luke," she said softly, "we've been having the same discussion all week, and it's got to come to an end." Luke faced her and their eyes met with an impact that shocked her. "Luke, I think you're a wonderful man—I have for years and years," she continued. "But I don't love you, at least not the way you deserve to be loved."

Luke's eyebrows soared, then his brow furrowed. He seemed about to argue, but Kate stopped him before he had the chance.

"I refuse to be coerced into a wedding simply because *you* feel it's the best thing for me—because you feel I need looking after. Frankly, I don't believe marriage is a good idea for us—at least not to each other."

"Kate, love—"

Lowering her lashes in an effort to disguise her frustration, Kate reminded him for what seemed the thousandth time, "I am not your 'love.'"

His eyes became sharper, more intent. "Then explain," he said slowly, "why it feels so right when I hold you? How do you answer that?"

She avoided his gaze, her eyes focusing a fraction below his. "I can't explain it any more than I can deny it." She'd admit that much. "I do enjoy it when you kiss me, though I don't know why, especially since I'm still in love with Clay. My guess is that we've lived all these years in close proximity and we're such good friends that it was a natural, comforting, thing to do. But I don't think it should continue."

His nostrils flared briefly, and she could tell he was angered by her words.

"I'm begging you, Luke, pleading with you, if you—"

"Kate, would you listen to me for once?"

"No," she said, holding her ground. "I'm asking for only one thing from you. I want you to drop this incessant pressure to marry you."

"But—"

"Give me your word, Luke."

His entire expression changed, and just looking at him told Kate how difficult he was finding this. "All right," he said heavily. "You have my word. I won't mention it again."

Kate sighed shakily and all her muscles seemed to go limp. "Thank you," she whispered. "That's all I want."

Luke lunged to his feet and reached for Silver Shadow's reins. He eased himself back into the saddle, then paused to look down at her, his face dark and brooding. "What about what *I* want, Kate? Did you stop to consider that?"

Six

Kate felt good. The lethargy and depression she'd been feeling since Clay's wedding had started to dissipate. She'd completely adjusted to the idea of her father's impending marriage. And even the sale of the Circle L—to Luke of all people—no longer seemed so devastating. Clearing the air between them had helped, too.

"Evening, Nellie," Kate called as she entered the small, homey café. She'd arrived home from school to discover a message from her father suggesting she meet him for dinner at Nellie's at six sharp.

"Howdy, Kate," Nellie called from behind the counter.

Kate assumed her father would be bringing Dorothea so they could discuss last-minute plans for their wedding, which was scheduled for Friday evening at the parsonage. Minnie Wilkins, Pastor Wilkins's wife, and Dorothea were close friends. Kate would be standing up for Dorothea and Luke for her father in the small, private ceremony.

Carrying a water glass in one hand, a coffeepot in the other and a menu tucked under her arm, Nellie followed Kate to the booth. "I'm expecting my dad and Dorothea Murphy to join me," Kate explained.

"Sure thing," Nellie said. "The special tonight is Yankee pot roast, and when your daddy gets here, you tell him I pulled a rhubarb pie out of the oven no more than fifteen minutes ago."

"I'll tell him."

"Nellie, I could use a refill on my coffee," Fred Garner said. Sitting at the table closest to the window, he nodded politely in Kate's direction. "Good to see you, Kate."

"You, too, Fred." She smiled at the owner of Garner Feed and Supply and the two ranchers who were dining with him. Glancing at her watch, Kate realized her father was a few minutes late, which wasn't like him.

To pass the time she began reading the menu; she was halfway through when the door opened. Smiling automatically, she looked up and saw Luke striding toward her. He slid into the booth across from her.

"Where's your dad?"

"I don't know. He asked me to meet him here for dinner."

"I got the same message."

"I think it has something to do with the wedding."

"No," Luke muttered, frowning. "I've got some bank forms he needs to sign."

Nellie brought another glass of water, then poured coffee for both of them.

"Evening, Nellie."

"Luke Rivers, I don't see near enough of you," the older woman said coyly, giving him a bold wink as she sauntered away with a swish of her hips.

Astonished that Nellie would flirt so openly with

Luke, Kate took a sip of her coffee and nearly scalded her tongue. Why, Nellie had a good fifteen years on Luke!

"Does she do that often?" Kate asked, in a disapproving whisper.

"You jealous?"

"Of course not. It's just that I've never known Nellie to flirt quite so blatantly."

"She's allowed." Luke gazed down at his menu and to all appearances, was soon deep in concentration.

Kate managed to squelch the argument before it reached her lips. There wasn't a single, solitary reason for her to care if a thousand women threw themselves at Luke Rivers. She had no claim on him, and wanted none.

The restaurant telephone pealed, but with four plates balanced on her arms, Nellie let it ring until someone in the kitchen answered it.

A minute later, she approached their table. "That was Devin on the phone. He says he's going to be late and you two should go ahead and order." She pulled a notepad from the pocket of her pink uniform. "Eat hearty since it's on his tab," she said, chuckling amiably.

"The roast-beef sandwich sounds good to me," Kate said. "With a small salad."

"I'll have chicken-fried steak, just so I can taste those biscuits of yours," Luke told the café owner, handing her the menu. "I'll start with a salad, though."

"I got rhubarb pie hot from the oven."

"Give me a piece of that, too," Luke said, grinning up at Nellie.

"Kate?"

"Sure," she said, forcing a smile. "Why not?"

Once Nellie had left, an awkwardness fell between Kate and Luke. To Kate it felt as though they'd become strangers, standing on uncertain ground.

Luke ventured into conversation first. "So how's school?"

"Fine."

"That's good."

She laughed nervously. "I've started washing down cupboards at the house, clearing out things. I've got two piles. What Dad's going to take with him and what I'll need when I move."

Instead of pleasing Luke, her announcement had the opposite effect. "You're welcome to live on the ranch as long as you want," he said, his dark eyes narrowing. "There's no need to move."

"I know that, but the Circle L belongs to you—or it will soon."

"It's your home."

"It won't be much longer," she felt obliged to remind him. "I'm hoping to find a place in town. In fact, I'm looking forward to the move. You know what the roads are like in the winter. I should have done this years ago."

"You wouldn't have to move if you weren't so damn stubborn," Luke muttered from between clenched teeth. "I swear, Kate, you exasperate me. The last thing I want to do is take your home away from you."

"I know that." She hadn't considered relocating to town earlier for a number of reasons, foremost being that her father had needed her. But he didn't anymore, and it was time to exhibit some independence.

Nellie brought their tossed green dinner salads, lingering at the table to flirt with Luke again. He waited until she'd left before he leaned forward, speaking to

Kate in a low, urgent voice. His eyes were filled with regret. "Kate, please stay on at the ranch. Let me at least do this much for you."

She thanked him for his concern with a warm smile, but couldn't resist adding, "People will talk." After all, Luke had pointed that very fact out to her when she'd made her foolish proposal. The night of Clay's wedding...

"Let them talk."

"I'm a schoolteacher, remember?" she whispered. She felt genuinely grateful for his friendship and wanted to assure him that all this worry on her behalf was unnecessary, that she was fully capable of living on her own.

Their dinner arrived before they'd even finished the salads. Another silence fell over them as they ate. Several possible subjects of conversation fluttered in and out of Kate's mind as the meal progressed. Her fear was that Luke would divert the discussion back to the ranch no matter what she said, so she remained silent.

A sudden commotion came from the pavement outside the café.

"It's Harry Ackerman again," Fred Garner shouted to Nellie, who was busy in the kitchen. "You want me to call the sheriff?"

"No, let him sing," Nellie shouted back. "He isn't hurting anyone."

Harry Ackerman was the town drunk. Back in his and Nellie's high-school days, they'd dated seriously, but then Harry went into the military and returned to Nightingale more interested in the bottle than a wife and family. Within six months, Nellie had married a mechanic who'd drifted into town. Problem was, when he drifted out again, he didn't take Nellie or their two children with him. But Nellie hadn't seemed to miss him much, and had supported her family by opening the café, which did a healthy business from the first.

Fifteen years had passed, and Harry was still courting Nellie. Every time he came into town, he took it upon himself to sing love songs from the pavement outside the café. He seemed to believe that would be enough of an inducement for her to forget the past and finally marry him.

"Actually his singing voice isn't that bad," Kate murmured to Luke.

Luke chuckled. "I've heard better."

Fred Garner stood up and strolled toward the cash register. He nodded in Luke's direction and touched the rim of his hat in greeting. "I've been hearing things about the two of you," Fred said, grinning broadly.

Kate concentrated on her sandwich, refusing to look up from her plate.

Luke made some vague reply that had to do with the ranch and not Kate, and she was grateful.

"Be seeing you," Fred said as he headed toward the door. As he opened it, Harry's latest love ballad, sung off-key, could be heard with ear-piercing clarity.

Fred left and soon Harry Ackerman came inside. He stared longingly at Nellie, placed his hand over his heart and started singing again at the top of his lungs.

"You get out of my restaurant," Nellie cried, reaching for the broom. "I don't want you in here bothering my customers." She wielded the broom like a shotgun, and before she could say another word Harry stumbled outside. He pressed his forlorn face to the glass, content to wait until his one true love returned to his waiting arms.

"Sorry, folks," Nellie muttered, replacing the broom.

"No problem," Luke answered, and she threw him a grateful smile, then hurried over to refill their coffee cups.

The disturbance died down when Harry wandered down the street to find a more appreciative audience. Luke sighed as he stirred his coffee. "I don't think your father has any intention of showing up tonight," he began. "In fact—"

"That's ridiculous," Kate said, cutting him off. "Dad wouldn't do that."

"He's trying to tell you something," Luke insisted.

"I can't imagine what." She could, but decided to pretend otherwise.

For a long moment, Luke said nothing. "You're smart enough to figure it out, Kate." He finished off the last bite of his pie and pushed the plate aside. "I've got some things to attend to, so I'd best be leaving." The corners of his eyes crinkled with amusement as he glanced out the café window. "Who knows, you might be singing me love songs in a couple of years if you don't come to your senses soon."

Kate ignored the comment. "My father will be here any minute."

"No, Princess," Luke said, and the smile left his eyes. He leaned across the table to brush his hand gently against her cheek. "But his message is coming across loud and clear."

Kate stayed at the café another half-hour after Luke had gone and it took her that long to admit he was right. Her father *had* been giving her a message, this one no more subtle than the rest. Expelling her breath in disgust, Kate dredged up a smile and said goodbye to Nellie.

Kate didn't see Luke again until Friday evening, when they met at the Wilkins home for her father's wedding. Kate arrived with Devin, and Luke followed a few minutes later. Kate was busy arranging freshly baked cookies on a tray for the small reception to be held after the ceremony, when Luke walked into the dining room. Dorothea was with Minnie Wilkins in the back bedroom, and her father and Pastor Wilkins were talking in the office.

"Hello, Kate," Luke said from behind her.

"Hi," she responded, turning to give him a polite smile. Her breath caught in her throat at the elegant yet virile sight he made. He was dressed in a dark, three-piece suit that did nothing to disguise his strong, well-formed body, and his light blue silk tie enhanced the richness of his tan. Kate suspected that Luke was basking in the wonder she was unable to conceal, and yet she couldn't stop staring at him.

Her heart skipped a beat, then leaped wildly as his penetrating brown eyes looked straight into hers. She felt the tears well up, knowing that only Luke truly understood how difficult this evening was for her.

Many of her emotions tonight were identical to the ones she'd experienced at Clay and Rorie's wedding. All day, she'd worried her stomach into a knot of apprehension. The acceptance and strength of purpose she'd so recently been feeling had fled. Tonight, she was reminded again that everything she loved, everything familiar, had been taken from her life. First the man she'd planned to marry, now her father, and soon, so very soon, her childhood home. It was too much change, too quickly.

Just as she had at Clay's wedding, Kate forced herself to show pleasure, to behave appropriately. She *was* happy for her father and Dorothea—just as she'd been for Clay and Rorie. But why did everyone else's happiness need to cost Kate so much?

Luke must have read the distress in her eyes, because he hurried to her side. "Everything's going to be all right," he told her quietly. He'd said the same thing at Clay's wedding.

"Of course it is," she agreed, braving a smile. She turned back to the flowers, although her fingers were trembling. "I couldn't have chosen a better wife for Dad myself. Dorothea's wonderful."

Luke's hands rested on her shoulders and began to caress them gently. "So are you, Princess."

It demanded every ounce of fortitude Kate possessed not to whirl around and bury her face in Luke's chest, to absorb his strength. But this was exactly how she'd lost control before; she had to remember that.

A sound came from behind them, and Luke released her with a reluctance that echoed her own. She needed Luke now, just as she'd needed him a few weeks before. But this time, she was determined to be stronger.

The ceremony itself was brief. Kate felt almost wooden as she stood next to the woman her father had chosen to replace her mother. Memories of the lovely, soft-spoken Nora, and of their happy, close-knit family, almost overwhelmed Kate. Twice she felt tears threaten, but managed to hold them back. Both times she found Luke's eyes on her, his gaze warm with empathy.

When Pastor Wilkins closed his Bible and announced that Devin and Dorothea were now husband and wife, Devin took his bride in his arms and kissed her. Minnie Wilkins dabbed at her eyes with a lace hankie.

"You look so lovely," the woman murmured, hugging her friend.

Soon they were all hugging each other. When Kate's arms slipped around Luke it felt…comfortable. In fact, it felt *too* comfortable, too familiar, and that frightened her. She stiffened and let her arms drop. Luke would have none of that, however. Locking his hands on her upper arms, he drew her back to him.

"What I wouldn't give for a full moon and some champagne," he whispered in her ear.

Kate could have done without his teasing, but she refused to satisfy him with a response.

The small reception began immediately afterward, and Kate was busy for the next hour, dishing up pieces of wedding cake, passing trays of sugar cookies and pouring coffee.

Her father came to see her in the kitchen, his eyes bright with happiness. "You're going to be fine, aren't you, Princess?"

"You know I am," she said, flashing him a brilliant smile.

"Dorothea and I will be leaving soon." He placed his arm around her shoulders and hugged her. "Don't forget I love you. You'll always be my little girl."

"You'll always be my hero."

Devin chuckled. "I think Luke would like to fill that position and I'd be pleased if he did. He's a good man, sweetheart. You could do a lot worse."

"Dad," she groaned, closing her eyes. "Luke is wonderful, and I understand your concern. You'd like all the loose ends neatly tied up before you leave for your honeymoon, but I'm just not ready for a commitment."

"You'd make a lovely country bride, Princess. I want you to be happy, that's all."

"I will be," she said, standing on the tips of her toes to kiss his cheek.

By the time Devin and Dorothea were ready to leave, more than twenty close friends had gathered at the parsonage. They crowded onto the porch to send the newlyweds off with a flourish of kisses and enthusiastic waves. Almost everyone returned to the warmth of the house but Kate lingered, not wanting to go back inside when tears were blurring her eyes.

Luke joined her, standing silently at her side until she'd composed herself.

"Your father asked me to see you home."

Kate nodded and swallowed a near-hysterical laugh. Despite their conversation Devin was still attempting to throw her together with Luke.

"You mean you aren't going to argue with me?" Luke asked with exaggerated surprise.

"Would it do any good?"

"No," he said and chuckled lightly. Then, suddenly, his strong arms encircled her stiff body. "It's been a long time since you let me kiss you," he said, his warm breath moving closer and closer to her mouth.

Kate stared at his chest, refusing to raise her eyes to his. Gathering her resolve, she snapped her head up to demand he release her. But Luke smothered her words with his mouth. Her hands tightened into fists as soon as the initial shock had subsided and she fully intended to push him away. But once his mouth had settled over hers, he gentled the kiss, and her resolve all but disappeared.

Again and again his mouth sought hers. Luke's sweet, soft kisses seemed to erase all the pain from her heart. Only a moment before, she'd been intent on escaping. Now she clung to him, tilting her face toward him, seeking more. He deepened his kiss, sending jolts of excitement through her.

When he stopped abruptly, Kate moaned her dissatisfaction.

"Kate…" he warned.

"Hmm… Luke, don't stop."

"I'm afraid we've attracted an audience," he returned mildly.

Sucking in her breath, Kate dropped her arms and whirled around so fast she would have stumbled if Luke's arms hadn't caught her. Eyes wide, she stared into the faces of the twenty or so guests who'd stepped outside, preparing to leave.

"I thought Taylor Morgenroth should play the Indian chief," Kate was saying to Linda when Sally Daley walked into the faculty lounge Monday afternoon. The two were discussing the final plans for their Thanksgiving play.

"Taylor's the perfect choice," Linda agreed.

"I see you girls are busy," Sally commented. "This play is such an ambitious project. You two are to be commended."

"Thanks." Linda answered for them both, trying to ignore the other woman as much as possible.

"Wasn't that Rorie Franklin I saw you with the other day, Kate, dear?"

"Yes. We had coffee at Nellie's." She resumed her discussion with Linda, not wanting to be rude to Sally, but at the same time, hoping to dissuade her from further conversation.

But Sally refused to be thwarted. She settled in the chair opposite Kate and said in confidential tones, "You're completely over Clay Franklin now, aren't you, dear?"

Kate shared an exasperated look with Linda and nearly laughed out loud when the third-grade teacher playfully rolled her eyes toward the ceiling. To hear Sally talk, anybody would think Kate had recently recovered from a bad case of the flu.

"Sally!" Kate exclaimed when she realized how avidly the other woman was waiting for her reply. "How am I supposed to answer that?" She covered her heart dramatically with one hand and assumed a look meant to portray misery and anguish. "Do you want me to tell you that my pride's been shattered and I'll never love again?"

Sally shook her head. "I wouldn't believe it, anyway."

"Then why ask?" Linda prompted.

"Well, because we all love Kate. She's such a dear, and she's been through so much lately."

"Thank you," Kate said graciously, then returned her attention to the Thanksgiving project.

"Most of the fuss about you and Eric Wilson and Luke Rivers has died down now," Sally assured her, as if this should lessen the embarrassment of that Friday night.

"I take it you haven't talked to Eric lately?" Linda asked, surprising Kate with her sudden interest. There'd been plenty of opportunity to inquire about him, but Linda hadn't done so until now.

"Talked to him?" Kate echoed with a short, derisive laugh. "I don't even shop at the Safeway store for fear of running into him again."

"I don't think you need to worry," Sally said blandly. "From what I hear, he's avoiding you, too."

Linda snickered softly. "No doubt. I'm sure Luke Rivers put quite a scare into him."

"How do you mean?" Kate demanded, already angry with Luke.

"You don't know?" Sally asked, her eyes sparkling with excitement.

"Know what?" Kate swung her gaze first to Linda, then to Sally. "Did Luke threaten him?" If he had, he was going to hear about it from her.

"I haven't got the foggiest idea what Sally's talking about," Linda said quickly.

"I didn't hear anything specific," Sally confirmed sheepishly. "I thought maybe you…" The older teacher's expression suggested that she hoped Kate would fill in the succulent details herself. "My dear, surely you understand that everyone in town is speculating about you and Luke," she continued.

"Rumors have been floating around since Clay's wedding," Linda added.

"But Sally just finished telling me those were dying down," Kate snapped, irritated with the entire discussion.

"The rumors aren't about you and that Wilson fellow," Sally rushed to explain. "As far as your one date with him is concerned, it's history. He's too smart to cross Luke."

"I'm sure he is," Kate said, anxious to quell the woman's gossip. "Aren't we about finished here, Linda?" she asked pointedly.

"Ah…yes."

"Now folks are talking about seeing you and Luke together at Nellie's last week, just before your father's wedding, and there've been a few rumors flying about the two of you at Pastor Wilkins's, too."

As fast as her hands would co-operate, Kate gathered up their materials. Sally seemed to accept that she was about to lose her audience. If she'd come to pump Kate for information she'd just have to realize Kate wasn't talking. Standing, Sally gave a deep sigh, clearly disappointed. She collected her purse and headed out the door, pausing to look back. "Frankly, I think Fred Garner's carrying this thing about you and Luke a bit too far. I consider what he's doing in poor taste." With that, she left the room.

"Fred Garner?" Linda echoed after a stunned second. "What's that old coot doing now?"

"Fred Garner owns the feed store," Kate said in a puzzled voice.

"Yes, but what's he got to do with anything?"

"Beats me." Still, Kate couldn't help wondering. Fred had seen them at the restaurant, and he'd been at the reception for her father and Dorothea. Although she hadn't seen him on the porch when a number of guests had found her in Luke's arms, she had very little doubt that he was there.

When Kate drove home an hour later, Luke was working in the yard. She climbed out of the car, took two steps toward him and halted abruptly. The lump in her throat was so large she could hardly swallow, let alone speak.

The trembling had started the minute she left Garner Feed and Supply. She'd dropped in at the store following Sally's remark, and from then on everything had grown progressively worse. The way she felt right now, she could slam her bag over Luke's head, or do something equally violent, and feel completely justified.

"Kate?" he asked, looking concerned. "What's wrong?"

She knew her emotions were written on her face. She'd never been more scandalized in her life, which was saying a great deal, considering the fiasco with Eric Wilson.

In fact, the blow her dignity had been dealt by Luke Rivers during that incident paled in comparison with this latest outrage. There was only one thing for her to do. She'd have to move away from Nightingale.

"This is all your doing, isn't it?" she demanded in a shaking voice. She held her head high, although it was a struggle to preserve her composure. Her pride was all she had left, and that was crumbling at her feet.

Luke advanced several steps toward her. "What are you talking about?"

She ground her fist into her hip. "I just got back from the feed store. Does that tell you anything?"

"No."

"I'll bet."

He frowned. "Kate, I swear to you, I don't know what you're talking about."

She made a doubting noise that came out sounding and feeling like a sob. Yet hc appeared so bewildered. She didn't know how any man could cause her such life-shattering embarrassment and maintain that look of faithful integrity.

The tears wouldn't be restrained any longer, and they fell from her eyes, running down her face. They felt cool against her flushed cheeks.

"Kate? What's wrong?"

Kate turned and walked rapidly away from Luke rather than allow him to witness her loss of control. She hurried into the house and slumped in a chair, hiding her face in her hands as she battled the terrible urge to weep hysterically. The painful sensation in the pit of her stomach grew more intense every time she took a breath.

The door opened and she said, "Go away."

"Kate?"

"Haven't…you…done…enough?" Each word rolled from her tongue on the end of a hiccuping sob.

He knelt in front of her and wrapped his arms around her, holding her close, but she pushed him away, refusing the comfort he offered.

Kate's shoulders still heaved. With an exasperated sigh, Luke got up. He stood back on his boot heels and buried his hands in his pockets. "All right, tell me about it."

"Pastor… Wilkins…bet…twenty…dollars…on… December," she told him between sobs. Her fingers curled into fists. "Even… Clay…put in a…wager."

Seeing his name on that huge blackboard had hurt more than anything.

"Kate, I swear to you I don't know what you're talking about."

Furiously she wiped the tears from her face and tried

to marshal her self-control enough to speak clearly. "The…feed store," she managed.

"What about the feed store?"

"They're taking bets—it's a regular lottery," she cried, all the more furious with him because he was making her spell out this latest humiliation.

"Bets on what?" Luke's frown was growing darker, and Kate could tell that he was dangerously close to losing his patience.

"On *us!*" she wailed, as if that much, at least, should be obvious.

"For what?"

"When we're going to be married!" she shouted. "What else? Half the town's gambling on the date of our wedding."

Luke moaned, closing his eyes, as if he couldn't quite believe what she was telling him.

"You honestly didn't know?"

"Of course not." He was beginning to look perturbed as only Luke could. His dark eyes took on a cold glare that would intimidate the strongest of men. "How'd you find out?"

"Sally Daley said something about it after school, and then in the school car park one of the mothers told me March is a lovely time of year for a wedding. March sixteenth, she said. Then…then I made the mistake of stopping in at the feed store on my way home to…to check out what was going on."

Luke nodded, but Kate had the impression he was only half listening to her.

"As far as I'm concerned, there's just one thing for me to do," she said, gaining strength from her decision.

"I'll offer my resignation to the school board tomorrow morning and leave the district this weekend."

Luke sent her a quick, angry look. "That won't be necessary. I'll take care of this my own way."

Seven

At one time Kate spent as many hours at Elk Run, the Franklin stud farm, as she did at the Circle L. But when she arrived Tuesday night for dinner, Elk Run no longer felt familiar. It seemed like years instead of weeks since her last visit. Kate's enthusiasm for this dinner with Clay and Rorie had never been high, but now she felt decidedly uncomfortable.

"Kate, welcome." Rorie flew out the door the minute Kate pulled into the driveway. She stepped from the car into Rorie's hug.

Clay Franklin followed his wife and briefly held Kate close, smiling down on her the same way he always had from the time she was thirteen. Back then, she'd worshipped him from afar, and she'd worshipped him more with each passing year. Kate paused, waiting for the surge of regret and pain she'd been expecting; to her astonishment, it didn't come.

"We're so glad you could make it," Rorie said as she opened the door.

Recognising Kate, Clay's old dog, Blue, ambled over

for his usual pat. Kate was more than happy to comply and bent down to scratch his ears.

Mary, the Franklins' housekeeper, bustled about the kitchen, dressed in her bib apron, hair twisted into thick braids and piled on top of her head. Kate could scarcely remember a time she hadn't seen Mary in an apron. The scent of freshly baked pie permeated the room, mingling with the hearty aroma of roast beef and simmering vegetables.

"I hope that's one of your award-winning pies I'm smelling, Mary," Kate said. "I've had my heart set on a piece all day."

"Oh, get away with you," Mary returned gruffly, but the happy light that sparked from her eyes told Kate how gratified the housekeeper was by her request.

"When are you going to give me your recipe?" Kate asked, although she didn't know whom she'd be baking pies for now that her father had remarried. "No one can bake an apple pie like yours."

"Mary won't share her secret with me, either," Rorie said, giving a soft laugh. "I don't think she's willing to trust a city slicker yet."

"I never wrote down any recipe," Mary grumbled, casting Rorie a stern look. "I just make my pies the same way my mother did."

"I wish I could bake like Mary does," Rorie said, slipping her arm around her husband's waist. They exchanged a meaningful glance. Clay's smile showed he couldn't care less whether or not she could bake a pie.

Once more Kate braced herself for the pain of seeing them together, gentle and loving, but to her surprise she didn't feel so much as a pinprick of distress. She relaxed, wondering at what was happening—or rather, wasn't—and why.

"Where's Skip?" she asked suddenly. She missed Clay's younger brother almost as much as she did Clay. They'd been friends for years.

"Football practice," Clay explained. "He's quarterback this year and proud as a peacock. He'll be home later."

"About the time Mary serves her pie," Rorie whispered to Kate. Skip's appetite for sweets was legendary.

The small party headed into the homey living room. The piano stood against one wall, and Kate noted the music on the stand. She'd always been the one who'd played that piano, but it was Rorie who played for Clay now. There'd been a time when Kate and Clay had sung together, their voices blending in a melodious harmony. But Clay sang with Rorie now.

Kate expected the knowledge to claw at her insides, and she did feel a small twinge of regret—but that was all.

"Skip's hoping to catch you later," Rorie said.

"As I recall, you played quarterback your senior year of high school," Kate reminded Clay as she claimed the overstuffed chair. "That was the first year the Nightingale team made it to the state finals."

Rorie smiled delightedly at her husband. "You never told me that."

"There wasn't much to tell," Clay said with a short laugh. "We were eliminated in the first round." He sat beside Rorie and draped his arm around her shoulders, as if he had to keep touching her to believe she was here at his side.

Mary carried in a tray of wineglasses and an unopened bottle of a locally produced sparkling white. "I take it Devin and Dorothea arrived safely in California?" she asked as she uncorked the wine.

"Yes, Dad phoned when they arrived at Dorothea's daughter's house."

"We didn't get a chance to say more than a few words to you at the reception," Rorie apologized. "You were so busy pouring coffee, there wasn't much opportunity to chat."

"I know. It was good of you and Clay to come."

"We wouldn't have missed it for the world," Clay said.

"I wanted to tell you how nice your father and Dorothea looked together. And for that matter, you and Luke, too," Rorie added.

"Thank you," Kate said simply, wondering if her friends had heard about the incident on the Wilkins's front porch. It still embarrassed Kate to think of all her father's friends seeing her and Luke together…like that. "So much has happened in the last month," she said, trying to change the subject before either of them mentioned her father's wedding again. "Who'd ever have believed Luke would end up buying the ranch?"

"It must've come as a shock to you," Clay said evenly, "but I've been after him for years to get his own spread."

"What are your plans now that the Circle L's been sold?" Rorie asked.

"I'm looking for a place in town," she said, and sipped her wine.

"From what Luke told me, he'd rather you continued living on the ranch," Clay said, studying her as though he knew something she didn't.

"I know," Kate admitted. "It's very generous of him, but I'd prefer to get an apartment of my own."

"Good luck finding one," Clay murmured.

They were both aware that a decent apartment might be difficult to locate. Nightingale was a place of family dwellings, not singles' apartments.

They chatted easily as they waited for Mary to announce dinner. Every now and then, Kate saw Clay glance over at Rorie. His look was tender and warm and filled with the deep joy that came from loving completely and knowing that love was returned.

When Rorie Campbell had arrived in their midst, Kate had seen almost immediately that Clay was attracted to her. That was understandable, after all, since Rorie was a beautiful woman. In the beginning, Kate had done everything she could to combat her jealousy. Rorie had been due to leave Elk Run in a few days and once she was gone, Kate had told herself, their lives and feelings would return to normal.

Eventually Rorie did go back to San Francisco, but Clay couldn't forget her. Kate had done her best to pretend; she'd even talked Clay into setting a wedding date, pressuring him in a not-so-subtle way to marry her quickly. They'd been talking about it for years, and Kate wanted the deed done before Rorie realized what she'd given up. Their getting married seemed the perfect solution. Then, if Rorie did come to Nightingale again, it would be too late.

Kate's strategy had been a desperate one, planned by a desperate woman. And as often happened in such cases, her scheme backfired.

Kate didn't think she'd ever forget the day Clay told her he wanted to break their engagement. The words had scarred her soul like lye on tender skin. He'd come to the ranch, and from the minute he'd asked to talk to her, Kate had known something was terribly wrong. She'd tried to ease the tension with talk of bridesmaids' dresses and floral arrangements, but Clay had stopped her.

He'd sat with his hands folded, his eyes regarding her sadly. "I wouldn't hurt you for anything," he'd said, and his words rang with truth and regret.

"Clay, you could never hurt me." Which was a lie, because he was already inflicting pain.

He'd told her then, simply and directly, that it would be wrong for them to marry. Not once did he mention Rorie's name. He didn't need to. Kate had known for weeks that Clay was in love with the other woman. But she'd chosen instead to involve her heart in a painful game of pretend.

Instead of accepting the truth when Clay had come to her with his decision, she'd insisted he was mistaken, that they *were* right for each other and had been all their lives. The memory humbled her now. She'd tried to convince him that all they needed was a little more time. By the next week, or maybe the next month, Clay would understand that he'd made a mistake and he'd want to go through with the wedding. She could afford to be patient because she loved him so much. Kindly, and as gently as possible, Clay had told her time wouldn't alter the way he felt. Then he'd left, although she'd pleaded with him to stay.

In the week that followed, Kate had felt as though she was walking around in a fog. She laughed, she smiled, she slept, she ate. The school year hadn't started yet, so there was little else to occupy her mind. The days bled into each other, one indistinguishable from the next.

Soon after he'd broken their engagement, Clay headed for San Francisco, purportedly to attend a horse show. In her heart, she'd expected Clay to return with Rorie at his side. As hard as it had been, she'd tried to accept the fact Clay loved Rorie and nothing was ever going to change that.

To everyone's surprise, Clay came home alone, and there was no mention of Rorie. Kate didn't know what had happened between them. Hope stirred in her heart, and she'd briefly entertained thoughts of Clay resuming their engagement, the two of them marrying and settling down together, the way she'd always dreamed.

Instead she stood helplessly by as Clay threw himself into his work, making unreasonable demands on himself and his men. At first she believed the situation would change. She began stopping off at Elk Run, trying to be the friend she knew Clay needed. But Clay didn't want her. He didn't want anyone.

Except Rorie.

Only then did Kate recognize that it was in her power to help this man she loved. She talked over her idea with Luke, even before she approached her father. Luke, and Luke alone, had seemed to understand and appreciate her sacrifice. When she couldn't hold back the tears any longer, it had been Luke who'd held her in his arms and who'd beamed with pride over the unselfishness of what she'd done.

As she sat, listening to the predinner conversation, even contributing now and then, she reminded herself that Luke had been the one who'd made it possible to survive that difficult time.

Luke.

Losing Clay had threatened to destroy her, mentally and physically. But Luke hadn't allowed that to happen. It was then he'd started bullying her, she realized. She'd thought of him as a tyrant, with his unreasonable demands and his gentle harassments. Kate had been so furious with him for assuming command of her life that she'd overlooked the obvious. Only now could she understand and appreciate his strategy. Gradually, the fire had returned to her eyes and her life, although it had been fuelled by indignation. Nevertheless it was there, and Luke had been the person responsible.

She'd been furious with him when she should've been grateful. Luke had never stopped being her friend—the best friend she'd ever had. She'd leaned heavily on him in the days and weeks before Clay married Rorie, though she'd never understood how much he'd done for her, how much he cared.

The wineglasses were replenished and Kate proposed a toast. "To your happiness," she said sincerely. It pained her to remember that Clay and Rorie had nearly lost each other. Because of her…

Nightingale had needed a librarian, and with her father's help, Kate had convinced the town council to offer the job to Rorie Campbell. When she'd turned them down, Kate herself had called Rorie, and together they'd wept over the phone and later in each other's arms.

So Rorie had returned to Nightingale, and she and Clay had been married. In October. The same month Kate had planned for her own wedding to Clay.

Kate's thoughts were pulled back to the present when

Clay said, "Rorie has a piece of good news." He cast a proud look at his wife.

"What's that?" Kate asked.

Rorie blushed becomingly. "Clay shouldn't have said anything. It's not certain yet."

"Rorie," Kate said, studying her carefully, "are you pregnant? Congratulations!"

"No, no." Rorie rushed to correct that impression. "Good grief, we've been married less than a month."

"It's about Rorie's book," Clay explained.

Vaguely Kate recalled that Rorie wrote children's books. In fact, she'd been on her way to a writers' conference when the car she was driving broke down on the road not far from Elk Run.

"Has one of your stories been accepted for publication?" Kate asked eagerly.

"Not exactly," Rorie said.

"An editor from New York phoned and asked for a few revisions, but she sounded enthusiastic about the book and there was talk of a contract once the revisions are done," Clay said. His fingers were twined with his wife's and he looked as excited as if he'd created the story himself.

"Oh, Rorie, that's wonderful." Kate felt pleased and proud for her friend. "What's the book about?"

"Well, the story involves Star Bright and the night we delivered Nightsong, and it's told from the foal's point of view," Rorie said.

"I know I'm her husband," Clay broke in, "but I read it, and I don't mind telling you, the book's gripping. Any editor worth her salt would snap it up in a minute."

"Oh, Clay, honestly!"

"When will you know if it's sold?" Kate asked. "I

don't think Nightingale's ever had an author living here before. Dad could convince the town council to commission a sign. You might even become a tourist attraction. Who knows where this could go?"

They all laughed, but Rorie cautioned, "It could be months before I hear, so don't go having your father commission any signs."

"You should've seen her after she got the call," Clay said, his eyes twinkling with merriment. "I didn't know what to think. Rorie came running out of the house and started shrieking and jumping up and down."

"So I was a little excited."

Playfully Clay rolled his eyes. "A little! That's got to be the understatement of the year."

"I'd behave the same way," Kate said. "And you seem pretty thrilled about all this yourself, Clay Franklin."

Clay admitted it, and then the discussion turned to the awards Clay had accumulated in several national horse shows in the past year.

A few minutes later, Mary announced that dinner was ready and they moved into the dining room. The meal was lively, and conversation flowed easily around the table.

Kate had been dreading this dinner from the moment Rorie had issued the invitation. Now she was pleasantly surprised by how enjoyable the evening had become. She'd been convinced that seeing Clay and Rorie's happiness would deepen her own pain. It hadn't happened. She'd expected to spend this evening nursing her wounds behind a brave front. Instead she felt giddy with a sense of release.

She *had* loved Clay, loved him with a youthful innocence. But she didn't feel the same way toward him now. Clay belonged to Rorie and Rorie to him. The tender relationship Kate had once shared with him was part of the past. He would always be a special person in her life, but those old feelings, that adulation she'd felt for him, were relegated to her adolescent fantasies.

Kate Logan was a woman now.

She wasn't sure exactly when the transformation had taken place, but it had. She'd struggled with it, fought the metamorphosis, because change, as always, was both painful and difficult. Kate realized for the first time that all the pain, all the uncertainty, had not been for nothing.

"Kate?" Luke called, as he let himself into the kitchen. "You around?"

"Here." She was at the back of the house, packing away the library of books her father kept in his den. Every night she did a little more to get the main house ready for Luke to move in and her to move out.

She straightened and tucked in a few wisps of hair that had escaped the red bandanna. She wore blue jeans and an old gray sweatshirt and no doubt looked terrible. Despite that, she was pleased to see Luke, eager to talk to him. She was wiping her dusty palms on her jeans when he walked in.

"What are you doing?" He stood just inside the door, a frown creasing his forehead.

"What does it look like?" she said. "I'm packing."

He hesitated, then said, "I told you, I want you to live here, at least to the end of the school year. I thought you understood that."

"I do, Luke. It's just that this place is yours now—or will be soon, and there's no reason for me to stay on."

For one despairing moment, she was swept away on a crashing wave of disbelief and misery at everything she'd lost in so short a time. She could barely walk through her home and not feel an aching throb at the prospect of leaving it behind. But the sale of the ranch was part of the new reality she was learning to face.

"Of course there's a reason for you to stay here," Luke insisted, his voice sharp with impatience. "It's where you belong—where I want you. Isn't that reason enough?"

Kate forced a laugh. "Come on, Luke, there's no excuse for me to continue living here. You don't need a housekeeper, or a cook or anything else. You're completely self-sufficient. And I could do without all the gossip my living here would start in town." She paused a moment, then added gently, "I really *can* manage on my own, you know. I'm a big girl, Luke, and I don't need anyone to take care of me."

He wanted to argue with her; Kate could sense it with every breath he drew. But when he spoke next, his remarks had nothing to do with her moving.

"I suppose I should tell you about the feed store," he said. His voice was controlled, though Kate heard a hint of anger in his words. He'd been just as incensed as she was over the incident. Once she'd come to grips with her own outrage, she'd seen how furious Luke was.

"No…well, yes, I guess I am curious to hear how you handled that. Would you like some coffee?"

"Please."

Kate led the way into the kitchen and filled two ceramic mugs. After giving Luke his, she walked into the living room and sat on the sofa. Relaxing, she slipped off her shoes and tucked her feet underneath her. It felt good to sit here with Luke—almost like old times. So often over the years, they'd sat and talked like this. Friends. Confidants. Companions. She cradled the mug in both hands, letting the warmth seep up her arms.

"I had dinner with Clay and Rorie last night," she said, wanting to share with Luke what she'd discovered.

"Yes, I heard. Listen, you can close the door on the situation with Fred Garner. You don't need to worry about it anymore."

Kate lowered her eyes. "Thanks," she murmured. There was so much she wanted to tell Luke. "I had a great time at Elk Run last night, although I honestly didn't expect to."

"I can personally guarantee the matter with Garner is over. If it isn't a dead issue, it soon will be."

Kate would rather not talk about the wedding lottery. The subject had become an embarrassing memory—a very embarrassing one—but as Luke said, it was finished. There were other, more important issues to discuss.

"All day I'd worried about that dinner," she said, starting over. "I wondered how I'd ever be able to sit at a table with Clay, knowing he was married to Rorie. But I did. Oh, Luke, I can't tell you how happy they are. Deep down, I knew they would be, and I had to brace myself for that, expecting to find it unbearably painful. But something incredible happened. During the evening, I learned a valuable lesson about—"

"Good." Luke's response was clipped, detached.

Kate hesitated. From the moment he'd walked into her father's office, she'd felt something was wrong, but she hadn't been able to put her finger on it. "Luke, what is it?"

"Nothing. I'd prefer not talking about Clay and Rorie, all right?"

"I…suppose so," she said, feeling hurt. After an awkward moment, she attempted conversation once more. "You'll never guess who I got a letter from today." If Luke didn't want to talk about Clay and Rorie, then she'd try another topic that was sure to pique his interest. "Eric Wilson. Remember him?"

A slight smile touched Luke's mouth. "I'm not likely to forget him. What'd he have to say?"

"He's moved back to Portland and is talking to his ex-wife. Apparently she's been just as miserable as he has since their divorce. It looks as if they might get back together."

"That's good news."

"He asked me to give you his regards, and sends his thanks." Kate paused. "But he didn't say what I was supposed to thank you for?" She made the statement a question, hoping Luke would supply an answer.

"We talked."

"Oh."

"I told him he was wasting his time on you because you're in love with me."

Kate was outraged. "Luke, you didn't! Please tell me you're joking."

He smiled briefly, then his eyes took on the distant look he'd been wearing a moment earlier. Kate couldn't ignore it any longer. "Luke, please, tell me what's bothering you."

"What makes you think anything is?"

"You don't seem yourself tonight." Something in his voice puzzled her. A reserved quality. It was as if he was distancing himself from her and that was baffling.

After Clay's wedding, Luke had actually insisted they get married, and now he was treating her like some casual acquaintance.

Kate took another sip of coffee while she collected her thoughts. Luke was sitting as far away from her as he could. His shoulders were stiff and his dark eyes a shade more intense than usual. Gone was the laughing devilry she adored.

"I'll be out of town for a few days next week," he said abruptly. "I'm hoping to pick up a few pieces of new equipment from a wholesaler in New Mexico."

"When will the bank close the deal on the ranch?"

Luke paused and his eyes pinned hers. "Your father and I signed all the papers the day before he married Dorothea Murphy."

Kate felt like bolting from her chair, the shock was so great. "Why didn't you tell me?" she demanded, her heart racing. "Why didn't my father? I shouldn't even be here now. This is your home. Yours. Bought and paid for and—"

"Kate." He set his mug aside and wearily rubbed the back of his neck. "You're welcome to stay as long as you need. If you insist on leaving, that's fine, too, but there's no rush."

She brought her hands to her cheeks, which were feverishly hot one minute, numb and cold the next. "I'll be out as…as soon as I can find someplace to move."

"Kate, for heaven's sake, why do you persist in being so stubborn?"

She shook her head, hardly understanding it herself. All she knew was that this house, which had been a part of her from the time she was born, no longer belonged to her family. Despite everything Luke said, she couldn't stay on at the Circle L, and she had nowhere else to go.

Eight

Kate had just finished correcting a pile of math papers when her friend Linda Hutton entered her classroom. Linda's third-grade class had been on a field trip and the two friends had missed talking at lunchtime.

"Hi," Kate said, smiling up at her. "How'd the tour of the jail and fire station go?"

Linda pulled up a child-size chair and sank down on it, then started massaging her temples with her fingertips. "Don't ask. By noon I was ready to lock up the entire third-grade class and lose the key."

"It certainly was quiet around school."

Linda gave a soft snicker. "Listen, I didn't come in here to learn what a peaceful day *you* had. The only reason I'm not home in bed curled up with aspirin and a hot-water bottle is so I can tell you I was at Garner Feed and Supply yesterday afternoon."

"Oh?"

"Yes, and you aren't going to like what happened. While I was there, Mr. Garner asked me if I wanted to place a wager on the Rivers-Logan wedding."

Kate's heart stopped cold. "He didn't!"

"I'm afraid so."

"But Luke told me he'd taken care of the problem. He said it was a dead issue and I shouldn't worry about it anymore." It wasn't like Luke to make careless promises.

"I wish I didn't have to tell you this," Linda said, with a sympathetic sigh.

"But Luke told me he'd personally talked to Fred Garner."

"He did. Mr. Garner made a point of telling me that, too," Linda confirmed. "He claimed Luke was hotter than a Mexican chili pepper. Said Luke came into his place, ranted and raved and threatened him within an inch of his life. But, Kate, the whole time old Garner was talking to me, he wore a grin so wide I could've driven a Jeep through it."

Kate sagged against the back of her chair.

"Then Garner told me that the harder a man fights marriage, the faster he falls. Apparently he's taking bets from as far away as Riversdale and south."

Kate pressed a hand over her eyes. "What am I going to do now?"

Linda shook her head. "I don't know. At least Garner's taken it off the blackboard, but when I said something about that, he told me he had to, since half the county wants in on the action. It seems the betting outgrew his blackboard space."

"If nothing else, it proves how desperate this community is for entertainment," Kate muttered. "If the good people of Nightingale have nothing better to do than waste their time and money on something as silly as this, then it's a sad commentary on our lives here."

Kate's friend cleared her throat and looked suspiciously guilty.

Kate hesitated, studying Linda. No, she told herself. Not Linda. Her closest childhood friend wouldn't place a wager. Her expression confirmed that she would.

"You chose a date yourself, didn't you?" Kate demanded.

Linda's gaze darted all over the room, avoiding Kate's completely.

"You did, didn't you?" Kate exclaimed.

Linda's fingers were curling and uncurling in her lap. "You're my oldest, dearest friend. How could I ever do anything like that?" she wailed.

"I don't know, Linda. You tell me."

"All right, all right," Linda confessed. "I did put a wager on June. The first part of summer is such a lovely time of year for a wedding…."

"I can't believe I'm hearing this." Kate had the sinking suspicion that her father had probably gotten in on the action, too, before he left on his honeymoon.

"I had no intention of betting," Linda hurried to explain. "In fact I never would have, but the odds were so good for June. For a five-dollar bet, I could collect as much as five hundred if you were to marry around the middle of the month—say the sixteenth. It's a Saturday. Weekends are always best for weddings, don't you think?"

Kate wasn't about to answer that. "You know, I suspect this whole thing is illegal. Each and every one of you should thank your lucky stars I don't call the sheriff."

"He's betting himself—on March. Said his own wedding anniversary is March tenth and he thinks Luke will be able to persuade you early in the spring. According to Fred, the sheriff figures that once Luke gets you to agree, he won't wait around for a big wedding. He'll want to marry you before you can change your mind."

Kate sent her a furious look. "If you're telling me this to amuse me, you've failed miserably."

"I'm sorry, Kate, I really am. The only reason I went into the feed store was so I could assure you the whole betting thing was over, but I can't and—"

"Instead you placed a bet of your own."

"I feel guilty about that," Linda admitted, her voice subdued.

"Why don't we both forget it and concentrate on the Thanksgiving play?" Instead of upsetting herself with more talk of this wedding lottery, Kate preferred to do something constructive with her time.

"I might be able to make it up to you, though," Linda murmured, fussing with the cuffs of her long-sleeved blouse.

"Whatever it is will have to be good."

"It is." Linda brightened and pulled a slip of paper from her purse. "I got this information from a friend of a friend, so I can't confirm how accurate it is, but I *think* it's pretty much for sure."

"What's for sure?" she asked when Linda handed her the paper. A local phone number was carefully printed on it.

Linda's sheepish look departed. "It's Mrs. Jackson's number—she's the manager of the apartment complex on Spruce Street. They may have a vacancy coming up next week. If you're the first one to apply, you might have a decent chance of getting it."

"Oh, Linda, that's great!"

"Am I forgiven?"

Kate laughed. "This makes up for a multitude of sins."

"I was counting on that."

Kate called five times before she got through. Mrs. Jackson seemed surprised to be hearing from her.

"I thought you were marrying that Rivers chap," the elderly woman said. "Can't understand why you'd want to rent an apartment when you're engaged to that man. The whole town says it's just a matter of time."

"Mrs. Jackson," Kate said loudly, because everyone knew the old woman was hard of hearing, "could I look at the apartment soon?"

"Won't be cleaned up for another day or two. I'll let you know once it's ready to be shown, but I can't help feeling it's a waste of time. Don't know what's wrong with you young women these days. In my day, we'd snap up a good man like Luke Rivers so fast it'd make your head spin."

"I'd still like to see the apartment," Kate said.

"Saturday, I guess. Yes, Saturday. Why don't you plan to come over then? I'll need a deposit if you decide to take the place."

"Will a check be all right?"

"Good as gold when it's got your name on it," Mrs. Jackson said, chuckling. "Don't suppose you have any season or month you're particularly partial to for weddings, would you?"

"No, I can't say I do."

"Well, me and Ethel Martin think you and that Rivers fellow will tie the knot in April. April seems a mighty nice month for a country wedding."

"I'm sure it is," Kate said, clenching her teeth.

"Good. Now listen, soon as the word gets out, someone else'll be wanting that apartment, so if you aren't here by noon Saturday, I'm going to have to give it to whoever shows up. You understand?"

"I'll be there before noon."

"See you then."

"Goodbye, Mrs. Jackson."

"You keep thinking about April, you hear?"

"Yes, I will," Kate murmured, rolling her eyes as she replaced the receiver.

That night, Luke stopped in shortly after Kate had finished dinner, which consisted of a sandwich eaten while she emptied the living-room bookcases. She filled box after box with books, her own and her father's, as well as complete sets of Dickens, Thackeray and George Eliot that had belonged to her mother. The physical activity gave her time to think. She'd realized the night she had dinner at the Franklins' that she wasn't in love with Clay. That same evening, Kate had also realized how much Luke had done for her in the weeks following her broken engagement. It troubled her to acknowledge how unappreciative she'd been of his support.

At Clay's wedding, she'd only added to the problem by asking Luke to marry her. He'd been willing to comply, willing to continue taking care of her through these difficult emotional times. In his own way, he did love her; Kate didn't question that. But he seemed far more concerned with protecting her from the harsh realities of life.

All the talk about weddings had brought the subject to the forefront of Kate's mind. She tried to picture what her life would be like if she were to marry Luke. From the night of Clay's wedding, Luke had been telling her she was in love with him. It came as a shock to realize how right he was. She *did* love him, a thousand times more than she'd ever dreamed.

Luke claimed he loved her, too. If that was true, why was she fighting him so hard? For one thing, Luke had delivered his declaration of love in such a matter-of-fact, unromantic way, it was hard to believe he really meant it. If she could be sure that his feelings were rooted in more than sympathy and physical attraction, she'd feel more confident. But Luke kept trying to shield her, as though she were a child. Now that she was moving into a place of her own, she'd be able to analyze her changing emotions more objectively. She'd be completely independent, away from the environment they'd always shared. Once they were apart, once it was clear that she could manage by herself, Luke would be free to pursue a relationship with her as an equal, an adult woman—not a little girl who needed looking after.

"I see you're at it again," he said, standing in the doorway between the kitchen and the living room.

"Luke—" she slapped her hand over her heart "—you startled me!" Her thoughts had been full of him and then suddenly he was there.

As he did more and more often of late, Luke was frowning, but Kate wasn't going to let that destroy her mood. She was thrilled with the prospect of moving into her own apartment and settling into a different kind of life.

"I have good news. I'm going to look at an apartment on Saturday morning." She dragged a heavy box of books across the carpet. "So," she said, huffing, "I'll probably be out of here sooner than we figured."

Luke interrupted her, effortlessly picking up the

cardboard box and depositing it on the growing stack at the far side of the room.

"Thanks," she murmured, grateful for his help.

"You shouldn't be doing this heavy work by yourself."

"It's fine," she said, rubbing the dust from her hands. "The only trouble I'm having is with these books. We've got so many."

"Kate, dammit, I wish you'd listen to reason."

"I'm being reasonable," she said, fixing a reassuring smile on her face. "All I'm doing is giving you what's rightfully yours."

Luke's frown grew darker, and he dragged a hand through his hair. "Listen, I think we may have more of a problem with Fred Garner than I thought."

"Yes, I know," Kate said, already filling the next box. "Linda told me after school that he's doing a thriving business."

Luke knelt on the floor beside her. "You're not upset?"

"Would it do any good? I mean, you obviously did your best and that just seemed to encourage the betting. As far as I can see, the only thing that will resolve this issue is time." She kept her gaze averted and added, "When six months pass and we're still not married, everyone will accept that nothing's going on between us."

"Nothing?" Luke asked bitterly.

Hope stirred briefly within her. "I like to think we'll always be friends." An absent smile touched her lips. "Now that I've decided to distance my emotions from this lottery nonsense, I find it all rather comical. You should do the same."

"This amuses you?"

"The good citizens of Nightingale are amused. Everyone seems to assume that because Clay and Dad both got married and the ranch has been sold, I should swoon into your arms."

"Personally, I don't think that's such a bad idea."

"Oh?" She chuckled and tucked a few more books in the box. Her heart was racing. If Luke was ever really going to declare his love, it would be now. "That wasn't the message I got the other night. I tried to have a serious talk with you about my evening with Clay and Rorie, and all you could do was glower at me." She glanced up, shaking her head. "Like you're doing now."

Luke walked away from her. He stood staring out the window, although Kate suspected the view was of little interest to him. "I just wish you'd be sensible for once in your life," he snapped.

"I didn't know I had a habit of not being sensible," she said conversationally, disheartened by his attitude. She rose and walked over to the larger bookcase, but even standing on her toes, she couldn't quite reach the trophies stored on the top shelf. Not to be defeated, she rolled the ottoman in front of the empty bookcase and climbed onto the thick cushioned seat. She stretched up and her fingers were about to grasp the first trophy when she heard Luke's swift intake of breath.

"Kate!"

Just as he spoke the ottoman started to roll out from under her. She flailed her arms in a desperate effort to maintain her balance.

Kate had never seen Luke move faster. His hands closed around her waist in an iron grip. Her cry of alarm caught in her throat as she was slammed against his solid chest.

"Of all the stupid, idiotic things I've ever seen—"

"I would've been perfectly fine if you hadn't called my name." Her heart was pounding so hard she could barely breathe.

Luke's hold relaxed. "You're all right?"

She nodded.

He closed his eyes, exhaling a ragged sigh. When he opened them, he assessed her carefully; apparently he concluded that she was unhurt because he gave her an impatient little shake. "Whatever possessed you to climb up on that ottoman in the first place?" he demanded.

"I couldn't reach the trophies."

"Couldn't you have asked me to get them for you? Why do you have such a difficult time accepting help from me?"

"I don't know," she admitted softly.

Still he held her and still Kate let him, trying to resist the comfort she felt in his arms. Her hands were braced against his powerful shoulders, but then she relaxed, unconsciously linking her fingers behind his neck.

Neither moved for a long moment.

Slowly Luke ran a provocative finger down the length of her cheek, and Kate's eyes drifted shut. She felt herself drawn inexorably toward him. Her lips parted and trembled, awaiting his kiss. When she realized what she was doing, she opened her eyes and broke away from him so quickly that she would've stumbled had his hands not righted her.

Embarrassed now, she stepped back. Luke brought down the trophies and handed them to her, but she saw that his eyes had become distant and unreadable.

"That's enough packing for tonight," she murmured,

her voice breathless even while she struggled to sound cheerful and bright.

He nodded slightly, then without another word stalked from the room. Kate didn't know what possessed her to follow him, certainly the last thing she should have done.

"Luke?"

He stopped halfway through the kitchen and turned toward her. His eyes were steely and intense, and just seeing that harsh edge drove her to take a step backward in retreat.

"You wanted something?" he asked when she didn't immediately explain.

"Just to say..." She could barely talk coherently. It occurred to her to ask if he loved her the way a man loves his wife, but she lacked the courage. "I thought maybe, I mean, I wanted to know if there was anything I could do for you before I left the house. Paint the living room...or something?"

"No."

Briefly she toyed with the idea of following him outside. For all his words about wanting her to stay, he couldn't seem to get away from her fast enough. The thought of not having Luke for her friend anymore felt crippling. Her pride was the problem. Luke had told her repeatedly that she needed him, and she knew now that she did. But not in the way he meant. Not just as a friend who was willing to offer her the protection and peace of marriage, a friend who felt obliged to take care of her.

"I don't want you to move from the ranch," he said.

Her heart was begging him to give her a reason to stay—the reason she longed to hear. "Luke, please accept that I'm only doing what I think is best for my life."

"I know that, but dammit, Kate, why are you being so stubborn? Why do you resist me when all I want is to make things easier for you? We could be married, and you could settle down in the house, and nothing needs to change. Yet you insist on causing all this turmoil in your life."

There wasn't anything Kate could say.

"You can't tell me we aren't physically attracted to each other. The electricity between us is powerful enough to light up Main Street."

"I…know."

"Say it, Kate. Admit that it felt good when I held you just now."

"I…"

Luke reached for her then, and Kate felt as if she'd lost some strategic battle. When his mouth found hers, her stomach tightened and fluttered wildly. Against her will, her lips parted, and before she understood what was happening she slid her arms tightly around his hard, narrow waist, wanting to hold on to him forever.

Luke moaned, then suddenly tore his lips from hers. She felt a tremor go through him before he raised his head and gazed tenderly into her face, his eyes dark and gentle.

"Is it so difficult to say?" he asked.

Nine

"This is the second bedroom," Mrs. Jackson was saying as she led Kate through the vacant rooms. From the moment she'd walked in the door, Kate had known that this apartment would suit her needs perfectly.

"I can't understand why you'd be wanting a two-bedroom place, but that's none of my business," Mrs. Jackson went on. Her hair was tightly curled in pink plastic rollers. To the best of her ability, Kate couldn't remember ever seeing the woman's hair *without* rollers.

"What did that Rivers fellow say when you told him you were moving into town?" She didn't wait for a response, but cackled delightedly. "Frankly, I wasn't sure you'd show up this morning. My friend Ethel and me talked about it, and we figured Rivers would tie a rope around you and hightail it to Nevada and marry you quick. Offhand, I can't remember who's got money on November."

"You said to be here before noon," she murmured, ignoring the other comments.

"Well, if Luke didn't stop you, I expected that snowstorm would, the one the weatherman's been talking about for the last two days."

"Do you really think it's going to snow?" Kate asked anxiously. The sky had been dark all morning, and the temperature seemed to be dropping steadily. Normally Kate wouldn't have chanced driving into town by herself with weather conditions this uncertain, but if she hadn't come, she might have missed getting the apartment.

"If I was you, I'd stick around town for a while," Mrs. Jackson advised. "I'd hate the thought of you getting trapped on the road in a bad storm."

"I'm sure I'll be all right." She'd driven her father's four-wheel-drive truck, and even if the storm did materialize, she shouldn't have any trouble getting home. The Circle L was only twenty minutes away, and how much snow could fall in that time?

"Would you like me to write you a check now?" Kate asked, eager to be on her way.

"That'd be fine. There's still some cleaning to be done, but it'll be finished before the first of the month. Fact is, you can start moving your things in here next week if you want."

"Thanks, I appreciate that."

Mrs. Jackson bundled her coat around her thin shoulders as they stepped outside. She glanced at the sky and shook her pink-curlered head. "If you are going home, I suggest you do it quick. I don't like the look of them clouds."

"Then I'd better write that check and head out."

No more than five minutes later, Kate was sitting in her father's truck. The sky was an oyster gray and darkening by the minute. Shivering from the cold, she zipped her jacket all the way up to her neck and drew on a pair of fleece-lined leather gloves.

Kate started the engine and shifted the gears. The radio was set on her dad's favorite country station and the music played softly. When she left the outskirts of town, she hit a couple of rough patches in the road and bounced so high her head nearly banged into the roof of the cab. After that she kept her speed down. She drove at a steady pace, her gaze focused on the road ahead, scanning the horizon for any sign of snow.

When she was about ten miles from the ranch, the storm began. Light, fluffy flakes whirled around the windshield. The morning sky darkened until it resembled dusk and Kate was forced to turn on the headlights.

A love song came on the radio, one the band at the Red Bull had played that fateful Friday night. The night Luke had lifted her in his arms and carried her off the dance floor. Embarrassed by the memory, she reached for the radio dial, intending to change the station.

She didn't see the rock that had rolled onto the road, not until she was almost on top of it, and then it was too late. Her instincts took control. She gripped the wheel with both hands, then swerved and slammed into the embankment. The truck stopped with a sudden jerk, and the engine went dead.

For a stunned moment, Kate couldn't breathe. Her heart was in her throat and her hands clenched the steering wheel so tightly her fingers felt numb.

Finally, when she was able to move, Kate released a long, shaky breath, grateful the accident hadn't been worse. She took a moment to compose herself and tried to restart the engine, but nothing happened. Twice more she tried to get the engine to kick over, but it wouldn't even cough or sputter.

Frustrated, she smacked the cushioned seat with her gloved hand and closed her eyes. The snow was coming down thick and fast now.

"Don't worry," she muttered, opening the door and climbing out. "Stay calm." Although everything Kate knew about the internal workings of engines would fit on a Post-it note, she decided to see if she could find the problem.

The snow and wind struck at her viciously, as though to punish her for not listening to Mrs. Jackson and staying in town.

After considerable difficulty locating the latch, Kate raised the hood. With a prayer on her lips, she looked everything over, then touched two or three different parts as if that would repair whatever was broken. Certain that she was destined to sit out the storm huddled in the cab, she returned and tried the key again.

The engine gave one sick cough and promptly died.

"Damn!"

Nothing remained but to sit and wait for someone to drive past. Leaving the truck and attempting to make her way to the house would be nearly as insane as driving around in a snowstorm in the first place.

Kate could almost hear Luke's lecture now. It would be hot enough to blister her ears. All she could do was hope her father never found out about this—or she'd get a lecture from him, too.

A half hour passed and, hoping against hope, Kate tried the engine again. Nothing. But it was snowing so hard now that even if the truck had started, she probably wouldn't have been able to drive in these conditions. She tried to warm herself by rubbing her hands and hugging her arms close to her body. It had become cold, the coldest weather she could remember.

With very little to take her mind off the freezing temperature, she laid her head back and closed her eyes, trying to relax. There was nothing to do but sit patiently and wait….

She must have dozed off because the next thing she knew, the truck door was jerked open and her arm gripped in a sudden, painful hold.

"Have you lost your mind?" The fury in Luke's voice was like a slap in the face.

"Luke… Luke." She was so grateful to see him that she didn't question where he'd come from or how he'd found her. It all felt like a dream. Moving was difficult, but she slid her arms around his neck and hugged him, laughing and crying at the same time. "How did you ever find me?"

"Don't you realize I was about to have heart failure worrying about you?"

"You're sick?" Her mind was so muddled. Of course he'd be worried. How had he known where she was? And he seemed so angry, but that was nothing new. For the past few days, he'd been continually upset with her.

Her arms tightened around his neck and she breathed in his fresh, warm scent. When she sat up and looked around, she was shocked by how dark it had become; if it weren't for the blowing, swirling snow, the stars would be twinkling. The storm had abated somewhat, but not by much.

"I can't believe you'd do anything so stupid." His voice was low and angry, his face blanched with concern. "Don't you know you could've frozen to death out here? If you don't want to consider your own life, then what about Devin away on his honeymoon? If anything happened to you, he'd never forgive himself."

Kate bore up well under Luke's tirade, refusing to cry even though she was trembling with shock and cold and the truth of his words. As for the part about being frozen, she was already halfway there, but he didn't seem to notice that.

"Kate, I don't know what I would've done if you'd left the truck and tried to make it back to the house on foot."

"I knew enough to stay here at least." She'd been a fool not to have taken the danger more seriously. "I'm sorry," she whispered.

He pulled her to him and held her so tight she couldn't move. His face was buried in her hair, one ungloved hand gently stroking her forehead, her cheek, her chin, as if he had to touch her to know he'd found her safe. When he lifted his head, he gazed into her eyes, his own dark and filled with unspoken torment. "Are you all right?"

She nodded and tried to talk, but her teeth began to chatter. Luke shrugged out of his coat and draped it over her shoulders.

"Tell me what happened."

"I swerved to miss a rock and hit…the embankment. It was already snowing and I…the song… I changed stations and that's when it happened… I don't know what I did, but after I turned so sharply, the truck wouldn't start."

"I've got to get you to the house." He half carried her to his truck and placed her in the passenger seat. He climbed into the driver's side and leaned over to wrap a warm blanket around her, then began to rub some warmth back into her hands.

"What about Dad's truck?" Kate asked, shocked by how tired and weak she felt.

"We'll worry about that later. I'll send someone to fix it when the storm's over."

The blast from the heater felt like a tropical wind and Kate finally started to relax. She was terribly cold but dared not let Luke know.

All the way back to the ranch he didn't say a word. Driving was difficult, and she didn't want to disturb his concentration. So she sat beside him, her hands and feet numb despite the almost oppressive warmth, and her eyes heavy with weariness.

Several of the ranch hands ran toward the front porch when Luke pulled into the yard. Kate found the flurry of activity all centered on her disconcerting, but she tried to thank everyone and apologized profusely for the concern she'd caused.

If Luke had been impatient and demanding when he rescued her, it didn't compare to the way he rapped out orders once she was inside the house.

"A bath," he said, pointing toward the bathroom as if she'd never been there before. "Warm water, not hot."

Bill Schmidt, Luke's newly appointed foreman, followed them to the doorway of the tiny room, looking pale and anxious. Kate felt so weak that she simply stood, leaning against the sink, while Luke ran the bathwater, testing it several times to check the temperature.

"It's stopped snowing. Do you think I should contact one of her female friends? Maybe Miz Franklin?" Bill asked, shifting awkwardly from foot to foot. When

Luke nodded, Bill charged out of the house, slamming the door behind him.

Luke turned off the bathwater and straightened. He shook his head, arms limp and at his sides, mouth stern and tight. "Kate, Kate, what could have possessed you to drive in from town during the worst storm of the year? Can you imagine what went through my mind when I was looking for you?"

It took all her strength just to manage a few words. "How'd…you know…where I was?"

"You told me you were going to town to look at an apartment on Saturday. Remember? When you weren't back after the blizzard hit, I called around town until I learned you were renting one of the apartments on Spruce Street. Mrs. Jackson told me she'd warned you herself and that you'd left a few hours earlier. Also that she's fond of April because of all the flowers, whatever the hell that means."

"I'm…sorry I worried you."

His hands gripped her shoulders and the anguish he'd endured during the past few hours was written plainly on his face. The anger and pain in his eyes told her about the panic he'd felt. A rush of emotion crossed his expression and he pulled her close, wrapping his arms around her.

He didn't speak for a long moment. Instead, quietly, gently, he stroked her hair as he dragged in several deep breaths.

Kate's heart pounded wildly in her chest. She longed to look at him, to gaze into his eyes again. She was puzzled by the intensity she'd seen there. Fear, yes, doubt and anger, too, but there was something more, something deeper that she didn't recognize.

She longed to tell him she loved him, just the way he claimed she did, but the thought didn't make it to her lips. Love was a strange, unpredictable emotion, so painful and difficult. Her eyes held his and she tried to smile, but her mouth wouldn't cooperate.

Her fingertips mapped out the lines of his face, as she strove to reassure him with her touch when her words couldn't. He captured her wrist and brought her palm to his lips.

She'd just opened her mouth to speak, when Bill Schmidt came crashing into the room. "Rorie Franklin will be over as soon as she can."

"Thanks, Bill," Luke said without looking away from Kate.

"Uh, I'll be leaving now, if you don't need me."

"Fine. Thanks again for your help."

"No problem. Glad you're all right, Kate." He touched his hat and then was gone.

"Someone should help you out of those clothes," Luke said, half smiling, "and I don't think I should be the one to do it."

"I'm fine. I can undress myself."

Luke didn't seem inclined to challenge her statement. She floated toward the bathroom door and ushered him out, then shut it softly.

Once she started undressing, she discovered that Luke hadn't been too far wrong when he'd suggested she needed help. By the time she sank into the warm water, she was shivering, exhausted and intensely cold again. But the water felt wonderful, although it stung her tender skin. When the prickling sensation left her, she was almost overwhelmed by the sensation of comfort. She sighed deeply, closed her eyes and lay back in the tepid water.

"Kate," Luke called from the other side of the door, "are you okay in there?"

"I'm fine."

"Do you need anything?"

"No," she assured him.

A sudden thought made her bolt upright, gasping. *Luke could have died searching for me.* She closed her eyes and whispered a prayer of thanks that the events of this traumatic afternoon had turned out as they had.

She must have sobbed because Luke called out, "What's wrong? It sounds like you're crying."

"You…could have died trying to find me."

"I didn't."

"I know," she said hoarsely, biting her lip. "I'm glad. I wouldn't want you to die."

"That's encouraging," he answered with a soft laugh.

Dressed in her flannel pyjamas and long robe, her hair hanging wetly against her shoulders, Kate let herself out of the bathroom. She looked like something the cat had proudly dragged onto the porch, but at least she felt better. A thousand times better.

Luke was sitting in the kitchen, nursing a shot glass of whiskey. Kate had very rarely seen Luke drink straight liquor.

"I blame myself," he muttered. "I knew about the storm and didn't warn you."

"Warn me? That wouldn't have made any difference. I would've gone into town anyway. I had to be there before noon if I was going to get the apartment. You couldn't have stopped me, Luke. You know that."

Luke shook his head grimly. "What I can't understand is why moving away from here is so all-fired important that you'd risk your fool neck to do it."

"Mrs. Jackson said she'd have to give the apartment to someone else if I wasn't there."

"She wouldn't have understood if you'd phoned? You had to go look at it in a blizzard?" He urged her into a chair and poured a cup of hot coffee, adding a liberal dose of whiskey before handing her the cup.

"I already told you I couldn't wait. Besides, it wasn't snowing when I drove there," Kate said patiently. "Please don't be angry, Luke." She reached for his hand, needing to touch him.

He clutched her fingers with his own. "Kate, if anything should convince you we ought to get married, this is it. You need me, Princess, can't you see that?" He released her hand to brush the damp curls from her forehead. "How many times do I have to tell you that before you'll believe it?"

"Oh, Luke," she moaned, feeling close to tears.

"I want to take care of you, Kate. What nearly happened today, plus the fiasco with Eric Wilson, should tell you something."

She stared at him, feeling lost and disoriented. "There are women in this community, women my age, who already have children." Even as she spoke, she knew she wasn't making sense.

Luke blinked in confusion. "You want children? Great, so do I. In fact, I'm hoping we'll have several."

"That's not what I meant," Kate said, exasperated. She tried again. "These women don't live with a guardian." Was that clearer? she wondered.

"Of course they don't—they're married," Luke countered sharply.

Kate shut her eyes. "Don't you understand? I'm old enough to be on my own. I don't need someone to protect me."

"We're not discussing your age."

"You don't *love* me," she blurted. "You feel sorry for me, that's all. You think because Clay's married to Rorie and...and Dad married Dorothea that I don't have anyone. But I do! There's Linda and lots of other friends. I've got a good life. I don't need to get married."

Luke sprang from the chair and walked to the sink, pressing both hands against the edge, hunching his shoulders, his back toward her. He said nothing for several minutes and when he finally spoke, his voice was cool, detached. "All I can say is that you must feel a lot more strongly about this than I realized. Apparently you're willing to risk your life to get away from me."

"I didn't go to town knowing I was in any danger," she objected, but he didn't seem to hear.

"Then leave, Kate. I won't try to keep you any longer, despite the fact that I love you and want to marry you. If you want your independence so badly, then take it."

"Luke, please, you don't love me—not the way you should."

"Oh, and what do you know about that? Obviously nothing."

"I know you keep saying you want to take care of me."

"That's so wrong?"

"Yes! A woman needs more. She needs to be an equal. She—"

"My love and my life are all I've got to offer you, Kate," he broke in. "It's a take-it-or-leave-it proposition."

"That's not fair," she said. "You make it sound as

though I'm going to live my life alone if I don't marry you within the next ten minutes."

Slowly he turned to face her. His eyes were piercing and as dark as she'd ever seen them. "Fine. You've made your choice. I'm not going to stand here arguing with you. It's over, Kate. This is the last time we'll talk about marriage."

She tried to say something, but couldn't think coherently. Even if she'd been able to work out her thoughts and give them voice, she doubted Luke was in any mood to listen. He avoided looking at her as he stalked out of the house.

A fire was blazing in the fireplace and Kate stretched out on the nearby sofa, intending to mull over Luke's words. But her eyes felt as heavy as her heart, and almost as soon as she laid her head on the pillow, she was asleep.

Someone working in the kitchen stirred Kate to wakefulness, and when she glanced at her watch she was shocked to see that she'd slept for almost two hours.

Her heart soared when she thought it must be Luke. He'd been so angry with her earlier, although she supposed his anxiety about finding her in the snowstorm explained his attitude. She hoped they could clear the air.

But it wasn't Luke. Instead, Rorie peered into the living room, her eyes concerned.

"I hope you don't mind. Luke let me in."

"You're always welcome here, Rorie, you know that."

"Bill Schmidt called with an incredible story about you being lost in the storm. I could hardly believe it.

Clay drove me over as soon as he could, but to be honest I don't know who was worse off—you or Luke."

At the mention of his name, Kate lowered her gaze to the multicolored quilt spread across her lap. Idly she smoothed the wrinkles, trying not to think about Luke.

"How are you feeling?"

"I'm okay. I just have a headache."

"A bad one from the look of you. I've never seen you this pale."

Kate's hands twisted the edge of the homemade quilt. "Luke was furious with me for going into town—I found an apartment, Rorie. He said it was over between us." She began to cry. "He said he'd be glad when I was gone and that he'd…never bother me again." By the time Kate had finished, her voice was reduced to a hoarse whisper.

"I see," Rorie murmured.

"I don't even recognize Luke anymore. We used to be able to talk to each other and joke together, but lately we can't seem to discuss anything in a rational manner. I've tried, Rorie, I really have, but Luke makes everything so difficult."

"Men have a habit of doing that."

"I wanted to tell Luke about the night I had dinner with you and Clay and—" She stopped abruptly when she realized what she'd almost said.

"What about it?" Rorie coaxed.

"It's just that I'd dreaded the evening because I was afraid of being with Clay again. I'm sorry, I don't want to upset you, Rorie, but I loved Clay for a long time, and getting over him was much harder than I thought it would be. Until the night we were all together." The words came rushing from her. "I saw Clay with you and

I assumed I'd feel all this pain, but instead I felt completely free. You're both so happy, and I knew, then and there, that I never loved Clay the way you do. True, I adored him for years, but it was more of an adolescent infatuation. Clay was part of my youth. When I understood all these things about myself, all these changes, I felt such hope, such excitement."

"Oh, Kate, I'm so pleased to hear that." A shy smile dented Rorie's cheeks.

"I wanted to explain all this to Luke, but I never got the chance, and now it's all so much worse. I don't know if we'll ever be able to talk to each other again."

"Of course you will."

"But he sounded so angry."

"I'm sure that's because of his concern for your safety."

"I can't talk to him," Kate repeated sadly. "At least not yet and maybe not ever…"

"Yes, you will, and it'll be sooner than you think," Rorie said. "You won't be able to break off all those years of friendship, and neither will he. He'll be around in a day or two, ready to apologize for being so harsh. Just you wait and see."

Kate shook her head. "You make it all seem so easy."

"Trust me, I know it isn't. When I think back to the way things went between Clay and me, I empathize all the more with what you're going through now."

Kate remembered the dark days following Clay's visit to California. Neither Rorie nor Clay had ever told her what happened. Clay had gone to San Francisco, intending to bring Rorie back with him, and instead had returned alone.

"Maybe we need to get away from each other for a

while," Kate said. "Maybe if we aren't in such close proximity, we'll be able to sort out what we really feel for each other."

"When are you moving to town?"

"Monday," Kate said, looking at the cardboard boxes stacked against the opposite wall.

"Do you need help? Skip, Clay and I could easily lend a hand."

"That would be wonderful."

The rest of the weekend passed in a blur. Kate didn't see Luke once. So much for Rorie's assurances that he'd come by soon to talk everything out. Apparently he meant what he'd said.

Monday morning, when she was about to leave for school, Kate paused before she got into her car, deciding she should at least say goodbye to Luke before she moved out.

Luke wasn't in the barn, but Bill Schmidt was.

"Good morning, Bill."

"Howdy, Kate," he said with a wide grin. "Glad to see there's no ill effects from your accident."

"None, thanks. Is Luke around?"

Bill settled his hands in the pockets of his bib overalls. "No. Thought you knew. He left yesterday afternoon for New Mexico to look at some new equipment. He won't be back until Thursday."

Ten

Kate was carrying the last of the cardboard boxes to the recycling bins outside the apartment building on Thursday evening when she saw Luke's pickup turn onto Spruce Street. He came to a grinding halt at the curb, vaulted out of the cab and stood there scowling. His features were contorted, but for the life of her Kate couldn't understand why he was so irritated. Didn't he *tell* her to move? Wasn't this what he wanted?

She was about to make her presence known, but before she could act, Luke brought his fist down on the bonnet. She heard the sound from where she was standing. It must have smarted because he rubbed his knuckles, gazing intently at the redbrick building. Then, tucking his hands in the back pockets of his jeans, he squared his shoulders and strode toward it. He stopped abruptly, then retreated to his truck. Opening the door, he balanced one foot on the side rail, as if he was about to leap into the cab.

Kate leaned forward on the tips of her toes and stretched out her hand to stop him. It took everything in her not to rush forward. She was afraid she'd burst into tears. Viewing Luke's behavior had touched something deep within her.

If Luke had planned to drive away, he apparently changed his mind, because he slammed the door shut and resolutely faced the building again.

Knowing that the time to make her move was now, Kate casually turned the corner.

"Kate."

"Luke," she said, pretending surprise.

For a moment, Luke didn't say a word. "I just got back to the ranch and discovered that the main house was empty. I thought you'd be there when I returned."

"Mrs. Jackson said I could have the apartment Monday, and since Rorie, Clay and Skip were able to help me move, I couldn't see any reason to delay."

"You might've told me."

Kate lowered her eyes, feeling a little guilty, since they'd parted on such unfriendly terms. "I tried, but you'd already left for New Mexico."

"Bill did say you wanted to talk to me," he conceded.

"Would you like to come inside?" she asked, opening the door for him.

"All right." He sounded reluctant.

Once in the apartment they stood looking at each other, and Kate felt suddenly awkward. Luke's eyes were dark and luminous and his face had never seemed so dear to her—familiar, yet in some exciting new way, not fully known. She would've liked nothing better than to walk into his arms. She wanted to tell him how sorry she was about the way they'd parted, to tell him she was ready to accept his proposal on any terms. But her pride made that impossible.

"Nice place," he said when the silence became painful. He tucked his fingers in his back pockets again.

"Can I take your coat?"

"Please." He took it off and gave it to her.

She motioned toward the sofa. "Would you like to sit down?"

He nodded and sat on the edge of the cushion. Leaning forward, he balanced his hands between his knees and rotated his hat with his fingers. Luke had sat on this very same sofa a thousand times, but he'd never looked as uncomfortable as he did now.

"I came to apologize for the last time we spoke."

"Oh, Luke," she whispered, sitting in the overstuffed chair across from him. "I felt bad, too. Why do we argue like that? Some days I feel we're growing further and further apart, and I don't want that."

"I'd like to suggest we put an end to this nonsense, but you've made your views plain enough."

"You still want to take care of me?"

"I don't think that's so wrong."

"I know." She sighed, tired of repeating the same arguments. "But I'm fully capable of doing that myself."

"Right," he said with deadly softness. "You took care of yourself pretty well during that snowstorm, didn't you?"

"Why don't you throw Eric Wilson in my face while you're at it? I thought you came because you regretted our last argument, but it looks to me as if you're trying to start another one."

"All right," he shouted, "I'll stop! You asked me not to bring up the distasteful subject of marriage and I agreed. It's just that—" He clamped his mouth shut.

"We're better off dropping the subject entirely," he finished stiffly.

"I hate when we argue," Kate said.

"So do I, Princess."

Although his tone was light, Kate heard the distress in his voice. It filled her with regret, and she longed for something comforting to say, something that would ease this awkwardness between them, and restore a sense of balance to their relationship.

"Do you need anything, Kate?"

"No. I'm fine," she rushed to assure him. She might occasionally date the wrong men and take foolish risks in snowstorms, but she could manage her own life!

Luke glanced around the room, then slowly nodded as if accepting the truth of her words.

"It was kind of you to stop by… I mean, it's good to see you and I really am grateful you wanted to clear the air, too."

"Are you saying you missed me while I was away?"

She had, terribly, but until that moment, Kate hadn't been willing to admit it, even to herself. Unconsciously she'd been waiting for Thursday, hoping to hear from Luke—but not really expecting to. For the past few days, she'd worked frantically to unpack her things and make her apartment presentable. And all along it had been an effort to prove to Luke how efficient and capable she actually was. After falling on her face so many times, she wanted this transition from the ranch house to her first apartment to go off without a hitch. It was a matter of pride.

They were like polite strangers with each other. Kate couldn't think of a single clever remark or probing question to reduce the tension between them.

"Have you eaten?" Luke asked brusquely. "I thought I'd take you to dinner. I realize I'm not giving you much notice and I read somewhere that women don't like a man to take things for granted, so if you don't want to go, I'll understand."

He sounded as though he assumed she'd reject his invitation. "I'd love to have dinner with you," she said, unable to hide a smile.

Luke seemed shocked by her easy acquiescence.

Kate stood up, stretching luxuriously. "If you'll give me a moment, I'll freshen up." She couldn't keep the happiness out of her voice.

Luke rose then, and his presence seemed to dwarf her small living room. Only a few scant inches separated them. With one finger, he tilted up her chin and looked deep into her eyes. "You honestly missed me?" he whispered.

For some reason, her throat squeezed shut and Kate was forced to answer him without words. She cradled his face between both hands and gazed up at him, nodding fervently.

Luke's eyes darkened and she thought he meant to kiss her. Just when she was prepared to slip into his arms and raise her mouth to his, he pulled loose from her light grasp and stepped back. Kate swallowed her disappointment.

"I was thinking about that pizza parlour in Riversdale," he said gruffly.

"Pizza would be wonderful," Kate said.

"Then it's settled."

Kate didn't bother to change clothes, but ran a brush through her hair and refreshed her make-up. A few minutes later, she was ready to leave. Luke stood at the door, and as she approached him, his appreciative look sent small flutters of awareness through her body.

Companionably they drove the thirty miles to Riversdale. By unspoken agreement they avoided any subject that would cause them to disagree.

The restaurant, Pizza Mania, was known throughout the county for its excellent Italian food. The room was dimly lit, and the wooden tables were covered with red-checkered cloths. Since it was a weeknight, the restaurant wasn't especially busy.

Luke guided her to a table in the middle of the homey room. Service was prompt and they quickly placed their order for a large sausage-and-black-olive pizza. Kate also ordered a raw vegetable platter with yogurt-herb dip, and she laughed at the disdainful expression on Luke's face. Then she laughed again.

"What's so funny now?"

"I was remembering the last time I ate pizza from here. It was when Rorie had just arrived, and she and I were making dinner for Clay and Skip. I made a lemon meringue pie and Rorie spent the entire afternoon preparing this fancy seafood dish."

"Where does the pizza come in?"

Kate told Luke about the disastrous dinner, and he smiled slightly, shaking his head. "Rorie must've been devastated."

"Actually she was a pretty good sport about the whole thing. We called Pizza Mania, ordered two large pizzas that Skip offered to pick up, and afterward we sat around the piano for a while."

That night was when she'd realized how hard Clay was fighting not to fall in love with Rorie. All evening he'd tried not to even glance in her direction. Then, later, when he drove Kate home, he'd said barely a word and gently kissed her cheek after he'd walked her to the door. A peck on the cheek, the way he'd kiss a younger sister.

"What's wrong?" Luke asked.

"Nothing." Kate summoned a smile. "What makes you ask?" She was relieved at the appearance of their vegetable appetizer, immediately reaching for a carrot stick.

"Your eyes looked kind of sad just now."

Kate concentrated on munching her carrot, astonished at the way Luke so often seemed to know what she was thinking. But then, sometimes he didn't.... "That night was when I knew I was losing Clay to Rorie. My whole world was about to fall apart and I felt powerless to do anything about it. It didn't mean I stopped trying, of course—it hurt too much to accept without putting up a fight." She paused and helped herself to a zucchini strip. "Enough about me. It seems I'm the only one we ever discuss. How was your trip to New Mexico?" she asked brightly, determined to change the subject.

"Good." He didn't elaborate. His eyes held hers, the mood warm and comfortable. "There are going to be a few changes around the Circle L in the coming months. I don't want you to be surprised when you find out I'm adding a couple of outbuildings and doing some remodelling on the house."

Although he spoke in a conversational tone, Kate wasn't fooled. "The Circle L belongs to you now. I expect there'll be plenty of changes, but don't worry about offending me or Dad."

He nodded and his eyes brightened with his dreams

for the future. "I intend to turn it into one of the top cattle ranches on the West Coast."

"I'm sure you'll do it, Luke." And she was.

He seemed pleased by her confidence in him. Kate couldn't help believing in Luke. In the ten years he'd worked for her father, he'd initiated several successful breeding programs. With each passing year, Devin had turned more and more of the ranch business over to Luke. Her father had become a figurehead. Kate had often heard Devin say that he couldn't understand why Luke would continue working for him when he was completely capable of maintaining his own spread. At one time, Kate had thought money was the issue, but that obviously wasn't the case.

"Why'd you delay buying your own ranch for so long?" Kate asked, just as their pizza arrived. Their waitress remained standing at their table and studied them so blatantly that Luke turned to her.

"Is something wrong?" he asked sharply.

"No…not at all. Enjoy your dinner." She backed away from their table and hurried over to the counter, where two other employees were waiting. Almost immediately the three of them huddled together and started whispering.

Luke chose to ignore their waitress's strange behavior and lifted a steaming piece, thick with melted cheese and spicy sausage, onto her plate. Then he served himself.

"Now, where were we?" Luke murmured.

"I asked why you didn't buy your own ranch before now."

"You don't want to know the answer to that, Princess."

"Of course I do. I wouldn't have brought it up otherwise," she insisted.

"Fine." Luke settled back in his chair. He looked at her, eyes thoughtful. "I had a minor problem. I was in love with the boss's daughter and she was crazy about me, only she didn't know it. In fact, she'd gotten herself engaged to someone else. I was afraid that if I moved away she'd never realize how I felt—or how she did—and frankly, I didn't think I could ever love anyone the way I do her."

Kate focused her attention on her meal. The lump in her throat was almost choking her. "You're right about…me not loving Clay," she told him softly. No matter how hard she tried, she couldn't raise her eyes high enough to meet his.

"What did you say?"

"I… You were right about me and Clay. I could never feel for him the things a wife should feel for her husband. I'd adored him for years, but that love was just a teenage fantasy."

She was well aware of the seriousness of her admission. The room seemed to go still; the music from the juke box faded, the clatter from the kitchen dimmed and the voices from the people around them seemed to disappear altogether.

"I didn't think I'd ever hear you admit that," Luke said, and his face filled with tenderness.

"I tried to tell you the night after I had dinner with Clay and Rorie, but you were so angry with me…because I was moving." She laughed, hoping to break the unexpected tension that had leaped between them.

"Does this also mean you're admitting you love *me?*"

"I've never had a problem with that—"

Kate was interrupted by an elderly man who strolled up to their table. With considerable ceremony, he lifted a violin to his chin and played a bittersweet love song.

"I didn't know they had strolling violinists here," Kate said when the man had finished. Everyone in the restaurant stopped to applaud.

"This next song is dedicated to the two of you," the man announced, "that the love in your hearts will blossom into a bouquet of *May* flowers."

It wasn't until he'd finished the third song that Kate noticed he didn't go to any of the other tables. He seemed to be playing only for them. Some of the customers had apparently noticed this, too, and gathered behind Luke and Kate in order to get a better view of the musician.

"Thank you," Kate said as the last notes faded.

The man lowered his instrument to his side. "You two have become quite a sensation in Nightingale and beyond. We at Pizza Mania are honored that you've chosen our restaurant for a romantic evening. We want to do our part to bring you together in wedded bliss."

"And you're suggesting the month of May?" Kate asked, referring to his comment about a bouquet of flowers.

"That would be an excellent choice," the violinist said, grinning broadly.

"It's time we left," Luke said, frowning. He pulled out his wallet, but the violinist stopped him. "Please, your pizza's on the house. We are delighted that you chose to dine in our humble establishment."

From the tight set of Luke's mouth, Kate could tell he wanted to argue, but more urgent was his need to escape. He took her by the hand and charged for the door.

"Your leftover pizza!" Their waitress ran after them, handing Luke a large white box as she cast Kate an envious glance.

Luke couldn't seem to get out of the car park fast enough. Kate waited until they were on the road before she spoke. "So this is the first time that's happened to you?"

Luke laughed shortly. "Not really, only I didn't pick up on it as quickly as you did. Several people have made odd comments about certain months, but until now, I didn't get what they were actually saying."

"It's funny when you think about it. Half the county's got money riding on our wedding day, and Fred Garner's making a killing raising and lowering the odds." Suddenly the lottery was the most hilarious thing Kate had ever heard of, and she started to laugh. She slumped against the side of the cab, holding her sides. She was laughing so hard, her stomach hurt. Tears ran down her cheeks and she wiped them away as she tried to regain control. The wedding lottery and everyone's interference wasn't all *that* funny, but Luke's disgruntled reaction was.

"Come on, Luke," she said, still chuckling. "There's a lot of humor in this situation."

He snorted.

"Don't be such a killjoy. I've been getting free advice from the butcher, Sally Daley, the paperboy and just about everyone else in town. It's only fair that you put up with a few of their comments, too."

"One might think you'd take some of that free advice," he muttered.

"What?" she cried. "And ruin their fun?"

Luke was oddly quiet for the remainder of the trip

into Nightingale. He stopped at her building, walked her to her door with barely a word, then turned and walked away. No goodnight kiss, no mention of seeing her again.

This was the last thing she'd expected. For the entire drive home, she'd been imagining how good it would feel when Luke kissed her. She'd decided to invite him in for coffee, hoping he'd accept. But this was even worse than Clay's peck on the cheek all those months ago.

"Luke..."

He stopped abruptly at the sound of her voice, then turned back. His eyes seemed to burn into hers as he came toward her, and she stumbled into his arms. His mouth, hot and hungry, sought hers in a kiss that scorched her senses.

His fingers plunged into her hair, releasing the French braid and ploughing through the twisted strands of blond hair.

Instinctively Kate reached up and slid her arms around his shoulders, feeling so much at home in his arms that it frightened her. She trembled with the knowledge, but she didn't have time to analyze her feelings. Not when her world was in chaos. She clung to him as though she were rocketing into a fathomless sky.

Luke broke away from her, his face a study of hope and confusion. "I never know where I stand with you, Kate." With that, he stroked her hair and quickly returned to his truck.

Kate was still reeling from the effects of Luke's kiss. If she hadn't leaned against her door, she might have fallen onto the walkway, so profound was her reaction.

"Luke," she called, shocked by how weak her voice

sounded. "Would you like to come inside for coffee? We could talk about…things."

Slowly a smile eased its way across his handsome features. "I don't dare, Princess, because the way I feel right now, I might not leave until morning. If then."

Flustered by his words, Kate unlocked her door and let herself inside.

She gulped a deep breath and stood in the middle of the living room with her hand over her rampaging heart. "You're in love with him, Kate Logan," she told herself. "Head over heels in love with a man and fighting him every step of the way."

Groaning, she buried her face in her hands. She didn't understand *why* she'd been fighting him so hard. She did realize that Luke wouldn't have spent years building up her father's ranch if he hadn't loved her. He could have left anytime, gone anywhere to buy his own ranch, but he'd stayed at the Circle L. He honestly loved her!

Now she knew what she wanted, but she didn't know what to do about it.

She guessed Luke was planning to court her, to use that charming old-fashioned term. If so, one more dinner with him would be enough. They'd be officially engaged by the end of the evening. She'd bet on it!

To her disappointment, Kate didn't hear from him the following day. Fridays were generally busy around the ranch, so she decided the next move would have to come from her.

Early Saturday morning she compiled a grocery list, intent on inviting Luke over for a home-cooked meal. She was reviewing her cookbooks, searching for a special dessert recipe, when she was suddenly distracted by the memory of their kiss. Closing her eyes, she relived the way she'd felt that night. She smiled to herself, admitting how eager she was to feel that way again.

If only she'd been listening to her heart instead of her pride…

She tried phoning Luke, but there was no answer, so she decided to do the shopping first. She put on her coat, hat and gloves, and walked the few blocks to the Safeway store.

It must've been her imagination, but it seemed that everyone stopped to watch her as she pushed her cart down the aisles.

When she'd finished buying her groceries, she headed over to the pharmacy and bought a couple of scented candles. Once again, everyone seemed to stop and stare at her.

"Kate," Sally Daley said, hurrying toward her. The older woman was shaking her head, eyes brimming with sympathy. "How are you doing, dear?"

"Fine," Kate said, puzzled.

Sally's mouth fell open. "You don't know, do you?"

"Know what?"

"Luke Rivers took Beth Hammond to dinner yesterday, and the two of them danced all night at the Red Bull. Why, everyone in town's talking about it. People are saying he's lost patience with you and is going to marry Beth. Really, dear, every woman in town thinks you'd be crazy to let a man like Luke Rivers get away."

Kate was so shocked she could hardly breathe. "I see," she murmured, pretending it didn't matter.

"You poor child," Sally said compassionately. "Don't let your pride get in the way."

"I won't," Kate promised, barely able to find her voice.

"I do worry about you, Kate. I have this terrible feeling that you're going to end up thirty and all alone."

Eleven

Thirty and all alone. The words echoed in Kate's mind as she walked the short distance to her apartment. Tears burned her eyes, but somehow she'd dredged up the courage to smile and assure Sally that Luke was free to date whomever he pleased. In fact, she'd even managed to laugh lightly and say that she hoped Luke's dating Beth would finally put an end to all this wedding-lottery nonsense.

Moving at a fast pace, she kept her head lowered and went directly back to her apartment, clutching her purchases. By the time she let herself in the door, her face was streaked with tears.

No doubt Sally would spread the story of her meeting with Kate all over town by evening. Not that it made much difference. By now, the residents of Nightingale should be accustomed to hearing gossip about her and Luke.

Luke. At the mere thought of him, her heart constricted painfully. He'd given up on her and now she'd lost him. Only it hurt so much more than when Clay had broken their engagement.

Wiping the tears from her eyes, she struggled to take in everything that had happened in the past few weeks. It seemed every time she found her balance and secured her footing, something would send her teetering again. Would it never end? Was her life going to be an endless struggle of one emotional pain after another?

She set her bags on the floor, and without bothering to remove her coat, slumped into the overstuffed chair.

"Okay," she said aloud. "Luke took Beth Hammond out to dinner and dancing. It doesn't have to mean anything."

But it did. In her heart Kate was sure Luke planned to do exactly as Sally suggested. He'd made it plain from the first that he wanted a wife, and like a fool Kate had repeatedly turned him down. He loved her, or so he claimed, and Kate had doubted him. Now she wondered if perhaps he didn't love her enough. But over and over again, Luke had insisted she needed him—and he'd been right.

Closing her eyes, she tried to picture her life without Luke. A chill ran down her spine as an intense wave of loneliness swept over her.

Someone pounded at the door, but before Kate could answer it, Luke strode into the apartment. Having to face him this way, when she was least prepared, put her at a clear disadvantage. Hurriedly she painted on a bright smile.

"Hello, Luke," she said, trying to sound breezy and amused. "What's this about you and Beth Hammond?"

"You heard already?" He looked stunned.

"Good heavens, yes. You don't expect something like that to stay quiet, do you?"

"When…who told you?"

"I went to the grocery store and ran into Sally Daley."

"That explains it," he said, pacing her carpet with abrupt, impatient steps. He stopped suddenly and turned to study her. "It doesn't bother you that I'm seeing Beth?"

"Not at all," she lied. "Should it? Would you like some coffee?"

"No."

Desperate for a chance to escape and compose herself, Kate almost ran into the kitchen and poured herself a cup, keeping her back to him all the while.

"You seem to be downright happy about this," he accused, following her into the small, windowless room.

"Of course I'm pleased. I think it's wonderful when two people fall in love, don't you?"

"I'm not in love with Beth," he said angrily.

"Actually I think dating Beth is a wonderful way to kill all the rumors floating around about us," she said, finally turning toward him. She held her coffee cup close.

Rubbing his neck, Luke continued his pacing in the kitchen. "I thought you might be…jealous."

"Me?" She refused to admit she'd been dying inside from the moment Sally had told her. "Now, why would I feel like that?"

"I don't know," Luke barked. "Why would you?"

Before Kate could answer, he stormed out of the apartment, leaving her so frustrated she could have cried.

"You should've told him how you feel," she reprimanded herself. "Why are you such a fool when it comes to Luke Rivers? Why? Why? Why?"

* * *

"I saw Luke yesterday," Rorie said, watching Kate closely as they sat across from each other in a booth at Nellie's.

"That's nice," she said, pretending indifference and doing a good job of it.

"He was with Beth Hammond."

Kate's breath caught in her throat at the unexpected rush of pain. "I…see."

"Do you?" Rorie inquired. "I swear I could shake the pair of you. I've never met two more stubborn people in my life. You look like one of the walking wounded, and Luke's got a chip on his shoulder the size of a California redwood."

"I'm sure you're mistaken." Kate concentrated on stirring her coffee and avoided Rorie's eyes. Her heart felt like a ball of lead.

"When's the last time you two talked?"

"A couple of days ago."

"Honestly, Kate, I can't understand what's wrong with you. Clay and I thought…we hoped everything would fall into place after you moved to the apartment. Now it seems exactly the opposite has happened."

"Luke's free to date whomever he pleases, just the way I am."

"There's only one person you want and that's Luke Rivers and we both know it," Rorie said with an exasperated sigh. "I shouldn't have said that. It's just that I hate the idea of you two being so miserable when you're in love with each other."

"Is love always this painful?" Kate asked, her question barely audible.

Rorie shrugged. "It was with Clay and me, and sometimes I feel it must be for everyone sooner or later. Think about it, Kate. If you really love Luke, why are you fighting the very thing you want most?"

"I don't know," she admitted reluctantly.

When they parted shortly afterward, Kate felt a new sense of certainty and resolve. She *did* love Luke and if she didn't do something soon, she was going to lose him.

She drove to the Circle L, her heart in her throat. Luke's truck was parked behind the house, and she left her car beside it, hurrying through the cold to the back door. Luke didn't respond to her knock, which didn't surprise her, since it was unusual for him to be in at this time of day. But she couldn't find him outside, either, and even Bill didn't know where he was.

Making a rapid decision, she let herself into the house and started preparations for the evening meal. It gave her a way of passing the time. Dinner was in the oven and she was busy making a salad, when the back door opened and Luke walked into the kitchen.

Apparently he hadn't noticed her car because he stopped dead, shock written on every feature, when he saw her standing at the sink.

Kate held her breath for a moment, then dried her hands on the dish towel she'd tucked into her waistband. She struggled to give the impression that she was completely at ease, tried to act as though she made dinner for him every evening.

"Hello, Luke," she said to break the silence that had been growing heavier by the second.

He blinked. "I suppose you're looking for an explanation."

Kate wasn't sure what he meant.

"Taking Beth out on Friday night was a mistake."

"Then why'd you do it?"

"So you'd be jealous. The night you and I went out, I was furious at the way you started laughing, and talking as if you were never going to marry me. I wanted you to know you weren't the only fish in the sea. Only my plan backfired."

"It did?" Not as far as Kate was concerned—she'd been pretty darn worried.

"That wasn't all that went wrong. Beth saw I was in town on Saturday and started following me," he explained. "I swear I had no intention of seeing her again, but before I knew it, her arm was linked with mine and we were strolling through the middle of town together."

"Beth's a nice girl."

He frowned. "Yes, I suppose she is. I'd forgotten it doesn't bother you who I date. You've never been one for jealousy."

"I was so jealous I wanted to die."

"You were? You could've fooled me."

"Believe me, I tried to," Kate murmured.

"So what are you doing here?"

"I made dinner," Kate said sheepishly. She'd admitted how she felt about Luke seeing Beth and she couldn't stop there. "I've got pork chops in the oven, along with scalloped potatoes and an acorn squash," she rattled off without pausing for breath. Then, gathering her resolve, she casually added, "And if you're still asking, I'll marry you."

Luke stared at her. When he finally spoke he sounded strangely calm. "What did you just say?"

"There's pork chops and potatoes and—"

"Not that. The part about marrying me."

She struggled to hold on to what remained of her tattered pride. "If you're still asking me to marry you, the answer is yes."

"I'm still asking."

Kate dropped her gaze. "You've been right about so much. I do need you. I guess I was waiting for you to admit you needed *me,* only you never did."

Luke rubbed a hand over his face. "Not need you?" he repeated, his voice filled with shock and wonder. "I think my life would be an empty shell without you, Kate. I couldn't bear the thought of living one day to the next if you weren't at my side to share everything with me—all the good things that are in store for us. I've waited so long, Kate."

"You do love me, don't you?" she whispered.

For a long, long moment Luke said nothing. "I tried not to. For years I stood by helplessly, watching you break out in hives with excitement every time you saw Clay Franklin. I realized it was a schoolgirl crush, but you never seemed to get over him. Instead of improving, things got worse. How could I let you know how I felt?"

"Couldn't you have said something? Anything?"

A flicker of pain crossed his face. "No. You were so infatuated with Clay I didn't dare. It wouldn't have done any good—although God only knows how you managed not to figure it out yourself. The first day Rorie met me, she guessed."

"Rorie knew all along?"

Luke shook his head in bewildered amusement. "We were quite a pair a few months back—Rorie in love with Clay and me crazy about you. All this time, I thought I'd kept my feelings secret, and then I discovered everyone in town knew."

"Beth Hammond didn't."

"No, but she should have. I've never wanted anyone but you, Kate Logan. I haven't for years. Somehow I always kept hoping you'd see the light."

"Oh, Luke." She took a step toward him, her eyes full of emotion. "Are you going to stand way over there on the other side of the room?"

For every step Kate took, Luke managed three. When they reached each other, she put her arms around his waist, hugging him tight. She felt the beating of his heart and closed her eyes, succumbing to the wave of love that seemed about to overwhelm her.

Luke's hand was gentle on her hair. "Do you love me, Kate?"

She couldn't speak, so she nodded her head wildly. Her hands framed his face and she spread light, eager kisses over his mouth and nose and eyes, letting her lips explain what was in her heart.

"I love you," he whispered. "If you marry me, I promise I'll do everything I can to make you happy." His eyes shone with delight and a kind of humility that touched Kate's very soul. Gone was the remoteness he'd displayed so often these past few weeks.

"Oh, Luke, I can hardly wait to be your wife," she said. "Didn't you say something about a December wedding?"

"Kate, that's only a few weeks from now."

"Yes, I know. But Christmas is such a lovely time of year for a wedding. We'll decorate the church with holly, and all the bridesmaids will wear long red dresses…."

"Kate, you mean it, don't you?" His voice was low and husky.

"I've never meant anything more. I love you, Luke Rivers. We're going to have a wonderful life together."

He kissed her then, with a hunger that spoke of his years of longing. Dragging his mouth from hers, he buried it in the curve of her neck.

"I want children, Kate. I want to fill this home with so much love that the walls threaten to burst with it."

For a breathless moment, they did nothing more than gaze at each other as they shared that dream.

Kate smiled up at him, and as her hands mapped his face, loving each strong feature, she was astonished at how easily this happiness had come to her once she'd let go of her pride.

Luke's mouth settled on hers, his kiss almost reverent, as though he couldn't yet believe she was in his home and eager to be his wife.

As Kate wrapped her arms around his neck, her glance fell on the calendar. She seemed to recall that Pastor Wilkins had placed a sizeable wager on the fifteenth of December. That sounded good to Kate.

Very good indeed.

Epilogue

The sun shone clear and bright in the late-July afternoon, two years after Rorie Campbell's car had broken down near Nightingale. Kate was making a fresh pitcher of iced tea when Rorie knocked on the back door.

"Come on in," Kate called. "The screen door's unlocked."

A moment later Rorie entered the kitchen, looking slightly frazzled. "How did your afternoon at the library go?" Kate asked, as she added ice cubes to the tall pitcher.

"Very well, thanks."

"Katherine's still sleeping," Kate told her.

Rorie's eyes softened as she gazed out at the newly constructed patio where her baby slept under the shade of the huge oak tree.

"It was such a lovely afternoon I kept her outside." Kate wiped her hands dry. She poured them each a glass of iced tea, and carried a tray of tea and cookies onto the patio.

The nine-month-old infant stirred when Rorie stood over the portable crib and protectively placed her hand on the sleeping baby's back. When she turned, her eyes fell on Kate's protruding abdomen. "How are *you* feeling?"

"Like a blimp." Kate's hands rested on her swollen stomach. "The doctor told me it'll probably be another two weeks."

"Two weeks!" Rorie said sympathetically.

"I know, and I was hoping Junior would choose this week to arrive. I swear to you, Rorie, when you were pregnant with Katherine you positively glowed. You made everything seem so easy."

Rorie laughed. "I did?"

"I feel miserable. My legs are swollen, my hands and feet look like they've been inflated. There isn't a single part of my body that's normal-sized anymore."

Rorie laughed again. "The last few weeks are always like that. I think the main difference is that Katherine was born in October, when the weather was much cooler."

With some difficulty Kate crossed her legs. "I only hope our baby will be as good-natured as Katherine. She barely fussed the whole time she was here."

"Her uncle Skip thinks she's going to start walking soon."

"I think he's right." Pressing a hand to her ribs, Kate shifted her position. She was finding it difficult to sit comfortably for longer than a few minutes at a time.

"Oh—" Rorie set her iced tea aside "—I almost forgot." She hurried back to the kitchen and returned with a hardbound children's book. "I received my first copies of *Nightsong's Adventures* in the mail yesterday. Kate, I can't even begin to tell you how thrilled I was when I held this book in my hands."

Kate laid the book on her lap and slowly turned the

pages. "The illustrations are fantastic. They really fit the story."

"The reviews have been excellent. One critic said he expected it to become a children's classic, which I realize is ridiculous, but I couldn't help feeling excited about it."

"It isn't ridiculous, and I'm sure your publisher knows that, otherwise they wouldn't have been so eager to buy your second book."

"You know, the second sale was every bit as exciting as the first," Rorie said with a smile.

"Just think, in a few years our children will be reading your stories and attending school together. They're bound to be the best of friends."

Before Kate could respond, the baby woke and they watched, delighted, as she sat up in the portable crib. When she saw her mother sitting next to Kate, she smiled, her dark eyes twinkling. She raised her chubby arms, reaching for Rorie.

Rorie stood and lifted Katherine out of the crib, kissing the little girl's cheeks. "I'd better get her home. Thanks so much for watching Katherine for me. I promised I'd pinch-hit for the new librarian if she ever needed me, and I didn't think I could refuse her even though it was at the last minute."

"It wasn't any problem, so don't worry. And tell Mary she should visit her sister more often so I get the opportunity to babysit every once in a while."

"Call me later and let me know how you're feeling."

Kate nodded.

Ten minutes after Rorie and Katherine left, Luke drove up and parked behind the house. Standing on the porch, Kate waved to her husband.

Luke joined her, placing an arm around what once had been a trim waist, and led the way into the kitchen. "You okay?" His gaze was tender.

Kate wasn't sure how to answer that. She was miserable. Excited. Frightened. Eager. So many emotions were coming at her, she didn't know which one to mention first.

"Kate?"

"I feel fine." There was no need to list her complaints, but all of a sudden she felt *funny.* She didn't know any other way to describe it. As Rorie had said, there were a dozen different aches and pains the last few weeks of any pregnancy.

Luke kissed her, his mouth soft. "Did you have a busy day with Katherine?"

"She slept almost the entire time, but I think Rorie knew she would." Leaning forward, Kate kissed her husband's jaw. "I made some iced tea. Want some?"

"Please."

When Kate reached inside the cupboard for a glass, a sharp pain split her side. She let out a cry.

"Kate?"

Clutching her swollen abdomen, Kate stared at Luke. "Oh, my goodness. I just felt a pain."

Luke paled. "You're in labor?"

Smiling, wide-eyed, she nodded slowly. "I must be. I didn't expect them to start off so strong."

In an instant, Luke was across the kitchen beside her. "Now what?"

"I think I should call the doctor."

"No." Luke's arm flew out as if that would halt the course of nature. "I'll call. Stay there. Don't move."

"But, Luke—"

"For heaven's sake, Kate, don't argue with me now. We're about to have a baby!"

He said this as if it were a recent discovery. As he reached for the phone, she saw that he'd gone deathly pale. When he finished talking to the doctor, he gave her a panicked look, then announced that Doc Adams wanted them to go straight to the hospital. As soon as the words left his mouth, he shot to the bedroom, then returned with her suitcase. He halted abruptly when he saw she'd picked up the phone.

"Who are you calling?"

"Dad and Dorothea. I promised I would."

"Kate, would you let me do the phoning?"

"All right." She handed him the receiver and started toward the bedroom to collect the rest of her things. If he thought that talking on the phone was too taxing for her, fine. She'd let him do it. The years had taught her that arguing with Luke was fruitless.

"Kate," he yelled. "Don't wander off."

"Luke, I just want to get my things before we leave." A pain began to work its way around her back and she paused, flattening her hands across her abdomen. She raised her head and smiled up at her husband. "Oh, Luke, the baby..."

Luke dropped the receiver and rushed to her side. "Now?"

"No." She laughed and touched his face. "It'll be hours yet. Oh! I just felt another pain—a bad one."

He swallowed hard and gripped both her hands in his own. "I've been looking forward to this moment for nine months, but I swear to you, Kate, I've never been more frightened in my life."

"Don't worry." Her hands caressed his face and she kissed him, offering what reassurance she could.

He exhaled noisily, then gave her a brisk little nod. Without warning, he lifted her in his arms, ignoring her protests, and carried her out the door to the truck. Once he'd settled her in the seat, he returned to the house for her bag.

"Luke," she called after him, "I really would like to talk to Dad and Dorothea."

"I'll phone them from the hospital. No more arguing, Kate. I'm in charge here."

Only another sharp pain—and her regard for Luke's feelings—kept her from breaking out in laughter.

Ten long hours later, Kate lay in the hospital bed, eyes closed in exhaustion. When she opened them, she discovered her father standing over her. Dorothea was next to him, looking as pleased and proud as Kate's father. Devin took his daughter's hand in his own and squeezed it gently. "How do you feel, little mother?"

"Wonderful. Did they let you see him? Oh, Dad, he's so beautiful!"

Her father nodded. For a moment he seemed unable to speak. "Luke's with Matthew now. He looks so big sitting in that rocking chair, holding his son."

"I don't think I've ever seen Luke wear an expression quite like that before," Dorothea murmured. "So tender and loving."

Devin concurred with a nod of his head. "When Luke came into the waiting room to tell us Matthew Devin had been born, there were tears in his eyes. I'll tell you, Kate, that man loves you."

"I know, Dad, and I love him, too."

Devin patted her hand. “You go ahead and rest, Princess. Dorothea and I’ll be back tomorrow.”

When Kate opened her eyes a second time, Luke was there. She held out her hand to him and smiled dreamily. “I couldn’t have done it without you. Thank you for staying with me.”

“Staying with you,” he echoed, his fingers brushing the tousled curls from her face. “Nothing on earth could have kept me away. I would’ve done anything to spare you that pain, Kate. Anything.” His voice was raw with the memory of those last hours.

Her smile was one of comfort. “It only lasted a little while and we have a beautiful son to show for it.”

“All these months when we’ve talked about the baby,” he said, his eyes glazed, “he seemed so unreal to me, and then you were in the delivery room and in so much agony. I felt so helpless. I wanted to help you and there was nothing I could do. Then Matthew was born and, Kate, I looked at him and I swear something happened to my heart. The love I felt for that baby, that tiny person, was so strong, so powerful, I could hardly breathe. I thought I was going to break down right there in front of everyone.”

“Oh, Luke.”

“There’s no way I could ever thank you for all you’ve given me, Kate Rivers.”

“Yes, there is,” she said with a smile. “Just love me.”

“I do,” he whispered, his voice husky with emotion. “And I always will.”

* * * * *

The Courtship of Carol Sommars

One

Carol Sommars swore the entire house shook from her fifteen-year-old son's sound system, which was blasting out his favorite rap song.

> I'm the Wizard MC and I'm on the mike
> I'm gonna tell you a story that I know you'll like
> 'Cause my rhymes are kickin', and my beats do flash
> When I go to the studio, they pay me cash

"Peter!" Carol screamed from the kitchen, covering her ears. She figured a squad of dive-bombers would've made less of a racket.

Realizing that Peter would never be able to hear her above the din, she marched down the narrow hallway and pounded on his door.

Peter and his best friend, Jim Preston, were sitting on Peter's bed, their heads bobbing in tempo with the music. They both looked shocked to see her.

Peter turned down the volume. "Did you want something, Mom?"

"Boys, please, that music is too loud."

Her son and his friend exchanged a knowing glance, no doubt commenting silently on her advancing age.

"Mom, it wasn't *that* bad, was it?"

Carol met her son's cynical look. "The walls and floors were vibrating."

"Sorry, Mrs. Sommars."

"It's okay, Jim. I just thought I'd save the stemware while I had a chance." Not to mention warding off further hearing loss…

"Mom, can Jim stay for dinner? His dad's got a hot date."

"Not tonight, I'm afraid," Carol said, casting her son's friend an apologetic smile. "I'm teaching my birthing class, but Jim can stay some other evening."

Peter nodded. Then, in an apparent effort not to be outdone by his friend, he added, "My mom goes out on hot dates almost every weekend herself."

Carol did an admirable job of disguising her laugh behind a cough. Oh, sure! The last time she'd gone out had been…she had to think about it…two months ago. And that had been as a favor to a friend. She wasn't interested in remarrying. Bruce had died nearly thirteen years earlier, and if she hadn't found another man in that time, she wasn't going to now. Besides, there was a lot to be said for the benefits of living independently.

She closed Peter's bedroom door and braced her shoulder against the wall as she sighed. A jolt of deafening music brought her upright once more. It was immediately lowered to a respectable level, and she continued back to the kitchen.

At fifteen, Peter was moving into the most awkward teenage years. Jim, too. Both boys had recently obtained their learner's permits from the Department of Motor Vehicles and were in the same fifth-period driver training class at school.

Checking the time, Carol hurried into the kitchen and turned on the oven before popping two frozen meat pies inside.

"Hey, Mom, can we drive Jim home now?"

The operative word was *we,* which of course, meant Peter would be doing the driving. He was constantly reminding her how much practice he needed if he was going to pass the driving part of the test when he turned sixteen. The fact was, Peter used any excuse he could to get behind the wheel.

"Sure," she said, forcing a smile. These "practice" runs with Peter demanded nerves of steel.

Actually, his driving skill had improved considerably in the last few weeks, but the armrest on the passenger side of the car had permanent indentations. Their first times on the road together had been more hair-raising than a horror movie—another favorite pastime of her son's.

Thanks to Peter, Carol had been spiritually renewed when he'd run the stop sign at Jackson and Bethel. As if to make up for his mistake, he'd slammed on the brakes as soon as they'd cleared the intersection, catapulting them both forward. They'd been saved from injury by their seat belts.

They all clambered into her ten-year-old Ford.

"My dad's going to buy me a truck as soon as I get my license," Jim said, fastening his seat belt. "A red four-by-four with flames painted along the sidewalls."

Peter tossed Carol an accusing glare. With their budget, they'd have to share her cantankerous old sedan for a while. The increase in the car insurance premiums with an additional driver—a male teenage driver—meant frozen meat pies every third night as it was. As far as Carol was concerned, nurses were overworked, underpaid and underappreciated.

"Mom—hide!"

Her heart vaulted into her throat at the panic in her son's voice. "What is it?"

"Melody Wohlford."

"Who?"

"Mom, please, just scoot down a little, would you?"

Still not understanding, she slid down until her eyes were level with the dashboard.

"More," Peter instructed from between clenched teeth. He placed his hand on her shoulder, pushing her down even farther. "I can't let Melody see me driving with my *mother!*"

Carol muttered under her breath and did her best to keep her cool. She exhaled slowly, reminding herself *this, too, shall pass.*

Peter's speed decreased to a mere crawl. He inadvertently poked her in the ribs as he clumsily lowered the window, then draped his left elbow outside. Carol bit her lower lip to prevent a yelp, which probably would've ruined everything for her son.

"Hey, Melody," he said casually, raising his hand.

The soft feminine greeting drifted back to them. "Hello, Peter."

"Melody," Jim said, leaning across the backseat. He spoke in a suave voice Carol hardly recognized.

"Hi, Jimmy," Melody called. "Where you guys off to?"

"I'm driving Jim home."

"Yeah," Jim added, half leaning over Carol, shoving her forward so that her head practically touched her knees. "My dad's ordered me a truck, but it hasn't come in yet."

"Boys," Carol said in a strangled voice. "I can't breathe."

"Just a minute, Mom," Peter muttered under his breath, pressing down on the accelerator and hurrying ahead.

Carol struggled into an upright position, dragging in several deep gulps of oxygen. She was about to deliver a much-needed lecture when Peter pulled into his friend's driveway. Seconds later, the front door banged open.

"James, where have you been? I told you to come directly home after school."

Carol blinked. Since this was the boys' first year of high school and they'd come from different middle schools, Carol had never met Jim's father. Now, however, didn't seem the appropriate moment to leap out and introduce herself.

Alex Preston was so angry with Jim that he barely glanced in their direction. When he did, he dismissed her and Peter without a word. His dark brows lifted derisively over gray eyes as he scowled at his son.

Carol suspected that if Jim hadn't gotten out of the car on his own, Alex would have pulled him through the window.

Carol couldn't help noting that Alex Preston was an imposing man; he had to be easily six-two. His forehead was high and his jaw well-defined. But his eyes were what immediately captured her attention. They held his son's with uncompromising authority.

There was an arrogant set to his mouth that Carol

found herself disliking. Normally she didn't make snap judgments, but one look told her she wasn't going to get along with Jim's father, which was unfortunate since the boys had become such fast friends.

Not that it really mattered. Other than an occasional phone conversation, there'd be no reason for them to have any contact with each other.

She didn't know much about the man, other than his marital status (single—divorced, she assumed) and the fact that he ran some sort of construction company.

"I told you I was going out tonight," Alex was saying. "The least you could've done was have the consideration to let me know where you were. You're lucky I don't ground you for the next ten years."

Jim dropped his head, looking guilty. "Sorry, Dad."

"I'm sorry, Mr. Preston," Peter said.

"It's not your fault."

To his credit, Alex Preston glanced apologetically at Peter and Carol as if to say he regretted this scene.

"It might be a good idea if you hurried home yourself," Alex told her son.

Carol stiffened in the front seat. She felt like jumping out of the car and informing him that they had no intention of staying anyway. "We should leave now," she said to Peter with as much dignity as she could muster.

"Later," Peter called to his friend.

"Later," Jim called back, still looking chagrined.

Peter had reversed the car out of the driveway and was headed toward the house before either of them spoke.

"Did you know Jim was supposed to go home right after school?" Carol asked.

"How could I know something like that?" Peter flared.

"I asked him over to listen to my new CD. I didn't know his dad was going to come unglued over it."

"He's just being a parent."

"Maybe, but at least you don't scream at me in front of my friends."

"I try not to."

"I've never seen Mr. Preston blow his cool before. He sure was mad."

"I don't think we should be so hard on him," she said, feeling generous despite her earlier annoyance. Adults needed to stick together. "He was obviously worried."

"But, Mom, Jim's fifteen! You shouldn't have to know where a kid is every minute of the day."

"Wanna bet?"

Peter was diplomatic enough not to respond to that.

By the time they'd arrived at the house and Carol had changed clothes for her class, their dinner was ready.

"Mom," Peter said thoughtfully as she brought a fresh green salad to the table. "You should think about going out more yourself."

"I'm going out tonight."

"I mean on dates and stuff."

"Stuff?" Carol repeated, swallowing a smile.

"You know what I mean." He sighed loudly. "You haven't lost it yet, you know."

Carol wasn't sure she did. But she was fairly certain he meant to compliment her, so she nodded solemnly. "Thanks."

"You don't even need to use Oil of Olay."

She nodded, although she didn't appreciate such close scrutiny of her skin.

"I was looking at your hair and I don't see any gray, and you don't have fat folds or anything."

Carol couldn't help it—she laughed.

"Mom, I'm serious. You could probably pass for thirty."

"Thanks… I think."

"I'm not kidding. Jim's dad is going out with someone who's twenty-one, and Jim told me she's tall and blonde and pretty with great big…you know." He cupped his hands over his chest.

Carol sat down at the table. Leaning her elbows on it, she dangled her fork over her plate. "Are you suggesting I find myself a twenty-one-year-old guy with bulging muscles and compete with Jim's dad?"

"Of course not," Peter said scornfully. "Well, not exactly. I'm just saying you're not over the hill. You could be dating a whole lot more than you do. And you should before…well, before it's too late."

Carol pierced a fork full of lettuce and offered a convenient excuse. "I don't have time to get involved with anyone."

Peter took a bite of his own salad. "If the right guy came along, you'd make time."

"Perhaps."

"Mr. Preston does. Jim says his dad's always busy with work, but he finds time to date lots of women."

"Right, but most of the women he sees are too young to vote." Instantly feeling guilty for the catty remark, Carol shook her head. "That wasn't nice. I apologize."

"I understand," Peter said, sounding mature beyond his years. "The way I see it, though, you need a man."

That was news to her. "Why? I've got you."

"True, but I won't be around much longer, and I hate the thought of you getting old and gray all alone."

"I won't be alone. Grandma will move in with me

and the two of us will sit side by side in our rocking chairs and crochet afghans. For entertainment we'll play bingo every Saturday afternoon." Even as she spoke, Carol realized how ridiculous that was.

"Grandma would drive you crazy in three days," Peter said with a know-it-all smile, waving his fork in her direction. "Besides, you'd get fat eating all her homemade pasta."

"Maybe so," Carol agreed, unwilling to argue the point. "But I have plenty of time before I have to worry about it. Anything can happen in the next few years."

"I'm worried *now,*" Peter said. "You're letting your life slip through your fingers like…like the sand in an hourglass."

Carol's eyes connected with her son's. "Have you been watching soap operas again?"

"Mom," Peter cried, "you're not taking me seriously."

"I'm sorry," she said, trying to hide the smile that raised the corners of her mouth. "It's just that my life is full. I'm simply too busy to spend time developing a relationship." One look from her son told her he didn't accept her explanation. "Sweetheart," she told him, setting her fork aside, "you don't need to worry about me. I'm a big girl. When and if I decide to see another man, I promise it'll be someone muscular so you can brag to your friends. Would a wrestler be all right?"

"The least you could've done was get married again," he muttered, his patience clearly strained. "Dad would've wanted that, don't you think?"

Any mention of Peter's father brought with it a feeling of terror and guilt. They'd both been far too young and foolish to get married. They were high school seniors when Carol learned she was pregnant. Given her very traditional Catholic family, marriage had seemed the only option. She'd also believed her love and their baby would change Bruce. For those reasons, Carol had agreed to marry him. But from that point to the moment Bruce had died in a terrible car accident three years later, Carol's life had been a living hell. She'd have to be crazy to even consider remarriage.

"Peter," she said, pointedly glancing at her watch and pushing her plate away. "I'm sorry to end this conversation so abruptly, but I've got to get to class."

"You're just being stubborn, but fine. It's your decision."

Carol didn't have time to argue. She dumped the remainder of her meal in the garbage, rinsed off her plate and stuck it in the dishwasher. She left Peter after giving him instructions to take care of his own dishes, then she hurried into the bathroom.

She refreshed her makeup and ran a brush though her shoulder-length dark hair, then examined her reflection in the mirror.

"Not bad," she muttered, eyeing herself critically. Thirty-four wasn't exactly retirement age.

Releasing her breath, Carol let her shoulders fall. "Who are you kidding?" she said with a depressed sigh. She faced the mirror and glared at her image again. Peter might not think she needed Oil of Olay, but the dew was definitely off the rose.

Tugging at the skin on her cheekbones until it was stretched taut, she squinted at her reflection, trying to remember what she'd looked like at eighteen. Young. Pretty. Stupid.

She wasn't any one of those now. And even if she'd had the opportunity, she wouldn't go back. She'd made plenty of mistakes, but there wasn't a single, solitary thing she'd change about her current life. Although after Peter got his driver's license, she might modify that thought.

No, the only option open to her was the future, and she'd face that, sagging skin and all.

"Hey, Mom." Peter's voice cut into her musings. "Can I invite a friend over tonight?"

Carol opened the bathroom door and frowned at her son. "I can't believe you'd even ask that. You know the rules. No one's allowed here when I'm not home."

"But, Mom," he whined.

"No exceptions."

"You don't trust me, do you?"

"We're not discussing this now. I have a class to teach, and I'm already five minutes behind schedule." She blamed Peter for that. If he hadn't tried to convince her how attractive she was, she wouldn't be late in the first place.

Class went well. They were into the third week of the eight-week course sponsored by Ford Hospital in a suburb of Portland, Oregon. The couples were generally first-time parents, and their eagerness and excitement for the adventure that lay before them filled each session with infectious enthusiasm.

If Carol had known when she was carrying Peter that he was to be her one and only pregnancy, she would've taken time to appreciate it more.

Since she was the last to leave the building, Carol turned off the lights and hauled her material out to her car. The parking lot was well lit, and she hurried through the rain, sliding inside the car. She drew in a deep breath and turned the ignition key. The Ford coughed and objected before roaring to life. Her car had been acting a little funny lately, but it was nothing she could pinpoint. Satisfied that there wasn't anything too terribly wrong, she eased into traffic on the busy street.

It wasn't until she'd stopped for the red light at the first intersection that her car released a series of short pathetic coughs, only this time it really sounded…sick.

"What's wrong?" she cried as the light turned green. Pushing down on the accelerator, she leaped ahead, but it was apparent that the problem, whatever it might be, was serious.

"All right, all right," she said, "I get the message. You need a mechanic and fast." A quick glance down the business-lined thoroughfare revealed there wasn't a single service station in sight.

"Great," she moaned. "How about if I promise not to let Peter behind the wheel for a while. Will that help?"

The ailing car belched loudly and a plume of black smoke engulfed the rear end.

"Okay, so you're not interested in a deal." Turning into the first driveway she happened upon, Carol found herself in a restaurant parking lot. The minute she entered an empty space, the car uttered one last groan and promptly died. And of course she'd left her cell phone charging—at home.

For a full minute Carol just sat here. "You can't do this to me!" Her car disagreed. Climbing out, she walked around it, as if she'd magically discover a cure lying on the ground. The rain was coming down in sheets, and within seconds, she was drenched.

In an act of angry frustration, she kicked a tire, then

yelped when the heel of her pump broke off. She wanted to weep.

With no other alternative, she limped into the restaurant, intent on heading for the ladies' room. Once she composed herself, she'd deal with the car and call Peter to tell him she was going to be late.

Alex thought that if his date giggled one more time, he'd have to walk away from the table. Thanks to this woman, he was going slowly insane. He should know by now never to accept a blind date.

The first thing Bambi did when they were seated at the restaurant was to pick up the saltshaker and start discussing the "amazing" qualities of crystal.

It took Alex five minutes to make the connection. The saltshaker was made of crystal.

"I'm crazy about hot tubs," Bambi said, leaning forward to offer him a generous view of her ample breasts.

"They're...hot, all right," Alex murmured, examining the menu without much enthusiasm. His friend—at least someone he *used* to consider a friend—claimed Bambi was every man's dream. Her name should have been his first clue. Once they'd met, he'd learned her given name was Michelle, but she'd started calling herself Bambi because she loved forest animals so much. Animals like deer and chipmunks and hamsters.

Alex didn't have the heart to tell her that in all the years he'd been camping, he had yet to stumble upon a single family of hamsters grazing in a meadow.

When the waitress came to take their order, it took Bambi five minutes to explain how she wanted her salad served. Okay, he was exaggerating. Four minutes. He ordered a steak and asked for it rare.

"I'm on a diet," Bambi said, once the waitress had left.

He smiled benignly.

"Do you think I'm fat, Alex?" she asked.

Her big brown eyes appealed to him to lie if he must. Once more she bunched her full breasts together and leaned toward him. It was more than obvious that she wasn't wearing a bra. He suspected that he was supposed to swoon at the sight.

"You do think I'm fat, don't you?" Bambi asked, pouting prettily.

"No," Alex told her.

"You're just saying that to be nice," she purred, and demurely lowered her lashes against the high arch of her cheek.

Alex smoothed out the linen napkin on his lap, thinking he was getting old. Far too old for someone like Bambi/Michelle. His teenage son might appreciate her finer qualities, but he suspected even James had better sense than that.

"Do you have a hot tub?"

Alex was so caught up in his thoughts, mentally calculating how long it would take to get through dinner so he could drive her home, that he didn't immediately realize she'd directed the question at him.

"I love hot tubs," she reminded him. "I even carry a swimsuit with me just in case my date has a tub. See?" She reached inside her purse and held up the skimpiest piece of material Alex had seen in his entire life. It was all he could do not to grab it out of her hand and shove it back in her purse.

"I don't have a hot tub," he said, making a strenuous effort to remain civil.

"Oh, that poor, pathetic thing," Bambi said, looking past him to the front of the restaurant.

"I beg your pardon?"

Bambi used this opportunity to lean as far forward as possible, drape her breasts over his arm and whisper, "A bag lady just came into the restaurant. She's drenched, and I think she might be hurt because she's limping pretty bad."

Although he really wasn't interested, Alex glanced over his shoulder. The instant his gaze connected with the woman Bambi was referring to, he twisted his chair around for a better view. "That's no bag lady," he said. "I know that girl."

"You do?"

"Yes, she was with my son and his best friend this afternoon. I think she's another friend of theirs." He paused. "She might be in some kind of trouble." He wasn't in the business of rescuing maidens in distress, but someone had to do something. "Will you excuse me a moment?"

"Alex," Bambi cried, reaching out for his arm, stopping him. Half the restaurant turned to stare at them—including the woman at the front. Even from halfway across the room, Alex could feel her eyes on him.

"You can't involve yourself in other people's problems," Bambi insisted.

"She's just a kid." He pulled his arm free.

"Honey, one look at her and I can tell you she's no kid."

Disregarding Bambi's unsought advice, Alex dropped his napkin on the table, stood and walked away.

"Hello, again," he said when he reached his son's friend. Bambi was right about one thing. She looked terrible—nothing like the way she'd looked earlier. Her hair fell in wet tendrils that dripped on her jacket. Her mascara had left black streaks down her face, and she held the heel of her shoe in one hand. "I'm James's dad—we met briefly this afternoon." He held out his hand to her. "Do you remember me?"

"Of course I do," she said stiffly, clearly resenting this intrusion. She glanced longingly at the ladies' room.

"Is something wrong?"

"Wrong?" she echoed. "What could possibly be wrong?"

She thrust out her chin proudly, but he resisted the urge to shake some sense into her. Sarcasm always set his teeth on edge. "I'd like to help if I could."

"I appreciate the offer, but no thanks. Listen, I think you'd better get back to your date." She nodded toward Bambi, and a smile quivered at the corners of her mouth. She had difficulty meeting his eyes.

Briefly Alex wondered what she found so amusing. But then again…he knew.

"I thought she was supposed to be tall," she said next, and it sounded like she was trying not to laugh outright. Alex didn't appreciate her sense of humor, but he wasn't going to respond in kind. She was the one standing there looking like a drowned rat. Not him.

Her brows rose as she studied Bambi. "Actually two out of three isn't bad."

Alex had no idea what she was talking about. His expression must have said as much because she added, "Jim was telling Peter how your date for this evening was tall and blonde and had big—"

She stopped abruptly, and Alex could swear she was blushing. A bright pink color started creeping up her neck and into her cheeks. "I'm sorry, that was uncalled for."

Bambi apparently wasn't about to be the center of their conversation while sitting down. She pushed back her chair, joined them near the hostess desk and slipped her arm through Alex's. "Perhaps you'd care to introduce us, Alex darling."

Alex wanted to roll his eyes at the way she referred to him as "darling." They'd barely met. He doubted Bambi knew his last name. He certainly didn't remember hers.

Since he wasn't sure of anyone's name, Alex gestured toward Carol and said, "This is a friend of my son's…."

"Carol Sommars," she supplied.

Alex was surprised. "I didn't know Peter had a sister."

Carol shot him a look. "I'm not his sister. I'm his mother."

Two

"His mother," Alex echoed, clearly distressed. "But I thought… I assumed when you were with the boys that…"

"She's got to be *way* over thirty!" the blonde with her arm wrapped around Alex's exclaimed, eyeing Carol as possible competition.

Unwilling to be subjected to any debate over her age, Carol politely excused herself and headed blindly toward the ladies' room. The way her luck had been going this evening, it shouldn't be any shock that she'd run into Alex Preston of all people—and his infamous "hot date."

As soon as Carol examined herself in the mirror, she groaned and reached for her purse, hoping to repair the worst of the damage. No wonder Alex had mistaken her for a teenager. She looked like Little Orphan Annie on a bad day.

To add to her consternation, he was waiting for her when she left the restroom.

"Listen," he said apologetically. "We got off to a bad start. Can I do something to help?"

Carol thanked him with a smile. "I appreciate that, but I don't want to ruin your evening. My car broke down and I don't have my cell. I'm just going to call the auto club from here and have them deal with it." She already had the phone number and a quarter in her hand. The pay phone was just outside the restrooms.

"All right." Carol was grateful when he left. She was horrified by the way she'd spoken to him earlier and wanted to apologize—later. Alex had caught her at a bad moment, but he'd made up for it by believing she was Peter's sister. That was almost laughable, but exceptionally flattering.

She finished her call and tried three frustrating times to get through to Peter, but the line was busy. Sitting in the restaurant foyer, she decided to give her son a few more minutes before calling again.

Alex strolled toward her. "Is the auto club coming?"

"They're on their way," she answered cheerfully, flashing him a smile.

"Did you get hold of Peter?"

Her facade melted away. "I tried three times and can't get through. He's probably talking to Melody Wohlford, the love of his life."

"I'll contact James on my cell and have him get in touch with Peter for you. That way, you won't have to worry about it."

"Thank you." She was more gracious this time. "Knowing Peter, he could be on the phone for hours."

Alex stepped away and returned a minute later. "Jim was talking to Peter. Fortunately we have call waiting so I got through to him." He shook his head slightly. "They're doing their algebra homework together, which is probably good because Jim needs all the help he can get."

"In this case it's the blind leading the blind."

Alex grinned, and the mouth she'd found so arrogant and haughty earlier now seemed unusually appealing. His smile was sensual and affable at the same time and Carol liked it a whole lot. It had been a good many years since she'd caught herself staring at a man's mouth. Self-conscious, she dragged her gaze away and looked past him into the restaurant.

Alex glanced uncomfortably at his table, where the other woman was waiting impatiently. "Would you like to join us and have something to eat?" he asked eagerly.

"Oh, no," Carol said, "I couldn't do that."

Alex's gray eyes reached out to hers in blatant appeal. "*Please* join us."

Carol wasn't sure what was going on between Alex and his date, and she was even less sure about putting herself in the middle of it, but… Oh, well, why not?

"All right," she agreed in a tentative voice.

Alex immediately looked grateful. He glanced back at the woman who was glaring at him, clearly displeased that he was paying so much attention to Carol.

However, if her disapproval bothered him, he didn't show it. He led Carol back to the table and motioned for the waitress to bring a menu.

"I'll just have coffee."

As soon as the waitress was gone, Alex introduced the two women. "Bambi, Carol. Carol, Bambi."

"I'm pleased to make your acquaintance," Bambi said formally, holding out her hand. Carol thought she'd never seen longer nails. They were painted a fire engine red and were a good inch in length.

"Alex and I have sons the same age," Carol explained. Her coffee arrived, and she quickly took a sip to disguise her uneasiness.

"Eat your dinner, Alex," Bambi instructed. "There's no need to let our evening be ruined by Carol's problems."

"Yes, please," Carol said hurriedly. "By all means, don't let me keep you from your meal."

Alex reached for the steak knife. "Is Peter trying out for track this year?"

"He wouldn't miss it. I'm positive that's the only reason he's managed to keep his grades up. He knows the minute he gets a D, he's off the team. Who knows what'll happen next year when he takes chemistry."

"Jim's decided to take chemistry his junior year, too."

"I took chemistry," Bambi told them. "They made us look inside a worm."

"That's biology," Carol said kindly.

"Oh, maybe it was."

"I need to apologize for the way I blew up this afternoon," Alex continued. "I felt bad about it afterward. Yelling at Jim in front of his friends was not the thing to do. It's just that there are times my son frustrates me no end."

"Don't worry about it. I feel the same way about Peter when he does something I've specifically asked him not to do." Feeling guilty for excluding Bambi from the conversation, Carol turned toward her and asked, "Do you have children?"

"Heavens, no. I'm not even married."

"Children can be extremely wonderful and extremely frustrating," Carol advised Bambi, who seemed far more interested in gazing lovingly at Alex.

"Jim only has one chore around the house during the week," Alex went on to say. "He's supposed to take out the garbage. Every week it's the same thing. Garbage starts stacking up against the side of the refrigerator until it's as high as the cabinets, and Jim doesn't even notice. I end up having to plead with him to take it out."

"And two days later he does it, right? Peter's the same."

Alex leaned forward and braced his forearms against the table, pushing his untouched steak aside. "Last week, I didn't say a word, wanting to see how long it would take him to notice. Only when something began to stink did he so much as—"

"Pass the salt," Bambi said, stretching her arm between Carol and Alex and reaching for it herself. She shook it over her salad with a vengeance, then slammed it down on the table.

Apparently Alex felt contrite for having ignored his date. He motioned toward her salad. "Bambi's on a diet."

"I am not fat!" Bambi cried. "You said so yourself."

"I…no, I didn't mean to imply that you *needed* to be on a diet, I was just…making small talk."

"Well, if you don't mind, I'd prefer it if you didn't discuss my eating habits."

"Where's the protein?" Carol asked, examining Bambi's plate of greens. "You should be having some protein—eggs, lean meat, that sort of thing."

"Who are you?" Bambi flared. "Jenny Craig?"

"You're right, I'm sorry. It's just that I'm a nurse, and I work with pregnant women, and nutrition is such an important part of pregnancy that—"

"Are you suggesting I'm pregnant?"

"Oh, no, not in the least." Every time Carol opened

her mouth, it seemed she made an even worse mess of the situation. "Look, I think the auto club might need some help finding me. If you'll both excuse me, I'll wait outside."

"You should," Bambi said pointedly. "You're over thirty, so you can take care of yourself."

Carol couldn't get away fast enough. The rain was coming down so hard it was jitterbugging across the asphalt parking lot. Standing just inside the restaurant doorway, Carol buried her hands in her pockets and shivered. She hadn't been there more than a few minutes when Alex joined her.

Before she could say anything, he thrust his hands in his own pockets, sighed and said, "I gave her money for a taxi home."

Carol wasn't sure how to respond. "I hope it wasn't on account of me."

"No." He gave her another of his warm, sensual smiles. "It was a blind date. I should've known better than to let myself get talked into it."

"I went out on one a while ago, and it was a disaster, too." It got worse the longer she was single. Her friends seemed to believe that since she'd been alone for so many years, she should be willing to lower her standards. "How long have you been single?" she asked Alex.

"Two years. What about you?"

"Thirteen."

He turned to face her. "That's a long time."

"So Peter keeps telling me. According to him, I'm about to lose it and need to act fast. I haven't figured out precisely what *it* is, but I have a good idea."

"Jim keeps telling me the same thing. Between him

and Barney—that's the guy who arranged this date—they're driving me crazy."

"I know what you mean. My brother's wife calls me at least once a week and reads me ads from the personal columns. She's now progressed to the Internet, as well. The one she picked out last week really got me. It was something like—Male, thirty-five, dull and insecure, seeks exciting, wealthy female any age who's willing to love too much. Likes string cheese and popcorn. If you can do *Sudoku for Dummies,* I'm the man for you."

"Maybe we should introduce him to Bambi."

They laughed together, and it felt natural.

"Give me your car keys," Alex said suddenly. "I'll check it out and if it's something minor, I might be able to fix it."

"I don't think it is. When the engine died, it sounded pretty final." Nevertheless, she handed him her key ring and stood under the shelter while Alex ran across the parking lot to test her car. She stood on her tiptoes and watched him raise the hood, disappear under it for a few minutes and then close it and come running back to her.

"I think you're right," he said, rubbing the black grease from his hands with a white handkerchief.

"Excuse us, please," a soft feminine voice purred from behind Carol. Bambi slithered past them, her arm looped through that of a much older gentleman. She cast Carol a dirty look and smiled softly in Alex's direction before turning her attention to her most recent admirer. "Now, what were you saying about your hot tub?"

The two were barely out of earshot when Alex started to chuckle. "It didn't take her long, did it?"

"I really am sorry," Carol felt obliged to say. "I feel terrible…as though I personally ruined your evening."

"No," he countered. "On the contrary, you saved me. By the time you arrived, I was trying to figure out how long my patience was going to hold out. I had the distinct impression that before the evening was over I was going to be fighting her off."

Carol laughed. It didn't require much imagination to see Bambi in the role of aggressor. Come to think of it, Carol had dealt with a handful of Bambi's male counterparts over the years.

The rain had diminished and it was drizzling when the auto club van arrived. Alex walked the driver to Carol's car, and together the two men tried to determine what was wrong with her faithful Ford. They decided that whatever the problem was, it couldn't be fixed then and there and that the best thing to do was call a tow truck.

Carol agreed and signed on the dotted line.

"I'll give you a lift home," Alex volunteered.

"Thanks." She was already in his debt; one more thing wouldn't matter.

Within minutes, they were sitting inside Alex's car with the heater running full blast. Carol ran her hands up and down her arms to warm them.

"You're cold."

"I'll be fine in a minute. If I wasn't such a slave to fashion," she said with self-deprecating humor, "I would've worn something heavier than this cotton jacket. But it's the same pale green as my slacks and they go so well together."

"You sound just like Jim. It was forty degrees yesterday morning, and he insisted on wearing a shirt from last summer."

They smiled at each other, and Carol was conscious

of how close they were in the snug confines of Alex's sports car. Her dark eyes met his warm gray ones. Without warning, the laughter faded from Alex's lips, and he studied her face. After viewing the damage earlier, Carol knew her hair hung in springy ringlets that resembled a pad used to scrub pots and pans. She'd done the best she could, brushing it away from her face and securing it at the base of her neck with a wide barrette she'd found in the bottom of her purse. Now she was certain the tail that erupted from her nape must be sticking straight out.

A small lump lodged in her throat, as though she'd tried to swallow a pill without water. "You never did get your dinner, did you?" she asked hastily.

"Don't worry about it."

"Listen, I owe you. Please…stop somewhere and let me treat you. It's after nine—you must be starved." She glanced at her watch and felt a blush heat her cheeks. It'd been longer than she could recall since a man had unsettled her quite this much.

"Don't worry about it," he said again. "I'm a big boy. I'll make myself a sandwich once I get home."

"But—"

"If you insist, you can have me over to eat sometime. All right? When it comes to dinner, Jim and I share the duties. A good home-cooked meal would be welcome."

Carol didn't have any choice but to agree, and she did so by nodding her damp head briskly until she realized she was watering the inside of his car. "Oh, sure, I'd like that." She considered saying that she came from a large Italian family and was an excellent cook, but that would sound too much like the personal ads her sister-in-law, Paula, insisted on reading to her.

"You *do* cook?"

"Oh, yes." Once more she held her tongue. Whereas a few moments earlier she'd been cold, now she felt uncomfortably warm. Her hands were clammy and her stomach was filled with what seemed like a swarm of bees.

They chatted amicably on the rest of the drive to her house. When Alex pulled into her driveway, she turned and smiled at him, her hand on her door handle. "I'm really grateful for all your help."

"No problem."

"And… I'm sorry about what happened with Bambi."

"I'm not," he said, then chuckled. "I'll give you a call later, all right? To check on your car…."

The question seemed to hang between them, heavy with implication. It was the "all right" that told her he was referring to something beyond the state of her car.

"Okay," she said almost flippantly, feeling more than a little light-headed.

"So, tell me about this man who brings color back to my little girl's cheeks," Angelina Pasquale said to Carol as she carried a steaming plate of spaghetti to the table.

Carol's mother didn't know how to cook for three or four; it was twelve or fifteen servings for each and every Sunday dinner. Her two older sisters lived in California now, and only Tony and Carol and their families came religiously for Sunday dinner. Her mother, however, continued to cook as if two or three additional families might walk in unannounced for the evening meal.

"Mama, Alex Preston and I just met last week."

"That's not what Peter said." The older woman wiped her hands on the large apron tied around her thick waist.

Her dark hair, streaked with gray, was tucked into a neat bun. She wore a small gold crucifix that had been given to her by Carol's father forty-two years earlier.

Carol brought the long loaves of hot bread from the oven. "Alex is Jim's father. You remember Peter's friend, don't you?"

"He's not Italian."

"I don't know what he is. Preston might be an English name."

"English," Angelina said as if she was spitting out dirty dishwater. "You gonna marry a non-Italian again?"

"Mama," Carol said, silently laughing, "Alex helped me when my car broke down. I owe him dinner, and I insisted on taking him out to repay him. We're not stopping off at the church to get married on the way."

"I bet he's not even Catholic."

"Mama," Carol cried. "I haven't the faintest clue where he attends church."

"You taking a man to dinner instead of cooking for him is bad enough. But not even knowing if he's Catholic is asking for trouble." She raised her eyes as if pleading for patience in dealing with her youngest daughter; when she lowered her gaze, they fell to Carol's feet. She folded her hands in prayerlike fashion. "You wear pointed-toe shoes for this man?"

"I didn't wear these for Alex. I happen to like them—they're in style."

"They're gonna deform your feet. One day, you'll trip and end up facedown in the gutter like your cousin Celeste."

"Mama, I'm not going to end up in a gutter."

"Your cousin Celeste told her mother the same thing,

and we both know what happened to her. She had to marry a foot doctor."

"Mama, please don't worry about my shoes."

"Okay, but don't let anyone say your mama didn't warn you."

Carol had to leave the room to keep from laughing. Her mother was the delight of her life. She drove Carol crazy with her loony advice, but Carol knew it was deeply rooted in love.

"Carol," Angelina said, surveying the table, "tell everyone dinner's ready."

Peter was in the living room with his younger cousins, who were watching the Dodgers play Kansas City in a hotly contested baseball game.

"Dinner's on the table, guys."

"Just a minute, Mom. It's the bottom of the eighth, with two out." Peter's intense gaze didn't waver from the screen. "Besides, Uncle Tony and Aunt Paula aren't back from shopping yet."

"They'll eat later." Carol's brother Tony and his wife had escaped for the afternoon to Clackamas Town Center, a large shopping mall south of Portland, and they weren't expected back until much later.

"Just a few more minutes," Peter pleaded.

"Mama made zabaglione," Carol said.

The television went off in a flash, and four children rushed into the dining room, taking their places at the table like a rampaging herd of buffalo. Peter was the oldest by six years, which gave him an air of superiority over his cousins.

Sunday dinner at her mother's was tradition. They were a close-knit family and helped one another without question. Her brother had lent her his second car while hers was being repaired. Carol didn't know what she'd do without him. She'd have her own car back in a few days, but Tony's generosity had certainly made her life easier.

Mama treasured these times with her children and grandchildren, generously offering her love, her support and her pasta. Being close to her family was what had gotten Carol through the difficult years following Bruce's death. Her parents had been wonderful, helping her while she worked her way through college and the nursing program, caring for Peter when she couldn't and introducing her to a long list of nice Italian men. But after three years of dealing with Bruce's mental and physical abuse, she wasn't interested. The scars from her marriage ran deep.

"I'll say grace now," Angelina said. They all bowed their heads and closed their eyes.

No one needed any encouragement to dig into the spaghetti drenched in a sauce that was like no other. Carol's mother was a fabulous cook. She insisted on making everything from scratch, and she'd personally trained each one of her three daughters.

"So, Peter," his grandmother said, tearing off a thick piece from the loaf of hot bread. "What do you think of your mother marrying this Englishman?"

"Aw, Grandma, it's not like that. Mr. Preston called and Mom's treating him to dinner 'cause he gave her a ride home. I don't think it's any big deal."

"That was what she said when she met your father. 'Ma,' she told me, 'it's just dinner.' The next thing I know, she's standing at the altar with this non-Italian and six months later the priest was baptizing you."

"Ma! Please," Carol cried, embarrassed at the way

her mother spoke so freely—although by now she should be used to it.

"Preston." Her mother muttered the name again, chewing it along with her bread. "I could accept the man if he had a name like Prestoni. Carol Prestoni has a good Italian ring to it…but Preston. Bah."

Peter and Carol exchanged smiles.

"He's real nice, Grandma."

Angelina expertly wove the long strands of spaghetti around the tines of her fork. "Your mama deserves to meet a nice man. If you say he's okay, then I have to take your word for it."

"Mama, it's only one dinner." Carol wished she'd never said anything to her mother. Alex had called the night before, and although he sounded a little disappointed that she wouldn't be making the meal herself, he'd agreed to let her repay the favor with dinner at a local restaurant Monday night. Her big mistake was mentioning it to her mother. Carol usually didn't say anything to her family when she was going out on a date. But for some reason, unknown even to herself, she'd mentioned Alex as soon as she'd walked in the door after church Sunday morning.

"What color eyes does this man have?"

"Gray," Carol answered and poured herself a glass of ice water.

Peter turned to his mother. "How'd you remember that?"

"I… I just recall they were…that color." Carol felt her cheeks flush. She concentrated on her meal, but when she looked up, she saw her mother watching her closely. "His eyes are sort of striking," she said, mildly irritated by the attention her mother and her son were lavishing on her.

"I never noticed," Peter said.

"A boy wouldn't," Angelina told him, "but your mother, well, she looks at such things."

That wasn't entirely true, but Carol wasn't about to claim otherwise.

As soon as they were finished with the meal, Carol's mother brought out the zabaglione, a rich sherry-flavored Italian custard thick with eggs. Angelina promptly dished up six bowls.

"Mama, zabaglione's high in fat and filled with cholesterol." Since her father's death from a heart attack five years earlier, Carol worried about her mother's health, although she wasn't sure her concern was appreciated.

"So zabaglione's got cholesterol."

"But, Mama, cholesterol clogs the veins. It could kill you."

"If I can't eat zabaglione, then I might as well be dead."

Smiling wasn't what Carol should have done, but she couldn't help it.

When the dishes were washed and the kitchen counters cleaned, Carol and her mother sat in the living room. Angelina rocked in the chair her mother's mother had brought from Italy seventy years earlier. Never one for idle hands, she picked up her crocheting.

It was a rare treat to have these moments alone with her mother, and Carol sat on the sofa, feet tucked under her, head back and eyes closed.

"When am I gonna meet this Englishman of yours?"

"Mama," Carol said with a sigh, opening her eyes, "you're making me sorry I ever mentioned Alex."

"You didn't need to tell me about him. I would have asked because the minute you walked in the house I could see a look in your eyes. It's time, my *bambina.* Peter is growing and soon you'll be alone."

"I… I'm looking forward to that."

Her mother discredited that comment with a shake of her head. "You need a husband, one who will give you more children and bring a sparkle to your eyes."

Carol's heart started thundering inside her chest. "I… I don't think I'll ever remarry, Mama."

"Bah!" the older woman said. A few minutes later, she murmured something in Italian that Carol could only partially understand, but it was enough to make her blush hotly. Her mother was telling her there were things about a man that she shouldn't be so quick to forget.

The soft Italian words brought a vivid image to Carol's mind—an image of Alex holding her in his arms, gazing down at her, making love to her. It shocked her so much that she quickly made her excuses, collected Peter and drove home.

Her pulse rate hadn't decreased by the time she arrived back at her own small house. Her mother was putting too much emphasis on her dinner date with Alex… far more than necessary or appropriate.

As soon as Peter went over to a neighbor's to play video games, Carol reached for the phone. When voice mail kicked in on the fourth ring, she immediately hung up.

On second thought, this was better, she decided, and

dialed again, planning to leave a message. "You're a coward," she muttered as she pushed down the buttons.

Once more the recorded message acknowledged her call. She waited for the greeting, followed by a long beep.

"Hello… Alex, this is Carol… Carol Sommars. About our dinner date Monday night… I'm sorry, but I'm going to have to cancel. Something…has come up. I apologize that thisissuchshortnotice. Bye." The last words tumbled together in her haste to finish.

Her face was flushed, and sweat had beaded on her upper lip as she hung up the phone. With her hand on the receiver, she slowly expelled her breath.

Her mother was right. Alex Preston was the one man who could bring the light back into her eyes, and she'd never been more frightened in her life.

Three

Carol's hand remained closed around the telephone receiver as she heaved in a giant breath. She'd just completed the most cowardly act of her life.

Regretting her actions, she punched out Alex's phone number again, and listened to the recorded message a third time while tapping her foot. At the beep, she paused, then blurted out, "I hope you understand… I mean…oh…never mind." With that, she replaced the receiver, pressed her hand over her brow, more certain than ever that she'd just made a world-class idiot of herself.

Half an hour later, Carol was sorting through the dirty clothes in the laundry room when Peter came barreling into the house.

He paused in the doorway, watching her neatly organize several loads. "Hey, Mom, where's the TV guide?"

"By the television?" she suggested, more concerned about making sure his jeans' pockets were empty before putting them in the washer.

"Funny, Mom, real funny. Why would anyone put it there?"

Carol paused, holding a pair of dirty jeans to her chest. "Because that's where it belongs?" she said hopefully.

"Yeah, but when's the last time anyone found it there?"

Not bothering to answer, she dumped his jeans in the washing machine. "Did you look on the coffee table?"

"It's not there. It isn't by the chair, either."

"What are you so keen to watch, anyway? Shouldn't you be doing your homework?"

"I don't have any…well, I do, but it's a snap."

Carol threw another pair of jeans into the churning water. "If it's so easy, do it now."

"I can't until Jim gets home."

At the mention of Alex's son, Carol hesitated. "I… see."

"Besides, it's time for wrestling, but I don't know what channel it's on."

"Wrestling?" Carol cried. "When did you become interested in *that?*"

"Jim introduced me to it. I know it looks phony and stuff, but I get a kick out of those guys pounding on each other and the crazy things they say."

Carol turned and leaned against the washer, crossing her arms. "Personally I'd rather you did your homework first, and if there's any time left over you can watch television."

"Of course you'd prefer that," Peter said. "You're a mom—you're supposed to think that way. But I'm a kid, and I'd much rather watch Mr. Muscles take on Jack Beanstalk."

Carol considered her son's argument for less than two seconds. "Do your homework."

Peter sighed, his shoulders sagging. "I was afraid you'd say that." Reluctantly he headed toward his bedroom.

It was still light out, and with the wash taken care of, Carol ventured into the backyard, surveying her neatly edged flower beds. Besides perennials, she grew Italian parsley, basil and thyme and a few other herbs in the ceramic pots that bordered her patio. One of these days she was going to dig up a section of her lawn and plant an honest-to-goodness garden.

"Mom…" Peter was shouting her name from inside the house.

She turned, prepared to answer her son, when she saw Alex walk out the back door toward her. Her heart did a somersault, then vaulted into her throat and stayed there for an uncomfortable moment.

"Hello, Alex," she managed to say, suspecting that her face had the look of a cornered mouse. She would gladly have given six months' mortgage payments to remove her messages from his voice mail. It wasn't easy to stand there calmly and not run for the fence.

"Hello, Carol." He walked toward her, his gaze holding hers.

He sounded so…relaxed, but his eyes were a different story. They were like the eyes of an eagle, sharp and intent. They'd zeroed in on her as though he was about to swoop down for the kill.

For her part, Carol was a wreck. Her hands were clenched so tightly at her sides that her fingers ached. "What can I do for you?" she asked, embarrassed by the way her voice pitched and heaved with the simple question.

A brief smile flickered at the edges of Alex's mouth. "You mean you don't know?"

"No…well, I can guess, but I think it would be best if you just came out and said it." She took a couple of steps toward him, feeling extraordinarily brave for having done so.

"Will you offer me a cup of coffee?" Alex asked instead.

The man was full of surprises. Just when she was convinced he was about to berate her for behaving like an utter fool, he casually suggested she make coffee. Perhaps he often confronted emotionally insecure women who left him nonsensical messages.

"Coffee? Of course…come in." Pleased to have something to occupy her hands, Carol hurried into the kitchen. Once she'd added the grounds to the filter and filled the coffeemaker with water, she turned and leaned against the counter, hoping to look poised. She did an admirable job, if she did say so herself—at least for the first few minutes. After all, she'd spent the last thirteen years on her own. She wasn't a dimwit, although she'd gone out of her way to give him that impression, and she hadn't even been trying. That disconcerted her more than anything.

"No, I don't understand," Alex said. He opened her cupboard and took down two ceramic mugs.

"Understand what?" Carol decided playing dumb might help. It had worked with Bambi, and who was to say it wouldn't with her? However, she had the distinct notion that if she suggested they try out a hot tub, Alex would be more than willing.

"I want to know why you won't have dinner with me."

Carol was completely out of her element. She dealt

with pregnancy and birth, soon-to-be mothers and terrified fathers, and she did so without a pause. But faced with one handsome single father, she was a worthless mass of frazzled nerves. Fearing her knees might give out on her, she walked over to the table, pulled out a chair and slumped into it. "I didn't exactly say I wouldn't go out with you."

"Then what did you say?"

She lowered her gaze, unable to meet his. "That… something came up."

"I see." He twisted the chair around and straddled it. The coffeemaker gurgled behind her. Normally she didn't even notice it, but now it seemed as loud as the roar of a jet plane.

"Then we'll reschedule. Tuesday evening at six?"

"I… I have a class… I teach a birthing class to expectant parents on Tuesday evenings." Now, that was brilliant! Who else would attend those classes? But it was an honest excuse. "That's where I'd been when my car broke down in the parking lot of the restaurant where I met you…last Tuesday…remember?"

"The night I helped you," Alex reminded her. "As I recall, you claimed you wanted to repay me. Fact is, you insisted on it. You said I'd missed my dinner because of you and that you'd like to make it up to me. At first it was going to be a home-cooked meal, but that was quickly reduced to meeting at a restaurant in separate cars, and now you're canceling altogether."

"I…did appreciate your help."

"Is there something about me that bothers you? Do I have bad breath?"

"Of course not."

"Dandruff?"

"No."

"Then what is it?"

"Nothing," she cried. She couldn't very well explain that their one meeting had jolted to life a part of her that had lain dormant for years. To say Alex Preston unsettled her was an understatement. She hadn't stopped thinking about him from the moment he'd dropped her off at the house. Every thought that entered her mind was linked to those few minutes they'd spent alone in his car. She was an adult, a professional, but he made her forget everything—except him. In thinking about it, Carol supposed it was because she'd married so young and been widowed shortly afterward. It was as though she didn't know how to behave with a man, but that wasn't entirely true, either. For the past several years, she'd dated numerous times. Nothing serious of course, but friendly outings with "safe" men. One second with Alex, and she'd known instantly that an evening with him could send her secure, tranquil world into a tailspin.

"Wednesday then?"

Carol looked warily across the kitchen, wanting to weep with frustration. She might as well be a good sport about it and give in. Alex wasn't going to let her off the hook without a fuss.

"All right," she said, and for emphasis, nodded. "I'll see you Wednesday evening."

"Fine." Alex stood and twisted the chair back around. "I'll pick you up at seven." He sent her one of his smiles and was gone before the coffee finished brewing.

Once she was alone, Carol placed her hands over her face, feeling the sudden urge to cry. Closing her eyes, however, was a mistake, because the minute she did, her mother's whispered words, reminding her of how good lovemaking could be, saturated her thoughts. That subject was the last thing Carol wanted to think about, especially when the man she wanted to be making love with was the one who had so recently left her kitchen.

Abruptly she stood and poured herself a cup of coffee. It didn't help to realize that her fingers were shaking. What was so terrific about men and sex, anyway? Nothing that *she* could remember. She'd been initiated in the backseat of a car at eighteen with the boy she was crazy in love with. Or the boy she *thought* she was in love with. More likely it had been hormones on the rampage for both of them.

After she'd learned she was pregnant, Carol was never convinced Bruce had truly wanted to marry her. Faced with her hotheaded father and older brother, he'd clearly regarded marriage as the more favorable option.

In the last of her three years with Bruce, he'd been drunk more than he was sober—abusive more than he was considerate. Lovemaking had become a nightmare for her. Feeling violated and vaguely sick to her stomach, she would curl up afterward and lie awake the rest of the night. Then Bruce had died, and mingled with the grief and horror had been an almost giddy sense of relief.

"I don't want a man in my life," she said forcefully.

Peter was strolling down the hallway to his room and stuck his head around the doorway. "Did you say something?"

"Ah..." Carol wanted to swallow her tongue. "Nothing important."

"You look nice," Peter told Carol on Wednesday when she finished with her makeup.

"Thanks," she said, smiling at him. Her attitude toward this evening out with Alex had improved now that she'd had time to sort through her confused emotions. Jim's father was a nice guy, and to be honest, Carol didn't know what had made her react the way she did on Sunday. She was a mature adult, and there was nothing to fear. It wasn't as though she was going to fall into bed with the man simply because she was attracted to him. They'd have the dinner she owed him and that would be the end of it.

But, as much as she would've liked to deny it, Alex was special. For the first time since she could remember, she was physically attracted to a man. And what was wrong with that? It only went to prove that she was a normal, healthy woman. In fact, she should be grateful to Alex for helping her realize just how healthy she was.

"Where's Mr. Preston taking you?" Peter asked, plopping himself down on the edge of the tub.

"Actually I'm taking him, and I thought we'd go to Jake's." Jake's was a well-known and well-loved Portland restaurant renowned for its Cajun dishes.

"You're taking Mr. Preston to Jake's?" Peter cried, his voice shrill with envy. "Are you bringing me back anything?"

"No." As it was, she was stretching her budget for the meal.

"But, Mom—Jake's? You know that's my favorite restaurant in the whole world." He made it sound as though he were a global traveler and connoisseur of fine dining.

"I'll take you there on your birthday." The way she had every year since he was ten.

"But that's another five months," Peter grumbled.

She gave him what she referred to as her "Mother Look," which generally silenced him.

"All right, all right," he muttered. "I'll eat frozen pot pie for the third time in a week. Don't worry about me."

"I won't."

Peter sighed with feeling. "You go ahead and enjoy your *étouffée*."

"I'm sure I will." She generally ordered the shrimp dish, which was a popular item on the menu.

Peter continued to study her, his expression revealing mild surprise. "Gee, Mom, don't you have a heart anymore? I used to be able to get you with guilt, but you hardly bat an eyelash anymore."

"Of course I've got a heart. Unfortunately I don't have the wallet to support it."

Peter seemed about to speak again, but the doorbell chimed and he rushed out of the tiny bathroom to answer it as though something dire would happen if Alex was kept waiting more than a few seconds.

Expelling a sigh, Carol surveyed her appearance in the mirror one last time, confident that she looked her best. With a prepared smile on her face, she headed for the living room.

The instant she appeared, Alex's gaze rushed to hers. The impact of seeing him again was immediate. It was difficult to take her eyes off him. Instead, she found herself thinking that his build suggested finely honed muscles. He was tall, his shoulders were wide and his chest solid. Carol thought he was incredibly good-looking in his pin-striped suit. His face was weathered from working out of doors, his features bronzed by the sun.

So much for the best-laid plans, Carol mused, shaking from the inside out. She'd planned this evening down to the smallest detail. They would have dinner, during which Carol would subtly inform him that she wasn't interested in anything more than a casual friendship, then he'd take her home, and that would be the end of it. Five seconds after she'd walked into the living room, she was thinking about silk sheets and long, slow, heart-melting kisses.

Her mother was responsible for this. Her outrageous, wonderful mother and the softly murmured Italian words that reminded Carol she was still young and it was time to live and love again. She was alive, all right. From the top of her head to the bottom of her feet, she was *alive.*

"Hello, Carol."

"Alex."

"Mom's taking you to Jake's," Peter muttered, not bothering to hide his envy. "She can't afford to bring me anything, but that's okay."

"Peter," she chastised, doubting Alex had heard him.

"Are you ready?"

She nodded, taking an additional moment to gather her composure while she reached for her jacket and purse. Glancing at her son, she felt obliged to say, "You know the rules. I'll call you later."

"You don't need to phone," he said, making a show of rolling his eyes as if to suggest she was going overboard on this parental thing.

"We'll be back early."

Alex cupped her elbow as he directed her to the door. "Not too early," he amended.

By the time they were outside, Carol had bridled her fears. Her years of medical training contributed to her skill at presenting a calm, composed front. And really, there wasn't a reason in the world she should panic....

They talked amicably on the drive into downtown Portland, commenting on such ordinary subjects as the weather, when her car would be fixed and the approach of summer, which they both dreaded because the boys would be constantly underfoot.

Alex managed to find parking on the street, which was a feat in its own right. He opened her car door and took her hand, which he didn't release.

Since Carol had made a reservation, they were immediately seated in a high-backed polished wood booth and greeted by their waiter, who brought them a wine list and recited the specials of the day.

"Jim tells me you're buying him a truck," Carol said conversationally when they'd placed their order.

"So he'd like to believe."

Carol hesitated. "You mean you aren't?"

"Not to the best of my knowledge," Alex admitted, grinning.

Once more, Carol found herself fascinated by his smile. She found herself wondering how his mouth would feel on hers. As quickly as the thought entered her mind, she discarded it.

"According to Jim it's going to be the latest model, red with flames decorating the sidewalls."

"The boy likes to dream," Alex said, leaning back. "If he drives any vehicle during the next two years, it'll be because he's impressed me with his grades and his maturity."

"Oh, Alex," Carol said with a sigh, "you don't know how relieved I am to hear that. For weeks, Peter's been making me feel as though I'm an abusive mother because I'm not buying him a car—or, better yet, a truck. Time and time again he's told me that *you're* buying one for Jim and how sharing the Ford with me could damage his self-esteem, which might result in long-term counseling."

Alex laughed outright. "By the way," he added, "Jim isn't Jim anymore, he's James."

"James?"

"Right. He noticed that his learner's permit listed his name as James Preston, and he's insisting everyone call him that. Actually, I think he came up with the idea after I spoke to him about driving and his level of maturity. Apparently, James is more mature-sounding than Jim."

"Apparently," Carol returned, smiling. "Well, at least if Peter does end up having to go to a counselor, he'll have company."

Their wine arrived and they both commented on its delicious flavor and talked about the quality of Walla Walla area wineries.

Their meal came soon after. The steaming *étouffée* was placed before her, and she didn't experience the slightest bit of guilt when she tasted the first bite. It was as delicious as she remembered.

"Have you been a nurse long?" Alex asked, when their conversation lagged.

"Eight years. I returned to school after my husband was killed, and nursing was a natural for me. I was forever putting Band-Aids on my dolls and treating everyone from my dog to my tolerant mother."

"Next time I have a cold, I'll know who to call," Alex teased.

"Oh, good. And when I'm ready to put the addition on the house, I'll contact you," Carol told him.

They both laughed.

The evening wasn't nearly as difficult as Carol had feared. Alex was easy to talk to, and with the boys as common ground, there was never a lack of subject matter. Before Carol was aware of it, it was nearly ten.

"Oh, dear," she said, sliding from the booth. "I told Peter I'd check in with him. Excuse me a minute."

"Sure," Alex said, standing himself.

Carol was in the foyer on her cell, waiting for Peter to answer when she looked over and saw that Alex was using his own cell phone.

"Hello."

"Peter, it's Mom."

"Mom, you said you were going to phone," he said, sounding offended. "Do you know what time it is? When you say you're going to phone you usually do. James is worried, too. Where have you guys been?"

"Jake's—you knew that."

"All this time?"

"Yes. I'm sorry, sweetheart, the evening got away from us."

"Uh-huh," Peter said and paused. "So you like Mr. Preston?"

Carol hedged. "He's very nice," she murmured.

"Do you think you'll go out with him again? What did you guys talk about? Just how long does it take to eat dinner, anyway?"

"Peter, this isn't the time or place to be having this discussion."

"Were there any leftovers?"

"None."

Her son sighed as if he'd actually been counting on her to bring home her untouched dinner—a reward for the supreme sacrifice of having to eat chicken pot pie, which just happened to be one of his favorites.

"When will you be home? I mean, you don't have to rush on my account or anything, but you'd never let *me* stay out this late on a weeknight."

"I'll be back before eleven," she promised, ignoring his comment about the lateness of the hour. Sometimes Peter forgot who was the adult and who was the child.

"You *do* like Mr. Preston, don't you?" His tone was too smug for comfort.

"Peter," she moaned. "I'll talk to you later." She was about to replace the receiver when she heard him call her name. "What is it now?" she said sharply, impatiently.

He hesitated, apparently taken aback by her brusqueness. "Nothing, I just wanted to tell you to wake me up when you get home, all right?"

"All right," she said, feeling guilty.

She met Alex back at their table. "Everything okay at home?" he asked.

"Couldn't be better." There was no need to inform Alex of the inquisition Peter had attempted. "What about Jim—James?"

"He's surviving."

"I suppose we should think about getting home," Carol suggested, eager now to leave. The evening had flown by. At some point during dinner, her guard had slipped and she'd begun to enjoy his company. There'd been none of the terrible tension that had plagued her earlier.

"I suppose you're right," Alex said with enough reluctance to alarm her. He'd obviously enjoyed their time as much as she had.

They had a small disagreement over the check, which Alex refused to let her take. He silenced her protests by reminding her that she owed him a home-cooked meal and he wasn't accepting any substitutes. After a couple of glasses of wine and a good dinner, Carol was too mellow to put up much of an argument.

"Just don't let Peter know," she said as they walked toward the car. Alex held her hand, and it seemed far too natural, but she didn't object.

"Why?"

"If Peter discovers you paid, he'll want to know why I didn't bring anything home for him."

Alex grinned as he unlocked his car door and held it open. He rested his hand on the curve of her shoulder. "You *will* make me that dinner sometime, won't you?"

Before she realized what she was doing, Carol found herself nodding. She hadn't had a chance to compose herself by the time he'd walked around the front of the car and joined her.

Neither of them spoke on the drive back to her house. Carol's mind was filled with the things she'd planned to tell him. The things she'd carefully thought out beforehand—about what a nice time she'd had, and how she hoped they'd stay in touch and what a good boy Jim—James—was and how Alex was doing a wonderful job raising him. But the trite, rehearsed words refused to come.

Alex pulled into her driveway and turned off the engine. The living room was dark and the curtains drawn. The only illumination was the dim light on her front porch. When Alex turned to face her, Carol's heart exploded with dread and wonder. His look was warm, eager enough to make her blood run hot…and then immediately cold.

"I had a good time tonight." He spoke first.

"I did, too." How weak she sounded, how tentative…

"I'd like to see you again."

They were the words she'd feared—and longed for. The deep restlessness she'd experienced since the night her car had broken down reverberated within her, echoing through the empty years she'd spent alone.

"Carol?"

"I…don't know." She tried to remind herself of what her life had been like with Bruce. The tireless lies, the crazy brushes with danger as though he were courting death. The anger and impatience, the pain that gnawed at her soul. She thought of the wall she'd so meticulously constructed around her heart. A wall years thick and so high no man had ever been able to breach it. "I… don't think so."

"Why not? I don't understand."

Words could never explain her fear.

"Let me revise my statement," Alex said. "I *need* to see you again."

"Why?" she cried. "This was only supposed to be one night…to thank you for your help. I can't give you any more… I just can't and…" Her breath scattered, and her lungs burned within her chest. She couldn't deny the things he made her feel.

"Carol," he said softly. "There's no reason to be afraid."

But there was. Except he wouldn't understand.

He reached up and placed his calloused palm against her cheek.

Carol flinched and quickly shut her eyes. "No…

please, I have to go inside… Peter's waiting for me." She grabbed the door handle, and it was all she could do not to escape from the car and rush into the house.

"Wait," he said huskily, removing his hand from her face. "I didn't mean to frighten you."

She nodded, opening her eyes, and her startled gaze collided with his. She watched as he slowly appraised her, taking in her flushed face and the rapid rise and fall of her breasts. He frowned.

"You're trembling."

"I'm fine…really. Thank you for tonight. I had a marvelous time."

His hand settled over hers. "You'll see me again."

It wasn't until she was safely inside her living room and her heart was back to normal that Carol realized his parting words had been a statement of fact.

Four

"So, Dad, how did dinner go with Mrs. Sommars?" James asked as he poured himself a huge bowl of cornflakes. He added enough sugar to make eating it worth his while, then for extra measure added a couple of teaspoons more.

Alex cupped his steaming mug of coffee as he considered his son's question. "Dinner went fine." It was afterward that stayed in his mind. Someone had hurt Carol and hurt her badly. He'd hardly touched her and she'd trembled. Her dark brown eyes had clouded, and she couldn't seem to get out of his car fast enough. The crazy part was, Alex felt convinced she was attracted to him. He knew something else—she didn't want to be.

They'd spent hours talking over dinner, and it had seemed as though only a few moments had passed. There was no need for pretense between them. She didn't pretend to be anything she wasn't, and he was free to be himself as well. They were simply two single parents who had a lot in common. After two years of dealing with the singles scene, Alex found Carol a refreshing change. He found her alluringly beautiful and at the same time shockingly innocent. During the course of their evening, she'd argued with him over politics, surprised him with her wit and challenged his opinions. In those few hours, Alex learned that this intriguing widow was a charming study in contrasts, and he couldn't wait to see her again.

"Mrs. Sommars is a neat lady," James said, claiming the kitchen chair across from his father. "She's a little weird, though."

Alex looked up from his coffee. "How's that?"

"She listens to opera," James explained between bites. "Sings it, too—" he planted his elbows on the tabletop, leaned forward and whispered "—in Italian."

"Whoa." Alex was impressed.

"At the top of her voice. Peter told me she won't let him play his rap CDs nearly as loud as she does her operas."

"The injustice of it all."

James ignored his sarcasm. "Peter was telling me his grandmother's a real kick, too. She says things like 'Eat your vegetables or I'm calling my uncle Vito in Jersey City.'"

Alex laughed, glanced at his watch and reluctantly got to his feet. He finished the last of his coffee, then set the mug in the sink. "Do you have your lunch money?"

"Dad, I'm not a kid anymore. You don't have to ask me stuff like that."

"Do you?" Alex pressed.

James stood and reached inside his hip pocket. His eyes widened. "I...guess I left it in my room."

"Don't forget your driver's permit, either."

"Dad!"

Alex held up both hands. "Sorry."

He was all the way to the front door when James's shout stopped him.

"Don't forget to pick me up from track practice, all right?"

Alex pointed his finger at his son and calmly said, "I'll be there."

"Hey, Dad."

"What now?" Alex complained.

James shrugged and leaned his shoulder against the door leading into the kitchen. "In case you're interested, Mrs. Sommars will be there, too."

Alex was interested. Very interested.

He left the house and climbed inside his work van, sitting in the driver's seat with his hands on the steering wheel. He mulled over the events of the night before. He'd dated several women recently. Beautiful women, intelligent women, wealthy women. A couple of them had come on hot and heavy. But not one had appealed to him as strongly as this widow with the dark, frightened eyes and the soft, delectable mouth.

A deep part of him yearned to stroke away the pain she held on to so tightly, whatever its source. He longed to watch the anxiety fade from her eyes when she settled into his arms. He wanted her to feel secure enough with him to relax. The urge to hold her and kiss her was strong, but he doubted Carol would let him.

"Okay, Peggy, bear down...push...as hard as you can," Carol urged the young mother-to-be, clutching her hand. Peggy did as Carol asked, gritting her teeth, arching forward and lifting her head off the hospital pillow. She gave it everything she had, whimpering softly with the intensity of the labor pain. When the contraction had passed, Peggy's head fell back and she took in several deep breaths.

"You're doing a good job," Carol said, patting her shoulder.

"How much longer before my baby's born?"

"Soon," Carol assured her. "The doctor's on his way now."

The woman's eyes drifted closed. "Where's Danny? I need Danny."

"He'll be back in a minute." Carol had sent her patient's husband out for a much-needed coffee.

"I'm so glad you're here."

Carol smiled. "I'm glad I'm here, too."

"Danny wants a son so much."

"I'm sure he'll be just as happy with a little girl."

Peggy smiled, but that quickly faded as another contraction started. She reached for Carol's hand, her face marked by the long hours she'd struggled to give birth. Carol had spent the past hour with her. She preferred it when they weren't so busy and she could dedicate herself to one patient. But for more days than she cared to remember, the hospital's five labor rooms had been full, and she spent her time racing from one to the other.

Peggy groaned, staring at a focal point on the wall. The technique was one Carol taught in her classes. Concentrating on a set object helped the mother remember and practice the breathing techniques.

"You're doing just fine," Carol said softly. "Take a deep breath now and let it out slowly."

"I can't do it anymore… I can't," Peggy cried. "Where's Danny? Why's he taking so long?"

"He'll be back any second." Now that her patient was

in the final stages of labor, the pains were stronger and closer together.

Danny walked into the room, looking pale and anxious…and so very young. He moved to the side of the bed and reached for his wife's hand, holding it to his cheek. He seemed as relieved as Peggy when the contraction eased.

Dr. Adams, old and wise and a hospital institution, sauntered into the room, hands in his pockets, smiling. "So, Peggy, it looks like we're going to finally have that baby."

Peggy grinned sheepishly. "I told Dr. Adams yesterday I was sure I was going to be pregnant until Christmas. I didn't think this baby ever wanted to be born!"

Phil Adams gave his instructions to Carol, and within a few minutes the medical team had assembled. From that point on, everything happened exactly as it should. Before another hour had passed, a squalling Danny, Jr., was placed in his father's arms.

"Peggy…oh, Peggy, a son." Tears of joy rained down the young man's face as he sobbed unabashedly, holding his son close.

Although Carol witnessed scenes such as this day in and day out, the thrill of helping to bring a tiny being into the world never left her.

When her shift was over, she showered and changed clothes, conscious of the time. She had to pick Peter up from track practice on her way home, and she didn't want to keep him waiting, although she was the one likely to be twiddling her thumbs.

The first thing Carol noticed when she pulled into the school parking lot was a van with Preston Construction printed in large black letters on the side. Alex. She drew in a shaky breath, determined to be friendly but reserved. After the way she'd escaped from his car the night before, it was doubtful he'd want anything to do with her, anyway.

The fact was, she couldn't blame him. She wasn't sure what had come over her. Then again, she did know…and she didn't want to dwell on it.

She parked a safe distance away, praying that either Peter would be finished soon and they could leave or that Alex wouldn't notice her arrival. She lowered the window to let in the warm breeze, then turned off the ignition and reached for a magazine, burying her face in its pages. For five minutes nothing happened.

When the driver's side of the van opened, Carol realized her luck wasn't going to hold. She did her best to concentrate on a recipe for stuffed pork chops and pretend she hadn't seen Alex approach her. When she glanced up, he was standing beside her car. Their eyes met for what seemed the longest moment of her life.

"Hello again." He leaned forward and rested his hands on her window.

"Hello, Alex."

"Nice day, isn't it?"

"Lovely." It wasn't only his smile that intrigued her, but his eyes. Their color was like a cool mist rising off a pond. Would this attraction she felt never diminish, never stop? Three brief encounters, and she was already so tied up in knots she couldn't think clearly.

"How was your day?" His eyes were relentless, searching for answers she couldn't give him to questions she didn't want him to ask.

She glanced away. "Good. How about yours?"

"Fine." He rubbed a hand along the back of his neck. "I was going to call you later."

"Oh?"

"To see if you'd like to attend the Home Show with me next Friday night. I thought we could have dinner afterward."

Carol opened her mouth to refuse, but he stopped her, laying his finger across her lips, silencing her. The instant his hand touched her, the warm, dizzy feeling began. As implausible, as preposterous as it seemed, a deep physical sensation flooded her body. And all he'd done was lightly press his finger to her lips!

"Don't say no," Alex said, his voice husky.

She couldn't, at least not then. "I… I'll have to check my schedule."

"You can tell me tomorrow."

She nodded, although it was an effort.

"Good… I'll talk to you then."

It wasn't until he'd removed his finger, sliding it across her moist lips, that Carol breathed again.

"What do you mean you can't pick me up from track?" Peter complained the next morning. "How else am I supposed to get home? Walk?"

"From track practice, of all things." She added an extra oatmeal cookie to his lunch because, despite everything, she felt guilty about asking him to find another way home. She was such a coward.

"Mom, coach works us hard—you know that. I was so stiff last night I could barely move. Remember?"

Regretfully, Carol did. A third cookie went into the brown-paper sack.

"What's more important than picking me up?"

Escaping a man. If only Alex hadn't been so gentle. Carol had lain awake half the night, not knowing what was wrong with her or how to deal with it. This thing with Alex, whatever it was, perplexed and bewildered her. For most of her life, Carol had given and received countless hugs and kisses—from relatives, from friends. Touching and being touched were a natural part of her personality. But all Alex had done was press his finger to her lips, and her response…her response still left her stunned.

As she lay in bed, recalling each detail of their brief exchange, her body had reacted again. He didn't even need to be in the same room with her! Alone, in the wee hours of the morning, she was consumed by the need to be loved by him.

She woke with the alarm, in a cold sweat, trembling and frightened, convinced that she'd be a fool to let a man have that kind of power a second time.

"Mom," Peter said impatiently. "I asked you a question."

"Sorry," she said. "What was it you wanted to know?"

"I asked why you aren't going to be at track this afternoon. It's a simple question."

Intuitively Carol knew she wouldn't be able to escape Alex, and she'd be a bigger fool than she already was even to try.

She sighed. "I'll be there," she said, and handed him his lunch.

Peter stood frozen, studying her. "Are you sure you're not coming down with a fever?"

If only he knew…

When Carol pulled into the school parking lot later that same day, she saw Alex's van in the same space as the day before. Only this time he was standing outside, one foot braced against it, fingers tucked in his pockets. His jeans hugged his hips and fit tight across his thighs. He wore a checked work shirt with the sleeves rolled up past his elbows.

When she appeared, he lowered his foot and straightened, his movement leisurely and confident.

It was all Carol could do to slow down and park her car next to his. To avoid being placed at a disadvantage, she opened her door and climbed out.

"Good afternoon," she said, smiling so brightly her mouth felt as though it would crack.

"Hello again."

A lock of his dark hair fell over his forehead, and he threaded his fingers through its thickness, pushing it away from his face.

His gaze tugged at hers until their eyes met briefly, intently.

"It's warmer today than it was yesterday," she said conversationally.

"Yes, it is."

Carol lowered her eyes to his chest, thinking she'd be safe if she practiced what she preached. Find a focal point and concentrate. Only it didn't work as well in situations like this. Instead of saying what had been on her mind most of the day, she became aware of the pattern of his breathing, and how the rhythm of her own had changed, grown faster and more erratic.

"Have you decided?"

Her eyes rushed to his. "About…"

"Going to the home show with me."

She wished it could be the way it had been in the restaurant. There was something about being with a crowd that relaxed her. She hadn't felt intimidated.

"I…don't think seeing each other is such a good idea. It'd be best if we…stayed friends. I can foresee all kinds of problems if we started dating, can't you?"

"The Home Show's going to cause problems?"

"No…our seeing each other will."

"Why?"

"The boys—"

"Couldn't care less. If anything, they approve. I don't understand why there'd be any problems. I like you and you like me—we've got a lot in common. We have fun together. Where's the problem in that?"

Carol couldn't very well explain that when he touched her, even lightly, tiny atoms exploded inside her. Whenever they were within ten feet of each other, the air crackled with sensuality that grew more intense with each encounter. Surely he could feel it, too. Surely he was aware of it.

Carol held a hand to her brow, not knowing how to answer him. If she pointed out the obvious, she'd sound like a fool, but she couldn't deny it, either.

"I…just don't think our seeing each other is a good idea," she repeated stubbornly.

"I do," he countered. "In fact, it appeals to me more every minute."

"Oh, Alex, please don't do this."

Other cars were filling the parking lot, and the two of them had quickly become the center of attention. Carol glanced around self-consciously, praying he'd accept her refusal and leave it at that. She should've known better.

"Come in here," Alex said, opening the side panel to his van. He stepped inside and offered her his hand.

She joined him before she had time to determine the wisdom of doing so.

Alex closed the door. "Now, where were we...ah, yes. You'd decided you don't want to go out with me again."

That wasn't quite accurate, but she wasn't going to argue. She'd rarely wanted anything more than to continue seeing him, but she wasn't ready. Yet... Bruce had been dead for thirteen years. If she wasn't ready by now, she never would be. The knowledge hit her hard, like an unexpected blow, and her eyes flew to his.

"Carol?" He moved toward her. The walls of the van seemed to close in around her. She could smell the scent of his after-shave and the not unpleasant effects of the day's labor. She could feel the heat coming off his body.

Emotion thickened the air, and the need that washed through her was primitive.

She backed as far as she could against the orderly rows of tools and supplies stacked on the shelves. Alex towered above her, studying her with such tenderness and concern that she had to repress the urge to weep.

"Are you claustrophobic?"

She shook her head.

His eyes settled on her mouth, and Carol felt her body's reaction. She unconsciously held her breath so long that when she released it, it burned her chest. If she hadn't been so frightened, she would have marveled at what was happening between them, enjoyed the sensations.

Gently Alex whisked back a strand of hair from her face. At his touch, Carol took a deep breath, but he seemed to gain confidence when she didn't flinch away from him. He cupped her cheek.

Her eyes momentarily drifted shut, and she laid her own hand over his.

"I'm going to kiss you."

She knew it and was unwilling to dredge up the determination to stop him.

His hands slipped to her shoulders as he slowly drew her forward. She considered ending this now. At the least amount of resistance, he would have released her; she didn't doubt that for a second. But it was as if this moment had been preordained.

At first all he did was press his lips to hers. That was enough, more than enough. Her fingers curled into his shirt as he swept his mouth over hers.

She whimpered when he paused.

He sighed.

Her breathing was shallow.

His was harsh.

He hesitated and lifted his head, eyes wide and shocked, his brow creased with a frown. Whatever he'd decided, he didn't share, letting her draw her own conclusions.

Her hands were braced against his chest when he sought her mouth again. This time, the force of his kiss tilted back her head as he fused their lips together, giving her no choice but to respond. The heat, hot enough to scorch them both, intensified.

He kissed and held her, and her lungs forgot it was necessary to breathe. Her heart forgot to beat. Her soul refused to remember the lonely, barren years.

From somewhere far, far away, Carol heard voices. Her ears shut out the sound, not wanting anything or anyone to destroy this precious time.

Alex groaned, not to communicate pleasure but

frustration. Carol didn't understand. Nor did she comprehend what was happening when he released her gradually, pushing himself away. He turned and called, "The door's locked."

"The door?" she echoed. It wasn't until then that she realized Alex was talking to the boys. Peter and Jim were standing outside the van, wanting in. She'd been so involved with Alex that she hadn't even heard her own son calling her name.

"Please open that door," she said, astonished by how composed she sounded. The trembling hadn't started yet, but it would soon, and the faster she made her escape, the better.

"I will in just a minute." He turned back to her and placed his hands on her shoulders. "You're going with me next Friday night. Okay?"

"No..."

He cradled her face with his hands and kissed her once more, forcefully.

She gasped with shock and pleasure.

"I'm not going to argue with you, Carol. We've got something good between us, and I'm not about to let you run away from it."

Standing stock-still, all she could do was nod.

He kissed the tip of her nose, then turned again and slid open the van door.

"What are you doing with Mrs. Sommars?" Jim demanded. "I've been standing out here for the past five minutes."

"Hi, Mom," Peter said, studying her through narrowed eyes. "Everyone else has gone home. Did you know you left your keys in the ignition?"

"I... Mr. Preston was showing me his...van." She

was sure her face was as red as a fire truck, and she dared not meet her son's eyes for fear he'd know she'd just been kissed. Good heavens, he probably already did.

"Are you all right?" Peter asked her.

"Sure. Why?" Stepping down onto the pavement she felt as graceful as a hippo. James climbed in when she'd climbed out; she and Peter walked over to her car.

"I think you might be coming down with something," Peter said as he automatically sat in the driver's seat, assuming he'd be doing the honors. He snapped the seat belt into place. "There were three cookies in my lunch, and no sandwich."

"There were?" Carol distinctly remembered spreading peanut butter on the bologna slices—Peter's favorite sandwich. She must have left it on the kitchen countertop.

"Not to worry, I traded off two of the cookies." He adjusted the rearview mirror and turned the key. He was about to pull out of the parking space when a huge smile erupted on his face. "I'm glad you and Mr. Preston are getting along so well," he said.

Alex sat at his cluttered desk with his hands clasped behind his head, staring aimlessly into space. He'd finally kissed her. He felt like a kid again. A slow, easy smile spread across his face, a smile so full, his cheeks ached. What a kiss it had been. Seductive enough to satisfy him until he could see her again. He was going to kiss her then, too. He could hardly wait.

The intercom buzzed. "Mr. Powers is here."

Alex's smile brightened. "Send him in." He stood and held out his hand to Barney, his best friend. They'd been in college together, roommates their senior year, and had been close ever since. Barney was a rare kind of friend, one who'd seen him through the bad times and the good times and been there for both in equal measure.

"Alex, great to see you." He helped himself to a butterscotch candy from the bowl on the edge of the desk and sat down. "How you doing?"

"Fine." It was on the tip of his tongue to tell Barney about Carol, but everything was so new, he didn't know if he could find the words to explain what he was feeling.

"I've decided to forgive you."

Alex arched his eyebrows. "For what?"

"Bambi. She said you dumped her at the restaurant."

"Oh, that. It wouldn't have worked, anyway."

"Why not?" Barney said, unwrapping the candy and popping it in his mouth.

"I don't have a hot tub."

"She claimed you left with another woman. A bag lady?"

Alex chuckled. "Not exactly."

"Well, you needn't worry, because ol' Barn has met Ms. Right and is willing to share the spoils."

"Barn, listen…"

Barney raised his hand, stopping him. "She's perfect. I swear to you she's bright, beautiful and buxom. The three *b*'s—who could ask for anything more?"

"As I recall, that's what you told me about Bambi," Alex countered, amused by his friend's attempts to find him a wife. It wouldn't be quite as humorous if Barney could stay married himself. In the past fifteen years, his friend had gone through three wives. Each of them bright, beautiful and buxom.

They might've been the best of friends, but when it came to women, their tastes were as dissimilar as could be. Barney went for breasts, whereas Alex was far more interested in brains.

"You're going to let me introduce her, aren't you? I mean, the least you can do is meet Babette."

"No, thanks." The guy had an obsession with *B*-words, Alex thought. The next woman would probably be named Brandy. Or Barbie.

"You won't even have a drink with her?"

"Sorry, not interested."

Barney leaned back and crossed his legs, sucking on the butterscotch candy for a few seconds before he spoke. "She was first runner-up for Miss Oregon several years back. Does that tell you anything?"

"Sure," Alex said, reaching for a candy himself. "She looks terrific in a swimsuit and is interested in world peace."

Barney slowly shook his head. "I don't understand it. I thought you were ready to get back into dating."

"I am."

"Listen, buddy, take a tip from me. Play the field, sample the riches available, then settle down. I'm happier when I'm married, and you will be, too. Frankly, with your looks and money, I don't think you'll have much of a problem. There are plenty of willing prospects out there. Only I notice you aren't doing anything to meet one."

"I don't have to, with you around. You're worse than a matchmaker."

Barney ignored that. "It's time, Alex. You said so

yourself. Just how long are you going to wait? Gloria's been gone two years now. She wouldn't have wanted this."

"I know." At the mention of his late wife, Alex felt a twinge of pain. Time had healed the worst of it, but he'd always remember the agony of watching the woman he loved die.

"You want me to give you Babette's phone number?" his friend asked gently.

Alex shook his head. "Don't bother to introduce me to any more of your women friends."

Barney's mouth sagged open. "But you just admitted I was right, that it's time to get out there and—"

"Remember the bag lady Bambi was telling you about?" Alex asked, interrupting his friend before he could deliver the entire five-minute lecture.

"Yeah, what about her?"

"I'm going to marry her."

Five

"You know, Mom, I like Mr. Preston," Peter announced over dinner as though this was a secret he'd been waiting to share.

"He seems very nice," Carol agreed, reaching for a slice of tomato. She didn't want to say anything more to encourage this topic, so she changed it. "How was school?"

"Fine. James was telling me about all the neat things him and his dad do together, like camping and fishing and stuff like that."

"Your uncle Tony takes you with him."

"Not camping or fishing and besides, it's not the same," Peter murmured. "Uncle Tony's my *uncle*."

Carol paused, her fork over the plump red tomato. "Now, that was profound."

"You don't know what I mean, do you?"

"I guess not," Carol said.

"Going camping with Mr. Preston would be like having a dad."

"How's that?" She took a bite of her roast, then braced her elbows on the tabletop.

"You know."

"No, I don't."

Peter lapsed into silence as he mulled over his thoughts. "I guess what I'm trying to say is that James and I talked it over and we decided we'd like it if the two of you got married."

Carol was so shocked by her son's statement that she stopped eating. Peter was staring at her intently, waiting for some sign or reaction.

"Well?" he pressed. "Is it going to happen? I can tell you like each other."

Chewing furiously, Carol waved her fork at her son, letting it speak for her. The meat, which had been so tender a moment before, took on the quality of leather. The faster she chewed, the more there seemed to be.

"You may think I'm still a kid and I don't know much," Peter continued, "but it didn't take James and me long to figure out what was going on inside his dad's van."

The piece of meat finally slid down Carol's throat. She blinked, uncertain if she could speak normally.

Peter was grinning from ear to ear. "I wish you could've seen your face when Mr. Preston opened the door of the van." Peter didn't bother to disguise his amusement. "If I hadn't been arguing with James, I would've started laughing right then."

"Arguing with James?" Those three words were all she could force past her lips. From the moment the two boys had met on the first day of high school, they'd been the best of friends. In all the months since September, Carol couldn't remember them disagreeing even once.

"We had an argument when we couldn't get his dad to open the van," Peter admitted, his mouth twitching. "Your face was so red, and you had this stunned look, like an alien had hauled you inside his spaceship." Peter's deepening voice vibrated with humor.

"Peter," she demanded, furiously spearing another piece of meat. "What did you argue about?"

"We argued over what his father was doing with you in that van. What kind of son would I be if I didn't defend your…honor?"

"What did James say?"

Peter shrugged. "That his dad wouldn't do anything you didn't want him to."

"*Those* were fighting words?"

Peter shrugged again. "It was the way he said them."

"I see."

Peter scooped himself a second helping of the scalloped potatoes. "Getting back to the marriage part. What do you think?"

"That you need to finish your peas and carrots."

Peter's eyes rushed to hers, but only for a moment. Then he grinned. "Oh, I get it—you want me to mind my own business. Right?"

"Exactly."

"But think about it, Mom. Promise me you'll at least do that much. Meeting Mr. Preston could be the greatest thing that's ever happened to us."

"And when you're finished with your dinner, I want you to stack the dirty dishes in the dishwasher," Carol said without a pause. She ate the last bite of her roast, although it tasted more like rubber.

"Every time I mention Mr. Preston, are you going to give me another job to do?"

Her son was a quick study, Carol would grant him that.

"But you *are* going to sce him again, aren't you?" he asked hopefully.

"The garbage should be taken out, and I noticed that the front flower beds should be weeded. I know you worked out there last Saturday, but—"

"All right, all right," Peter cried, throwing his hands in the air. "Enough—I get the message."

"I certainly hope so," she said and got up to carry her plate to the sink.

Carol waited until Peter was busy with his homework and the dishes were done before she snuck into the kitchen and turned off the light. Then she called Alex. She wasn't sure what she'd do if James answered.

"Hello."

"Alex?" She cupped her hand over the receiver and kept her eye on the doorway in case Peter strolled past. "I can't talk long. Listen, did James happen to have a heart-to-heart discussion with you about...us?"

"Not exactly. He said something about the two of them having a talk about you and me. Why?"

"That's what I'm talking about," she whispered, ignoring his question. "Over dinner Peter threw a grenade at my feet."

"He did *what?*"

"It's a figure of speech—don't interrupt me. He said the two of them argued when you didn't open the van door and afterward decided it would be just great if the two of us...that's you and me...got *married*." She could barely get the words past the growing lump in her throat.

"Now that you mention it, James did say something along those lines."

Carol pressed her back to the kitchen wall, suddenly

needing its support. "How can you be so casual about this?" she burst out.

"Casual?"

"My son announced that he knew what was going on inside the van and that I should've seen my face and that fishing and camping with you would be like having a father." She paused long enough to draw in a breath.

"Carol?"

"And then when I try to calmly warn you what these two are plotting, you make it sound like… I don't know… like we're discussing basketball or something."

"Carol, slow down, I can barely understand you."

"Of course you can't understand me—I'm upset!"

"Listen, this is clearly disturbing you. We need to talk about it. Can you meet me for lunch tomorrow?"

"I'm working tomorrow. And can't go out for lunch, for heaven's sake—I'm a nurse."

"Okay, I'll meet you in the hospital cafeteria at noon."

Just then Peter strolled nonchalantly into the kitchen. He stood in the doorway, turned on the light and stared curiously at his mother.

"Sure, Mama, whatever you say," Carol said brightly—too brightly.

"Mama?" Alex echoed chuckling. "Okay, I get the picture. I'll see you tomorrow at noon."

Agreeing to meet Alex at the hospital was a mistake. Carol should have realized it immediately, but she'd been so concerned with the shocking news Peter had delivered over dinner that she didn't stop to consider what could happen once she was spotted with Alex in the gossip-rich cafeteria at Ford Memorial.

"Sorry I'm late," Carol murmured as she joined him

at a table for two, sliding her orange tray across from his. A couple of nurses from surgery walked past, glanced at Alex, then at Carol, and then back at Alex. Carol offered her peers a weak smile. Once she returned to the obstetrics ward, she was in for an inquisition that could teach the Spaniards a lesson.

"I haven't been here long." Alex grinned and reached for his ham sandwich. "How much time do you have?"

Carol checked her watch. "Forty-five minutes."

He opened a carton of milk. "All right. Do you want to tell me what upset you so much about last night?"

"I already did."

"Refresh my memory."

Carol released a slow sigh. Several more of her friends had seen her and Alex, including Janice Mandle, her partner in the birthing classes. By this time, the probing stares being sent their way were rattling Carol's shaky composure. "Apparently James and Peter have come to some sort of agreement…about you and me."

"I see." Humor flashed through his eyes like a distant light.

"Alex," she cried. "This is serious. We've gone out to dinner *once,* and our sons are talking about where the four of us are going to spend our honeymoon."

"And that bothers you?"

"Of course it does! And it should bother you, too. They already have expectations about how our relationship's going to develop. I don't think it's a healthy situation, and furthermore, they know about next Friday." She took a bite of her turkey sandwich and picked up her coffee.

"You mean that we're going to the Home Show?"

Carol nodded. "Yes, but I think we should forget the

whole thing. We're looking at potential trouble here, and I for one have enough problems in my life without dealing with the guilt of not giving my son a father to take him fishing." She breathed deeply, then added, "My brother doesn't camp or fish. Actually no one in our family does."

Alex held his sandwich in front of his mouth. He frowned, his eyes studying hers, before he lowered his hands to the plate. "I beg your pardon?"

Carol shook her head, losing patience. "Never mind."

"No," he said after a thoughtful pause. "Explain to me what taking Peter fishing has to do with us seeing each other Friday night and your brother Tony who doesn't camp and hunt."

"Fish," Carol corrected, "although he doesn't hunt, either."

"That part makes sense."

Curious stares seemed to come at Carol from every corner of the room. Alex had finished his sandwich, and Carol wasn't interested in eating any more of hers.

"Do you want to go outside?" she suggested.

"Sure."

Once they'd disposed of their trays, Carol led him onto the hospital grounds. The weather had been beautiful for April. It wouldn't last much longer. The rains would return soon, and the "Rose City" would blossom into the floral bouquet of the Pacific Northwest.

With her hands in the front pockets of her uniform, Carol strolled in the sunshine, leading them away from the building and toward the parking lot. She saw his van in the second row and turned abruptly in the opposite direction. That construction van would be nothing but a source of embarrassment to her now.

"There's a pond over this way." With its surrounding green lawns, it offered relative privacy.

An arched bridge stretched between its banks, and goldfish swam in the cold water. Sunlight rippled across the pond, illuminating half, while the other half remained in enigmatic shadow. In some ways, Carol felt her budding relationship with Alex was like sun and shadow. When she was with him, she felt as though she was stepping into the light, that he drew her away from the shade. But the light was brilliant and discomfiting, and it illuminated the darkest corners of her loneliness, revealing all the imperfections she hadn't noticed while standing numbly in the shadows.

Although gentle, Alex had taught her painful lessons. Until she met him, she hadn't realized how hungry she was to discover love in a man's arms. The emptiness inside her seemed to echo when she was with him. The years hadn't lessened the pain her marriage had brought into her life, but seemed to have intensified her self-doubts. She was more hesitant and uncertain now than she'd been the year following Bruce's death.

With his hand on her elbow, Alex guided her to a park bench. Once they were seated, he reached for her hand, lacing their fingers together.

"I don't want you to worry about the boys," he said.

She nodded and lowered her eyes. She couldn't help being worried, but Alex didn't understand her fears and revealed no distress of his own. That being the case, she couldn't dwell on the issue.

He raised her fingers to his mouth. "I suppose what I'm about to say is going to frighten you even more."

"Alex…no."

"Shh, it needs to be said." He placed his finger across

her lips to silence her, and who could blame him, she mused. It had worked so well the first time. "The boys are going to come to their own conclusions," he continued, "and that's fine, they would anyway. For Peter to talk so openly with you about our relationship is a compliment. Apparently he felt comfortable enough to do so, and that reflects well on the kind of mother you are."

Carol hadn't considered it in those terms, but he was right. She and Peter were close.

"Now, about you and me," Alex went on, "we're both adults."

But Carol felt less mature than an adolescent when it came to Alex. She trembled every time she thought of him, and that was far more often than she would've liked. When he touched and kissed her, her hormones went berserk, and her heart seemed to go into spasms. No wonder she was frightened by the things Alex made her experience.

"I like you, and I'm fairly confident you like me."

She agreed with a sharp nod, knowing it wouldn't do any good to deny it.

"The fact is, I like everything about you, and that feeling increases whenever we're together. Now, if it happens that this attraction between us continues, then so be it. Wonderful. Great. It would be a big mistake for us to allow two teenage boys to dictate our relationship. Agreed?"

Once more, Carol nodded.

"Good." He stood, bringing her with him. "Now we both have to get back to work." Tucking her hand in the crook of his arm, he strode back toward the parking lot, pausing when he came to his van. He opened the door, then turned to face her.

"It seems to me we should seal our agreement."

"Seal it? I don't understand." But she did.... His wonderful, mist-gray eyes were spelling out exactly what he meant.

He caressed her cheek, then traced the outline of her lips. Whatever it was about his touch that sent her heart into such chaos, Carol couldn't understand. She reacted by instinct, drawing his finger between her lips, touching it with the tip of her tongue. The impact of her action showed in his eyes with devastating clarity.

He leaned forward and slipped his finger aside, replacing it with his mouth. His kiss was exquisitely slow and wildly erotic.

When he broke away they were both shaking. Carol stared up at him, her breath ragged, her lips parted and eager.

"I've got to get back to work...." she whispered.

"I know," Alex said. But he didn't make any effort to leave.

Instead he angled his head and dropped tiny kisses on her neck, then her ear, taking the lobe in his mouth before trailing his lips in heart-stopping increments back to hers. She was ready for him this time, more than ready.

The sound of a car door slamming somewhere in the distance abruptly returned them to the real world. Carol leaped back, her eyes startled, her breathing harsh and uneven. She smoothed her hands down the front of her uniform, as though whisking away wrinkles. She'd been kissing him like a lover and in broad daylight! To her chagrin, Alex didn't look at all dismayed by what had happened between them, just pleased.

"I wish you hadn't done that," she said, knowing he

wasn't the only one to blame—but at the moment, the most convenient.

"Oh, baby, I don't regret a thing."

She folded her arms over her chest. "I've got to get back inside." But she had to wait until the flush of desire had left her face and her body had stopped trembling.

"It seems to me," Alex said with a smile of supreme confidence, "that if kissing you is this good, then when we finally make love it'll be downright dangerous." With that, he climbed into the driver's seat, closed the door and started the engine.

"You didn't call me," Carol's mother complained the following Friday evening. "All week I waited for you to phone and tell me about your date with the non-Italian."

"I'm sorry, Mama," Carol said, glancing at the kitchen clock. Alex was due to pick her up for the Home Show in ten minutes. Peter was staying overnight at a friend's, and she was running behind schedule as it was. The last thing she wanted to do was argue with her mother.

"You *should* be sorry. I could have died this week and you wouldn't have known. Your uncle in Jersey City would've had to call you and tell you your mother was dead."

"Mama, Peter started track this week, and we've gotten home late every single night."

"So don't keep me in suspense. Tell me."

Carol paused. "About what?"

"Your date with that Englishman. Did he take you to bed?"

"Mama!" Sometimes the things her mother said actually shocked Carol. "Of course not."

"It's a shame. Are you seeing him again? But don't wear those shoes with the pointed toes or he'll think you're a loose woman. And to be on the safe side, don't mention your cousin Celeste."

"Mama, I can't talk now. Alex will be here any minute—we're going to the Home Show. His company has a booth there, and it'd be impolite to keep him waiting."

"Do you think he'll convert?"

"Mama, I'm not marrying Alex."

"Maybe not," her mother said with a breathless sigh, "but then again, who knows?"

The doorbell chimed, and Carol, who'd been dreading this evening from the moment she'd agreed to it, was flooded with a sense of relief.

"Bye, Mama."

Angelina said her farewells and added something about bringing Alex over to try her pasta. Carol was putting down the receiver by the time her mother had finished issuing her advice.

The doorbell rang again as Carol hurried into the living room. She rushed to open the door. "I'm sorry it took me so long to answer. My mother was on the phone."

"Did she give you any advice?" Alex teased.

"Just a little. She said it might not be a good idea if I mentioned my cousin Celeste."

"Who?"

"Never mind." Carol laughed a little nervously. Alex looked too good to be true, and the warm, open appreciation in his eyes did wonders for her self-esteem.

"You were worth the wait."

Carol could feel the blush in her cheeks. She wasn't used to having men compliment her, although her family was free with praise and always had been. This was different, however. Alex wasn't family.

His eyes compelled her forward, and she stepped toward him without question, then halted abruptly, realizing she'd very nearly walked into his arms.

"I'll…get my purse." She turned away, but his hand at her shoulder turned her back.

"Not yet."

"Alex… I don't think we should—"

But that was all the protest she was allowed. She closed her eyes as he ran his hand through her hair, then directed her mouth to his with tender restraint. He kissed her lightly at first, until she was pliant and willing in his arms….

When he pulled away from her, she slowly, languorously, opened her eyes to meet his.

"Don't look at me like that," he groaned. "Come on, let's get out of here before we end up doing something we're not ready to deal with yet."

"What?" Carol asked, blinking, still too dazed to think coherently.

"I think you know the answer to that."

They were in Alex's car before either of them spoke again. "If it's okay with you, I've got to stop at the office and pick up some more brochures," Alex said. "We're running low already."

"Of course it's okay," Carol told him. It was a good thing she was sitting down because her legs seemed too weak to support her. She was sure her face was flushed, and she'd rarely felt this shaky.

Her mind became her enemy as Alex headed toward the freeway. Try as she might, she couldn't stop thinking about how he'd felt against her. So strong and warm.

A thin sheen of perspiration moistened her upper lip, and she swiped at it, eager to dispel the image that refused to leave her mind.

"How far is your office?" Carol asked after several strained minutes had passed. Alex seemed unusually quiet himself.

"Another quarter of an hour."

Not knowing how else to resume the conversation, she dropped it after that.

"Peter's staying with Dale tonight?" he finally asked.

"Yes. James, too?"

"Yes."

That was followed by ten more minutes of silence. Then Alex exited the freeway.

Carol curled her fingers around the armrest when he stopped at the first red light. The district was an industrial area and well lit.

As soon as he pulled into a side street, she saw his company sign. She'd never asked about his business and was impressed when she saw a small fleet of trucks and vans neatly parked in rows outside. He was apparently far more successful than she'd assumed.

Unlocking the door, Alex let her precede him inside. He flicked a switch, and light immediately flooded the office. One entire wall was lined with filing cabinets. Three desks, holding computers, divided the room. Carol didn't have time to give the room more than a fleeting glance as Alex directed her past the first desk and into another large office. She saw his name on the door.

The room was cluttered. The top of his desk looked as if a cyclone had hit it.

"The brochures are around here someplace," he muttered, picking up a file on a corner of the credenza. "Help yourself to a butterscotch candy."

"Thanks." As Carol reached for one, her gaze fell on the two framed photographs hidden behind a stack of computer printouts. The top of a woman's head showed on one of the photos, but that was all she could see. The second one was of James.

"I've got to get organized one of these days," Alex was saying.

Curious, Carol moved toward the credenza and the two photographs. "Who's this?" She asked, lifting the picture of the woman. She was beautiful. Blonde. Blue-eyed. Wholesome. Judging by the hairstyle and clothes, the picture had been taken several years earlier.

Alex paused. "That's Gloria."

"She was your wife?"

Alex nodded, pulled out the high-backed cushioned chair and sank into it. "She died two years ago. Cancer."

It was all Carol could do to hold on to the picture. The pain in his voice stabbed through her.

"I… I thought you were divorced."

"No," Alex said quietly.

Carol continued to study the beautiful woman in the photo. "You loved her, didn't you?"

"So much that when the time came, I wanted to die with her. Yes, I loved her."

With shaking hands, Carol replaced the photograph. Her back was to Alex, and she briefly closed her eyes. She made a rigorous effort to smile when she turned to face him again.

He frowned. "What's wrong?"

"Nothing," she said breezily.

"You look pale all of a sudden. I thought you knew.... I assumed James or Peter had told you."

"No—neither of them mentioned it."

"I'm sorry if this comes as a shock."

"There's no reason to apologize."

Alex nodded, sighed and reached for her hand, pulling her down into his lap. "I figured you'd understand better than most what it is to lose someone you desperately love."

Six

"Gloria had problems when James was born," Alex began. His hold on Carol's waist tightened almost painfully, but she was sure he wasn't aware of it. "The doctors said there wouldn't be any more children."

"Alex, please, there's no need to tell me this."

"There is," he said. "I want you to know. It's important to me…."

Carol closed her eyes and pressed her forehead against the side of his head. She knew intuitively that he didn't often speak of his late wife, and that he found it difficult to do so now.

Alex wove his fingers into her hair. "In the years after Jim's birth, Gloria's health was never good, but the doctors couldn't put their finger on what was wrong. She was weak and tired a lot of the time. It wasn't until Jim was in junior high that we learned she had leukemia—myelocytic leukemia, one of the most difficult forms to treat." He paused and drew in an unsteady breath.

"Alex," she pleaded, her hands framing his face. "Don't, please—this is obviously so painful for you."

But the moment her eyes met his, she knew nothing she said or did would stop him. She sensed that only sharing it now, with her, would lessen the trauma of his memories.

"We did all the usual things—the chemotherapy, the other drugs—but none of it helped, and she grew steadily worse. Later, when it was clear that nothing else could be done, we opted for a bone-marrow transplant. Her sister and mother flew in from New York, and her sister was the better match. But…that didn't work, either."

Carol stroked his cheek, yearning to do anything she could to lessen the pain.

He hesitated and drew in a quavering breath. "She suffered so much. That was the worst for me to deal with. I was her husband, and I'd sworn to love and protect her, and there wasn't a thing I could do…not a single, solitary thing."

Tears moistened Carol's eyes, and she struggled to keep them at bay.

Alex's voice remained firm and controlled, but Carol recognized the pain he was experiencing. "I didn't know what courage was until I watched Gloria die," he whispered. He closed his eyes. "The last three weeks of her life, it was obvious she wasn't going to make it. Finally she fell into a coma and was put on a respirator. The doctors knew she'd never come out of it and so did the nurses. I could see them emotionally removing themselves, and I couldn't bear it. I became a crazy man, refusing to leave her side, letting no one care for her but me. I held on to her hand and silently willed her to live with every breath I took. I honestly believe I kept her alive by the sheer force of my will. I was afraid to leave her, afraid that when I did, she'd slip silently into death. Eventually that was exactly what happened. I left her because Jim needed me and because I knew that at some point I'd have to leave. I sat in the hospital waiting room with my son, telling him about his mother, and suddenly a pain, an intense stabbing pain, shot through me—" he hesitated and gave a ragged sigh "—and in that instant, I knew she was gone. I've never felt anything like it. A few minutes later, a nurse came for me. I can remember that scene so vividly—my mind's played it back so many times.

"I stood up and Jim stood with me, and I brought my son as close to my side as I could, looked the nurse in the eye and said, 'She's gone, isn't she?' The nurse nodded and Jim started to cry and I just stood there, dazed and numb. I don't remember walking back to Gloria's room, but somehow I found myself there. I lifted her into my arms and held her and told her how sorry I was that I'd been so stubborn and selfish, keeping her with me those three weeks, refusing to let her die. I told her how I would much rather have been with her, how I'd wanted to hold her hand as she stepped from one life into the next."

By now Carol was weeping softly, unabashedly.

Alex's fingers stroked her hair. "I didn't mean for you to cry," he whispered, and his regret seemed genuine. "You would have liked her."

Carol had felt the same way from the first moment she'd seen Gloria's photograph. Nodding, she hid her face in the strong curve of his neck.

"Carol," he whispered, caressing her back, "look at me."

She sniffled and shook her head, unwilling to let

him witness the strength of her emotion. It was one thing to sit on his lap, and entirely another to look him in the eye after he'd shared such a deep and personal part of himself.

His lips grazed the line of her jaw.

"No," she cried softly, her protest faint and nearly inaudible, "don't touch me…not now." He'd come through hell, suffered the torment of losing his wife, and he needed Carol. He was asking for her. But her comfort could only be second-best.

"Yes," he countered, lifting her head so he could look at her. Against her will, against her better judgment, her gaze met his. His eyes were filled with such hunger that she all but gasped. Again and again, they roamed her face, no doubt taking in the moisture that glistened on her cheeks, the way her lips trembled and the staggering need she felt to comfort him. Even if that comfort was brief, temporary, a momentary solace.

"I'm sorry I upset you." He wove his fingers into her hair and directed her lips to his. His mouth was warm and moist and gentle. No one had ever touched her with such tenderness and care. No kiss had ever affected her so deeply. No kiss had ever shown her such matchless beauty.

Tears rained down Carol's face. Sliding her fingers through his hair, she held him close. He was solid and muscular and full of strength. His touch had filled the hollowness of her life and, she prayed, had helped to ease his own terrible loneliness.

"Carol," he breathed, sounding both stunned and dismayed, "what is it? What's wrong?"

"Nothing," she whispered. "Everything."

"I'm sorry…so sorry," he said in a low voice.

Confused and uncertain, Carol turned to face him. "You are? Why?"

"For rushing you. For thinking of my own needs instead of yours."

"No…" She shook her head, incapable of expressing what she felt.

"Are you going to be all right?"

She nodded, still too shaken to speak.

He placed his hands on the curve of her shoulder and kissed the crown of her head. "Thank you."

"For what?" Reluctantly her eyes slid to his.

"For listening, for being here when I needed you."

All she could manage in response was a tremulous smile.

For the rest of the evening, Alex was a perfect gentleman. He escorted her to the Home Show, where they spent several hours wandering from one display to another, discussing the ideas and products represented. They strolled hand in hand, laughing, talking, debating ideas. Carol was more talkative than usual; it helped disguise her uneasiness. She told him about her plan to dig up a portion of her back lawn and turn it into an herb garden. At least when she was talking, her nerve endings weren't left uncovered and she didn't have to deal with what had happened a few hours before…

After they'd toured the Home Show, Alex took her out to eat at a local Greek restaurant. By that time of the evening, Carol should have been famished, since they were having dinner so late. But whatever appetite she'd had was long gone.

When Alex dropped her off at the house, he kissed

her good-night, but if he was expecting an invitation to come inside, he didn't receive one.

Hours later, she lay staring at the ceiling, while shadows of the trees outside her window frolicked around the light fixture like dancing harem girls. Glaring at the clock radio, Carol punched her pillow several times and twisted around so she lay on her stomach, her arms cradling her head. She *should* be sleepy. Exhausted. Drained after a long, trying week. Her job took its toll in energy, and normally by Friday night, Carol collapsed the moment she got into bed, waking refreshed Saturday morning.

She would've liked to convince herself that Alex had nothing to do with this restless, trapped feeling. She tried to analyze what was bothering her so much. It wasn't as though Alex had never kissed her before this evening. The impact he had on her senses shouldn't come as any surprise. She'd known from the first night they'd met that Alex had the power to expose a kaleidoscope of emotions within her. With him, she felt exhilarated, excited, frightened, reborn.

Perhaps it was the shock of passion he'd brought to life when he'd kissed her. No, she mused, frowning, she'd yearned for him to do exactly that even before they'd arrived at his office.

Squeezing her eyes closed, she tried to force her body to relax. She longed to snap her fingers and drift magically into the warm escape of slumber. It was what she wanted, what she needed. Maybe in the morning, she'd be able to put everything into perspective.

Closing her eyes, however, proved to be a mistake. Instead of being engulfed by peace, she was confronted with the image of Alex's tormented features as he told her about Gloria. *I figured you'd understand better than most what it is to lose someone you desperately love.*

Carol's eyes flew open. Fresh tears pooled at the edges as her sobs took control. She'd loved Bruce. She'd hated Bruce.

Her life ended with his death and her life had begun again.

It was the end; it was the beginning.

There hadn't been tears when he'd died—not at first but later. Plenty of tears, some of profound sadness, and others that spoke of regrets. But there was something more. A release. Bruce had died, and at the same moment, she and Peter had been set free from the prison of his sickness and his abuse.

The tears burned her face as she sobbed quietly, caught in the horror of those few short years of marriage.

Bruce shouldn't have died. He was too young to have wasted his life. Knowing he'd been drunk and with another woman hadn't helped her deal with the emotions surrounding his untimely death.

I figured you'd understand better than most what it is to lose someone you desperately love. Only Carol didn't know. Bruce had destroyed the love she'd felt for him long before his death. He'd ravaged all trust and violated any vestiges of respect. She'd never known love the way Alex had, never shared such a deep and personal commitment with anyone—not the kind Alex had shared with Gloria, not the kind her mother had with her father.

And Carol felt guilty. Guilty. Perhaps if she'd been a better wife, a better mother, Bruce would have stopped drinking. If she'd been more desirable, more inventive in the kitchen, a perfect housekeeper. Instead she felt guilty. It might not be rational or reasonable but it was how she felt.

"Well?" Peter asked as he let himself in the front door the next morning. He dumped his sleeping bag on the kitchen floor, walked over to Carol and dutifully kissed her cheek.

"Well, what?" Carol said, helping herself to a second cup of coffee. She didn't dare look in the mirror, suspecting there were dark smudges under her eyes. At most, she'd slept two hours all night.

"How did things go with Mr. Preston?"

Carol let the steam rising from her coffee mug revive her. "You never told me James's mother had died."

"I didn't? She had leukemia."

"So I heard," Carol muttered. She wasn't angry with her son, and Alex's being a widower shouldn't make a whole lot of difference, but for reasons she was only beginning to understand, it did.

"James said it took his dad a long time to get over his mother's death."

Carol felt her throat muscles tighten. He wasn't over her, not really.

"James keeps a picture of her in his room. She was real pretty."

Carol nodded, remembering the bright blue eyes smiling back at her from the framed photograph in Alex's office. Gloria's warmth and beauty were obvious.

"I thought we'd work in the backyard this morning," Carol said, as a means of changing the subject.

"Aw, Mom," Peter groaned. "You know I hate yard work."

"But if we tackle everything now, it won't overwhelm us next month."

"Are you going to plant a bunch of silly flowers again? I don't get it. Every year you spend a fortune on that stuff. If you added it all up, I bet you could buy a sports car with the money."

"Buy who a sports car?" she challenged, arms akimbo.

"All right, all right." Peter clearly didn't want to argue. "Just tell me what I have to do."

Peter's attitude could use an overhaul, but Carol wasn't in the best of moods herself. Working with the earth, thrusting her fingers deep into the rich soil, was basic to her nature and never more than now.

The sun was out when Carol, dressed in her oldest pair of jeans and a University of Oregon sweatshirt, knelt in front of her precious flower beds. She'd tied a red bandanna around her head, knotting it at the back.

Peter brought his portable CD player outside and plugged it into the electrical outlet on the patio. Next, he arranged an assortment of CDs in neat piles.

Carol glanced over her shoulder and groaned inwardly. She was about to be serenaded with music that came with words she found practically impossible to understand. Although maybe that was a blessing…

"Just a minute," Peter yelled and started running toward the kitchen.

That was funny. Carol hadn't even heard the phone ring. Ignoring her son, she knelt down, wiping her wrist under her nose. The heat was already making her perspire. Bending forward, she dug with the trowel, cultivating the soil and clearing away a winter's accumulation of weeds.

"Morning."

At the sound of Alex's voice, Carol twisted around to confront him. "Alex," she whispered. "What are you doing here?"

"I came to see you."

"Why?"

He joined her, kneeling beside her on the lush, green grass. His eyes were as eager as if it had been weeks since he'd seen her instead of a few hours.

"What are you doing here?" she demanded again, digging more vigorously than necessary. She didn't want to have this conversation. It was too soon. She hadn't fully recovered from their last encounter and was already facing another one.

"I couldn't stay away," he said, his voice harsh and husky at once, and tinged with a hint of anger as if the lack of control bothered him. "You were upset last night, and we both ignored it instead of talking about it the way we should have."

"You were imagining things," she said, offering him a false smile.

"No, I wasn't. I felt guilty, too."

"Guilty?" she cried. "Whatever for?"

"Because I told you about Gloria and didn't ask about your husband. It would've been the perfect time for you to tell me."

Carol's stomach lurched. "That was a long time ago…and best forgotten."

"But you loved him and were saddened by his death, and I should've realized that talking about Gloria would be especially painful for you. I should have been more sensitive."

She shut her eyes. "There's no reason to feel guilty.

You talked openly and honestly, and I appreciated knowing about your wife."

"Maybe so," Alex conceded, "but I frightened you, and now you're feeling confused."

"Nothing could be further from the truth." She continued to work, dragging the trowel through the damp soil.

Alex chuckled softly. He gripped her shoulders and turned her toward him as he scanned her features. "You shouldn't lie, Carol Sommars. Because you blush every time you do."

"That's ridiculous." As if on cue, she felt her cheeks grow pink. Carol groaned inwardly, furious with Alex and even more so with herself.

"No, it isn't ridiculous." He paused, and his mouth quivered as he studied her. "You're doing it now."

"Where are the boys?"

Alex's chuckle deepened. "Don't try changing the subject—it isn't going to work."

"Alex, please."

"Hey, Mom, you'll never guess what!"

Grateful for the distraction, Carol dragged her eyes away from Alex and turned to her son, who stood on the patio, looking exceptionally pleased.

"What is it, Peter?"

"James and Mr. Preston brought over one of those fancy, heavy-duty tillers. They're going to dig up that garden space you've been talking about for the past two summers."

Carol's gaze flew back to Alex's, full of unspoken questions.

"You said something last night about wanting to grow an herb garden, didn't you?"

"Yes, but why… I mean, you don't have to do this." She felt flustered and surprised and overwhelmed that he'd take a casual comment seriously and go out of his way to see that her wish was fulfilled.

"Of course I don't have to, but I want to. Peter and James and I are your willing servants, isn't that right, boys?" Neither bothered to answer, being far more interested in sorting through the CDs Peter had set out.

Two hours later, Carol had been delegated to the kitchen by all three men, who claimed she was a world-class nuisance.

"Mom," Peter said, "do something constructive like make lunch. You're in the way here."

Slightly taken aback by her son's assessment of her role, Carol muttered under her breath and did as he asked. Her ego suffered further when James sent his friend a grateful glance. Even Alex seemed pleased to have her out from under their capable feet.

Twenty minutes later, Alex entered the kitchen. He paused when he saw her stacking sandwiches on a platter. He walked over to her, slipped his arms around her waist and nuzzled her neck.

"Alex," she protested in a fierce whisper, "the boys will see you."

"So?"

"So, what they're thinking is bad enough without you adding fuel to the fire."

"They're too busy to care."

"I care!"

His growl was low as he slid his hand from her navel up her midriff. "I know."

"If you don't stop I'll… I'll… I'm not sure what I'll do—but it won't be pleasant." Her threat was an empty one, and Alex knew it as well as she did. She was trembling the way she always did when he touched her. The more intimate the caress, the more she shivered.

"I told the boys I was coming inside to pester you, and I'm nothing if not a man of my word," Alex informed her, clearly relishing her shyness.

"Alex..."

"Don't say it," he murmured. "I already know—this isn't the time or the place. I agree, but I don't have to like it." Slowly and with great reluctance, he released her.

Carol was aware of every nuance of this man. He made the most innocent caress sweet with sensations. His touch only created a need for more. Much more.

Once he'd released her, Carol sighed with relief—or was it regret? She no longer had any idea. She carried the platter of sandwiches to the table and brought out a pitcher of fresh lemonade.

Alex pulled out a chair and sat down. "I like watching you move," he whispered. "I like touching you even more."

"Alex...please don't. You're making me blush."

He laughed lightly. "I like that, too. Being with you makes me feel alive again. I hadn't realized how...desensitized I'd become to life. The first time we kissed I discovered what I'd been missing. All those arranged dates, all those wasted evenings—and all that time you were right under my nose and I didn't even know it."

"I... I think I'll put out two kinds of chips," Carol said, completely unsettled by the way he spoke so openly, so frankly.

"You're beautiful." His eyes were dark, filled with the promise of things to come. "So beautiful..."

"Alex, please." She leaned against the counter, overwhelmed by his words.

"I can't help it. I feel as though I've been granted a second chance at life. Tell me I'm not behaving like an idiot. Tell me you feel it, too."

She did feel everything he did, more profoundly than she dared let him know. "We've both been alone too long," she said. "People in situations like ours must think these kinds of thoughts all the time."

Her comment didn't please him. He frowned and slowly stood. "You may find this difficult to believe, Carol, but there hasn't been anyone since Gloria who made me feel the things you do. And trust me, there've been plenty who tried."

Gulping, Carol whirled around and made busy work opening a bag of potato chips.

Alex joined her, leaning against the counter and facing her so she couldn't ignore him. "You, on the other hand, don't even need to touch me to make me respond. You might not want to admit it, but it's the same for you."

"When you decide to pester someone, you don't do it by half measures, do you?" she muttered.

"Admit it, Carol."

"I..."

He slid his lips across hers. "Are you ready to admit it yet?"

"No, I—"

He bent forward and kissed her again.

Carol's knees buckled and she swayed toward him.

Alex instantly reached for her. Without question, without protest, Carol fell into his arms, so hungry for his touch, she felt as if she were on fire.

The sound of someone clearing his throat was followed by, "Hey, we're not interrupting anything, are we?" Peter was standing just inside the kitchen. "In case you two haven't noticed, it's lunchtime."

Seven

Alex pressed one knee down on the green and stretched out his putter, judging the distance to the hole with a sharp eye. He'd been playing golf with Barney every Sunday afternoon for years.

"So when do I get to meet this female dynamo?" Barney asked after Alex had successfully completed the shot.

"I don't know yet," Alex said as he retrieved his golf ball. He inserted the putter back inside his bag before striding toward the cart.

"What do you mean, you don't know?" Barney echoed. "What's with you and this woman? I swear you've been a different man since you met her. You stare off into space with this goofy look on your face. I talk to you and you don't hear me, and when I ask you about her, you get defensive."

"I'm not defensive, I'm in love."

"Alex, buddy, listen to the voice of experience. You're not in love, you're in lust. I recognize that gleam in your eye. Ten to one you haven't slept with her yet. So I recommend that you get her in the sack and be done with it before you end up doing something foolish."

Alex's gaze fired briefly as he looked at his friend. How did Barney know the progress of his relationship with Carol?

"I have every intention of sleeping with her. Only I plan to be doing that every night for the rest of my life. Carol's not the type of woman to have a fling, and I refuse to insult her by suggesting one."

Barney stared at Alex as if seeing him for the first time. "I don't think I ever realized what an old-fashioned guy you are. Apparently you haven't noticed, but the world's become a lot more casual. Our clothes are casual, our conversations are casual and, yes, even our sex is casual. In case you hadn't heard, you don't have to marry a woman to take her to bed."

"Continue in this vein," Alex said, "and you're going to become a casual friend."

Barney rolled his eyes dramatically. "See what I mean?"

If three wives hadn't been able to change Barney's attitude, Alex doubted he could, either. "As I recall, the last time we had this conversation," Alex reminded him, "you said settling down was the thing to do. I'm only following your advice."

"But not yet," Barney said. "You haven't played the field enough. There are riches out there—" he gestured with his hands "—female gold nuggets just waiting to be picked up, then set gently back in place for the next treasure-hunter."

"You mean like Bambi and what was the name of the other one? Barbie?"

"Stop being clever," Barney snickered. "I have your

best interests at heart, and frankly I'm concerned. Two years after Gloria's gone, you suddenly announce it's time to start dating again. Man, I was jumping up and down for joy. Then you go out with a grand total of ten different women—most of them only once—and calmly inform me you've met *the one.* You plan to marry her, just like that, and you haven't even slept with her yet. How are you going to find out if you're sexually compatible?"

"We're compatible, trust me."

"You may think so now, but *bingo,* once she's got a wedding band, it's a totally different story."

"Stop worrying, would you?" Alex eased his golf cart into his assigned space. From the day he'd decided to look for another wife, Barney had been a constant source of amusement. The problem was, his most hilarious moments had come in the form of women his friend had insisted he meet.

"But, Alex, I *am* worried about you," Barney muttered as he lifted his clubs from the back of the cart. "You don't know women the way I do. They're scheming, conniving, money-hungry, and how they get their clutches into you is by marriage. Don't be so eager to march up the aisle with Carol. I don't want you to go through what I have."

After three wives, three divorces and child support payments for two separate families, Barney was speaking from experience—of a particularly negative sort.

"Gloria was special," his longtime friend said. "You're not going to find another one like her. So if it's those qualities that attract you to Carol, look again. You may only be seeing what you want to see."

* * *

"You wanna yell?" Angelina Pasquale shouted from the doorway of the kitchen into the living room where her grandchildren were squabbling. "Then let's have a contest. But remember—I've been doing it longer. They can hear me all the way in Jersey City."

Peter and his younger cousins ceased their shouting match, and with a nod of her head, Angelina returned to the kitchen, satisfied that a single threat from her was enough to bring about peace that would last through the afternoon.

Carol was busy slicing tomatoes for the salad, and her sister-in-law, Paula, was spreading garlic butter on thick slices of French bread.

The sauce was warming on the stove, and the water for the long strands of fresh pasta was just starting to boil. The pungent scent of basil and thyme circled the kitchen like smoke from a campfire. From Carol's earliest memory, her mother had cooked a pot of spaghetti sauce every Saturday evening. The unused portion from Sunday's dinner was served in a variety of ways during the week. Leftover pot roast became something delectable with her mother's sauce over top. And chicken with Mama's sauce rivaled even the Cajun chicken at Jake's restaurant.

"So, Carol," her mother began, wiping her hands on the ever-present apron. She took a large wooden spoon and stirred the kettle of simmering sauce. "I suppose your English friend thinks good spaghetti sauce comes from a jar," she said disparagingly. This was her way of letting Carol know the time had come to invite Alex and his son to Sunday dinner.

"Mama, Alex plays golf on Sundays."

"Every Sunday?"

Carol nodded.

"That's because he's never tasted my sauce." Angelina shook her head as though to suggest Alex had wasted much of his life walking from green to green when he could've been having dinner at her house.

Adding serving utensils to the salad, Carol set the wooden bowl on the dining room table.

Tony, Carol's brother, sauntered into the kitchen and slipped his arms around Paula's waist. "How much longer until dinner? The natives are getting restless."

"Eleven minutes," Angelina answered promptly. She tasted the end of the wooden spoon and nodded in approval.

Carol returned to the kitchen and noticed that her mother was watching her under the guise of waiting for the water to boil. The question Carol had expected all day finally came.

"You gonna marry this non-Italian?" her mother asked, then added the noodles, stirring with enough energy to create a whirlpool in the large stainless-steel pot.

"Mama," Carol cried. "I barely know Alex. We've only gone out a handful of times."

"Ah, but your eyes are telling me something different."

"The only thing my eyes are interested in is some of that garlic bread Paula's making," Carol said, hoping to divert her mother's attention from the subject of Alex.

"Here." Her sister-in-law handed her a slice. "But it's no substitute for a man." Paula turned her head to press a quick kiss on her husband's cheek.

Tony's hands slipped further around Paula's waist as he whispered in his wife's ear. From the way her sister-in-law's face flooded with warm color, Carol didn't need much of an imagination to guess what Tony had said.

Carol looked away. She wasn't embarrassed by the earthy exchange between her brother and his wife; instead, she felt a peculiar twinge of envy. The realization shocked her. In all the years she'd been alone, Carol had never once longed for a pair of arms to hold her or for a man to whisper suggestive comments in her ear. Those intimacies were reserved for the happily married members of her family.

Yet, here she was, standing in the middle of her mother's kitchen, yearning for Alex to stroll up behind her, circle her waist and whisper promises in her ear. The image was so vivid that she hurried into the living room to escape it.

It wasn't until later, when the dishes were washed, that Carol had a chance to sort through her thoughts. Tony and Peter were puttering around in the garage. Paula was playing a game of Yahtzee with the younger children. And Angelina was rocking in her chair, nimble fingers working delicate yarn into a sweater for her smallest grandchild.

"So are you gonna tell your mama what's troubling you?" she asked Carol out of the blue.

"Nothing's wrong," Carol fibbed. She couldn't discuss what she didn't understand. For the first time, she felt distanced from the love and laughter that was so much a part of Sunday dinner with her family. For years she'd clung to the life she'd built for herself and her son. These few, short weeks with Alex had changed everything.

Alex had discovered all her weaknesses and used

them to his own advantage. Digging up the earth for her herb garden was a good example. She could've asked her brother to do it for her. Eventually she probably would have. But Tony did so much to help her already that she didn't want to burden him with another request. It wasn't as if tilling part of the backyard was essential. But one casual mention to Alex, and next thing she knew, there was freshly tilled earth waiting for basil and Italian parsley where before there'd been lawn.

"You like this man, don't you?"

Carol responded with a tiny nod of her head.

A slow, easy smile rose from her mother's mouth to her eyes. "I thought so. You got the look."

"The look?"

"Of a woman falling in love. Don't fight it so hard, my *bambina.* It's time you met a man who brings color to your cheeks and a smile to your lips."

But Carol wasn't smiling. She felt confused and ambivalent. She was crazy about Alex; she prayed she'd never see him again. She couldn't picture her life with him; she couldn't picture her life without him.

"I lit a candle in church for you," her mother whispered. "And said a special prayer to St. Rita."

"Mama…"

"God and I had a good talk, and He told me it's predestined."

"What's predestined?"

"You and this non-Italian," her mother replied calmly.

"Mama, that doesn't make the least bit of sense. For years you've been telling me to marry a rich old man with one foot in the grave and the other on a banana peel. You said everyone loves a rich widow."

"Keep looking for the rich old man, but when you

find him, introduce him to me. With any luck his first wife made spaghetti sauce with tomato soup and he'll worship at my feet."

Carol couldn't keep from smiling. She wasn't so sure about her mother lighting candles on her behalf or deciding that marrying Alex was predestined, but from experience she'd learned there wasn't any point in arguing.

Tony, Paula and their two children left around five. Usually Carol headed for home around the same time, but this afternoon she lingered. The 1940s war movie on television held Peter's attention, and her eyes drifted to it now and again.

It wasn't until she felt the moisture on her cheeks that she realized she was crying.

Doing what she could to wipe away the tears so as not to attract attention to herself, she focused on the television screen. Her mother was right; she was falling in love, head over heels in love, and it was frightening her to death.

Silently Angelina set her knitting aside and joined Carol on the sofa. Without a word, she thrust a tissue into Carol's hand. Then she wrapped her arm around her daughter's shoulders and pressed her head tenderly to her generous bosom. Gently patting Carol's back, Angelina whispered soothing words of love and encouragement in a language Carol could only partially understand.

Alex didn't see Carol again until Monday afternoon when he pulled into the high school parking lot. He angled his van in front of the track, four spaces down from her car. He waited a couple of minutes, hoping she'd come and see him of her own free will. He should've known better. The woman wasn't willing to give an inch.

Deciding to act just as nonchalant, Alex opened his door, walked over to the six-foot-high chain-link fence and pretended to be watching the various groups participate in field events. Neither James nor Peter was trying out for any of those positions on the team.

Then he walked casually toward Carol, who was determined, it seemed, to ignore him, hiding behind the pages of a women's magazine.

"Hello, Carol," he said after a decent interval.

"Oh—Alex." She held the magazine rigidly in place.

"Mind if I join you?"

"Not at all." The hesitation was long enough to imply that she would indeed mind. Regardless, he opened the passenger door and slid inside her car. Only then did Carol bother to close the magazine and set it down.

By now, Alex told himself, he should be accustomed to her aloof attitude toward him. It was like this nearly every time they were together. She'd never shown any real pleasure at seeing him. He had to break through those chilly barriers each and every encounter. The strangest part was that he knew she was as strongly attracted to him as he was to her. And not just in the physical sense. Their lives were like matching bookends, he thought.

"Did you have a good day?" he asked politely.

She nodded and glanced away, as though she thought that sharing even a small part of her life with him was akin to admitting she enjoyed his company.

"I suppose it would be too much to hope that you missed me the last couple of days?" he asked.

"Yes."

Alex was almost embarrassed by the way his heart raced. "You missed me," he repeated, feeling like a kid who'd been granted free rein in a candy store.

"No," Carol said, clearly disconcerted. "I meant it would be too much to hope I did."

"Oh." The woman sure knew how to deflate his pride.

"It really was thoughtful of you to dig up that area in my backyard on Saturday. I'm grateful, Alex."

Crossing his arms, Alex leaned against the back of the seat and tried to conceal his injured pride with a lazy shrug. "It was no trouble." Especially since the two boys had done most of the work, leaving him free to "pester" Carol in the kitchen. With everything in him, he wished they were back in that kitchen now. He wanted her in his arms the way she'd been on Saturday afternoon, her lips moist and swollen with his kisses, her eyes dark with passion.

"The boys will be out any minute," Carol said, studying the empty field.

Alex guessed this was his cue to leave her car, but he wasn't taking the hint. When it came to Carol Sommars, he was learning that his two greatest allies were James and Peter.

It was time to play his ace.

Alex waited until the last possible minute. Both boys had walked onto the parking lot, their hair damp from a recent shower. They were chatting and joking and in a good mood. Climbing out of Carol's car, Alex leaned against the fender in a relaxed pose.

"Peter, did you say something about wanting to go camping?" he said, casting Carol a defiant look. "James and I were thinking of heading for the Washington coastline this coming weekend and thought you and your mother might like to go with us."

"We are?" James asked, delighted and surprised.

Peter's eyes widened with excitement. "Camping? You're inviting Mom and me to go camping?"

At the mention of the word *camping,* Carol opened her car door and vaulted out. Her eyes narrowed on Alex as if to declare a foul and charge him a penalty.

"Are you two free this weekend?" Alex asked with a practiced look of innocence, formally extending the invitation. The ball was in her court, and he was interested in seeing how she volleyed this one.

"Yes," Peter shouted. "We're interested."

"No," Carol said at the same moment. "We already have plans."

"We do?" her son moaned. "Come on, Mom, Mr. Preston just offered to take us camping with him and James. What could possibly be more important than that?"

"I wanted to paint the living room."

"What? Paint the living room? I don't believe it." Peter slapped his hands against his thighs and threw back his head. "You know how I feel about camping," he whined.

"Give your mother time to think it over," Alex urged, confident that Carol would change her mind or that Peter would do it for her. "We can talk about it tomorrow evening."

James gave Peter the okay signal, and feeling extraordinarily proud of himself, Alex led the way to his van, handing his son the keys.

"You're going to let me drive?" James asked, sounding more than a little stunned. "Voluntarily?"

"Count your blessings, boy, and drive."

"Yes, sir!"

Carol was furious with Alex. He'd played a faultless game, and she had to congratulate him on his fine closing move. All day she'd primed herself for the way she was going to act when she saw him again. She'd allowed their relationship to progress much further than she'd ever intended, and it was time to cool things down.

With her mother lighting candles in church and having heart-to-heart talks with God, things had gotten completely out of hand. Angelina barely complained anymore that Alex wasn't Catholic, and worse, not Italian. It was as if those two prerequisites no longer mattered.

What Carol hadn't figured on was the rush of adrenaline she'd experienced when Alex pulled into the school parking lot. She swore her heart raced faster than any of the runners on the track. She'd needed every ounce of determination she possessed not to toss aside the magazine she'd planted in the car and run to him, bury her face in his chest and ask him to explain what was happening to her.

Apparently Alex had read her perfectly. He didn't appear at all concerned about her lack of welcome. That hadn't even fazed him. All the arguments she'd amassed had been for naught. Then at the last possible minute he'd introduced the subject of this camping trip, in what she had to admire was a brilliant move. Her chain of resistance was only as strong as the weakest link. And her weakest link was Peter.

Grudgingly she had to admire Alex.

"Mom," Peter cried, restless as a first grader in the seat beside her. "We're going to talk about it, aren't we?"

"About the camping trip?"

"It's the chance of a lifetime. The Washington coast—I've heard it's fabulous—"

"We've got plans."

"To paint the living room? We could do that any old time!"

"Peter, please."

He was silent for a minute or so. The he asked, "Do you remember when I was eleven?"

Here it comes, Carol mused darkly. "I remember," she muttered, knowing it would've been too much to expect him not to drag up the lowest point of her life as a mother.

"We were going camping then, too, remember?"

He said *remember* as though it was a dirty word, one that would get him into trouble.

"You promised me an overnight camping trip and signed us up for an outing through the Y? But when we went to the meeting you got cold feet."

"Peter, they gave us a list of stuff we were supposed to bring, and not only did I not have half the things on the list, I didn't even know what they were."

"You could have asked," Peter cried.

"It was more than that."

"Just because we were going to hike at our own pace? They said we'd get a map. We could've found the camp, Mom, I know we could have."

Carol had had visions of wandering through the woods for days on end with nothing more than a piece of paper that said she should head east—and she had the world's worst sense of direction. If she could get lost in a shopping mall, how would she ever find her way through dense forest?

"That wasn't the worst part," Peter murmured. "Right there in the middle of the meeting you leaned over and asked me what it would cost to buy your way out of the trip."

"You said you wouldn't leave for anything less than a laser tag set," Carol said, tormented by the unfairness of it all. The toy had been popular and expensive at the time and had cost her a pretty penny. But her son had conveniently forgotten that.

"I feel like I sold my soul that day," Peter said with a deep sigh.

"Peter, honestly!"

"It wasn't until then that I realized how much I was missing by not having a dad."

The kid was perfecting the art of guilt.

"Now, once again," he argued, "I have the rare opportunity to experience the great out-of-doors, and it's like a nightmare happening all over again. My own mother's going to pull the rug out from under my feet."

Carol stopped at a red light and pretended to play a violin. "This could warp your young mind for years to come."

"It just might," Peter said, completely serious.

"Twenty years from now, when they lock those prison doors behind you, you can cry out that it's all my fault. If only I'd taken you camping with Alex and James Preston, then the entire course of your life would have been different."

A short pause followed her statement.

"Sarcasm doesn't suit you, Mother."

Peter was right, of course, but Carol was getting

desperate. At the rate this day was going, she'd end up spending Saturday night in front of a campfire, fighting off mosquitoes and the threat of wild beasts.

Because she felt guilty, despite every effort not to, Carol cooked Peter his favorite chicken-fried steak dinner, complete with gravy and mashed potatoes.

After the dishes had been cleared and Peter was supposed to be doing his homework, Carol found him talking on the phone, whispering frantically. It wasn't hard to guess that her son was discussing strategies with James. The three of them were clearly in cahoots against her.

Carol waited until Peter was in bed before she marched into the kitchen and righteously punched out Alex's phone number. She'd barely given him a chance to answer before she laid into him with both barrels.

"That was a rotten thing to do!"

"What?" he asked, feigning innocence.

"You know darn well what I'm talking about. Peter's pulled every trick in the book from the moment you mentioned this stupid camping trip."

"Are you going to come or is this war?"

"It's war right now, *Mister* Preston."

"Good. Does the victor get spoils? Because I'm telling you, Carol Sommars, I intend to win."

"Oh, Alex," she said with a sigh, leaning against the wall. She slid all the way down to the floor, wanting to weep with frustration. "How could you do this to me?"

"Easy. I got the idea when you told me it was too much to hope that you'd miss me."

"But I don't know anything about camping. To me, roughing it is going without valet service."

"It'll be fun, trust me."

Trusting Alex wasn't at the top of her priority list at the moment. He'd pulled a fast one on her, and she wasn't going to let him do it again.

"Is Peter sleeping?" Alex asked softly.

"If he isn't, he should be." She didn't understand where this conversation was heading.

"James is asleep, too," he said. "After the cold shoulder you gave me this afternoon, I need something to warm my blood."

"Try a hot water bottle."

"It won't work. Keep the door unlocked and I'll be right over."

"Absolutely not. Alex Preston, listen to me, I'm not dressed for company and—"

It was too late. He'd already disconnected.

Eight

Standing in front of her locked screen door, Carol had no intention of letting Alex inside her home. It was nearly eleven, and they both had to work in the morning. When his car pulled into the driveway, she braced her feet apart and stiffened her back. She should be furious with him. Should be nothing; she *was* furious!

But when Alex climbed out of his car, he stood in her driveway for a moment, facing the house. Facing her. The porch light was dim, just bright enough to outline his handsome features.

With his hands in his pockets, he continued to stand there, staring at her. But that seemed such an inadequate way to describe the intensity of his gaze as his eyes locked with her own. Not a muscle moved in the hard, chiseled line of his jaw, and his eyes feasted on her with undisguised hunger. Even from the distance that separated them, Carol saw that his wonderful gray eyes had darkened with need.

He wanted her.

Heaven help her, despite all her arguments to the contrary, she wanted him, too.

Before he'd marched two steps toward her, Carol had unlocked the screen door and held it open for him.

"I'm not going camping," she announced, her voice scarcely audible. Her lips felt dry and her hands moist. Once she'd stated her position, her breath escaped with a ragged sigh. She thought of ranting at him, calling him a coward and a cheat to use her own son against her the way he had, but not a word made it from her mind to her lips.

Alex turned and shut the front door.

The only light was a single lamp on the other side of the room.

They didn't move, didn't breathe.

"I'm not going to force you to go camping," Alex whispered. "In fact, I…" He paused as he lowered his eyes to her lips, and whatever he intended to say trailed into nothingness.

Carol felt his eyes on her as keenly as she had his mouth.

In an effort to break this unnatural spell, she closed her eyes.

"Carol?"

She couldn't have answered him had her life depended on it. Her back was pressed to the door, and she flattened her hands against it.

Not once during her marriage had Carol felt as she did at that moment. So…needy. So empty.

He came to her in a single, unbroken movement, his mouth descending on hers. Carol wound her arms around him and leaned into his solid strength, craving it as never before. Again and again and again he kissed her.

"Alex." She tore her lips from his. "Alex," she breathed again, almost panting. "Something's wrong…."

She could feel his breath against her neck and his fingers in her hair, directing her mouth back to his, kissing her with such heat, Carol thought she'd disintegrate.

Her tears came in earnest then, a great profusion that had been building inside her for years. Long, lonely, barren years.

With the tears came pain, pain so intense she could hardly breathe. Agony spilled from her heart. The trauma that had been buried within her stormed out in a torrent of tears that she could no more stop than she could control.

Huge sobs shook her shoulders, giant hiccupping sobs that she felt all the way to her toes. Sobs that depleted her strength. Her breathing was ragged as she stumbled toward the edge of hysteria.

Alex was speaking to her in soft, reassuring whispers, but Carol couldn't hear him. It didn't matter what he said. Nothing mattered.

She clutched his shirt tighter and tighter. Soon there were no more tears to shed, no more emotion to be spent. Alex continued to hold her. He slid his arms all the way around her, and although she couldn't understand what he was saying, his voice was gentle.

Once the desperate crying had started to subside, Carol drew in giant gulps of air in a futile effort to gain control of herself.

Slowly Alex guided her to the sofa and sat her down, then gathered her in his arms and held her tenderly.

Time lost meaning to Carol until she heard the clock chime midnight. Until then she was satisfied with being held in Alex's arms. He asked no questions, demanded no explanations. He simply held her, offering comfort and consolation.

This newfound contentment in his arms was all too short-lived, however. Acute embarrassment stole through the stillness, and fresh tears stung Carol's eyes. Her mind, her thoughts, her memories were steeped in emotions too strong to bear.

"I… I'll make some coffee," she whispered, unwinding her arms from him, feeling she had to escape.

"Forget the coffee."

She broke away and got shakily to her feet. Before he could stop her, she hurried into the kitchen and supported herself against the counter, not sure if she could perform the uncomplicated task of making a pot of coffee.

Alex followed her into the darkened room. He placed one hand on her shoulder and gently turned her around, so she had no choice but to face him. "I want to talk about what happened."

"No…please." She leveled her eyes at the floor.

"We *need* to talk."

"No." She shook her head emphatically. "Not now. Please not now."

A long, desperate moment passed before he gently kissed the crown of her head. "Fine," he whispered. "Not now. But soon. Very soon."

Carol doubted she could ever discuss what had happened between them, but she didn't have the strength or the courage to say so. That would only have invited argument.

"I… I think you should go."

His nod was reluctant. "Will you be all right?"

"Yes." A bold-faced lie if ever there was one. She

would never be the same again. She was mortified to the very marrow of her bones by her behavior. How could she ever see him again? And then the pain, the memories came rushing back…

No, she wouldn't be all right, but she'd pretend she was, the same way she'd been pretending from the moment she married Bruce.

The message waiting for Alex when he returned to his office the following afternoon didn't come as any surprise. His secretary handed him the yellow slip, and the instant he saw Carol's name, he knew. She was working late that evening and asked if he could pick up Peter from track and drop him off at the house.

The little coward! He sat at his desk, leaned back in his chair and frowned. He hadn't wanted to leave her the night before. Hadn't wanted to walk out of her kitchen without being assured she was all right. Carol, however, had made it clear that she wanted him to leave. Equally apparent was the fact that his being there had only added to her distress. Whatever Carol was facing, whatever ghost she'd encountered, was ugly and traumatic.

So he'd left. But he hadn't stopped thinking about her all day. The thought of her had filled every waking minute.

Even now, hours later, he could remember in vivid detail the way she'd started to unfold and blossom right before his eyes. Because of him. For him.

His frown deepened. She'd never talked about her marriage. Alex assumed it had to be the source of her anguish, but he didn't know why. He didn't even know her late husband's name. Questions bombarded him, and he cursed the lack of answers.

And now, his sweet coward had gone into hiding.

"Will you talk to her, Mr. Preston?" Peter begged as he climbed inside the van in the school parking lot. "Mom's never gone camping, and I think she'd probably like it if she gave it half a chance."

"I'll talk to her," Alex promised.

Peter sighed with relief. "Good."

Sounding both confident and proud, James said, "My dad can be persuasive when he wants to be."

Alex intended to be *very* persuasive.

"I tried to reason with Mom this morning, and you know what she said?" Peter's changing voice pitched between two octaves.

"What?"

"She said she didn't want to talk about it. Doesn't that sound just like a woman? And I thought Melody Wohlford was hard to understand."

Alex stifled a chuckle. "I'll tell you boys what I'm going to do. We'll pick up hamburgers on the way home, and I'll drop you both off at my house. Then I'll drive over to your place, Peter, and wait for your mother there."

"Great idea," James said, nodding his approval.

"But while I'm gone, I want you boys to do your homework."

"Sure."

"Yeah, sure," James echoed. "Just do whatever it takes to convince Mrs. Sommars to come on our camping trip."

"I'll do everything I can," Alex said.

* * *

Carol let herself in the front door, drained from a long, taxing day at the hospital and exhausted from the sleepless night that had preceded it. That morning, she'd been tempted to phone in sick, but with two nurses already out due to illness, there wasn't anyone to replace her. So she'd gone to work feeling emotionally and physically hungover.

"Peter, I'm home," she called. "Peter?"

Silence. Walking into the kitchen, she deposited her purse on the counter and hurried toward her son's bedroom. She'd contacted Alex and asked that he bring Peter home, with instructions to phone back if he couldn't. She hadn't heard from him, so she'd assumed he'd pick up her son and drop him off at the house.

Peter's room was empty, his bed unmade. An array of clean and dirty clothes littered his floor. Everything was normal there.

This was what she got for trying to avoid Alex, Carol mused, chastising herself. Peter was probably still waiting at the high school track, wondering where she could possibly be.

Sighing, she hurried back into the kitchen and reached for her purse. She had to get him his own cell phone, she decided—it would help in situations like this.

The doorbell rang as she walked through the living room. Impatiently she jerked open the door and her eyes collided with Alex's. She gasped.

"Hello again," he said in the warm, husky way that never failed to affect her. "I didn't mean to startle you."

"You didn't." He had, but she wasn't about to admit it. "Apparently you didn't get my message…. Peter must still be at the school."

"No. He's at my house with James."

"Oh." That hardly expressed the instant dread she felt. They were alone, and there was no escape, at least not by the most convenient means—Peter.

Alex stepped into the house and for the first time, she noticed he was carrying a white paper bag. Her gaze settled on it and she frowned.

"Two Big Macs, fries and shakes," he explained.

"For whom?"

Alex arched his eyebrows. "Us."

"Oh..." He honestly expected her to sit down and eat with him? It would be impossible. "I'm not hungry."

"I am—very hungry. If you don't want to eat, that's fine. I will, and while I'm downing my dinner, we can talk."

It wouldn't do any good to argue, and Carol knew it. Without another word, she turned and walked to the kitchen. Alex followed her, and his movements, as smooth and agile as always, sounded thunderous behind her. She was aware of everything about him. When he walked, when he breathed, when he moved.

His eyes seemed to bore holes in her back, but she ignored the impulse to turn and face him. She couldn't bear to look him in the eye. The memory of what had happened the night before made her cheeks flame.

"How are you?" he asked in that husky, caring way of his.

"Fine," she answered cheerfully. "And you?"

"Not so good."

"Oh." Her heart was pounding, clamoring in her ears. "I'm...sorry to hear that."

"You should be, since you're the cause."

"Me? I'm…sure you're mistaken." She got two plates from the cupboard and set them on the table.

As she stepped past him, Alex grabbed her hand. "I don't want to play word games with you. We've come too far for that…and we're going a lot further."

Unable to listen to his words, she closed her eyes.

"Look at me, Carol."

She couldn't do it. She lowered her head, eyes still shut.

"There's no need to be embarrassed."

Naturally he could afford to be generous. He wasn't the one who'd dissolved in a frenzy of violent tears and emotion. She was just grateful that Peter had slept through the whole episode.

"We need to talk."

"No…" she cried and broke away. "Couldn't you have ignored what happened? Why do you have to drag it up now?" she demanded. "Do you enjoy embarrassing me like this? Do you get a kick out of seeing me miserable?" She paused, breathless, her chest heaving. "Please, just go away and leave me alone."

Her fierce words gave birth to a brief, tense silence.

Grasping her chin between his thumb and forefinger, Alex lifted her head. Fresh emotion filled her chest, knotting in her throat as her eyes slid reluctantly to his.

"I don't know what happened last night," he said. "At least not entirely." His voice was gruff, angry, emotional. "All I know is that I've never felt closer to anyone than I did to you—and I've never felt more helpless. But we've got something special, Carol, and I refuse to let you throw it away. Understand?"

She bit her lower lip, sniffled, then slowly nodded.

The tension eased from Alex, and he reached for her,

gently taking her in his arms. She went without question, hiding her face against his neck.

Long, lazy moments passed before he spoke. "I want you to tell me about your marriage."

"No!" she cried and frantically shook her head.

He was silent again, and she could feel him withdrawing from her—or maybe she was the one withdrawing. She wanted to ask him to be patient with her, to give her breathing room, time to analyze what was happening between them.

Just when she was ready to speak, she felt him relax. He chuckled softly, his warm breath mussing her hair. "All right, I'll strike a bargain with you. If you go camping with me this weekend, I'll drop the subject—not forever, mind you, but until you're comfortable enough to talk about it."

Carol raised her head, her eyes meeting his. "You've got a black heart, Alex Preston."

He chuckled and kissed the tip of her nose. "When it comes to courting you, I've learned I need one."

"I can't believe I'm doing this," Carol muttered as she headed up the steep trail into the trees. The surf pounded the Washington beach far below. But directly in front of her was a narrow path that led straight into the rain forest.

"We don't have to wait for you guys, do we?" James whined. He and Peter were obviously eager to do some exploring on their own.

Carol was about to launch into a long list of cautions when Alex spoke. "Feel free," he told the two boys. "Carol and I will be back at camp in time for dinner. We'll expect you to be there then."

"Great!"

"All *right.*"

Within minutes both boys were out of sight, and Carol resumed the increasingly difficult climb. A mountain goat would've had trouble maneuvering this path, she told herself.

"You're doing fine," Alex said behind her. Breathless from the physical exertion required by the steep incline, Carol paused and took a couple of minutes to breathe deeply.

"I love it when you get all hot and sweaty for me."

"Will you stop," she cried, embarrassed and yet amused by his words.

"Never."

To complicate things, Alex moved with grace and skill, even while carrying a backpack. So far, he hadn't even worked up a sweat. Carol, on the other hand, was panting. She hadn't realized how out of shape she was until now.

"The view had better be worth all this effort," she said with a moan five minutes later. The muscles in her calves were beginning to protest, and her heart was pounding so hard it echoed in her ears.

To make matters worse, she'd worn the worst possible combination of clothes. Not knowing what to expect weatherwise, she'd donned heavy boots, jeans and a thick sweatshirt, plus a jacket. Her head was covered with a bright pink cap her mother had knitted for her last Christmas. Should they happen upon a snowstorm, Carol was prepared.

"It's worth the climb," Alex promised. "Do you want me to lead?"

"No way," she said, dismissing his offer. "I'd never be able to keep up with you."

A little while later, Carol staggered into a clearing. She stopped abruptly, astonished by the beauty that surrounded her. The forest she'd just left was dense with a variety of evergreens. Huge limbs were draped with mossy green blankets that hung down so far they touched the spongy ground. Moss-coated stumps dotted the area, some sprouting large white mushroom caps. Wildflowers carpeted the earth and a gentle breeze drifted through the meadow and, catching her breath, Carol removed her hat in a form of worship.

"You're right," she murmured. "This is wonderful… I feel like I'm standing in a cathedral…this makes me want to pray."

"This isn't what I wanted you to see," Alex said, resting his hand on the curve of her shoulder.

"It isn't?" she whispered in disbelief. "You mean there's something better than this?"

"Follow me."

Carol pulled off her jacket, stuffed her hat into one of the pockets and tied the sleeves around her waist. Eagerly she trailed Alex along the winding narrow pathway.

"There's a freshwater cove about a mile from here," he explained, turning back to look at her. "Are you up to the trek?"

"I think so." She felt invigorated. More than that, she felt elated. *Alive.*

"You're being a good sport about all this," Alex said, smiling at her.

"I knew I was going to be okay when I saw that you'd pitched the tents close to the public restrooms. I'm not comfortable unless I'm near something that goes flush in the night."

Alex laughed. They hiked for another twenty minutes and eventually came to the edge of a cliff that fell sharply into the water. The view of bright green waves, contrasted by brilliant blue skies, was beautiful enough to bring tears to Carol's eyes. The park department had set up a chain-link fence along the edge, as well as a rough-hewn bench that had been carved out of an old tree trunk.

Alex gestured for her to sit down. Spreading her coat on the bench, Carol sat down and gazed out at the vista before her.

"You hungry?"

"Starving."

"I thought you would be." He slipped off his pack and set it in front of them. Then he unfastened the zipper and removed a folded plastic bag that resembled the ones Carol used to line her garbage cans.

"What's that?" she asked.

"A garbage bag."

"Oh." Well, that was what it looked like.

Next, he took out a whistle, which he held up for her inspection. "A whistle," he announced unnecessarily. Finally he found what he was searching for and placed a thick chocolate bar and two apples on the bench.

"Without appearing completely stupid," Carol said, biting into her apple, "may I ask why you hauled a garbage bag all the way up here?"

"In case we get lost."

"What?" she cried in alarm. She'd assumed Alex knew his way back to their campsite. He'd certainly implied as much.

"Even the best of hikers have been known to get lost. This is just a precaution."

"When… I mean, I thought you were experienced."

He wiggled his eyebrows suggestively. "I am."

"Alex, this is no time to joke."

"I'm not joking. The garbage bag, the whistle and the chocolate are all part of the hug-a-tree program."

"Hug-a-tree?"

"It's a way of preparing children, or anyone else for that matter, in case they get lost in the woods. The idea is to stay in one place—to literally hug a tree. The garbage bag is for warmth. If you slip inside it, feet first, and crouch down, gathering the opening around your neck, you can keep warm in near-freezing temperatures. It weighs practically nothing. The whistle aids rescuers in locating whoever's lost, and the reason for the candy is obvious."

"Do you mean to tell me we're chowing down on our limited food rations?" Carol bit into her apple again before Alex could change his mind and take it away from her.

"Indeed we are, but then we're practically within sight of the campground, so I don't think we're in any danger of getting lost."

"Good." Too ravenous to care, Carol peeled the paper from the chocolate bar and took a generous bite.

"I was waiting for that," Alex murmured, setting aside his apple.

Carol paused, the candy bar in front of her mouth. "Why?"

"So I could kiss you and taste the chocolate on your lips." He reached for her, and his mouth found hers with such need, such hunger, that Carol groaned. Alex hadn't touched her in days, patiently giving her time to determine the boundaries of their relationship. Now she was starving for him, eager for his kiss, his touch.

His kiss was slow, so slow and deliberate. When he lifted his head Carol moaned and sagged against him.

"You taste sweet," he whispered, tugging at her lower lip with his teeth. "Even sweeter than I expected. Even sweeter than chocolate."

Nine

Her sleeping bag and air mattress didn't look as comfortable as a bed at the Hilton, but they appeared adequate, Carol decided later that night. At least Alex had enough equipment for the four of them. All Carol and Peter owned was one G.I. Joe sleeping bag, decorated with little green army men, and Carol wasn't particularly excited about having to sleep in that.

They'd hiked and explored most of the afternoon. By the time everything was cleared away after dinner, dusk had settled over Salt Creek Park. Carol was out of energy, but Peter and James insisted they couldn't officially call it camping unless everyone sat around the campfire, toasted marshmallows and sang silly songs. And so a lengthy songfest had ensued.

Carol was yawning when she crawled inside the small tent she was sharing with Peter. Alex and James's larger tent was pitched next to theirs. By the dim light of the lantern hanging from the middle of the tent, Carol undressed, cleaned her face and then slipped into the sleeping bag.

"Is it safe yet?" Peter yelled impatiently from outside the tent.

"Safe and sound," Carol returned. She'd just finished zipping up the bag when Peter pulled back the flap and stuck his head in.

Smiling, he withdrew, and she heard him whisper something to James about how unreasonable women could be. Carol didn't know what she'd done that could be considered unreasonable, and she was too drained to ask.

"Good night, everyone," Carol called out when Peter dimmed the lantern.

There was a mixed chorus of "good nights." Content, she rolled onto her stomach and closed her eyes.

Within minutes Carol was fast asleep.

"Carol."

She woke sometime later as her name was whispered close to her ear. Jerking her head up, she saw Alex kneeling just inside the tent, fully dressed. A shaft of moonlight showed her that he'd pressed his finger to his lips, indicating she should be quiet.

"What is it?"

"I want to show you something."

"Now?"

He grinned at her lack of enthusiasm and nodded.

"It can't wait until morning?" she said, yawning.

"It'll be gone by morning," he whispered. "Get dressed and meet me in five minutes."

She couldn't understand what was so important that she couldn't see it by the light of day.

"If you're not out here in five minutes," he warned

in a husky voice from outside her tent, "I'm coming in after you."

Carol grumbled as she scurried around looking for her clothes. It was difficult to pull on her jeans in the cramped space, but with a few acrobatic moves, she managed. Before she crawled out, she tapped Peter's shoulder and told him she'd be back in a few minutes.

Peter didn't seem to care one way or the other.

Alex was waiting for her. His lazy smile wrapped its way around her heart and squeezed tight. For all her moaning and complaining about this camping trip, Carol was having a wonderful time.

"This had better be good," she warned and ingloriously yawned.

"It is," he promised. He held a flashlight and a blanket in one hand and reached for hers with the other. Then he led her toward the beach. Although she was wearing her jacket, the wind made her shiver. Alex must have noticed, because he slid his arm around her shoulder and drew her closer.

"Where are we going?" She found herself whispering, not sure why.

"To a rock."

"A rock," she repeated, incredulous. "You woke me from a sound sleep so I could see a *rock?*"

"Not see, sit on one."

"I couldn't do this at noon in the warm sun?" she muttered, laughing at him.

"Not if you're going to look at the stars."

Carol's step faltered. "Do you mean to tell me you rousted me from a warm, cozy sleeping bag in the middle of the night to show me a few stars? The very same stars I could see from my own bedroom window?"

Alex chuckled. "Are you always this testy when you just wake up?"

"Always," she told him. Yawning again, she covered her mouth with one hand.

Although the campsite was only a few feet away, it was completely hidden behind a clump of trees. Carol could hear the ocean—presumably at the bottom of some nearby cliff—but she couldn't see it.

"I suppose I should choose a tree now. Which one looks the friendliest to you?" Carol asked.

"A tree? Whatever for?"

"To hug. Didn't you tell me this afternoon that if I ever get lost in the woods a tree is my friend? If we get separated, there's no way I'd ever find my way back to camp."

Alex dropped a kiss on her head. "I won't let you out of my sight for a minute, I promise."

"The last time I trusted a guy, I was eighteen and I was pregnant three weeks later." She meant it as a joke, but once the words were out they seemed to hang in the air between them.

"You were only eighteen when you got married?"

Carol nodded, pulled her hand free from his and shoved it in the pocket of her jacket. She could feel herself withdrawing from him. She drew inside herself a little more.

They walked in silence for several minutes.

Suddenly Alex aimed the flashlight at the ground and paused. "This way."

"Over there?" Carol asked. She squinted but couldn't see any rock.

"Just follow me," Alex said. "And no more wisecracks about what happened the last time you listened to a guy. I'm not your first husband, and it would serve us both well if you remembered that." His words were light, teasing, but they sent Carol reeling.

He reached for her hand, lacing his fingers through hers. She could almost hear the litany of questions in Alex's mind. He wanted her to tell him about Bruce. But no one fully knew what a nightmare her marriage had been. Not even her mother. And Carol wasn't about to drag out all the pain for Alex to examine.

Within a couple of minutes, Alex had located "his" rock. At first Carol thought it looked like all the other rocks, silhouetted against the beach.

He climbed up the side, obviously familiar with its shape and size, then offered Carol his hand. Once they were perched on top, he spread out the blanket and motioned for her to sit down.

Carol did and pulled her knees under her chin.

Alex settled down beside her. "Now," he said, pointing toward the heavens, "can you see *that* outside your bedroom window?"

Having forgotten the purpose of this outing, Carol cast her gaze toward the dark sky, then straightened in wonder and surprise. The sky was so heavy with stars—hundreds, no, thousands of them—that it seemed to sag down and touch the earth. "Oh, Alex," she breathed.

"Worth waking up for?" he asked.

"Well worth it," she said, thanking him with a smile.

"I thought you'd think so." His returning smile flew straight into her heart.

She'd been struck by so much extraordinary beauty in such a short while that she felt almost overwhelmed. Turning her head slightly, she smiled again at this man who had opened her eyes to life, to beauty, to love and whispered fervently, "Thank you, Alex."

"For what?"

"For the hike in the rain forest, for the view of the cove, for ignoring my complaints and showing me the stars, for…everything." For coming into her life. For leading her by the hand. For being so patient with her.

"You're welcome."

Lost in the magic, Carol closed her eyes and inhaled the fragrant scent of the wind, the ocean and the night. Rarely had she experienced this kind of contentment and uncomplicated happiness.

When the breeze came, the trees whispered, and the sound combined with the crashing of the surf below. The scents of pine and sea drifted over her. Throwing back her head, Carol tried to take it all in.

"I don't think I appreciated how truly beautiful you are until now," Alex murmured. His face was carved in severe but sensual lines, and his eyes had darkened with emotion.

Carol turned, and when she did, he brushed back the curls from her cheek. His hand lingered on her face, and Carol covered it with her own, closing her eyes at all the sensations that accompanied his touch.

He brought his free hand to her hair, which he threaded through his fingers as though the texture was pure silk. He traced her lower lip with his finger. Unable to resist, Carol circled it with the tip of her tongue….

Time seemed to stand still as Alex's eyes sought and held hers.

He kissed her, and it was excruciatingly slow. Exquisitely slow.

He pressed warm kisses in the hollow of her neck and

slipped his hands inside her jacket, circling her waist and bringing her closer. "The things you do to me," he said in a low voice.

"The things I do to *you?*" She rested her forehead against his own. "They can't compare to what you do—have always done—to me."

His lips twitched with the beginnings of a smile, and Carol leaned forward just enough to kiss him again.

Under her jacket Alex slid his hands up her back. He stopped abruptly, went still and tore his mouth from hers.

"What's wrong?" Carol asked, lifting her head. Her hands were on his shoulders.

"You're not wearing a bra, are you?"

"No. You said I had only five minutes to dress, so I hurried."

His eyes burned into hers, then moved lower to the snap of her jeans. "Did you…take any other shortcuts?"

"Wanna find out?"

He shook his head wildly. "I… I promised myself when you agreed to go camping that I'd do everything I could to keep my hands off you." Although she was still in his arms, Carol had to strain to hear him.

"I think that was a wise decision," she murmured, looking up at him. Alex's expression was filled with surprise. An inner happiness she'd banished from her life so long ago she hadn't known it was missing pulsed through her now.

When he finally released her, Carol was so weak with longing that she clung to him, breathing deeply.

"Carol," he said, watching her closely as she shifted positions. She climbed onto his lap, wrapped her legs around his waist and threw her arms around his neck.

"Oh… Carol." Alex moaned and closed his eyes.

"Shhh," she whispered, kissing him deeply. He didn't speak again for a long, long time. Neither did she…

Thursday afternoon, with a stethoscope around her neck, Carol walked down the hospital corridor to the nurses' station. Her steps were brisk and her heart heavy. She hadn't talked to Alex since late Sunday, when he'd dropped Peter and her at the house after their camping trip. There could be any number of excellent reasons why he hadn't called or stopped by. Maybe he was simply too busy; that made sense. Maybe he didn't want to see her again; perhaps he'd decided to start dating other women. Younger women. Prettier women. He was certainly handsome enough. Perhaps aliens had captured him, and he was trapped in some spaceship circling uncharted universes.

Whatever the reason, it translated into one glaring, inescapable fact. She hadn't seen or heard from Alex in four days. However, she reminded herself, she didn't need a man to make her happy. She didn't need a relationship.

"There's a call for you on line one," Betty Mills told her. "Want me to take a message?"

"Did the person give a name?"

"Alex Preston. He sounds sexy, too," Betty added in a succulent voice. "I don't suppose he's that handsome guy you were having lunch with a little while ago."

Carol's heart slammed against her ribs—first with alarm and then with relief. She'd done everything she could to ignore the gaping hole in her life without Alex there. All it would've taken was a phone call—she could have contacted him. She could've asked Peter to talk to

James. She could've driven over to his house. But she'd done none of those things.

"Carol? Do you want me to take a message or not?" Betty asked.

"No, I'll get it."

Betty laughed. "I would, too, if I were you." With that, she turned and marched away.

Carol moved to the nurses' station and was grateful no one else was around to overhear her conversation. "This is Carol Sommars," she said as professionally as she could manage.

"Carol, it's Alex."

His words burned in her ears. "Hello, Alex," she said, hoping she didn't sound terribly stiff. Her pulse broke into a wild, absurd rhythm at his voice, and despite her best efforts, a warm sense of happiness settled over her.

"I'm sorry to call you at the hospital, but I haven't been able to reach you at home for the past few nights."

"I've been busy." Busy trying to escape the loneliness. Busy ignoring questions she didn't want to answer. Busy hiding.

"Yes, I know," Alex said impatiently. "Are you avoiding me?"

"I… I thought you…if you want the truth, I assumed you'd decided not to see me again."

"Not *see* you," he repeated loudly. "Are you crazy? I'm nuts about you."

"Oh." Her mouth trembled, but whether it was from irritation or sheer blessed relief, Carol didn't know. If he was nuts about her, why had he neglected her all week? Why hadn't he at least left her a message?

"You honestly haven't figured out how I feel about you yet?"

"You haven't been at the school in the past few days, and since I didn't hear from you it made sense—to me, anyway—that you wanted to cool things down, and I don't blame you. Things are getting much too hot and much too…well, fast, and personally I thought that… well, that it was for the best."

"You thought *what?*" he demanded, his voice exploding over the wire. "When I get home the first thing I'm going to do is kiss some sense into you."

"When you get home?"

"I'm in Houston."

"Texas?"

"Is there any other?"

Carol didn't know. "What are you doing there?"

"Wishing I was in Portland, mostly. A friend of mine, another contractor, is involved in a huge project here and ran into problems. There must've been five messages from him when we returned from the camping trip. He needed some help right away."

"What about James? He isn't with you, is he?"

"He's staying with another friend of mine. I've probably mentioned him before. His name is Barney."

Vaguely Carol *did* remember either Alex or James mentioning the man, but she couldn't remember where or when she'd heard it. "How…long will you be gone?" She hated the way her voice fell, the way it made her need for him all too evident.

"Another week at least."

Her heart catapulted to her feet, then gradually righted itself. "A *week?*"

"I don't like it any better than you do. I can't believe how much I miss you. How much I needed to hear your voice."

Carol felt that, too, only she hadn't been willing to admit it, even to herself.

There was a slight commotion on Alex's end of the line and when it cleared, he said, "I'll try to call you again, but we're working day and night and this is the first real break I've had in three days. I'm glad I got through to you."

Her grip tightened on the receiver. "I'm glad, too."

"I have to go. Bye, Carol. I'll see you Thursday or so of next week."

"Goodbye, Alex…and thanks for phoning." She was about to hang up when she realized there was something else she had to say. She cried his name, desperate to catch him before he hung up.

"I'm here. What is it?"

"Alex," she said, sighing with relief. "I've… I want you to know I… I've missed you, too."

The sound of his chuckle was as warm and melodious as a hundred-voice choir. "It's not much, but it's something. Keep next Thursday open for me, okay?"

"You've got yourself a date."

Tuesday evening of the following week, Carol was teaching her birthing class. Ten couples were sprawled on big pillows in front of her as she led them through a series of exercises. She enjoyed this work almost as much as she did her daytime job at the hospital. She and Janice Mandle each taught part of the class, with Carol handling the first half.

"Everyone's doing exceptionally well tonight," Carol said, praising the teams. "Okay, partners, I have a question for you. I want you to tell me, in number of seconds, how long you think a typical labor pain lasts."

"Thirty seconds," one young man shouted out.

"Longer," Carol said.

"Sixty seconds," yelled another.

Carol shook her head.

"Ninety?"

"You don't sound too sure about that," Carol said, smiling. "Let's stick with ninety seconds. That's a nice round number, although in the final stages of labor it's not unusual for a contraction to last much longer."

The pregnant women eyed each other warily.

"All right, partners, I want you to show me your biceps. Tighten them as hard as you can. Good. Good," she said, surveying the room, watching as several of the men brought up their fists until the muscles of their upper arms bulged. "Make it as tight and as painful as you can," she continued. Most of the men were gritting their teeth.

"Very good," she went on to say. "Now, hold that until I tell you to relax." She walked to the other side of the room. "As far back as 1913, some doctors and midwives recognized that fear and tension could interfere with the birthing process. Even then they believed that deep breathing exercises and relaxation could aid labor." She paused to glance at her watch. "That's fifteen seconds."

The look of astonishment that crossed the men's faces was downright comical.

"Keep those muscles tightly clenched," Carol instructed. She strolled around the room, chatting amiably as the men held their arms as tight as possible. Some were already showing the strain.

"Thirty seconds," she announced.

Her words were followed by a low groan. Carol

couldn't help smiling. She hated to admit how much she enjoyed their discomfort, but this exercise was an excellent illustration of the realities of labor, especially for the men. The smile remained on her lips as the door in the back of the room opened to admit a latecomer. Carol opened her mouth to welcome the person, but the words didn't reach her lips.

There, framed inside the door, stood Alex Preston.

Ten

Carol stared at Alex. Alex stared at Carol.

The room went completely still; the air felt heavy, and the quiet seemed eerie, unnatural. It wasn't until Carol realized that several taut faces were gazing up at her anxiously that she pulled her attention away from Alex and back to her class.

"Now, where were we?" she asked, flustered and nervous.

"Ninety seconds," one of the men shouted.

"Oh. Right." She glanced at her watch and nodded. "Ninety seconds."

The relief could be felt all the way across the room.

A few minutes later Carol dismissed everyone for a fifteen-minute break. Janice strolled over to Carol and eyed the back of the room, where Alex was patiently waiting. He was leaning against the back wall, his ankles crossed and his thumbs hooked in the belt loop of his jeans.

"He's gorgeous."

Carol felt too distracted and tongue-tied to respond, although her thoughts had been traveling along those same lines. Alex was the sexiest man Carol had ever known. Unabashedly wonderful, too.

"He's…been out of town," she said, her eyes magnetically drawn to Alex's.

Janice draped her arm across Carol's shoulders. "Since your portion of tonight's class is finished, why don't you go ahead and leave?"

"I couldn't." Carol tore her eyes from Alex long enough to study her co-teacher. They were a team, and although they'd divided the class into two distinct sections, they stayed and lent each other emotional support.

"Yes, you can. I insist. Only…"

"Only what?" Carol pressed.

"Only promise me that if another gorgeous guy walks in off the street and looks at me like he's looking at you, you'll return the favor."

"Of course," Carol answered automatically.

Janice's voice fell to a whisper. "Good. Then we'll consider this our little secret."

Carol frowned. "I don't understand—what do you mean, our little secret?"

"Well, if my husband found out about this agreement, there could be problems."

Carol laughed. Janice was happily married and had been for fifteen years.

"If I were you I wouldn't be hanging around here talking," Janice murmured, giving Carol a small shove. "Don't keep him waiting any longer."

"Okay…thanks." Feeling unaccountably shy, Carol retrieved her purse and her briefcase and walked toward Alex. With each step that drew her nearer, her heart felt lighter. By the time she made her way to the back of the room, she felt nearly airborne.

He straightened, his eyes warm and caressing. "Hello."

"Hi."

"Peter told me you were teaching tonight and where. I hope you don't mind that I dropped in unexpectedly."

"I don't mind." *Mind?* Her heart was soaring with gladness. She could've flown without an airplane. No, she didn't mind that he'd dropped in—not in the least.

For the longest moment all they did was gaze at each other like starry-eyed lovers.

A noise at the front of the room distracted Carol. She glanced over her shoulder and saw several couples watching them with undisguised curiosity.

"Janice said she'd finish up here, and I could…should leave now."

Alex grinned, and with that, Carol could feel whole sections of the sturdy wall around her heart start to crumble. This man's smile was nothing short of lethal.

"Remind me to thank her later," Alex said. He removed the briefcase from her unresisting fingers and opened the door, letting her precede him outside.

They hadn't taken two steps out the door when Alex paused. Carol felt his hesitation and stopped, turning to face him. That was when she knew Alex was going to kiss her. It didn't matter that they were standing in front of a public building. It didn't matter that it was still light enough for any number of passersby to see them. It didn't matter that they were both respected professionals.

Alex scooped her into his arms and with a lavish sigh lowered his head and covered her lips in the sweetest, wildest kiss of her life.

"I've missed you," he whispered. "The hours felt like years, the days like decades."

Carol felt tears in the corners of her eyes. She hadn't thought about how empty her life had felt without him, how bleak and alone she was with him away. Now it poured out of her in a litany of sighs and kisses. "I… I missed you, too—so much."

For years she'd been content in her own secure world, the one she'd created for herself and her son. The borders had been narrow, confining, but she'd made peace with herself and found serenity. Then she'd met Alex, and he'd forced her to notice how cramped and limited her existence was. Not only that, he'd pointed toward the horizon, to a new land of shared dreams.

When Alex spoke again, his voice was heavy with need. "Come on, let's get out of here."

She nodded and followed him to his car, ready to abandon her own with little more than a second thought.

He unlocked the passenger door, then turned to face her. His eyes were dancing with excitement. "Let's dispense with formalities and elope. Now. Tonight. This minute."

The words hit her hard. She blinked at the unexpectedness of his suggestion, prepared to laugh it off as a joke.

But Alex was serious. He looked as shocked as Carol felt, but she noted that the idea had begun to gain momentum. The mischievous spark in his eyes was gone, replaced by a solemn look.

"I love you, Carol. I love you so much that my buddy in Texas practically threw me on the plane and told me to get home before I died of it. He said he'd never seen anyone more lovesick and made me promise we'd name one of our children after him."

The mention of a child was like a right cross to the

jaw after his punch to her solar plexus, and she flinched involuntarily.

Alex set his hands on her shoulders, and a smile touched his eyes and then his mouth. He smiled so endearingly that all of Carol's arguments fled like dust in a whirlwind.

"Say something."

"Ah…my car's parked over there." She pointed in the general vicinity of her Ford. Her throat was so tight she could hardly speak.

He laughed and hugged her. "I know this is sudden for you. I'm a fool not to have done it properly. I swear I'll do it again over champagne and give you a diamond so large you'll sink in a swimming pool, but I can't keep the way I feel inside anymore."

"Alex…"

He silenced her with a swift kiss. "Believe me, blurting out a proposal like this is as much of a surprise to me as it is to you. I had no idea I was going to ask you tonight. The entire flight home I was trying to figure out how I could make it as romantic as possible. The last thing I expected to do was impulsively shout it out in a parking lot. But something happened tonight." He reached for her limp hands and brought them to his lips, then kissed her knuckles with reverence. "When I walked into your class and saw you with all those pregnant women, I was hit with the most powerful shock of my life." His voice grew quiet. "All of a sudden, my mind conjured up the image of you pregnant with our child, and I swear it was all I could do not to break down and weep." He paused long enough to run his fingers through his hair. "Children, Carol…our children." He closed his eyes and sighed deeply.

Carol felt frozen. The chill worked its way from her heart, the icy circles growing larger and more encompassing until the cold extended down her arms and legs and into her fingers and toes.

"I know this is abrupt, and I'm probably ruining the moment, but say something," Alex urged. "Anything."

Carol's mind refused to function properly. Panic was closing in, panic and a hundred misgivings. "I...don't know what to tell you."

Alex threw back his head and laughed. "I don't blame you. All right," he said, his eyes flashing, "repeat after me. I, Carol Sommars." He glanced expectantly at her.

"I... Carol Sommars..."

"Am crazy in love with Alex Preston." He waited for her to echo his words.

"Am crazy in love with Alex Preston."

"Good," he whispered and leaned forward just enough to brush his mouth over hers. His arms slipped around her, locking at the small of her back and dragging her unresistingly toward him. "You know, the best part about those babies is going to be making them."

A blush rose up her neck, coloring her cheeks with what she felt sure was a highly uncomplimentary shade of pink. Her eyes darted away from his.

"Now all you need to do is say *yes,*" Alex said.

"I can't. I...don't know." To her horror, she started to sob, not with the restrained tears of a confused woman, but the harsh mournful cries of one in anguish.

Alex had apparently expected anything but tears. "Carol? What's wrong? What did I say?" He wrapped his arms around her and brought her head to his shoulder.

Carol wanted to resist his touch, but she so desperately needed it that she buried her face in the curve of his neck and wept. Alex's arms were warm and safe, his hands gentle. She did love him. Somewhere between his rescue the night her car broke down and the camping trip, her well-guarded heart had succumbed to his appeal. But falling in love was one thing; marriage and children were something else entirely.

"Come on," Alex finally said. He opened the car door for her.

"Where are we going?" she asked, sniffling.

"My house. James won't be home yet, and we can talk without being disturbed."

Carol wasn't sure what more he could say, but she agreed with a nod of her head and climbed inside. He closed the door for her, then paused and ran a hand over his eyes, slumping wearily.

Neither of them said much during the ten-minute drive. He helped her out of his car, then unlocked the front door to his house. His suitcases had been haphazardly dumped on the living room carpet. When he saw Carol looking at them, he said simply, "I was in a hurry to find you." He led the way into the kitchen and started making a pot of coffee.

Carol pulled out a stool at the counter and seated herself. His kitchen—in fact, his home—wasn't at all what she expected. A woman's touch could be seen and felt in every room. The kitchen was yellow and cheery. What remained of the evening light shone through the window above the sink, sending warm shadows across the polished tile floor. Matching ceramic canisters lined the counter, along with a row of well-used cookbooks.

"Okay, Carol, tell me what's on your mind," Alex urged, facing her from behind the tile counter. Even then Carol wasn't safe from his magnetism.

"That's the problem," she said, swallowing hard. "I don't *know* what's on my mind. I'm so confused…."

"I realize my proposal came out of the blue, but once you think about it, you'll understand how perfect we are for each other. Surely you've thought about it yourself."

"No," she said quickly, and for emphasis, shook her head. "I hadn't…not once. Marriage hadn't occurred to me."

"I see." He raised his right hand to rub his eyes again.

Carol knew he must be exhausted and was immediately overcome with remorse. She *did* love Alex, although admitting it—to herself as much as to him—had sapped her strength.

"What do you want to do?" he asked softly.

"I'm not sure," she whispered, staring down at her hands, which were tightly clenched in her lap.

"Would some time help?"

She nodded eagerly.

"How long?"

"A year. Several months. At the very least, three or four weeks."

"How about two weeks?" Alex suggested.

"Two weeks," she echoed feebly. That wasn't nearly enough. She couldn't possibly reach such an important decision in so little time, especially when there were other factors to consider. Before she could voice a single excuse, Alex pressed his finger to her lips.

"If you can't decide in that length of time, then I doubt you ever will."

A protest came and went in a single breath. There were so many concerns he hadn't mentioned—like their sons!

She was about to bring this up when Alex said, "I

don't think we should draw the boys into this until we know our own minds. The last thing we need is pressure from them."

Carol agreed completely.

The coffee had finished perking, and Alex poured them each a cup. "How about dinner Friday night? Just the two of us." At her hesitation, he added, "I'll give you the rest of this week to sort through your thoughts, and if you still have any questions or doubts by Friday, we can discuss them then."

"But not a final decision?" Carol murmured, uneasy with the time limitation. He'd said two weeks, and she was going to need every minute to make up her mind.

Carol woke around three with her stomach in painful knots. She lay on her side and at a breath-stopping cramp, she tucked her knees under her chin. A wave of nausea hit her hard, and she couldn't stifle a groan. Despite her flu shot last fall, maybe she'd caught one of the new strains that emerged every year.

She lay perfectly still in the fervent hope that this would ward off her growing need to vomit. It didn't work, and a moment later she was racing for the bathroom.

Afterward, sitting on the floor, her elbows on the edge of the toilet, she breathed deeply.

"Are you all right?" Peter asked from behind her.

"I will be. I just need a couple more minutes."

"What's wrong?" Peter asked. He handed her a warm washcloth, following that with a cup of water.

"The flu, I guess."

He helped her to her feet and walked her back to her

bedroom. "I appreciate the help, Peter, but it would be better if you went back to bed. I'll be fine by morning."

"I'll call work for you and tell them you're too sick to come in."

She shook her head. "No… I'll need to talk to them myself." Her son dutifully arranged the blankets around her, giving her a worried look before he slipped out of her bedroom.

Peter must have turned off her alarm because the next thing Carol knew it was eight-thirty. The house was eerily silent.

Sitting up, she waited for an attack of nausea. It didn't come. She'd slept without waking even once. She was astonished that she hadn't heard Peter roaming about. He was usually as noisy as a herd of rampaging buffalo. Perhaps he'd overslept as well.

In case he had, she threw the sheets back, sat on the edge of the bed and shoved her feet into slippers before wandering into the kitchen. The minute she stepped inside, it was obvious that her son had been up and about. A box of cold cereal stood in the middle of the kitchen table, along with a bowl half-filled with milk and crusts from several pieces of toast.

Posted on the refrigerator door was a note from Peter, informing her that he'd phoned the hospital and talked to her supervisor, who'd said Carol didn't need to worry about coming in. He proudly added that he'd made his own lunch and that he'd find a ride home from track practice, so she should stay in bed and drink lots of fluids. In a brief postscript he casually mentioned that he'd also called Grandma Pasquale.

Carol's groan had little to do with the way she was feeling. All she needed was her mother, bless her heart, hovering over her and driving her slowly but surely crazy. No sooner had the thought formed in her mind than the doorbell chimed, followed by a key turning in the lock and the front door flying open. Her mother burst into the house as though Carol lay on her deathbed.

"Carol," she cried, walking through the living room. "What are you doing out of bed?"

"I'm feeling much better, Mama."

"You look terrible. Get back in bed before the undertaker gets wind of how you look."

"Ma, please, I'm just a little under the weather."

"That's what my uncle Giuseppe said when he had the flu, God rest his soul. His wife never even got the chicken stewed, he went that fast." She pressed her hands together, raised her eyes to the ceiling and murmured a silent prayer.

"Peter shouldn't have phoned you," Carol grumbled. She certainly didn't need her mother fussing at her bedside, spooning chicken soup down her throat every time she opened her mouth.

"Peter did the right thing. He's a good boy."

At the moment Carol considered that point debatable.

"Now, back to bed before you get a dizzy spell." Her mother made a shooing motion with her hands.

Mumbling under her breath, Carol did as Angelina insisted. Not because she felt especially ill, but because arguing required too much energy. Carol might as well try to talk her mother into using canned spaghetti sauce as convince her she wasn't on her deathbed.

Once Carol was lying down, Angelina dragged the rocking chair into her bedroom and sat down. Before another minute had passed, she was busy with her knitting. Several balls of yarn were lying at her feet in case she wanted to start a second or third project in the next few hours.

"According to Peter you were sick in the middle of the night," Angelina said. Eyes narrowed, she studied Carol, as if staring would reveal the exact nature of her daughter's illness. She shook her head, then paused to count the neat row of stitches before glancing back at Carol, clearly expecting an answer.

"It must've been something I ate for dinner," she suggested lamely.

"Peter said you were looking at parts of a toilet no one should see that close up."

Her teenage son certainly had a way with words. "I'm feeling better," she said weakly.

"Your face is paler than bleached sheets. Uncle Giuseppe has more color than you, and he's been in his grave for thirty years."

Carol leaned back against the pillows and closed her eyes. She might be able to fool just about anyone else, but her mother knew her too well.

Several tense minutes passed. Angelina said not a word, patient to a fault. Yes, her mother knew; Carol was sure of it. She kept her eyes closed, afraid that another searching look would reveal everything. Oh, what the heck, Angelina would find out sooner or later.

"Alex asked me to marry him last night." Carol tried to keep her voice even, but it shook noticeably.

"Ah," her mother said, nodding. "That explains everything. From the time you were a little girl, you got an upset stomach whenever something troubled you, although why you should be troubled when this man tells you he loves you is a whole other question."

Carol didn't need to hear stories from her childhood to recognize the truth.

"So what did you say to him?"

"Nothing," she whispered.

"This man brings color to your cheeks and a smile to your eyes and you said *nothing?*"

"I…need time to think," Carol cried. "This is an important decision…. I've got more than myself and my own life to consider. Alex has a son and I have a son…. It isn't as simple as it sounds."

Her mother shook her head. Her rocker was going ninety miles an hour, and Carol was positive the older woman's thoughts were churning at equal speed.

"Don't be angry with me, Mama," she whispered. "I'm so frightened."

Angelina stopped abruptly and set her knitting aside. She reached for Carol's hands, holding them gently. A soft smile lit her eyes. "You'll make the right decision."

"How can you be so sure? I've been wrong about so many things—I've made so many mistakes in my life. I don't trust my own judgment anymore."

"Follow your heart," Angelina urged. "It won't lead you wrong."

But it would. She'd followed her heart when she married Bruce, convinced their love would see them through every difficulty. The marriage had been a disaster from the honeymoon on, growing more painful and more difficult with each passing day. The horror of those years with Bruce had shredded her heart and drained away all her self-confidence. She'd offered her husband everything she had to give, relinquished her pride and self-respect—and to what end? Bruce hadn't appreciated her sacrifices. He hadn't cherished her love, but turned it into something cheap and expendable.

"Whatever you decide will be right," her mother said once again. "I know it will be."

Carol closed her eyes to mull over her mother's confidence in her, which she was sure was completely unfounded. Angelina seemed to trust Carol's judgment more than Carol did herself.

A few minutes later, her mother started to sing softly, and her sweet, melodious voice harmonized with the clicking of the needles.

The next thing Carol knew, it was early afternoon and she could smell chicken soup simmering in the kitchen.

Angelina had left a brief note for her that was filled with warmth and encouragement. Feeling much better, Carol helped herself to a bowl of the broth and noodles and leisurely enjoyed her first nourishment of the day.

By the time Peter slammed into the house several hours later, she was almost back to normal.

"Mom," he said rushing into the room. His face was flushed and his eyes bright. It looked as though he'd run all the way home. His chest was heaving as he dropped his books on the table, then tried to catch his breath, arms waving excitedly.

"What is it?" Carol asked, amused by the sight her son made.

"Why didn't you *say* anything?" he demanded, kissing both her cheeks the way her mother did whenever she was exceptionally pleased. "This is great, Mom, really great! Now we can go fishing and camping and hiking all the time."

"Say anything about what?" she asked in bewilderment. "And what's this about fishing?"

"Marrying Mr. Preston."

Carol was half out of her seat before she even realized she'd moved. "Who told you…who so much as mentioned it was a possibility?"

"A possibility?" Peter repeated. "I thought it was a done deal. At least that's what James said."

"James told you?"

Peter gave her a perplexed look. "Who else? He told me about it first thing when I got to school this morning." He studied her, his expression cautious. "Hey, Mom, don't look so upset—I'm sorry if you were keeping it a secret. Don't worry, James and I think it's a great idea. I've always wanted a brother, and having one who's my best friend is even better."

Carol was so outraged she could barely talk. "H-he had no business saying a word!" she stammered.

"Who? James?"

"Not James. Alex." If he thought he'd use the boys to influence her decision, he had another think coming.

Carol marched into her bedroom, throwing on a pair of jeans and an old sweatshirt. Then she hurried into the living room without bothering to run a brush through her tousled hair.

"Where are you going?" Peter demanded. He'd ladeled himself a bowl of soup and was following her around the house like a puppy while she searched for her purse and car keys.

"Out," Carol stormed.

"Looking like that?" He sounded aghast.

Carol whirled around, hands on her hips, and glared at him.

Peter raised one hand. "Sorry. Only please don't let Mr. Preston see you, all right?"

"Why not?"

Peter raised his shoulder in a shrug. "If he gets a look at you, he might withdraw his proposal. Honestly, Mom, this is the best thing that's happened to us in years. Don't go ruining it."

Eleven

James answered the door, and a smile automatically came to his lips when he saw it was Carol. Then his eyes narrowed as though he wasn't sure it was her, after all. Carol realized he was probably taken aback by her appearance. Normally she was well-dressed and well-groomed, but what Alex had done—had tried to do—demanded swift and decisive action. She didn't feel it was necessary to wear makeup for this confrontation.

"Where is he?" Carol asked through gritted teeth.

"Who? Dad?" James frowned. "He's watching the news." The teenager pointed toward the family room, which was adjacent to the kitchen.

Without waiting for James to escort her inside, Carol burst past him, intent on giving Alex a piece of her mind. She was furious. More than furious. If he'd honestly believed that involving the boys would affect her decision, then he knew absolutely nothing about her. In fact, he knew so little, they had no business even considering marriage.

She refused to be pressured, tricked, cajoled or anything else, and before this day was over Alex would recognize that very clearly indeed.

"Carol?" Alex met her halfway into the kitchen. His eyes softened perceptibly as he reached for her.

Carol stopped just short of his embrace. "How dare you," she snapped.

"How dare I?" Alex repeated. His eyes widened with surprise, but he remained infuriatingly calm. "Would you elaborate, please, because I'm afraid I have no idea what you're talking about."

"Oh, yes, you do."

"Dad?" James ventured into the kitchen, giving Carol a wide berth. "Something must really be wrong," the boy said, and then his voice dropped to a whisper as he pointed to Carol's feet. "Mrs. Sommars is wearing two different shoes."

Carol's gaze shot downward, and she mentally groaned. But if either of the Preston men thought they'd throw her off her guard by pointing out that she'd worn a blue tennis shoe on her right foot and a hot-pink slipper on her left, then she had news for them both.

"I have the feeling Mrs. Sommars was in a hurry to talk to me," Alex explained. The smile that quivered at the corners of his mouth did little to quell her brewing temper.

James nodded. "Do you want me to get lost for a few minutes?"

"That might be a good plan," Alex replied.

James exchanged a knowing look with his father before discreetly vacating the room. As soon as Carol heard James's bedroom door close, she put her hands on her hips, determined to confront Alex.

"How dare you bring the boys into this," she flared.

"Into what?" Alex walked over to the coffeepot and got two mugs. He held one up to her, but she refused the offer with a shake of her head. "I'm sorry, Carol, but I don't know what you're talking about."

Jabbing her index finger at him, she took several steps toward him. "Don't give me that, Alex Preston. You know very well what I mean. We agreed to wait, and you saw an advantage and without any compunction, you took it! Did you really think dragging Peter and James into this would help? How could you be so foolish?" Her voice shook, but her eyes were as steady as she could make them.

"I didn't mention the possibility of our getting married to James, and I certainly didn't say anything to Peter." He leaned against the kitchen counter and returned her disbelieving glare with maddening composure.

Angrily Carol threw back her head. "I don't believe you."

His eyes hardened but he didn't argue with her. "Ask James then. If he heard that I'd proposed to you, the information didn't come from me."

"You don't expect me to believe that, do you?" she cried, not nearly as confident as she'd been earlier. The aggression had gone out of her voice, and she lowered her hands to her sides, less certain with each minute. The ground that supported her outrage started to shift and crumble.

"I told you I wouldn't bring the boys into this," he reminded her smoothly. "And I didn't." He looked over his shoulder and shouted for James, who opened his bedroom door immediately. Carol didn't doubt for an instant that he'd had his ear pressed to it the entire time they'd been talking.

With his hands in his jean pockets, James strolled casually into the room. "Yes, Dad?"

"Do you want to tell me about it?"

"About what?" James wore a look of complete innocence.

"Apparently you said something to Peter about the relationship between Mrs. Sommars and me. I want to know what it was and where you found out about it." Alex hadn't so much as raised his voice, but Carol recognized that he expected the truth and wouldn't let up until he got it.

"Oh…that," James muttered. "I sort of overheard you saying something to Uncle Barn."

"Uncle Barn?" Carol asked.

"A good friend of mine. He's the one I was telling you about who kept Jim while I was out of town."

"Call me *James,*" his son reminded him.

Alex lifted both hands. "Sorry."

"Anyway," James went on to say, "you were on the phone last night talking to him about the basketball game tonight, and I heard you say that you'd *asked* Carol—Mrs. Sommars. I'm not stupid, Dad. I knew you were talking about the two of you getting married, and I thought that Peter and I had a right to know. You should've said something to us first, don't you think?"

"For starters, this whole marriage business is up in the air—when and if anything's decided, you two boys will be the first to find out."

"What do you mean, the wedding's up in the air?" This piece of information obviously took James by surprise. "Why? What's the holdup? Peter and I think it's a great idea. We'd like it if you two got married. It'd be nice to have a woman around the house. For one thing, your cooking could use some help. But if you married Mrs. Sommars—"

"James," Alex broke in, "I think it's time for you to go back to your room before Carol decides she wants nothing more to do with the likes of us."

James looked affronted, but without further questions, he pivoted and marched back into his bedroom.

Alex waited until his son was out of sight. He sighed loudly and rammed his fingers through his hair. "I'm sorry, Carol. I had no idea James overheard my conversation with Barney. I thought he was asleep, but I should've been more careful."

"I…understand," Carol whispered, mollified.

"Contrary to what James just said," Alex continued, the line of his mouth tight and unyielding, "I don't want to marry you for your cooking skills. I couldn't care less if you never cooked again. I love you, and I'm hoping we can make a good life together."

James tossed open his bedroom door and stuck out his head. "Peter says she's as good a cook as his grandmother. She's—"

Alex sent his son a look hot enough to melt tar.

James quickly withdrew his head and just as quickly closed his door.

"I'll talk to Peter and explain the mix-up, if you'd like," Alex offered.

"No… I'll say something to him." Suddenly self-conscious, Carol swung her arms at her sides and retreated a couple of steps. "I suppose I should get home…."

"You were sick last night?" Alex asked, his expression concerned. "James told me when I picked him up after school. I would gladly have given Peter a ride, but he'd apparently found another way because he was gone before James could find him."

"Peter decided to run home."

"But you *had* been ill?"

She nodded. "I...must've caught a twenty-four-hour bug." Her eyes darted around the room. She felt so foolish, standing there with her hair a tangled mess, wearing the oldest clothes she owned, not to mention mismatched shoes.

"You're feeling better today?"

"A lot better. Thank you." She was slowly but surely edging toward the front door. The sooner she escaped, the better it would be for everyone involved. If Alex was merciful, he'd never mention this visit again.

She was all the way across the living room and had just reached the front door, when Alex appeared behind her. As she whirled around, he flattened his hands on either side of her head.

"Have you come to a decision?" he asked softly. His gaze dropped to her mouth. "Do you need any help?"

"The only thing I've managed to come up with is the flu," she murmured in a feeble attempt at humor. Alex wasn't amused, however, and she rushed to add, "Obviously you want to know which way I'm leaning, but I haven't had time to give your proposal much thought. I will, I promise I will...soon." She realized she was chattering, but couldn't seem to stop. "We're still on for Friday night, aren't we? We can discuss it then and—"

The doorbell chimed, frightening Carol out of her wits. She gasped and automatically catapulted herself into Alex's arms. He apparently didn't need an excuse to hold her close. When he released her several awkward seconds later, he smiled at her, then kissed the tip of her upturned nose.

"That'll be Barney now. It's time the two of you met."

"*That* was Carol Sommars?" Barney asked for the third time. He scratched his jaw and continued to frown. "No wonder Bambi mistook her for a bag lady. I'm sorry, man, you're my best friend and we've been buddies for a lot of years, but I've got to tell you, you can do better than that."

Chuckling, Alex dismissed his friend's statement and walked into the family room. If he lived to be a hundred, he'd never forget Carol's mortified look as she bolted from the house.

Barney certainly hadn't helped the situation any. Doing his best to keep a straight face, Alex had introduced the two. Barney's eyes had widened and his mouth had slowly dropped open in disbelief. It took a moment before he had the presence of mind to step forward and accept Carol's outstretched hand. Barney had mumbled that it was a pleasure to finally meet her, but his eyes had said something else entirely.

"Trust me," Alex felt obliged to explain, "she doesn't always look like that."

Barney stalked over to the refrigerator and opened it. He stared inside for a long time before he reached for a cold beer. "What time do the Trail Blazers play?"

Alex checked his watch. Both he and Barney were keen fans of Portland's professional basketball team. The team had been doing well this year and were in the first round of the play-offs. "Seven."

"So," Barney said, making himself comfortable in the overstuffed chair. He crossed his legs and took a long swig of beer. "What happened to her foot?" he asked casually. "Did she sprain it?"

"Whose foot?"

"Carol's," Barney said, casting Alex a questioning glance. "She was wearing a slipper—you mean you didn't notice? Did she twist her ankle?"

"Nah," James answered for Alex, wandering into the family room holding a bag of pretzels. He plopped himself down on the sofa, resting his legs on the coffee table. "Peter says she does weird stuff like that all the time. Once she wore his swimming goggles in the shower."

Barney raised his eyebrows. "Should I ask why?"

"It made sense—sort of—when Peter explained it. His mother had gone to one of those cosmetics stores and they put some fancy makeup on her eyes, and she didn't want to ruin it when she took a shower, so she wore Peter's rubber goggles."

"Why didn't she just take a bath?" Barney asked. He threw Alex a look that suggested his friend have his head examined.

"She couldn't take a bath because the faucet was broken," James said, "and her brother hadn't gotten around to fixing it yet."

"That makes sense," Alex said in Carol's defense.

Barney rolled his eyes and tipped the beer bottle to his lips.

To his credit, Barney didn't say anything else about Carol until James was out of the room. "You're really serious about *this* woman?" His question implied that Alex had introduced Barney to the wrong one, and that the whole meeting was a setup to some kind of joke that was to follow.

"I'm totally serious. I told you I asked her to marry me—I can't get any more serious than that."

"And she's *thinking* about it?" Barney asked mockingly. Being the true friend he was, Barn clearly couldn't understand why Carol hadn't instantly leaped at Alex's offer.

To be honest, Alex wondered the same thing himself. True, he'd blurted out his proposal in a parking lot. He still had trouble believing he'd done anything so crazy. As a contractor, he'd sold himself and his company hundreds of times. He'd prepared bids and presented them with polish and professionalism. He always had solid arguments that made his proposals sound attractive and intelligent. Carol deserved nothing less.

But something had happened to him when he'd visited her birthing class. Something enigmatic and profound. Even now he had to struggle not to get choked up when he thought about it.

After nearly two weeks in Texas, Alex had been starved for the sight of her, and he'd barely noticed the others in the class. In retrospect, he was sure his reaction could be attributed to seeing all those soon-to-be mothers.

In fifteen years Alex hadn't given babies more than a passing thought. He had a son and was grateful for that. He might have suffered a twinge of regret when he learned there'd be no more children, but he'd been more concerned about his wife's well-being than the fact that they wouldn't be adding to their family.

Then he'd watched Carol with those pregnant couples, and the desire for another child, a daughter, had suddenly overwhelmed him. He'd decided while he was in Texas that he loved Carol and wanted to marry her, but the idea of starting a family of their own hadn't so much as crossed his mind. But why not? They were both young enough and healthy enough to raise a houseful of children.

He'd been standing at the back of her class, waiting for her, when it happened. Out of nowhere, yet as clear as anything he'd ever seen or felt, Alex saw Carol pregnant with a child. *His* child. He'd realized at the time that this—he used the word *vision* for lack of a better one—was probably due to physical and emotional exhaustion. Wanting to hold on to the image as long as he could, he'd closed his eyes. He'd pictured her.... Her breasts were full, and when she smiled at him, her eyes had a radiance that couldn't be described. She'd taken his hand and settled it on her protruding stomach. In his fantasy he'd felt their child move.

This fantasy was what had prompted the abrupt marriage proposal. He wanted to kick himself now. If he'd taken her in his arms, kissed her and said all the things she deserved to hear, things might have gone differently. He hadn't meant to rush her, hadn't meant to be so pushy, but once he'd realized how resistant she was to the idea, he'd panicked. The two-week ultimatum was unfair. He'd tell her that on Friday night when they went out for dinner.

Then again, maybe he wouldn't. He'd wait to hear what she was thinking, which way she was leaning, before he put his foot any farther down his throat.

Then he began to smile. Perhaps it wasn't too late for a proper proposal, after all.

"Alex?"

His name seemed to be coming from some distance away.

"What?" he asked, pulling himself out of his thoughts.

"The game's started," Barney said. "Don't you want to see it?" He peered closely at Alex. "Is something wrong with you?"

Yes, something *was* wrong, and there was only one cure. Carol Sommars.

Carol dressed carefully for her dinner date with Alex Friday evening. After going through her closet and laying half of everything she owned across the bed, she chose a demure, high-necked dress of soft pink that buttoned down the front. That seemed safe enough, especially with a shawl.

She'd hardly ever felt this awkward. Trying to make her decision, she'd swayed back and forth all week. One day she'd decide she would be a fool *not* to marry him, and the next, she'd been equally convinced she'd be crazy to trust a man a second time.

Marrying Alex meant relinquishing her independence. It meant placing herself and her son at the mercy of another human being. Memories of her marriage to Bruce swiped at her viciously, and whenever she contemplated sharing her well-ordered life with another man, she broke into a cold sweat.

Years ago, someone had told her it took a hell of a man to replace no man. It wasn't until Carol graduated from college with her nursing degree and was completely on her own that she fully understood that statement. Her life was good, too good to tamper with, and yet…

Her thoughts were more confused than ever when the doorbell chimed. She paused, took a calming breath and headed across the room.

"Hello, Alex," she said, smiling stiffly.

"Carol."

He looked gorgeous in a three-piece suit. Her eyes took him in, and she felt some of the tension leave her muscles. It was when she met his eyes that she realized he was chuckling.

"We're going to dinner," he said, nodding at her dress, "not a baptism."

She blinked, not sure she understood.

"If that collar went any higher up your neck, it'd reach your nose."

"I… I was removing temptation," she said, embarrassed by the blush that heated her face.

"Honey, at this rate, the only thing we'll be removing is that dress."

Carol decided the best thing to do was ignore his remark. "Did you say where we're going for dinner?"

"No," he answered cryptically, and his warm eyes caressed her with maddening purposefulness. "I didn't. It's a surprise."

"Oh." After all the time they'd been together, after all the moments she'd spent in his arms, after all the dreams she'd had about Alex, she shouldn't feel this uncomfortable. But her heart was galloping, her hands felt damp, her breath was coming in soft gasps—and they hadn't even left her house yet.

"Are you ready?"

It was a question he shouldn't have asked. *No*, her mind screamed. *Yes*, her heart insisted. "I guess so," her lips answered.

Alex led her outside and held open his car door.

"It was thoughtful of you to drop the boys at the theater. Personally I don't think they were that keen on seeing a Disney movie," she said, slipping inside his car.

"Too bad. I gave them a choice of things to do this evening."

"Attending a kids' movie on the other side of town or being set adrift in the Columbia River without paddles probably isn't their idea of a choice."

Alex chuckled. "I don't want anyone disturbing us tonight."

Their eyes met. Alex's were hot and hazy and so suggestive, Carol's heart skipped a beat. For sanity's sake, she looked away.

"I hope you like steak."

"I love it."

"The champagne's cooling."

"You must've ordered in advance," she murmured, having difficulty finding something to do with her hands. Her fingers itched to touch him...*needed* to touch him. A need that only confused her more.

"I...hope you explained to Barney—your friend—that I...that I don't normally look the way I did the evening we met. When I got home and saw myself in the mirror...well, I could just imagine what he must've thought." Carol cursed the madness that had sent her rushing out of her house that evening to confront Alex.

"Barney understood."

"Oh, good."

A couple of minutes later, Alex turned into his own driveway. Carol looked at him, somewhat surprised. "Did you forget something?"

"No," he said.

A moment later, he let her into the house. She paused in the doorway, and her heart gave a sudden, sharp lurch. They weren't going to any restaurant. Alex had always planned to bring her back to his house.

The drapes were drawn, and the lights had been lowered. Carol saw that the dining room table was set with crystal and china. Two tapered candles stood in the middle of the table, waiting to be lit.

Alex went over to the stereo and pushed a single button. Immediately the room was drenched with the plaintive sound of violins.

Carol was still trying to assimilate what was happening when he walked over to the table and lit the candles. Tiny flames sent a golden glow shimmering across the pristine white cloth.

"Shall we?" Alex said, holding out his hands.

Carol was too numb to reply. He took the lacy shawl from her shoulders and draped it over the back of the sofa. Then he pulled her purse from her unresisting fingers and set it next to the shawl. When he'd finished, he turned and eased her into his arms.

Their bodies came gently together, and a shudder went through her. She wasn't a complete fool—she knew what Alex was planning. She lowered her eyelids. Despite her doubts and fears, she wanted this, too.

For a moment, she battled the feeling, then with a deep sigh, she surrendered.

Alex wrapped his arms around her. "Oh, baby," he whispered in her ear. "You feel so good."

She emptied her lungs of air as his hands slid down her back, to her waist.

There was music, such beautiful music, and then Carol realized they were supposed to be dancing. She rested her fingertips on his shoulders as his mouth moved toward hers. Carol sighed. Alex's breath was moist and warm, his hands gentle as they pressed her closer and closer.

When he kissed her, the moment of anticipation ended, and Carol felt a tremendous surge of relief. He groaned. She groaned. He leaned back and began to unfasten the buttons at her throat.

That all too brief pause helped Carol collect her scattered senses. "Alex," she whispered, "what are you doing?"

"Undressing you."

"Why?" she asked breathlessly, knowing what a stupid question it was.

"Why?" he repeated with amusement. "Because we're going to make love."

Her pulse went wild.

"I love you," he said. "You love me. Right?"

"Oh…yes."

"Good." He kissed her again, so passionately she could hardly resist—and yet she had to. She broke away from him with what little strength she still possessed.

"Alex…please don't."

"Tonight's a new beginning for us. I'm crazy in love with you. I need you so much I can't think straight anymore."

"You brought me here to make love to me, didn't you?"

"You mean it wasn't obvious?" he asked as he nibbled kisses along the side of her neck.

"Why now? Why not that night on the Washington coast…? Why tonight?"

"Carol, do we need to go through this evaluation?"

"I have to know," she cried, pushing herself away from him. Her hands trembled, and it was with some difficulty that she rebuttoned her dress. "The truth, Alex. I want the truth."

"All right," he murmured. "I thought… I believed that if we made love, it would help you decide you wanted to marry me."

Carol felt as though he'd tossed a bucket of ice water in her face. She raised her hand to her pounding heart. "Oh, no…" she whispered. "Not again."

"Carol? What's wrong?"

"Bruce did this to me, too…pressured me into giving in to him…then he hated me…punished me…." Blindly she reached for her purse and shawl, then headed for the front door.

Alex caught up with her before she made it outside. His hand clasped her shoulder as he turned her to face him. By then she was sobbing, her whole body trembling with terror. Stark terror—stark memories.

Alex took one look at her and hauled her into his arms. "Carol." He threaded his fingers through her hair. "It's all right, it's all right. I would *never* have forced you."

Twelve

All Carol could do was cry, and the pile of used tissues was mounting. Alex tried to comfort her, to help her, but everything he did seemed to make matters worse. One thing he'd immediately recognized—she didn't want him to touch her.

She'd curled herself up on his sofa and covered her face as she wept. She wouldn't talk to him. She wouldn't look at him. The only comprehensible statement she'd made in the last fifteen minutes had been a demand that he take her home.

Fear knotted his stomach. He had the inexplicable feeling that if he did as she asked, he'd never see her again. He had tonight and only tonight to repair the trust he'd unwittingly destroyed.

"Carol, I'm sorry." He must have told her that twenty times. It was true enough. Everything he tried to do with this woman was wrong. Tonight was the perfect example. For days he'd been searching for a way to prove to Carol how much he loved her and how right they were for each other.

This evening had seemed the perfect place and time.

He'd planned it all—the music, champagne, the carefully worded proposal, the diamond ring.

He'd thought that if everything went well, they'd make love, and afterward, they could discuss the details of their wedding and their lives. He wanted her in his bed, and although it was more than a little arrogant of him, he didn't think he'd have any problem getting her there.

He'd also come to the conclusion that once they made love, she'd be convinced that they belonged together, and their marriage would naturally follow.

At first, his plan had worked flawlessly. Carol had walked into the house, seen that the table was set and the candles ready to light. She'd looked at him with those huge eyes of hers and given him a seductive smile. Then, with barely a pause, she'd waltzed into his arms.

From there everything had gone downhill.

One minute he was kissing her, marveling at the power she had over his body, and the next, she was cold and trembling, demanding answers that should've been obvious.

"Would you like some coffee?" he asked her gently for the second—or was it the third?—time. Although his arms ached with the need to hold her, he resisted.

"No," she whispered. "I want to go home."

"We need to talk first."

"Not now. I *need* to go home." She rubbed her face and plucked a clean tissue from the nearby box. Apparently she'd regained her resolve because she stood, wrapped her shawl around her, and stumbled to the door. "If you won't drive me, then I'll walk."

Alex heard the desperation in her voice and was helpless to do anything other than what she asked. As he stood, the regret swept through him. If there was anything he could do to ease her pain, he would've done it. If there were any words he could have uttered to comfort her, he would've said them gladly. But all she wanted him to do was take her back to her own home. Back to her own bed. Her own life.

Who did he think he was? Some Don Juan who could sweep this beautiful, sensitive woman into his bed and make love to her? He felt sick to his stomach at the way he'd plotted, the way he'd planned to use her body against her, to exploit the attraction between them to serve his own ends.

Now he was losing her, and there wasn't anyone he could blame but himself. He'd known his chances weren't good the night he'd asked her to marry him. He'd hoped to see joy in her eyes when he suggested it. He'd longed to see happiness on her face. He'd wanted Carol to hurl herself into his arms, excited and overcome with emotion.

He should've known he'd been watching too many old movies.

He'd asked Carol to marry him, and none of the things he'd hoped for had happened. Instead, her eyes had reflected fear. And tonight…tonight he'd witnessed stark terror.

Alex was astute enough to realize the problem lay in Carol's brief marriage. Whatever had gone on had left deep emotional scars. Even when he'd felt the closest to her, Alex had learned very little about her relationship with her late husband. She'd let tidbits of information drop now and then, but every time she did, Alex had the feeling she'd regretted it.

On her way out the door, Carol grabbed a handful

of fresh tissues, and with nothing more to say, Alex led the way to his car.

He opened the passenger door, noticing how she avoided any possibility of their accidentally touching as she climbed inside.

The tension inside the car made the air almost too thick to breathe. He could hardly stand it and he wondered how she could.

When he braked at a stop sign, he decided to make one last effort.

"Carol, please, how many times do I have to tell you how sorry I am? I made a mistake. I behaved like a jerk. Tell me what you want me to do, because I'll do it. Anything you say. I love you! You've got to believe I'd never intentionally do anything to hurt you."

His pleas were met with more of the same strained, intolerable silence.

In frustration he pressed his foot to the gas, and they shot ahead. The seat belts were all that kept them from slamming forward with the car.

The fiercest argument of their courtship now ensued, and the crazy part was, neither of them uttered a word. Every once in a while, Alex could hear Carol drag a breath through her lungs, and he knew she was doing everything in her power not to cry. Each tear she shed, each sob she inhaled, felt like a knife wound.

He was losing her, and there wasn't a thing he could do about it. It wouldn't be so tragic if he didn't care for her so much. After Gloria's death, Alex had never truly believed he'd fall in love again. Even when he'd made the decision to remarry, he hadn't expected to find the depth of emotion he'd experienced with Carol.

And now it might be too late.

* * *

"Hey, Mom, did you and Mr. Preston have a fight or something?" Peter asked the following morning.

"W-why do you ask?"

Peter popped two frozen waffles in the toaster, then stood guard over them as though he expected Carol to snatch them out of his hands.

"I don't know. Mr. Preston was acting strange last night when he picked us up from the movie."

"Strange?"

"Sad. Mr. Preston's usually loads of fun. I like him, I mean, he's about the neatest adult I know. He doesn't treat me like I'm a kid, and he likes the same things I like and—I don't know—I just think he's an all-around great guy. Fact is, Mom, men don't come much better than James's dad."

"He is…nice, isn't he?" she agreed. She tightened her fingers around the handle of her coffee mug and looked anywhere but at her son.

Peter leaned toward her and squinted. "Have you been crying?"

"Don't be silly," she said lightly, trying to make a joke out of it.

"Your eyes are all puffy and red like you have an allergy or something."

"Pollen sometimes affects me that way." Which was the truth. It just didn't happen to be affecting her eyes at that particular moment.

The waffles popped up, and Peter grabbed them, muttering under his breath when he burned his fingers. He spread a thin layer of butter on them and followed that with a puddle of syrup. Once that task was complete, he added two more waffles to the toaster, then sat across the table from Carol.

"I kind of thought you and Mr. Preston might've had a fight," Peter said, obviously feeling it was safe to probe some more. "That would've been too bad because on the way to the movie he was telling us that he wanted to make this dinner the most romantic night of your life. Was it?"

"He…tried."

"How did the Baked Alaska taste?"

"The Baked Alaska?" Carol made a nondescript gesture. "Oh…it was great."

"Mr. Preston made everything himself. Right down to the salad dressing. James told me he'd been shopping for days. It would've been terrible if you'd had a fight and ruined it…. You love Mr. Preston, don't you?" Peter asked earnestly.

Carol closed her eyes to the emotion assaulting her from all sides. She would be lying if she didn't admit it. And her heart refused to let her lie. But no one seemed to understand that love wasn't a cure-all. She'd loved Bruce, too—or thought she did—and look where that had gotten her.

"Yes," she whispered. She'd averted her gaze, but she could hear Peter's sigh of relief.

"I knew you did," he said cheerfully, slicing into his waffle. "I told James you were wild about his dad and that whatever happened at dinner would be okay in the morning."

"I'm sure you're right," Carol murmured.

An hour later, Carol was working in the garden space Alex had tilled for her several weeks earlier. She was cultivating the soil, preparing it to plant several different herbs that afternoon. She'd done her homework and discovered a wide variety that grew well in the moist climate of the Pacific Northwest.

Her back was to the kitchen, and she hadn't heard the doorbell. Nor was there the usual commotion that occurred whenever Peter let someone in.

Yet without a doubt, she knew Alex was standing in the doorway watching her. She felt his presence in the same way she experienced his absence.

Running her forearm across her damp brow, she leaned back and removed her gloves. "I know what you want to say," she said, "and I think it would be best if we just dropped the whole issue."

"Unfortunately that's a luxury neither of us can afford."

"I knew you were going to say that," she sighed, awkwardly struggling to an upright position. The knees of her jeans were caked with mud and the sweat was pouring down her flushed face.

There'd probably been only two other times in her life when she'd looked worse, and Alex had seen her on both occasions.

With the cultivator gripped tightly in her fist, she walked over to the patio and sank down on a deck chair. "All right, say what you have to say."

Alex grinned. "Such resignation!"

"I'd rather be working in my garden."

"I know." He flexed his hands a couple of times. "I suppose I should start at the beginning."

"Oh, Alex, this isn't necessary, it really isn't. I overreacted last night. So, you made a mistake—you're only human and I forgive you. Your intentions weren't exactly honorable, but given the circumstances they were understandable. You wanted to take me into your bed and afterward make an honest woman of me." She made quotation marks with her fingers around the words *honest woman.* "Right?"

"Something like that," he mumbled. Although of course the issue was much more complicated than that....

"The thing is, I've been made an honest woman once and it was the biggest mistake of my life. I'm not planning to repeat it."

"What was your husband's name?" Alex asked without preamble.

"Bruce...why?"

"Do you realize you've never told me?"

She shrugged; she never talked about Bruce if possible.

"Tell me about him, Carol," Alex pleaded, "tell me everything. Start with the minute you noticed each other and then lead me through your relationship to the day you buried him."

"I can't see how that would solve anything."

"Tell me, Carol."

"No." She jumped to her feet, her heart in a panic. "There's nothing to say."

"Then why do you close up tight anytime someone mentions him?"

"Because!" She paced the patio. Stopping abruptly, she whirled around and glared at him, angry all over again. "All right, you want to know? I'll tell you. We were teenagers—young, stupid, naive. We made out in the back seat of a car...and when I got pregnant with

Peter we got married. Bruce died three years later in a car accident."

An eternity passed before Alex spoke again. "That's just a summary. Tell me what *really* happened in those three years you were married." His voice was soft and insistent.

Her chest constricted painfully. Would nothing satisfy him short of blood? How could she ever hope to describe three years of living in hell? She couldn't, and she didn't even want to try.

Alex wouldn't understand, and nothing she could ever say would help him. What purpose would it serve to dredge up all that misery? None that she could see.

Slowly she lowered herself onto the deck chair again, trying to still her churning thoughts, to nullify the agonizing memories. The pain was so distinct, so acute, that she opted for the only sane solution. She backed away.

Alex reached for her hand, holding it loosely. "I know this is difficult."

He didn't know *how* difficult.

"Bruce and I were married a long time ago. Suffice it to say that the marriage wasn't a good one. We were much too young...and Bruce had...problems." She bit her lip, not willing to continue. "I don't want to drag up the past. I don't see how it would do any good."

"Carol, please."

"No," she said sharply. "I'm not about to dissect a marriage that ended thirteen years ago simply because *you're* curious."

"We *need* to talk about it," he insisted.

"Why? Because I get a little panicky when you start pressuring me into bed? Trust me, any woman who's gone through what I did would react the same way. You know the old saying—once burned, twice shy." She tried to make light of it and failed. Miserably.

For the longest time Alex said nothing. He did nothing. He stared into the distance, and Carol couldn't tell where his thoughts were taking him.

"I never expected to fall in love again," he said.

Carol frowned at the self-derision in his words.

"Gloria knew I would, but then she always did know me better than I knew myself." He paused for a moment, and he gave a sad, bitter smile. "I'll never forget the last time we were able to talk. The next day she slipped into a coma, and soon afterward, she died. She knew she was dying and had accepted it. The hospital staff knew it was only a matter of time. But I couldn't let go of her. I had such faith that God would save her from this illness. Such unquestionable trust. He did, of course, but not the way I wanted."

"Alex…" Tears were beginning to blur her vision. She didn't want to hear about Gloria and the wonderful marriage he'd had with her. The contrast was too painful. Too bleak.

"Gloria took my hand and raised her eyes to mine and thanked me for staying at her side to the very end. She apologized because she'd been ill. Can you imagine anyone doing that?"

"No." Carol's voice was the faintest of whispers.

"Then she told me God would send another woman into my life, someone healthy and whole who'd love me the way I deserved to be loved. Someone who'd share my success and who'd love our son as much as she did." He paused and smiled again, but it was the same sad smile. "Trust me, this was the last thing I wanted to hear from my wife. First of all, I was in denial, and I refused to believe she was dying, and second, nothing could have convinced me I'd ever love another woman as much as I loved Gloria."

Carol shut her eyes tightly and took deep breaths to keep from weeping openly.

"She told me that when I met this other woman and decided to marry her, I shouldn't feel guilty for having fallen in love again. She must've known that would be something powerful I'd be dealing with later. She squeezed my fingers—she was so weak, and yet, so strong. And wise, so very wise. Within a few hours she was gone from me forever." He rubbed his eyes and hesitated before continuing. "I didn't believe her. I didn't think it would be possible to love anyone as much as I loved her.

"Then I met you, and before I knew it, I was falling in love all over again." Once more he brought a weary hand to his face. His expression was blank, his eyes unrevealing. "And again I'm relinquishing the woman I love." He paused. "I'll give you the two weeks to make your decision, Carol. In fact, I'll make it easy for you. I won't call or contact you until the seventh—that's exactly two weeks from the day we talked about it. You can tell me your decision then. All right?"

"All right," she agreed, feeling numb.

Slowly he nodded, then stood and walked out of her house.

"The way I see it," Peter said, holding a red Delicious apple in one hand and staring at his mother, "James's dad can adopt me."

Carol felt the fleeting pain that tore through her every

time Peter not-so-casually mentioned Alex's name. He seemed to plan these times with precision. Just when she least expected it. Just when she was sure she knew her own mind. Just when she was feeling overly confident. Then *pow*, right between the eyes, Peter would toss some remark carefully chosen for its effect. It was generally preceded by some bit of information about Alex or a comment about how wonderful life would be when they were one big, happy family.

"I'd have to marry Alex first, and I'm not sure that's going to happen," she said reproachfully. One challenging look defied him to contradict her.

"Well, it makes sense, doesn't it? *If* you marry him, naturally." Peter took a huge bite of the apple. Juice dribbled down his chin, and he wiped it away with the back of his hand. "I haven't heard from Dad's family in years, and they wouldn't even care if someone adopted me. That way we could all have the same last name. Peter Preston has a cool sound to it, don't you think?"

"Peter," she groaned, frustrated and angered by the way he turned a deaf ear to everything she said. "If this is another tactic to manipulate me into marrying Alex so you can go fishing, then I want you to know right now that I don't appreciate it."

She was under enough pressure—mainly from herself—and she didn't need her son applying any more.

"But, Mom, think about how good our lives would be if you married Mr. Preston. He's rich—"

"I've heard all of this conversation that I want to. Now sit down and eat your dinner." She dished up the crispy fried pork chop and a serving of rice and broccoli, and set the plate on the table.

"You're not eating?" Peter asked, looking mildly disappointed. "This is the third night you've skipped dinner this week."

Carol's appetite had been nil for the entire two weeks. "No time. I've got to get ready for class."

"When will these sessions be over?"

"Two more weeks," she said, walking into her bedroom. *Two weeks* seemed to be the magical time period of late. Alex had given her two weeks to decide if she'd accept his proposal. Two weeks that were up today. He'd granted her the breathing space she needed to come to a sensible decision. Only "sensible" was the last thing Carol felt. It shouldn't be this difficult. She wondered why she had so many doubts if she loved Alex—which she did. But Carol knew the answer to that.

Alex's marriage had been wonderful.

Hers had been a disaster.

He was hoping to repeat what he'd shared with Gloria.

She wanted to avoid the pain Bruce had brought into her life.

"Mom…phone."

Carol froze. She'd been on tenterhooks waiting for Alex to contact her. All day she'd felt a growing sense of dread. She'd expected Alex to come strolling out from behind every closed door, to suddenly appear when she least expected him.

The last thing she'd figured he'd do was phone.

With one shoe on, she hobbled over to her nightstand and picked up the phone, wondering what she was going to say.

"Hello."

"Carol, it's your mother."

"Hello, Ma, what can I do for you?" Relief must have been evident in her voice.

Angelina Pasquale said, "I was in church this morning, lighting a candle to St. Rita, when something happened to my heart."

"Did you see your doctor?" Carol's own heart abruptly switched gears. Her greatest fear was losing her mother to heart disease the way she'd lost her father.

"Why should I see a doctor?" her mother protested. "I was talking to God—in my heart—and God was telling me I should have a talk with my daughter Carol, who's deciding if she's going to marry this rich non-Italian or walk away from the best thing since the invention of padded insoles."

"Mama, I've got a class—I don't have time to talk."

"You've seen Alex?"

"Not...yet."

"What are you going to tell him?"

Her mother was being as difficult as Peter. Everyone wanted to make up her mind for her. Everyone knew what she should do. Everyone except Carol.

"You know he's not Catholic, don't you?" she told her mother, who had once considered that an all-important factor in choosing a husband. Religion and an equally vital question—whether her potential husband was allergic to tomatoes.

Her mother snickered. "I know he's not Catholic! But don't worry, I've got that all worked out with God."

"Mama, I'm sorry, but I have to leave now or I'll be late for my class."

"So be late for once in your life. Who's it gonna hurt? All day I waited, all day I said to myself, my *bambina's* going to call and tell me she's going to marry again. I want to do the cooking myself, you tell him that."

"Mama, what are you talking about?"

"At the wedding. No caterers, understand? I got the menu all planned. We'll serve—"

"Ma, please."

It took Carol another five minutes to extricate herself from the conversation. Glancing at her watch, she groaned. Rushing from room to room, she grabbed her purse, her other shoe and her briefcase. She paused on her way out the door to kiss Peter on the cheek and remind him to do his homework. Then she jumped in the car, still wearing only one shoe.

Her breathing was labored by the time she raced through traffic and pulled into the parking lot at the community center where the birthing classes were held.

She'd piled everything she needed in her arms, including her umbrella, when she realized she'd left her lecture notes at the house.

"Damn," she muttered. She took two steps before she remembered she was carrying her shoe.

"It might help if you put that on instead of holding it in your arms."

Carol froze. She whirled around, angry and upset, directing all her emotion at Alex. "This is *your* fault," she said, dropping her shoe to the ground and positioning it with her toe until she could slip her foot inside. "First, Peter's on my case, and now my mother's claiming she received a message directly from God and that He's worked out a deal with her, since you're not Catholic, and frankly, Alex—don't you dare laugh." She finished with a huge breath. "I swear, if you laugh

I wouldn't marry you if you were the last living male in the state of Oregon."

"I'm sorry," he said, holding up both hands.

"I should hope so. You don't know what I've been through this past week."

"Your two weeks are up, Carol."

"You don't need to tell me that. I know."

"You've decided?"

Her eyes shut, and she nodded slowly. "I have," she whispered.

Thirteen

"Before you tell me what you've decided," Alex said, moving toward Carol, his eyes a smoky gray, "let me hold you."

"Hold me?" she echoed meekly. Alex looked one-hundred-percent male, and the lazy smile he wore was potent enough to tear through her defenses.

"I'm going to do much more than simply hold you, my love," he whispered, inching his way toward her.

"Here? In a parking lot?"

Alex chuckled and slipped his arms around her waist, tugging her closer. Carol had no resistance left in her. She'd been so lonely, so lost, without him. So confused.

His mouth brushed hers. Much too briefly. Much too lightly.

Carol didn't want him to be gentle. Not when she was this hungry for his touch. Her lips parted in a firm and wanting kiss. Alex sighed his pleasure and she clung to him, needing him.

When they drew apart, she rested her forehead against his. "Okay," Alex said, his breath warm and heavy. "Tell me. I'm ready now."

"Oh, Alex," she murmured, and her throat constricted with ready tears. "I can't decide. I've tried and tried and tried, and the only thing I really know is I need more time."

"Time," he repeated. Briefly he closed his eyes. His shoulders sagged with defeat. "You need more time. How much? A week? A month? Six months? Would a year fit into your schedule?" He broke away from her and rubbed his hand along the back of his neck. "If you haven't made up your mind by now, my guess is you never will. I love you, Carol, but you're driving me insane with this waiting."

"Can't you see things from my point of view?" she protested.

"No, I can't," he said. "I'm grateful for this time we've had, because it's taught me something I hadn't been willing to recognize before. I'm lonely. I want someone in my life—someone permanent. I want you as my wife. I *need* you as my wife. But if you don't want what I'm offering, then I should cut my losses and look elsewhere."

A strangled cry erupted from her lips. He was being so unfair, pressuring her like this. Everything had to be decided in *his* time frame, without any allowance for doubts or questions. Something broke in Carol. Control. It was all about control. She couldn't—wouldn't—allow another man to control her the way Bruce had.

"I think you're right, Alex," she finally said. "Find yourself someone else."

The shock of her words hit him like a blow to the head. He actually flinched, but all the while his piercing eyes continued to hold hers. Carol saw the regret and the pain flash through his burning gaze. Then he buried his hands in his pockets, turned and marched away.

It was all Carol could do not to run after him, but she knew that if she did she'd be giving up her self-respect.

Janice Mandle stuck her head out the door and scanned the parking lot. She looked relieved when she saw Carol, and waved.

Carol waved back. Although she wanted nothing more than to be alone, she didn't have any choice but to teach her class.

Janice called, mentioning the time.

Still Carol couldn't seem to tear her gaze from Alex, holding on to him for as long as she could. He made her feel things she'd never known she was capable of experiencing. When he kissed her, she felt hot and quivery, as though she'd just awakened from a long, deep sleep. Spending time with him was fun and exciting. There'd been adventures waiting to happen with this man. Whole new worlds in the making. Yet something was holding her back. Something powerful. She wanted everything Alex was offering, and at the same time her freedom was too precious, too important.

Carol didn't see Alex again until the end of the week, when the boys were participating in the district track meet. James was running in the four-hundred-and eight-hundred-meter races, and Peter was scheduled for the 1500-meter. On their own, the two friends had decided to choose events in which they weren't competing together. Carol had been impressed with their insight into each other's competitive personalities.

Carol's mother had decided to attend the meet with her. Angelina was as excited as a kid at the circus.

They'd just settled themselves in the bleachers when out of the corner of her eye, Carol saw Alex. Since they both had sons involved in track, she knew avoiding him would be nearly impossible, but she hadn't expected to see him quite so soon. Although, in retrospect, she should've realized he'd be attending this important meet.

Preparing herself, she sat stiffly on the bleachers as Alex strolled past. Instantly her heart started to thunder. His friend was with him, the one she'd met briefly—Barney or Bernie… Barney, she decided. Her hands were tightly clenched in her lap, and she was prepared to exchange polite greetings.

To her consternation, Alex didn't so much as look in her direction. Carol knew it would've been nearly impossible for him to have missed seeing her. If he'd wanted to hurt her, he'd done so—easily.

"So when does the man running with the torch come out?" Angelina asked.

"That's in the Olympics, Mama," Carol answered, her voice weak.

Her mother turned to look in Carol's direction, and her frown deepened. "What's the matter with you?" she demanded. "You look as white as bleached flour."

"It's nothing."

"What is it?" Angelina asked stubbornly.

"Alex…just walked past us."

"Not *the* Alex?"

Carol nodded. Before she could stop her mother, Angelina rose to her feet and reached for Carol's binoculars. "Where is he? I want to get a good look at this man who broke my daughter's heart."

"Ma, please, let's not get into that again." The way

her mother had defended her had touched Carol's heart, although Angelina hadn't wasted any time berating her daughter's foolishness, either. She'd spent most of Sunday muttering at Carol in Italian. Carol wasn't fluent enough to understand everything, but she got the gist of it. Angelina thought Carol was a first-class fool to let a man like Alex slip through her fingers.

"I want one look at this Alex," Angelina insisted. She raised the binoculars to her face and twisted the dials until she had them focused correctly. "I'm gonna give this man the eye. Now, tell me where he's sitting."

Carol knew it would be easier to bend a tire iron than persuade her mother to remove the binoculars and sit down before she made a scene.

"He's on your left, about halfway up the bleachers. He's wearing a pale blue sweater," she muttered. If he glanced in her direction, she'd be mortified. Heaven only knew what interpretation he'd put on her mother glaring at him through a set of field glasses, giving him what she so quaintly called "the eye."

Her mother had apparently found him, because she started speaking in Italian. Only this time her comments were perfectly understandable. She was using succulent, suggestive phrases about Alex's sexual talents and how he'd bring Carol pleasure in bed.

"Ma, *please,*" Carol wailed. "You're embarrassing me."

Angelina sat down and put the glasses on her lap. She began muttering in Italian again, leaning her head close to Carol.

"Ma!" she cried, distressed by the vivid language her mother was using. "You should have your mouth washed out with soap."

Angelina folded her hands and stared at the sky. "Such beautiful *bambinos* you'd have with this man."

Carol closed her eyes at the image of more children—hers and Alex's. Emotion rocked through her.

Her mother took the opportunity to make a few more succinct remarks, but Carol did her best to ignore them. It seemed as if the track meet wasn't ever going to begin. Carol was convinced she'd have to spend the afternoon listening to her mother whispering in her ear. Just when she couldn't endure it any longer, the kids involved in the hurdle events walked over to the starting line. They shook their arms at their sides and did a couple of stretching exercises. Carol was so grateful to have her mother's attention on the field that it was all she could do not to rush out and kiss the coach.

The four-hundred-meter race followed several hurdle events. Carol watched James through the binoculars as he approached the starting line. He looked confident and eager. As they were taking their positions, he glanced into the stands and cocked his head just slightly, acknowledging his father's presence. When his gaze slid to Carol, his eyes sobered before he smiled.

At the gun, the eight boys leapt forward. Carol immediately vaulted to her feet and began shouting at the top of her lungs.

James crossed the finish line and placed second. Carol's heart felt as though it would burst with pride. Without conscious thought her gaze flew to Alex, and she saw that he looked equally pleased by his son's performance. He must have sensed her watching him because he turned his head slightly and their eyes met. He held on to hers for just a moment, and then with obvious reluctance looked away.

Carol sagged onto her seat.

"So who is this boy you scream for like a son?" her mother demanded.

"James Preston—the boy who finished second."

"So that was Alex's son?" Angelina asked slowly, as she took the binoculars and lifted them to her eyes once more. She was apparently satisfied with what she saw, because she grinned. "He's a fine-looking boy, but he's a little on the thin side. He needs my spaghetti to put some meat on those bones."

Carol didn't comment. She *did* love James like a son. That realization forced a lump into her throat. And her heart—her poor, unsuspecting heart—was fluttering hard enough to take flight and leave her body behind.

Feeling someone's eyes on her, she glanced over her shoulder. Instantly Alex turned away. Carol's hands began to tremble, and all he'd done was look in her direction....

James raced again shortly afterward, placing third in the eight-hundred-meter. For a high school sophomore, he was showing a lot of potential, Carol mused, feeling very proud of him.

When her own son approached the starting line for his race, Carol felt as nervous as she ever had in her life....

Since the 1500-meter meant almost four long turns around the track, it didn't have the immediacy of the previous races. By the time Peter was entering the final lap, Carol and her mother were on their feet, shouting their encouragement. Carol in English. Angelina in Italian. From a distance, Carol heard a loud male voice joining theirs. Alex.

When Peter crossed the finish line in a solid third

position, Carol heaved a sigh of pride and relief. Tears dampened her lashes, and she raised her hands to her mouth. Both the first-and second-place winners were seniors. As a sophomore, Peter had done exceptionally well.

Again, without any conscious decision on her part, Carol found herself turning to look at Alex. This time he was waiting for her, and they exchanged the faintest of smiles. Sad smiles. Lonely smiles. Proud smiles.

Carol's shoulders drooped with defeat. It was as if the worlds of two fools were about to collide.

He was pushy. She was stubborn.

He wanted a wife. She wanted time.

He refused to wait. She refused to give in.

Still their eyes held, each unwilling to pull away. So many concerns weighed on Carol's heart. But memories, too—good memories. She remembered how they'd strolled through the lush green foliage of the Washington rain forest. Alex had linked his fingers with hers, and nothing had ever felt more right. That same night they'd sat by the campfire and sung with the boys, and fed each other roasted marshmallows.

The memories glided straight to Carol's heart.

"Carol?"

Dragging her gaze away from Alex, Carol turned to her mother.

"It's time to leave," Angelina said, glancing into the stands toward Alex and his friend. "Didn't you notice? The stadium's almost empty, and weren't we supposed to meet Peter?"

"Yes..." Carol murmured, "we were...we are."

Peter and James strolled out of the locker room and onto the field together, each carrying a sports bag and a stack of school books. Judging by their damp hair, they'd just gotten out of the shower.

Carol and her mother were waiting where Peter had suggested. It seemed important to keep them as far away from the school building as possible for fear any of his friends would realize he had a family.

Alex didn't seem to be anywhere nearby, and for that Carol was grateful. And even if it made no sense, she was also regretful. She wanted to be as close to him as she could. And yet she'd happily move to the Arctic Circle to escape him. Her thoughts and desires were in direct contrast and growing more muddled every second.

Peter and James parted company about halfway across the field. Before they went their separate ways, they exchanged a brief nod, apparently having agreed or decided upon something. Whatever it was, Peter didn't mention it.

He seemed unusually quiet on the ride home. Carol didn't question her son until they'd dropped her mother off. "What's bothering you?"

"Nothing." But he kept his gaze focused straight ahead.

"You sure?"

His left shoulder rose and fell in an indecisive shrug.

"I see."

"Mr. Preston was at the meet today. Did you see him?"

"Ah..." Carol hedged. There was no reason to lie. "Yeah. He was sitting with his friend."

"Mr. Powers and Mr. Preston are good friends. They met in college."

Carol wasn't sure what significance, if any, that bit of information held.

"According to James, Mr. Powers's been single for the past couple years, and he dates beautiful women all the time. He's the one who arranged all those hot dates for James's dad…and he's doing it again."

"That's none of our business." Her heart reacted to that, but what else could she expect? She was in love with the man. However, it wasn't as if Alex hadn't warned her; he'd said that if she wasn't willing to accept what he was offering, it was time to cut his losses and look elsewhere. She just hadn't expected him to start so soon.

"James was telling me his dad's been going out every night this week."

"Peter," she said softly, "I think it would be best if we made it a rule not to discuss Alex or his dating practices. You know, and, I hope, have accepted, the fact that the relationship between James's dad and me is over…by mutual agreement."

"But, Mom, you really love this guy!"

She arched her eyebrows at that.

"You try to fool me, but I can see how miserable you've been all week. And Mr. Preston's been just as unhappy, James says, and we both think he's going to do something stupid on the rebound, like marry this Babette girl."

"Peter, I thought I just said I don't want to talk about this."

"Fine," he muttered, crossing his arms and beginning to sulk. Five minutes passed before he sighed heavily. "Babette's a singer. In a band. She's not like the run-of-the-mill bimbos Barney usually meets. Mom, you've got to *do* something. Fast. This woman is real competition."

"Peter!" she cried.

"All right. All right." He raised both hands in surrender. "I won't say another word."

That proved to be a slight exaggeration. Peter had ways of letting Carol know what was going on between Alex and his newfound friend without ever having to mention either name.

Saturday, after playing basketball with James in the local park, Peter returned home, hot and sweaty. He walked straight to the refrigerator and took out a cold can of soda, taking the first swallows while standing in front of the open refrigerator.

Carol had her sewing machine set up on the kitchen table. Pins pressed between her lips, she waved her hand, instructing her son to close the door.

"Oh, sorry," Peter muttered. He did as she asked, then wiped his face. "Ever hear of a thirty-six-year-old man falling head over heels in love with a twenty-three-year-old woman?" Peter asked disdainfully.

Stepping on a nail couldn't have been more painful—or more direct—than her son's question. "No. Can't say that I have," she said, so flustered she sewed a seam that was so crooked she'd have to immediately take it out. With disgust, she tossed the blouse aside, and when her son had left the room, she trembled and buried her face in her hands.

On Sunday morning, Peter had stayed in church a few extra minutes after Mass, walking up to the altar. When he joined Carol in the vestibule, she placed her hand on his shoulder and studied him carefully. She'd never seen her son quite so serious.

"What's on your mind, honey?"

He gave her another of his one-shoulder rolls. "I

thought if Grandma could talk to God, then I'd try it, too. While I was up there, I lit a candle to St. Rita."

Carol didn't respond.

After that, she and her son drove over to her mother's house. The tears started when she was in the kitchen helping Angelina with dinner. It surprised Carol, because she had nothing to cry about—not really. But that didn't seem to matter. Soon the tears were flowing from her eyes so hard and fast that they were dripping from her chin and running down her neck.

Standing at the sink washing vegetables helped hide the fact that she was weeping, but that wouldn't last long. Soon someone would see she was crying and want to know why. She tried desperately to stop, but to no avail. If anything, her efforts only made her cry more.

She must've made more noise than she realized, because when she turned to reach for a hand towel to wipe her face, she found her mother and her sister-in-law both staring at her.

Her mother was murmuring something to Paula in Italian, which was interesting since the other woman didn't understand a word of the language. But Carol understood each and every one. Her mother was telling Paula that Carol looked like a woman who was in danger of losing the man she loved.

With her arm around Carol's shoulders, Angelina led her into her bedroom. Whenever Carol was ill as a little girl, her mother had always brought her to her own bed and taken care of her there.

Without resistance, Carol let her mother lead her through the house. By now the tears had become soft sobs. Everyone in the living room stopped whatever they were doing and stared at her. Angelina fended off questions and directed Carol to her bed, pulling back the blankets. Sniffling, Carol lay down. The sheets felt cool against her cheeks, and she closed her eyes. Soon she was asleep.

She woke an hour later and sat bolt upright. Suddenly she knew what she had to do. Sitting on the edge of the bed, she held her hands to her face and breathed in deep, steadying breaths. This wasn't going to be easy.

Her family was still busy in the living room. The conversation came to an abrupt halt when Carol moved into the room. She picked up her purse, avoiding their curious eyes. "I…have to go out for a while. I don't know when I'll be back."

Angelina and Peter walked to the front door with her, both looking anxious.

"Where are you going?" her son asked.

She smiled softly, kissed his cheek and said, "St. Rita must have heard your prayers."

Her mother folded her hands and raised her eyes to heaven, her expression ecstatic. Peter, on the other hand, blinked, his gaze uncertain. Then understanding apparently dawned, and with a shout, he threw his arms around Carol's neck.

Fourteen

Alex was in the kitchen fixing himself a sandwich when the doorbell chimed. From experience, he knew better than to answer it before James did. Leaning against the counter, Alex waited until his son had vaulted from the family room couch, passed him and raced toward the front door.

Alex supposed he should show some interest in his unannounced guest, but frankly he didn't care—unless it was one stubborn Italian woman, and the chances of that were more remote than his likelihood of winning the lottery.

"Dad," James yelled. "Come quick!"

Muttering under his breath, Alex dropped his turkey sandwich on the plate and headed toward the living room. He was halfway through the door when he jerked his head up in surprise. It was Carol. Through a fog of disbelief, he saw her, dressed in a navy skirt and white silk blouse under a rose-colored sweater.

At least the woman resembled Carol. His eyes must be playing tricks on him, because he was sure this woman standing inside his home was the very one who'd been occupying his thoughts every minute of every hour for days on end.

"Hello, Alex," she said softly.

It sounded like her. Or could it be that he needed her so badly that his troubled mind had conjured up her image?

"Aren't you going to say anything?" James demanded. "This is Carol, Dad, Carol! Are you just going to stand there?"

"Hello," he finally said, having some trouble getting his mouth and tongue to work simultaneously.

"*Hello?* That's it? You aren't saying anything more than that?" James asked, clearly distressed.

"How are you?" Carol asked him, and he noticed that her voice was husky and filled with emotion.

Someday he'd tell her how the best foreman he ever hoped to find had threatened to walk off the job if Alex's foul mood didn't improve. Someday he'd let her know he hadn't eaten a decent meal or slept through an entire night since they'd parted. Someday he'd tell her he would gladly have given a king's ransom to make her his wife. In time, he *would* tell her all that, but for now, all he wanted to do was enjoy the luxury of looking at her.

"Carol just asked you a question. You should answer her," James pointed out.

"I'm fine."

"I'm glad," she whispered.

"How are you?" He managed to dredge up the polite inquiry.

"Not so good."

"Not so good?" he echoed.

She straightened her shoulders, and her eyes held

his as she seemed to be preparing herself to speak. "Do you…are you in love with her, because if you are, I'll… I'll understand and get out of your life right now, but I have to know that much before I say anything else."

"In love with her?" Alex felt like an echo. "With whom?"

"Babette…the singer you've been dating."

James cleared his throat, and, looking anxious, glanced at his father. "I…you two obviously need time alone. I'll leave now."

"James, *what* is Carol talking about?"

His son wore an injured look, as if to suggest Alex was doing him a terrible injustice by suspecting he had anything to do with Carol's belief that he was seeing Babette.

"James?" He made his son's name sound like a threat.

"Well," the boy admitted with some reluctance, "Mrs. Sommars might've gotten the impression that you were dating someone else, from…from something I said to Peter. But I'm sure whatever I said was very nebulous." When Alex glared at him, James continued. "All right, all right, Peter and I got to talking things over, and the two of us agreed you guys were wasting a whole lot of time arguing over nothing.

"Mrs. Sommars is way, way better than any of the other women you've dated. Sometimes she dresses a little funny, but I don't mind. I know Peter would really like a dad, and he says you're better than anyone his mom's ever dated. So when Uncle Barn started pressuring you to date that Babette, we… Peter and I, came up with the idea of…you know…"

"I don't know," Alex said sternly, lacing his words with steel. "Exactly what did you say to Carol?"

"I didn't," James was quick to inform him. "Peter did all the talking, and he just casually let it drop that you were dating again and..."

"And had fallen head over heels in love with someone else," Carol supplied.

"In the space of less than a week?" Alex demanded. Did she really think his love was so fickle he could forget her in a few short days? He'd only retreated to fortify himself with ideas before he approached her again.

"You said it was time to cut your losses and look elsewhere," she reminded him.

"You didn't believe that, did you?"

"Yes... I thought you must've done it, especially when Peter started telling me about you and...the singer. What else was I supposed to believe?"

"I'll just go to my room now," James inserted smoothly. "You two go ahead and talk without having to worry about a kid hanging around." He quickly disappeared, leaving only the two of them.

"I'm not in love with anyone else, Carol," Alex said, his eyes holding hers. "If you came because you were afraid I was seeing another woman, then rest assured it isn't true. I'll talk to James later and make sure this sort of thing doesn't ever happen again."

"It won't be necessary."

"It won't?" he asked, frowning. They stood across the room from each other, neither of them making any effort to bridge the distance. The way Alex felt, they might as well have been standing on opposite ends of a football field...playing for opposing teams.

Her eyes drifted shut, and she seemed to be gathering her courage. When she spoke, her voice was low and trembling. "Don't be angry with James..."

"He had no right to involve himself in our business."

"It worked, Alex. It…worked. When I believed I was losing you, when I thought of you with another woman in your arms, I… I wanted to die. I think maybe I did, just a little, because I realized how much I love you and what a fool I've been to think I could go on without you. I needed time, I *demanded* time, and you wouldn't give it to me…"

"I was wrong—I understood that later."

"No," she countered, "you were right. I would never have made up my mind because…because of what happened in my marriage. With Bruce."

The whole world seemed to go still as comprehension flooded Alex's soul. "Are you saying…does this mean you're willing to marry me?" he asked, barely able to believe what she was saying. Barely able to trust himself to stay where he was a second longer.

Alex didn't know who moved first, not that it mattered. All that did matter was Carol in his arms, kissing him with a hunger that seemed to consume them both.

"Yes…yes, I'll marry you," she cried between kisses. "When? Oh, Alex, I'm so anxious to be your wife."

Alex stifled the sudden urge to laugh, and the equally powerful urge to weep. He buried his face in the soft curve of her neck and swallowed hard before dragging several deep breaths through his lungs. He slid his hands into her hair as he brought his mouth to hers, exploring her lips in all the ways he'd dreamed of doing for so many sleepless nights.

Her purse fell to the floor, and she wound her arms around him, moved against him, whispering over and over how much she loved him.

"I missed you so much," he told her as he lifted her

from the carpet and carried her across the room. He was so famished for her love that he doubted he'd ever be satisfied.

"I thought I'd never kiss you again," she moaned. "I couldn't bear the thought of not having you in my life."

Alex made his way to the sofa, throwing himself on the cushions, keeping her in his lap. He stroked her hair as he gazed into her beautiful dark eyes. Unable to resist, he kissed her again.

When they drew apart, Alex rested his forehead against hers and closed his eyes, luxuriating in the warm sensations inside him. He didn't want to talk, didn't want to do anything but hold her and love her.

"Alex," she whispered. "You asked me about Bruce, and I didn't tell you. I was wrong to hold back, wrong not to explain before."

"It's all right, my…"

She gently stroked his face. "For both our sakes, I need to tell you."

"You're sure?"

She didn't *look* sure, but she nodded, and when she started speaking, her voice trembled with pain. "I was incredibly young and naive when I met Bruce. He was the most fun-loving, daring boy I'd ever dated. The crazy things he did excited me, but deep in my heart I know I'd never have married him if I hadn't gotten pregnant with Peter."

Alex kissed her brow and continued to stroke her hair.

"Although Bruce seemed willing enough to marry me," she began, "I don't know how much pressure my father applied." Her voice was gaining strength as she spoke. "It was a bad situation that grew worse after

Peter was born. That was when Bruce started drinking heavily and drifted from one job to another. Each month he seemed to be more depressed and more angry. He claimed I'd trapped him and he was going to make sure I paid for what I did." She closed her eyes and he heard her sigh. "I did pay, and so did Peter. My life became a nightmare."

Alex had suspected things were bad for her, but he'd no idea how ugly. "Did he beat you, Carol?"

Her eyes remained closed, and she nodded. "When Bruce drank, the demon inside him would give rise to fits of jealousy, fear, depression and hatred. The more he drank, the more the anger came out in violent episodes. There were times I thought that if I didn't escape, he'd kill me."

"Didn't your family know? Surely they guessed?"

"I hardly ever got to see them. Bruce didn't approve of me visiting my family. In retrospect, I realize he was afraid of my father. Had Dad or Tony known what was happening, they would've taken matters into their own hands. I must have realized it, too, because I never told them, never said a word for fear of involving them. It was more than that.... I was too humiliated. I didn't want anyone to know about the terrible problems we were having, so I didn't say anything—not even to my mother."

"But surely there was someone?"

"Once...once Bruce punched me so hard he dislocated my jaw, and I had to see a doctor. She refused to believe all my bruises were due to a fall. She tried to help me, tried to get me to press charges against him, but I didn't dare. I was terrified of what Bruce would do to Peter."

"Oh, Carol." The anger Alex was experiencing was so profound that he clenched his fists. The idea of someone beating this warm, vibrant woman filled him with impotent rage.

"I'd lost any respect I ever had for Bruce shortly after we were married. Over the next three years I lost respect for myself. What kind of woman allows a man to abuse her mentally and physically, day after day, week after week, year after year? There must've been something terribly wrong with me. In ways I can't even begin to understand, all the hurtful, hateful things Bruce accused me of began to seem valid."

"Oh, Carol..." Alex's chest heaved with the weight of her pain.

"Then Bruce didn't come home one night. It wasn't unusual. I knew he'd come back when he was ready, probably in a foul mood. That was what I'd braced myself for when the police officer came to tell me Bruce had been killed in an accident. I remember I stared up at the man and didn't say anything. I didn't feel anything.

"I was hanging clothes on the line, and I thanked him for letting me know and returned to the backyard. I didn't phone anyone, I didn't even cry."

"You were in shock."

"I suppose, but later when I was able to cry and grieve, mingled with all the pain was an overwhelming sense of relief."

"No one could blame you for that, my love," Alex said, wanting with everything in him to wipe away the memories of those years with her husband.

"Now...now do you understand why I couldn't tell you about Bruce?" she asked. "Your marriage to Gloria was so wonderful—it's what a marriage was meant to be. When she died, your love and James's love surrounded her. When Bruce died—" she hesitated, and her lips were trembling "—he was with another woman. It was the final rejection, the final humiliation." She drew in a ragged breath and turned, her eyes burning into his. "I don't know what kind of wife I'll be to you, Alex. Over the years I've thought about those three nightmarish years and I've wondered what would've happened had I done things differently. Maybe the fault *was* my own…maybe Bruce was right all along, and if I'd only been a better woman, he wouldn't have needed to drink. If I'd done things differently, he might've been happy."

"Carol, you don't truly believe that, do you?"

"I… I don't know anymore."

"Oh, love, my sweet, sweet love. You've got to realize that any problems Bruce had were of his own making. The reasons for his misery lay within himself. Nothing you could ever have done would've been enough." He cupped her face in his hands. "Do you understand what I'm saying?"

"I… I can't make myself fully believe that, and yet I know it's true. But Alex…this time I want everything to be right." Her eyes were clouded and uncertain, as if she suspected he'd be angry with her.

"It will be," he promised her, and there wasn't a single doubt in his heart.

Carol awoke when dawn silently slipped through the lush drapes of the honeymoon suite. She closed her eyes and sighed, replete, sated, unbelievably happy. Deliriously happy.

From the moment Carol had agreed to become Alex's

wife to this very morning, exactly one month had passed. One month. It hardly seemed possible.

In one month, they'd planned, arranged and staged a large wedding, complete with reception, dinner and dance.

True to her word, Carol's mother had prepared a reception dinner that couldn't have been surpassed. Angelina had started dragging out her biggest pots and pans the Sunday afternoon she brought Alex back to the house to introduce him to the family.

Last week, Carol's sisters and their families had all arrived. The wedding became a celebration of love, a family reunion, a blending of families, all at once.

At the reception, Alex had surprised her with the honeymoon trip to Hawaii. The boys were mildly put out that they hadn't been included. Hawaii would have been the perfect place to "check out chicks," as Peter put it. To appease them, Alex promised a family vacation over the Thanksgiving holiday. Peter and James had promptly started talking about a Mexican cruise.

Carol smiled as she savored memories of her wedding day. Peter and James had circulated proudly among the guests, accepting full credit for getting their parents together.

Alex stirred and rolled onto his side, slipping his hand around her waist and tucking his body against hers as naturally as if they'd been married three years instead of three marvelous days.

Carol had been crazy in love with Alex before she married him, but the depth of emotion that filled her after the wedding ceremony made what she'd experienced earlier seem weak by comparison.

Never had she been more in love. Never had she felt

so desirable. Just as she'd known it would be, Alex's lovemaking was gentle and unselfish while at the same time fierce and demanding. Thinking of how often and well he'd loved her in the last few days was enough to increase the tempo of her heart.

"Good morning," she whispered, as Alex turned to face her.

"Good morning."

Their eyes met and spoke in silent messages.

He was telling her he loved her. She was saying she loved him back. He was saying he needed her. She echoed that need.

Alex kissed her again, lightly, his lips as weightless as the creeping sunlight.

"Oh, love," he whispered reverently, spreading moist kisses over her face. "I don't think I'll ever get tired of making love with you."

"I certainly hope not." She smiled at him, brushing a stray curl from his brow. She fought back the ready tears that his love brought so easily to the surface. But it would've been impossible to restrain them. Alex didn't understand her tears, and Carol could find no way to explain.

He tenderly wiped the moisture from her face and kissed her eyes. "I can't bear to see you cry. Please tell me if there's anything I can do…."

"Oh, no…" After all the times they'd made love, learned and explored each other's bodies in the past three days, he still couldn't completely accept her tears, fearing he was the cause. Once again, Carol tried to make him understand. "I… I didn't realize making love could be so wonderful…so good."

Alex momentarily closed his eyes, his look full of

chagrin and something else she couldn't name. "We didn't take any precautions last night."

His words triggered a slow easy smile. "I know, and I'm glad."

"Why? I thought we decided to wait a few months before we even considered starting a family.

"What do you think your chances of getting pregnant are?" he asked after several minutes of kissing and touching.

She smiled again. "About a hundred percent."

The room went quiet. When Alex spoke, his voice was strangled. "How would you feel about that?"

"Unbelievably happy. I want your child, Alex."

His mouth found hers again for a kiss that grew wilder and wilder. Nestling her head against his strong shoulder, Carol sighed. She felt happier than she'd ever imagined possible. Happy with her husband, her family, herself.

Epilogue

After all the years Carol had worked as an obstetrical nurse, after all the birthing classes she'd taught, she should be able to recognize a contraction. Still, she wasn't a hundred percent sure and had delayed contacting Alex until she was several hours into labor.

Resting her hands on her distended abdomen, she rubbed it gently, taking in several relaxing breaths. Twins! She and Alex were having *twins*. He felt as excited, as ecstatic, as she did. Maybe even more so… Everything was ready for their babies. The nursery was furnished with two cradles, each with a different mobile hanging above it, and Alex had painted a mural, a forest scene, on the wall for his daughters. All their little sweaters and sleepers were stacked in twin dressers he'd lovingly refinished.

Carol took another deep breath as the next pain struck. Then, knowing she shouldn't delay much longer, she reached for the phone and called Alex at the office.

"Yes," he cried impatiently. This last week he'd been as nervous as…a father-to-be.

"It's Carol."

She heard his soft intake of breath. "Are you all right?"

"I'm fine."

"You wouldn't be calling me at the office if you were fine," he countered sharply. "Is something going on that I should know about?"

"Not really. At least not yet, but I think it might be a good idea if you took the rest of the afternoon off and came home."

"Now?"

"If you're in the middle of a project, I can wait," she assured him, but she hoped he'd be home soon, otherwise she was going to end up driving herself to the hospital.

"I'm not worried about *me*," he said. "Are the babies coming now? Oh, Carol, I don't know if I'm prepared for this."

"Don't worry. I am."

Alex expelled his breath forcefully. "I'll be there in ten minutes."

"Alex," she cried. "Don't speed."

She used the time before his arrival to make some phone calls, then collected her purse and her small suitcase—packed several weeks ago. Finally, she sank into her favorite chair, counting the minutes between contractions.

From a block away, Carol could hear the roar of his truck as he sped toward the house. The squealing of brakes was followed by the truck door slamming. Seconds afterward, Alex vaulted into the house, breathless and pale.

She didn't get up from her chair; instead, Carol held out both hands to him. "Settle down, big daddy."

He flew to her side and knelt in front of her, clasping her hands in his. It took him a moment to compose himself.

"This is it, isn't it? We're in labor?" he asked when he'd found his voice.

"We're in labor," Carol told him and stroked his hair.

"How can you be so calm about this?"

She smiled and bent forward to brush her lips over his. "One of us has to be."

"I know… I know…you need me to be strong for you now, but look at me," he said, holding out his hands for her inspection. "I'm shaking." Gently he laid those same shaking hands on Carol's abdomen, and when he glanced up at her, his eyes were bright with unshed tears. "I love these babies—our daughters—so much. I can't believe how lucky I am. And now that they're about to be born, I feel so humble, so unworthy."

"Oh, Alex…"

"I guess we'd better go. Is there anything we need to do first?"

"No. I've phoned my mother and the doctor, and my suitcase is by the door." She made an effort to disguise the intensity of her next contraction by closing her eyes and breathing slowly and deeply until it passed. When she opened her eyes, she discovered Alex watching her intently. If possible, he looked paler than he had before.

"Are you going to be all right?" she asked.

"I… I don't know. I love our babies, but I love you more than anything. I can't stand to see you in pain. I—"

His words were interrupted by the sound of another car pulling into the driveway and two doors slamming. James burst into the house first, followed by Peter, both looking as excited as if it were Christmas morning.

"What are you two doing home from school?" Carol demanded.

"We heard you were in labor. You don't think we'd miss this, do you?"

"You heard?" Carol echoed. "How? From whom?"

The two boys eyed each other. "We've got our sources," James said.

This wasn't the time or place to question them. "All right, we won't discuss it now. James, take care of your father. Peter, load up the car. I think it might be best if you drove me yourself. James, bring your father—he's in no condition to drive."

Their sons leaped into action. "Come on, Dad, we're going to have a couple of babies," James said, urging his father toward the late-model sedan the two boys shared.

By the time they got to Ford Memorial, Carol's pains had increased dramatically. She was wheeled to the labor room while James and Peter were left to fend for themselves in the waiting room.

Alex was more composed by now, more in control. He smiled shyly and took her hand, clutching it between both of his. "How are you doing?"

"Alex, I'm going to be fine and so are our daughters."

Janice Mandle came bustling in, looking pleased. "Okay, we all ready for this special delivery?" she asked.

"Ready," Carol said, nodding firmly.

"Ready," Alex echoed.

With Janice's help and Alex's love, Carol made it through her next contractions. As she was being taken into the delivery room, Alex walked beside her. The pains were coming faster, but she managed to smile up at him.

"Don't worry," she whispered.

"I love you," he whispered back. He reached for her hand again and they met, palm to palm, heart to heart.

"Grandma, can I have seconds on the zabaglione?" James called from the large family kitchen.

Angelina Pasquale's smile widened and her eyes met those of her daughter. "I told you my cooking would put some meat on his bones."

"That you did, Mama," Carol said, exchanging a private smile with her husband. She and the babies had been home for a week. Royalty couldn't have been treated better. James and Peter were crazy about their sisters, and so far the only tasks allotted Carol had been diaper-changing and breastfeeding. She was well aware that the novelty would wear off, but she didn't expect it to be too soon. Angie and Alison had stolen two teenage hearts without even trying.

"I brought you some tea," Alex said, sliding onto the sofa beside her. His eyes were filled with love. From the moment Carol was brought to the delivery room, the light in Alex's eyes hadn't changed. It was filled with an indescribable tenderness. As she gave birth, his hand had gripped hers and when their two perfect identical daughters were born, there'd been tears in both parents' eyes. Tears of joy. Tears of gratitude. They'd each been granted so much more than they'd ever dreamed. New life. New love. A new appreciation for all the good things in store for them and their combined families.

The soft lilting words of an Italian lullaby drifted toward Carol and Alex. Eyes closed, Carol's mother rocked in her chair, a sleeping infant cradled in each arm. The words were familiar to Carol; she'd heard her mother sing them to her as a child.

When she'd finished, Angelina Pasquale murmured a soft, emotional prayer.

"What did she say?" Alex asked, leaning close to Carol.

A smile tugged at the edges of Carol's mouth. Her fingers were twined with Alex's and she raised his knuckles to her lips and kissed them gently. "She was thanking St. Rita for a job well done."

* * * * *